I0740526

F. E. H. Haines

Jonas King

Missionary to Syria and Greece

F. E. H. Haines

Jonas King
Missionary to Syria and Greece

ISBN/EAN: 9783337239046

Printed in Europe, USA, Canada, Australia, Japan

Cover: Foto ©Andreas Hilbeck / pixelio.de

More available books at **www.hansebooks.com**

JONAS KING:

MISSIONARY

TO

SYRIA AND GREECE.

BY

F. E. H. H.

AMERICAN TRACT SOCIETY,
150 NASSAU STREET, NEW YORK.

COPYRIGHT, 1879,
BY AMERICAN TRACT SOCIETY.

CONTENTS.

CHAPTER V.
MISSION TO PALESTINE ACCEPTED.

CHAPTER VI.
THROUGH FRANCE AND THE MEDITERRANEAN.

CHAPTER VII.
EGYPT.

CHAPTER VIII.
THE DESERT AND JERUSALEM.

CHAPTER IX.
STUDY AND WORK IN PALESTINE.

CHAPTER X.
MOUNT LEBANON AND THE SAMARITANS.

CHAPTER XI.
LIFE IN PALESTINE CONTINUED.

CHAPTER XII.
HOMEWARD THROUGH EUROPE.

CHAPTER XIII.
MISSIONARY AGENCY IN AMERICA.

CHAPTER XIV.
POROS—GREECE.

CHAPTER XV.
ATHENS.

CHAPTER XVI.
MISSIONARY WORK NEEDED IN THE EAST.

CHAPTER XVII.
LIFE-WORK AT ATHENS.

CHAPTER XVIII.
LIFE-WORK AT ATHENS CONTINUED.

CHAPTER XIX.

FRUITS OF LABOR.

CHAPTER XX.

PERSECUTIONS.

CHAPTER XXI.

TOURS, TRAVELS, AND EVANGELICAL ALLIANCE.

CHAPTER XXII.

LAST VISIT TO AMERICA.

CHAPTER XXIII.

RETURN TO GREECE—DEATH IN 1869.

CHAPTER XXIV.

CONCLUSION.

INTRODUCTION.

"ALL glory be to God, the High, the Mighty, the Everlasting, who exists mysteriously and incomprehensibly as the Father and the Son and the Holy Ghost."

Thus begins the Journal of Jonas King, dated, Paris, September 1, 1822, followed by a copy in Greek, Hebrew, and English, of the commission under which he served, Matt. 28:19. This Journal embraces twenty-four volumes of closely-written manuscript, and is a library in itself. The first volume contains an account of his early life, written at the request of his friend, S. V. S. Wilder, who, in view of Dr. King's intended mission to Palestine, gave him the book, consecrating it formally "to the service of Christ."

These books are as a chain of exceeding beauty, of which only a shining link here and there can be lifted to the view of the present generation, which cannot take time to examine much into the past, so earnest is it in the present, so intent upon the future. The interest in biographies, however, is reviving ; they meet a want of the human heart, recognized in the many personal histories given us in the Old Testament and the New. It must be to the honor of our Lord that at the present day some record should be made of those typical men who were used by him in the early days of missionary effort.

Foundation work does not appear upon the surface. Now that the Eastern world is found honeycombed with truth, we begin to appreciate the labors in those Bible lands of the Bible-men, as they were called—Parsons, Fisk, King, Goodell, Eli Smith, Bird, and others. Old superstitions there are crumbling away. Christ's kingdom is becoming established as never before. Let us honor the pioneers in his service, who "out of weakness were made strong" through faith.

Delay in bringing before the church some of the facts regarding initial missionary work in Syria and Greece may be of no disadvantage. Its thorough and truly evangelical character, as time passes on and the superstructure rises to view, will appear. God is ever true to his promise. It could not be in vain that about half a century ago so many copies of the Bible and Testament were sown in that part of the world—those of one year amounting to 6,847 copies. Prayers also were offered, and religious conversation held with old and young; and the Lord has said, "My word 'shall not return unto me void." The laborers now cultivating those fields, and beginning to gather in the harvest, and even transient Christian travellers, often find traces here and there of the footsteps of those who sowed the precious seed long years ago, and who have passed on to be for ever with the Lord, and are now watching with him the great ingathering from every nation. Not "the least among these his brethren" is found, no doubt, the honored missionary, a succinct account of whose character and labors these pages are intended to record.

JONAS KING—the name is as a household word in many Christian homes in this and other lands. An almost romantic interest is connected with it. Many have a general impression, through the mists of long years ago, of the course of his life, starting as it did among the western hills of Massachusetts, where he received the rugged New England training that so well fitted him for the work which proved to be in store for him. After unwearied perseverance in obtaining an education, came rapid promotion to a professorship in Amherst College. Then followed his sojourn in Paris, where more than fifty-six years ago the young American preacher, through his very uncompromising honesty and simplicity of purpose, conjoined with singular courtliness of manner, attracted attention to the pure doctrines of the cross.

Next God, by unexpected means, led him up to Jerusalem, then far distant, and the road to it but little travelled. Thence he "passed into Achaia also," and upon Mars' Hill, the very seat of the god of war, proclaimed the advent of the Prince of Peace. The apostle Paul, long years ago, once stood on these same steps of the Areopagus. Some modern Plutarch, without putting the two speakers on a par, might well find occasion for a parallel.

Then comes a time of work and of persecution in Greece, during which, under God, the triumphant power of our American flag was shown to Europe and to all the world.

Several of his later years Dr. King was privileged to spend in this his own native land. Everywhere was he greeted with special reverence. Many Christian people, in meeting him, felt, as one minister well expressed it, "as if shaking hands with one of the old apostles," for from early childhood the name Jonas King had been almost as familiar to him as those to be found in the New Testament.

Dr. King passed away from earth in Athens, the city of his adoption, comforted in his last hours by the ministrations not only of members of his family, for others were also at hand who by his means had been brought out into pure gospel light.

Let the earnest Christian student be encouraged, as he notes the providences of God as manifested all through the life of Jonas King.

JONAS KING.

CHAPTER I.

EARLY HOME-LIFE.

Birth and Home Training at Hawley, Mass.—Early Reading of the Bible—Modern Thought—Youthful Ambition—Conviction and Conversion—Work in Revival—Letter by Rev. W. A. Hallock, D. D.—Persevering Efforts to obtain an Education—Experiences as Singing Master and Teacher.

Extracts taken consecutively from the "Journals of Jonas King," joined by a thread alone here and there, can best give graphic detail as to many parts of his life.

"I was born the 29th of July, 1792, at Hawley, an obscure town on the mountains of Franklin county, Massachusetts, about twenty-five miles from North-ampton.

"My father was noted for extreme sobriety in his manner of living, rigid adherence to the truth, even in the most trivial things; perfect uprightness in all his dealings with others; the most strict observance of the Sabbath and its duties, love for the Sacred Scriptures, which are almost the only book he has read for thirty years past, and which are his meat and drink day and night; and for a mind contemplative to such a degree

that he is seldom known to smile. From my earliest
recollection, his constant theme has been the love of
Christ, and salvation by grace. During the first eighteen
years and a half of my life, which I passed in the humble
mansion of my father, I can scarcely remember a single
day that he did not converse with me seriously morning
and evening in the house or in the field, and sometimes
by my bedside, speaking of the love of Christ, the glories
of heaven, the deceitfulness of the world. Every object
which arrested my attention, he endeavored to connect
with something spiritual. The command to parents in
the sixth chapter of Deuteronomy he almost literally
obeyed.

"Under his instruction, I found myself, at the age of
four years, able to read with considerable fluency. My
father then told me that if I would read all the Scriptures
of the Old and New Testament before I should be six
years old, he would make me some little present, which
to my great joy I received, having performed my task
within the time specified. From the age of six to sixteen,
I continued to read through the Bible once a year. This
I did because he desired it, and also because it was
almost the only book in his library. That and the
Primer, Watts' Psalms and Hymns, a few common school-
books, such as Webster's and Perry's Spelling-books and
Dictionaries, the American Preceptor, Pike's Arithmetic,
Alexander's Grammar, together with a few pamphlets,
comprised nearly all the library to which I had access
the first seventeen years of my life.

"My father's paternal inheritance consisted of one

hundred acres. There he spent the vigor of his youth, and impaired his health felling giant hemlocks, overgrown pines, and sturdy maples."

Rev. W. A. Hallock, D. D., long an honored Secretary of the American Tract Society, New York, and himself an early as well as life-long friend of Dr. King, writes as follows:

"NEW YORK, Nov. 22, 1869.

"You have asked me to state any facts of the early life of Rev. Dr. Jonas King, which, should I pass away, it would be difficult to get; but the main facts are given in the memoir of S. V. S. Wilder, the sketch of Dr. King by Mrs. Doremus, and elsewhere. In a word, there is no blot, or slur, or drawback whatever in his early life: all is fair and bright and creditable, as to morals, temperance, intelligence, fidelity to his parents and sister, and fulfilling all his relations in the school, the church, and the community.

"I knew him intimately from childhood; for though born in Hawley, his father's house was but half a mile from the town of Plainfield (Hampshire Co., Mass.), where my father, Rev. Moses Hallock, was sole pastor for more than forty years, including the first forty years of Jonas' life. With my father he fitted for college, and though he was about two years older than I, it was my privilege to hear his first lessons in the Latin Grammar. Plainfield and Hawley were settled almost wholly by intelligent, church-going farmers, all very much on a level with each other, all sober and well-to-do; all the children attending the common school, almost all the population attending church, not one servant in either town, nor one person who might not be welcome at the table of any other.

"Mr. Jonas King, Sr., and his wife were worthy members of the church, having but two children, Dr. Jonas and his sister ; and were above the average in intelligence and worth. Both the father and the son had active investigating minds on Christian doctrines, as well as in this world's knowledge. They were praying, devout, consistent Christians, as represented in my tract, 'The Only Son,' which is in Mr. Wilder's Memoir.

"Mr. King's farm was, I suppose, about one hundred acres, with comfortable plain buildings, and a large sugar orchard, from which I know we often had very white and pure maple-sugar. A spring of beautiful mountain water was ever running to accommodate the family and the passers-by.

"The father and son resembled each other in very many respects. Neither of them was robust, yet the father was able to cultivate his farm, and both lived to an advanced age.

"It was the first object of Dr. King's parents to help him to prepare for and to enter the ministry. Father, mother, and son united in striving after this great end ; and although they possessed but limited means, they were blessed in the attainment of it."

The Journal goes on as follows .

"From the age of five or six years I went to school all the time that the district school lasted. If a teacher had studied as far as the 'Square Roots,' or 'Double Position,' he was thought to have a wonderful genius for Mathematics. I attended school with eagerness, though sometimes with much difficulty through heaps piled on heaps of snow. . . . Many and many a time have I lain down in the field and wept till the fountain of tears was exhausted, in thinking of what I considered was a hard lot—to have a father sick, no brother to accompany me, to be obliged to tug alone, and perform tasks upon the farm which men alone are capable of performing with ease. But I now find that it is good for me to have borne the yoke in my youth. Had my father been prosperous, and had I enjoyed perfect health, I have little doubt but that I would have been ruined. . . . At a very early age, I found within my bosom those germs of iniquity, which, without some check, would have grown rank, and brought forth a fruitful harvest of sin and death.

" I wished sometimes my father was an unbeliever, that I might sin as others did without remorse. I sometimes doubted whether there was anything of reality in what I saw and read and heard. I well recollect, that about the time that I finished the first reading of the Bible, I stood gazing at the woods and mountains around me, and at the clear sky which seemed to touch them, till I felt lost in a kind of amazement; and said to myself, 'What does all this mean? Is it not possible that I am dreaming? I lie down at night, sleep and fancy that I am in such and such a place, and that I see and hear such and such things; and in the morning awake and find that all I supposed real was nothing. Perhaps I and all the rest of the world are in another kind of sleep, from which we shall by-and-by awake and find that what we now think is real, is nothing but a dream; that there are no woods, no mountains, no world, no heavens.' Such reflections as these, I consider as the young blossoms of infidelity."

What would some of the disciples of "modern thought" say to this young farmer-boy, sounding with untrained imagination into the dark though shallow depths of their philosophy?

Dr. King goes on to write of his own unbounded ambition : " My heart would beat for hours at the thought of shining as a general or as a man of science, or of having my name uttered with respect by every child, like that of Washington or Franklin. How to attain this, I did not know. But I had read of David called from the sheep-cote to the throne; of Moses, and of many men of Greece and Rome, and in our own country, who had gone from the plough, and attained the most distinguished honors. I knew that 'with God all things are possible.' I often read in the Proverbs of Solomon ; and there I found written, 'By humility and the fear of the Lord, are riches and honor and life.' I found also written, 'Seest thou a man diligent in business ? he shall stand before kings ; he shall not stand before mean men.' As I always received praise from my parents for diligence and faithfulness in everything they set me to do, I had the idea that one day I might be called to the court of some crowned prince. A few years of course informed me that these were idle fancies." Yet a few years more proved them to be almost prophetic.

But these early questionings were turned into a more practical channel by means of a month's dangerous sickness, when the young dreamer was about ten years old. The realities of eternity then pressed upon him, and great tenderness of conscience remained for about a year; which however passed away, when, through fear of being thought too serious or religious, he was persuaded by some young people much older than himself to attend a ball. The silent monitor in his heart then gradually ceased to perform its office.

At twelve years of age, his attention was again arrested by the unhappy death of a very gay young lady with whom he was acquainted; and who called in the hour of death upon her parents who professed religion, saying, "Oh, why did you not restrain me? Now it is too late. I am dying, and must be miserable for ever;" but the boy soon found rest by concluding that he had lived a very moral life, and that if he needed regeneration in order to be saved, God would certainly renew him.

Yet such comfort of course was but transient, for of his feelings soon after this, Dr. King writes,

"I regretted that my situation in life guarded me so effectually from the snares of vice; when suddenly the word of God pierced through my heart like a two-edged sword, and made me feel that I was a dying sinner. It was a sermon from this text, 'Quench not the Spirit.' I felt that I had done it; that God had called upon me time after time, and I had refused. From this time I was engaged for about three months in searching what I should do to inherit eternal life, reading the Scrip-

tures, praying, performing acts of mortification, sometimes refusing to eat fruit and other things pleasant
to the taste, that I might appear humble in the sight
of God and merit something in his sight.   I also bor-
rowed 'Alleine's Alarm,' and read it over and over
again, taking care always to conceal it if any one came
into the room where I was, and to appear as gay as
possible, that I might not be suspected of being serious.
For, though I knew it would afford my father the highest pleasure in the world to know what was in my mind,
I could not for shame disclose it to him.   At length,
however, I ventured to do it, but instantly regretted having done so, and thought I had acted like a fool, and
should now have to bear the stigma of being a religious
boy, and give up all the youthful amusements to which
I had looked forward with a high degree of pleasure.

"It was soon noised through the town, that I was
what is there called, under 'concern of mind.'   Christians rejoiced ; old men noticed me, asked me questions,
gave me advice, and spoke of me in a flattering manner ;
so that instead of losing anything in point of reputation,
I found that I was gaining.   Pride at once suggested to
me that this might be one means of rising in the world.
I found too, that twenty or thirty other young people
had, unknown to me, been awakened, and were soon to
make a public profession of their faith in Christ.   This
strengthened me, and I began to speak of religion without much shame, and to demand of others what I should
do to obtain the same hopes and joys which they professed.   All replied in the same manner, 'Repent, repent.'

This duty I was aware of ; but *how* to repent was the difficulty I wished solved. This they could not tell me. It seemed to me the height of folly to tell a man to repent, without telling him *how* to repent.

"At length I became vexed, and thought I was troubling myself about things in which there was no reality ; that all I read in the Bible might be a fiction ; that there might be no God, no state of retribution hereafter, no heaven, no hell ; that it would be a sorrowful thing to let my youth pass by the fountains of pleasure without tasting them, and at last find that annihilation closed the scene; that if there were a God and a Saviour, I had been seeking them long enough, and without success ; and if He cast me eternally from his presence, why then I must suffer, I could not help it. These feelings I endeavored to cherish, having heard others say that they had experienced much hardness of heart, and opposition to the divine character a little previous to regeneration.

"It was the first of September, 1807. Towards evening I walked out alone for the purpose of meditation. The day was fine; the sun was just sinking behind the western forests, and not a cloud was to be seen in the heavens. Everything was calm and silent. Scarcely the voice of a bird broke in upon the stillness. For awhile I walked on with slow and pensive step, musing on what I was, and what I might be hereafter ; then stopped, looked around, and asked myself, 'What holds up this mighty, ponderous world in the midst of space? What makes the sun hold on his way in such a

regular manner? and what sustains him?'   That moment light seemed to break in upon my soul, and I *felt*
that there is a God of almighty power, supporting, moving and directing all things with infinite wisdom.   I
reflected on his commands and they seemed just; on his
mercy through a Saviour, and it appeared lovely.   I was
astonished that I never before had the same view.   I
thought that if love to God, and love to Christ, and love
towards our fellow-men, were all that was required of us,
nothing could be more reasonable and nothing more easy.
My heart, which for several days had been hard and
unyielding, now seemed to soften, and with eyes uplifted
towards heaven I wept and prayed for mercy.

"This day I celebrated for several years, as the day
of my spiritual birth.   Whether I had at that time any
genuine piety, I cannot say.   Sure I am that I knew
but very little of my own heart, and had very incorrect
and low views of the great work of redemption.   I had indeed read the Bible through ten different times, was
familiar with its language, but had little acquaintance
with its spirit.   I am fully convinced that a man may
read the Sacred Scriptures, just as he reads the volume
of nature, without having the least view of that glory
which fills heaven and earth, and which is inscribed in
letters of light on everything around us.   I had read it,
for the most part, as a matter of duty, something meri-
torious in the sight of God, or as containing beautiful
history, interesting parables, and sublime descriptions."

At the time when Jonas King joined the church at
Plainfield, then under the care of Rev. Moses Hallock,

there was a revival there of much power. Jonas was called on to speak one evening, and he gave an account of how he had been led to Christ. He was called the next morning, long before day, by the lady of the house, begging him to come and pray for her and her children. She and her husband were both professors of religion. He found them in the sittingroom, singing a hymn, with tears streaming down their cheeks. A few neighbors were called in, and the journal goes on to say, "As the morning dawned upon us from the east, it saw fifteen or twenty of us bowing before Him who called the light out of darkness, beseeching him to cause the dayspring from on high to visit our souls."

A great blessing followed this early prayer-meeting, felt throughout the church and community.

"Though much occupied with religious concerns, I felt an increasing desire after knowledge, an inextinguishable thirst for study, and entertained some very feeble distant hope that I might at a future period of my life obtain a collegiate education—how, I knew not."

Before attending a regular high-school, Jonas learned the whole of the English grammar by heart, studying it while hoeing corn—and in his seventy-fifth year could still repeat the whole long list of prepositions.

The following statement comes from Rev. W. A. Hallock, D. D.

"The Hon. William H. Maynard, Senator of the state of New York, was a native of Conway, Mass., and fitted for college with Rev. Moses Hallock.

"In an address before the Utica Lyceum, Mr. Maynard related some interesting facts, which had come under his own observation, illustrating the success of self-made men.

"In December, 1807, Mr. Maynard was teaching school for a quarter in a district of Plainfield : as he entered the schoolhouse one cold, blustering morning, he observed a lad that he had not seen before, sitting on one of the benches. The lad soon made known his errand. He was fifteen years old, he said, and he wanted an education. His parents lived about six miles distant, and he had come from home on foot that morning, to see if Mr. Maynard could help him to contrive how to obtain it.

"Mr. Maynard asked him if his parents could help him to get an education. 'No, sir.' 'Have you any friends to assist you?' 'No, sir.' 'Well, how do you expect to get an education?' 'I do n't know, sir, but I thought I would come and see you.'

"Mr. Maynard told him to stay that day, and he would see what could be done. He perceived that the boy had good sense, though no uncommon brilliancy; and he was peculiarly struck with the cool and resolute manner in which he undertook to conquer difficulties which would have intimidated common minds.

"In the course of the day, Mr. Maynard made provision for having him boarded through the winter in the family with himself, the lad to pay for his board by his services out of school.

"He gave himself diligently to study, in which he made good proficiency, improving every opportunity of reading and conversation for acquiring knowledge, and thus spent the winter. He afterwards fitted for college with Rev. Moses Hallock.

"This was the early history of the Rev. Dr. Jonas King, whose exertions in the cause of Oriental learning, and in alleviating the miseries of Greece, have endeared him alike to the scholar and the philanthropist, and shed a bright ray of glory upon his native country."

At the age of seventeen young Jonas was pronounced by the minister and selectmen fully competent to take charge of a small school, some of the scholars being older than himself. In this school, he says, "I endeavored to be faithful; prayed with the children morning and night, and often labored to impress on their minds the importance of religion."

The money obtained in this way was given to his father, who was just then building a new house. The next winter found Jonas teaching school at an increased salary, at Cummington, Mass., a town near Hawley, and the native place of William Cullen Bryant. Dr. King's father now urged him to leave home, saying, "I want you should be in a situation to be more useful than I have been in the cause of our Lord and Saviour, who died for us. I think I am willing to let you go, though it seems hard."

"Such conversation used almost to break my heart, and I was obliged to retire and give way to my feelings by weeping, and in prayer to God for direction.

"At length I signified to my father my determination to give two years, after I should be of age, to the study of Greek and Latin. But my father said it would be better for me to go then, though, if I stayed with him while he lived, the farm would be my recompense. He could not advise me, only commend me to God.

"After a little consideration, I decided deliberately; packed what clothes and books I had, and set off in search 'of a better country,' feeling as if I were a kind of orphan in the world; and commending myself to Him who, I had been taught to believe, would never forsake 'the seed of the righteous,' nor leave those who put their trust in him.

"Sixteen miles distant lived a gentleman who taught music, and with whom I had, the year before, formed some acquaintance. With him I made arrangements to study Latin and music. I agreed to his conditions, and he, to make me a complete singing-master. So great was my eagerness in reading Virgil, that with about fifty-eight days' study, I finished the twelve books of the 'Æneid.' These I recited to a lawyer named Pepper, who treated me with much affection, and taught me many things which were afterwards of much use to me."

In the fall, after visiting his parents, Jonas found his way to Cape Cod, at a town called Dennis, working his way there with his own hands, as did the Apostle Paul, and much to the benefit of his health, as he had a little before raised blood, either from his too close application to study or from too much effort in singing.

Some friend in Hawley had sent word to Dennis of Jonas' coming. The first question asked him was, "Is your name King?" Next, "What can you eat?" Answer, "Anything but cabbage-stumps," some of which were just at hand in a barren garden. "You are the very man we want to live among us and teach our children," was the rejoinder; and soon Jonas was engaged for six months at $14 a month, and board; a large salary in those days for such a place; and this the committee made $14 50 when the time of payment came.

Here Jonas remained a year, having then $120 or $130 in his purse; and feeling about his money as did Jacob at the sight of Joseph's wagons. He hesitated whether to go on teaching for another year, so as to increase his store, or, as he writes, "to quit all, and go and study with some minister with a view to enter college. I was in my twenty-first year, and feared if I delayed study another year, I might be induced finally to relinquish it. This I feared the more, as I found a growing attachment to one of my pupils in music, whose voice in the treble I thought might prove like that of the Syrens, a means of turning me out of the course which I wished to pursue. I at once decided, went on board a packet for Boston, spent a week in viewing the wonders of the capital, purchased a few second-hand Greek books, and set out for Hawley. Thence I went to Halifax, Vt., and with the Rev. T. H. Wood, whose name I shall ever remember with affection, commenced the Greek Testament, and a review of Virgil, which had been entirely laid aside aside from the time I left Chesterfield.

"My eyes were weak, and I could study only by daylight. I used to rise at five o'clock, and think over my conjugations and grammar-rules till daylight appeared; then walk out about forty rods for exercise, and then study till the setting of the sun. Nothing but Greek was in my head. I dreamed of it, and, as my roommate often told me, talked of it in my sleep.

"By the blessing of God I was enabled, by what was reckoned about six weeks' study, to finish reading, for the first time, the New Testament in the original. The progress I made was owing to the continual high excitement of mind which I had in view of going to college. My health, however, became impaired, from want of exercise and by too intense application to study."

But this did not discourage the young student. He was still determined to obtain an education, if possible.

CHAPTER II.

COLLEGE AND SEMINARY LIFE.

Williams College—College Revival—Doctrinal Doubts Overcome—
College Honors—Andover Theological Seminary—Life of
Faith—Classmates.

BEING persuaded by his instructor to go to Williams College, Dr. King writes:

" I set off on foot to visit the seat of the muses among the mountains of Berkshire, to see if I could be admitted among them. I arrived in the midst of a snowstorm weary and fatigued, fearing what would be the issue of my journey. My first business was to call on the president, who demanded how long I had been studying, and how much Latin and Greek I had read. I told him frankly, and he shook his head, saying he could give me no encouragement of entering before another year. This was like a frost on the flowers of spring, and my opening hopes began to wither. If I waited another year, my little purse would be empty, and then I would be obliged to spend another year keeping school, in order to be able to enter; and that would bring me to such an age, that I would view the idea of obtaining a liberal education as almost hopeless.

" I went out from his presence with a heavy heart, but thought I would use one effort more; that was to call on the tutors and hear what they would say to me.

I found two of them together.   Both shook their heads, and one replied very shortly, that it was out of all question to think of entering, and left the room.   I then asked the other if I could not be admitted for a while on probation, and if my progress was not such that they could with honor admit me, be sent away at the end of the term.

"Mr. E. (the tutor) looked at me with attention, and then demanded if I had been studying with the Rev. Mr. Wood of Halifax.   I replied that I had.   'If,' said he, 'you are the same young man of whom I have heard him speak, I will guarantee that you will be admitted before the close of the year.   Come on, and I will speak to the president in your behalf.'   This was like the dawn of morning to a night-worn and weather-beaten sailor.   For, had I met with a complete repulse at this time, I think my spirits would have sunk under it, and I should have relinquished the learned halls and academic groves, and have gone back to the little cottage and woodlands of my father.

"I returned home with a light and gladsome heart, packed up my books and clothes which I had left there, and having received the prayers and benedictions of my parents, set out a second time for Williamstown.   It was, if I rightly recollect, some time in March.   A thaw had taken place, the snow was rapidly melting, the roads were filled with water and mud, which rendered it extremely unpleasant and wearisome travelling.   It began, more-over, to rain, but at length I saw the lights of the lamp of science beaming faintly on me through the intervening darkness, a fit likeness of my situation, and I marched on with a quicker step and at about eleven o'clock reached an inn near the college. The next day I began to reside within its walls, and was permitted to recite with the members of the Freshman class, who entered college some time before I had read a single word of the Greek Testament, or Græca Minora. 'Hic labor, hoc opus fuit.' I was obliged to study night and day, to read for the first time long lessons which they were reviewing. Two hundred lines of the Georgics, seven or eight sections of Cicero's Orations, together with a portion of the Græca Minora was an Herculean task for one day. It often seemed to me that my head would be crazed, or that I would sink into the earth under the burden laid upon me."

His health now suffered severely in consequence of so much study, living too as he did in a very economical way; but at the end of two wearisome months, he sustained a public examination, and was admitted to the Freshman class.

At the close of the Freshman year, having taken a good stand in his class, he made application in vain to two distinguished gentlemen to lend him two or three hundred dollars to help him along. "One of them gave me a dollar, with which I bought a hymn-book to remember him by; the other gave a few kind words only."

The next winter teaching school again during part of the term and in vacation, brought in money enough to carry him on till spring; after which he concluded to make one more effort to borrow money; but after a toilsome journey, taking with him a letter of recommendation, was actually "repulsed with rage." "This decided me to make no more such applications, but simply lay my case before my Heavenly Father, who would not repulse me in such a manner, and who had the silver and the gold in his hands, and the cattle on a thousand hills. In a few days, I unexpectedly received an invitation to take charge of a school in Catskill for six months, which I accepted. During a part of this time I also taught music two or three evenings a week. By this means, I gained money sufficient to defray my expenses for the ensuing year. And, though I had been absent from college nine months of my Sophomore year, I had been enabled, by the goodness of God, to pursue my studies in such a manner as to remain in my class.

"My college companions used sometimes to rally me a little, saying that I was a singular genius, to keep up with them, and yet be absent continually heaping up wealth; that, after I had defrayed my college expenses, I should unquestionably have money to put out at interest.

The third year I was perfectly at my ease. My mind was in a state of perpetual enchantment. I felt as if I had entered upon a new state of existence ; that I had come out of darkness into marvellous light. What I had learned before seemed only as a pebble on the shore, by the side of that vast ocean of Mathematics which now opened to my view. I was the more delighted with these studies, because they were considered very important; and I began to entertain some hope that, by a strict attention to them, I might secure the highest appointment at the end of my academical career. But, before the close of the year, my attention was arrested by something more interesting than Philosophy, Mathematics, and college honors. Though my deportment before the world was, for the most part, strictly according to my profession as a disciple of Christ, still I felt a want of spirituality in my devotions, and of faithfulness to those around me who had no hope in the great Redeemer of sinners, and whom I should one day meet at the bar of God. These feelings were increased by the return of my roommate (at the end of the spring vacation) the Rev. S. Eaton, whose heart now seemed enkindled with a fresh flame from heaven. He and I and one other met together one evening, talked over our unfaithfulness, prayed for refreshings from the presence of the Lord, and agreed to converse seriously each day with some one of our college companions ; also to spend an hour together each evening in prayer.

"The effect was astonishing. In about a week or fortnight, almost all in college were interested. Some mocked, some wept, and some, who had been very gay and thoughtless, were seen, in great anxiety, inquiring what they should do to be saved."

After times of "surprising grace," the enemy of souls often takes advantage of the young Christian, who may have relaxed in watchfulness, thinking the conflict over. From whatever cause, just after the college revival Jonas King passed as it were into the very shadow of the "mount of privilege." His feet were lifted away from the foundations of his faith. Doubts as to doctrine, and as to his own acceptance, assailed him.　But "the Lord knoweth them that are his," and will not suffer them to be tempted above that they are able.　This young soldier of the cross was soon brought to the alternative, either to reject the Bible, or to accept all its teachings. He looked unto God, and was lightened.　The victory was given.　"He restoreth my soul" became the song of deliverance of him, who was thus taught from his own experience how to meet the bitter and acute cavillings of many with whom, as missionary in the East, he was afterwards brought in contact.

At the end of the Junior year an English oration was assigned him.

Through the Senior year also, Jonas passed successfully, teaching a singing-school, and engaging as private instructor in a family residing about a mile and a half from the college.　At the close, he received the Philosophical oration.

"During the summer vacation I took a school, and in September, 1816, received my Bachelor's degree; and a few weeks after settled all my college bills.　Sophomore year I had received from a friend twenty dollars; Junior year about the same; Senior year sixty, and fifty more from the American Education Society.　In two instances I had received from private friends about one dollar and a half, or two dollars, not more.　This was all the aid I ever received, from the time I left my father's house till I left college.　I had furnished myself, or rather God had furnished me, with books, clothing, board, everything, except a suit of clothes my parents gave me at the age of twenty-one, which was called my freedom-suit. When I had studied one book, I sold that to purchase another, and at the close sold all I had left to bear my part of the expenses at Commencement.

"Thus the Lord had brought me along in a strange way, and I appeared as a wonder unto many. I often passed through trials and hardships, but out of all of them the Lord delivered me. I had often come down to the brink of the Red Sea, and had seen there no possible way of passing over. But the moment I stepped in the waves divided.

"I was many a time hungry and thirsty in the wilderness, but whenever I cried unto the Lord God of Israel, and smote the rock with the rod of faith, the waters gushed out, and the heavens rained down manna. Often I have lain down at night weeping, and joy came in the morning. It was not owing to any skill or merit of my own. It was all of God, and all the glory be unto his name. One thing I have often noticed, and which I think worth remarking. That is, when I have been straitened and pressed till I knew not which way to turn, I have generally been brought to a kind of resignation to the will of God a little before deliverance came.

"By the advice of President Moore, and with the aid of some charitable people in Chatham, New York, I made my way to the Theological Seminary at Andover, near Boston. Here I spent three years, receiving from a charitable fund of the seminary eighty dollars a year to defray the expense of board.

"I read but few commentaries, few polemical works,

and generally examined subjects by the Scriptures themselves. And this course I would recommend to every
young student in theology. It is far better to drink at
the pure fountain, than of the streams at a distance,
which bear along in their course much of this earth.
The latter part of the first year I lost much time by a
severe illness, the effects of which I felt for two years
after. The third year I devoted to writing sermons, and
to the study of pulpit oratory, though from the state of
my health and the state of my heart, I labored under
almost constant depression of mind."

Dr. King's journal, while at Andover, is a record truly
of a life of faith. In time of need and discouragement,
he still hopes in God, and help is sure to follow. He
writes, " January 20, 1818 : Other young men, when they
need pecuniary aid, have parents and friends to whom
they apply for assistance ; but I have nowhere to go, but
directly to the throne of grace, and there I find all my
wants richly supplied. Bless the Lord, O my soul.

"Oct: 31. Visited to-day Dr. Morse's, in Charlestown. How kind is my Redeemer in granting me so
many friends."

Then mention is made of a sermon on the Resurrection, by Rev. Sereno Dwight, and of dining at Dr. Morse's.
Again of books bought at Andover.

" Purchased of Mr. Stuart, Eichhorn's Einleitung. It
is a very great treasure. What reason have I to be
thankful, that a kind Providence supplies me with books !
Oh, that I might write HOLINESS upon them all ; that I
might consecrate them to the cause of Christ ! Lord,

grant that I may desire books and learning, only that I may make myself more extensively useful to the church and to the world.

"'T is astonishing to me, that my Creator bestows on me books and friends and innumerable other blessings, since I am so constantly ungrateful and do so little to promote his glory."

He speaks of ill-health, of pain in his head, which make him think of the poor pagans with no comfort, no Saviour, when they are called to suffer.

Then follow confessions of ambition, pride, earthly-mindedness, and love of self.

"Friday, Dec. 11, 1818, was observed by the Senior class, Andover, for the special purpose of examining the motives which were leading them into the gospel ministry." And Dr. King copies from Titus and Timothy direct Bible instruction on the subject.

Among these young men, thus looking to God, were Thurston and Bingham, afterward of the Sandwich Islands, Dr. Wayland of Brown University, Byington of the Indian Missions, Torrey, who translated Neander's Church History, Spalding and Winslow of Ceylon, and others, whose useful lives, as well as that of Jonas King, have certified God's promise to give wisdom to those who seek it in sincerity and faith.

CHAPTER III.

EARLY MISSIONARY EFFORTS IN THIS COUNTRY.

Work in Charlestown, Boston, and Portsmouth—Licensed to preach at Andover, 1819—Labors in Brimfield and Holland, Massachusetts, and Charleston, South Carolina.   Letter from Rev. Edward Palmer.

In Dr. King's case the youth was emphatically "the father of the man."   Even before finishing his course at Andover Theological Seminary, he as an evangelist began in this country personal efforts that not only very early showed the aggressive nature of his piety, but in addition proved to be the exact training needed for his subsequent work abroad.

His vacations were employed as follows:

"The first vacation I spent in visiting my parents; the second with Dr. Jedediah Morse of Charlestown, passing six weeks in his family, while making an abridgment of 'Walker on Elocution,' and selecting some fine specimens of eloquence from speeches delivered before Bible Societies, Missionary Societies, etc., which, together with some others, were afterwards published under the title of 'The Christian Orator.'   Two vacations I spent in Boston as a missionary, and one in Portsmouth.   I also spent two weeks of term time in Harvard."

Dr. King was licensed to preach by an association of ministers at Andover, July 6, 1819.

Upon finally leaving Andover, he was providentially led almost immediately into practical labor. His own wish was to study if possible three years longer; but he was in debt for books, clothing, etc., and justice demanded that he should first of all do what he could to bring in ready money. He felt unfit for the ministry in point of knowledge and piety. He was blamed by many for wishing to give more time to preparation, they accusing him of undue ambition to be a great man. He comforted himself with the thought that God knew his motives and feelings.

"At present," he writes, "whatever might be my attainments in knowledge and piety, I must in some way earn two hundred dollars. It had been so ordered that I was in the ministry. My health demanded relaxation from study. In view of the whole, I concluded to go for awhile and preach faithfully what I believed to be truth, hoping that God would bless his own word, though it should be delivered by one whose hopes of heaven were very faint and feeble.

"I first engaged to go on a mission six weeks to South Brimfield and Holland, under the direction of the Massachusetts Domestic Missionary Society. There it seemed as if the Spirit of the Lord came upon me, as upon Samson of old when among the Philistines. My faith seemed to be strengthened, and my hopes revived, and it pleased God to crown my labors with some success. I have been told that about twenty were hopefully converted.

"Having been recommended by the Rev. P. Fiske, I was next employed for six months by the Female Domestic Missionary Society of Charleston, South Carolina, to labor as missionary in that city, where, on my arrival, I was ordained as an evangelist. My business was to preach the Gospel to seamen and the poor, and to bind up the broken-hearted; a work truly noble, and to perform which the Son of God left the abodes of glory. The fishermen of Galilee, the publicans and sinners, the sick and the afflicted, were the objects of his particular attention.

"I preached often for Dr. Palmer, at the Circular church, and supplied the Second Presbyterian church for six weeks, during the illness of Dr. Flinn. By these means, I was thrown much into society with those who were considered the most polished people in the United States, and had opportunity for improvement in many ways.

"Nathaniel Russell, Esq., the father-in-law of Bishop Dehone, and Charles O'Neale, Esq., both gave me a hospitable welcome to their houses during my residence at Charleston. By Mr. and Mrs. O'Neale I was received and treated as a son.

"Having finished my labors at Charleston, I returned to the North, preached six or eight weeks at Park Street Church, Boston, during an absence of the Rev. Mr. Dwight, visited my parents, made them a present of fifty dollars, returned to Andover and resumed my studies."

Among Dr. King's early papers appear "Plans for doing good in Boston and other places.

" Explore every nook and corner of the town to find those that are destitute of Bibles. If any such be found, take their name and place of residence, and see that they have Bibles sent them immediately, accompanied by a serious address on the importance of its contents, and the necessity of immediately becoming acquainted with its doctrines. In these visits, take some religious friend with me.

"Meddle not with politics. 'Procul, O procul.' Avoid, as much as possible, disputes of every kind. They are seldom of any use.

"Speak to the heart. Use the artillery of Mount Sinai, till men begin to feel that they are sinners. Show them the spirituality of the Divine Law.

" Let all your conversation be kind and affectionate. Address sinners with all that earnestness and affection with which a pious father would address his children from a death-bed.

" Tracts must be circulated, and always attended, if possible, with a short, but serious and impressive address.

" The sick and dying must be .visited ; funerals attended ; and let an evening conference be appointed at the house of mourning as soon as may be convenient.

"Boston contains about 40,000 inhabitants, and twenty-four societies. Allowing 1,000 souls to each society, there will be left destitute of religious instruction, 16,000. The number of deaths in 1814, was 907; in the year preceding, 904.

" Houses for religious worship must be erected for

the convenience of sailors and the destitute who belong to the town.

" Let little associations be formed in different parts of the town for the purpose of ascertaining, (1,) what families are destitute of the Bible, (2,) those who do not attend public worship, whether families or individuals, (3,) who need instruction, (4,) what vices are prevalent. (5.) Let these little associations distribute Bibles, tracts, etc., comfort the sick and afflicted, persuade those who are able to attend public worship, and prevent by various means Sabbath-breaking, profaneness, intemperance, idleness, and vice of all kinds.

" Let there be little social praying circles as many as are convenient. It is prayer that must bring down all the blessings.

"The blacks must be attended to. Find some fit for schoolmasters or ministers."

A diary of visits made to the poor, of meetings held, and Sunday-school children gathered in, shows how thoroughly these plans were carried out in detail.

Again, in Portsmouth, we find the same efforts made; and the following plans for doing good added to the former list:

"Let every Christian converse with one or more impenitent sinners every day; and at the social prayer-meeting relate his success for the encouragement of others.

" Obtain subscribers for the 'Panoplist,' in order to extend religious information, and to aid Rev. Jeremiah Evarts.

"Make an effort to secure some support for Mr. Evarts, that he may devote all his time to missionary objects.

"Form a society among the young men, auxiliary to the American Education Society."

In Portsmouth Dr. King found many Christians who were a help to him in his work, and in his personal religious experience. Many names, both here and in Boston, he notes with interest and affection ; among others, those of Deacon Tappan and his daughter Eliza, relatives of the Tappan brothers so widely known. Indeed, these early diaries are kept with the system and fastidious correctness which afterwards were so characteristic of the records of his subsequent work abroad.

Plans for doing good in Charleston, S. C., Sept., 1819, also precede the journal of his stay there.

"Endeavor to excite Christians to frequent and fervent prayer.

"Let the members of little circles for prayer have a street or part of a street assigned them, in which it shall be their duty to visit and converse with the families, find out their situation, whether they have Bibles, whether they attend family prayer, and attend meeting on the Sabbath ; whether any have serious impression. When the members meet, let all the interesting cases be made a particular subject of prayer.

"Visit Sabbath-schools, and have weekly meetings of the instructors, to converse with them and advise them.

"Almshouse, orphanhouse, hospital and jail, must receive proper attention.

4*

"Seamen. Form a marine Bible Society. Converse with captains and officers, and try to show them the importance of attending prayers on board their vessels.

"Write for the 'Southern Evangelical Intelligencer,' on practical subjects of religion.

"Keep a list of the names of all the families that I visit.

"Seek out young men of piety and talents, and prevail on them, if possible, to engage in the gospel ministry.

"Inquire the state of schools and colleges. Make some plan for their improvement.

"In order to keep my mind vigorous and active, study a little Latin, French, and Arabic, every day."

While it was simply impossible for any one to carry out in full so many different efforts for good, yet the high aims and labor of this young theological student were not without gratifying results; for in this early part of his minority he was privileged in Charleston, as elsewhere, to gather gems to the honor of his Lord.

Let the following testimony speak for itself, as given by Rev. Edward Palmer of Barnwell, South Carolina, the father of Rev. B. C. Palmer, D. D., of New Orleans, and brother of Rev. Benjamin Palmer, D. D., in whose church, the Circular church of Charleston, Jonas King was ordained evangelist, Dec. 17, 1819; after which he returned to Andover, and spent about a year as Resident Licentiate.

"Barnwell, August 17, 1875.

".... Probably I am the only person now living who

can, from a personal knowledge of that great and good servant of God, give any details of him and his work while a missionary in Charleston. . . . His visits and his labors were welcomed and appreciated by all the pious with whom he became conversant, particularly by the ladies of the society in whose employ he was, and who were made glad by his untiring and successful work among the poor and spiritually needy of the city. In the family of my brother, Rev. Dr. Palmer, whose lady was the corresponding secretary of the society, and ·in my own family, the female head of which was the superintendent of the same, the visits of that dear brother were very frequent, and always most welcome and cheering. From personal and specific acquaintance with the missionary and his work, I can truthfully say, that he was conscientiously, ardently, faithfully, and perseveringly devoted to the arduous duties he had undertaken; always giving the highest satisfaction to the society in whose employ he was, as well as securing the approbation of all who wished well to the new and interesting enterprise; for, if I am not mistaken, that was the first society of the kind ever inaugurated in the place, undertaken and managed altogether under the auspices of ladies; so that, as in the first report of the missionary, he remarked, ‘The formation of this society I hail as a star over this city, like that at Bethlehem, and anticipate the time when this star shall increase in magnitude, till it shall attain the full-orbed effulgence of the meridian sun.’ . . .

“Dr. King’s departure to the North was universally

deplored. If you will allow me, I will relate a circumstance which may be interesting, not only as evincing his devotion to his Master, but as developing his desire to 'have laborers sent into the harvest.'

"At the time he was in Charleston, I was the principal of a flourishing academy in the city, and not unfrequently called upon to deliver public addresses to certain societies. On one occasion I delivered a missionary address before the 'Young Men's Missionary Society' in the city, at which Brother King was present. Accompanying me home, at the close of the same, he took me aside and asked, 'Have you ever thought of the ministry *yourself?*' to which I promptly replied, 'Look, dear sir, at a fond wife, and four lovely children, whom I am bound by every tender and loving tie, to support, and then see whether such a question can be asked.' He immediately rejoined, 'If the Lord shall call, he will open up the way,' and then begged me to give the subject a prayerful consideration. Forthwith he communicated with my brother and pastor, Rev. Dr. Palmer, Sen., and other pious friends ; especially with Dr. Porter, the senior professor of Andover Seminary, then on a southern visit for health; all of which, to bring this topic to a close, culminated in my going to Andover Seminary in 1821, and returning in 1824 a regularly-ordained minister, whom a kind Providence has permitted to labor in the vineyard over 51 years; and though no longer a settled pastor, having the last year resigned my pastorate, I am still preaching nearly every Sabbath, at the advanced age of nearly 87.

" Instrumentally, therefore, Dr. King ushered me into the ministry, and then, perhaps, through me, my two sons, laboring in New Orleans and Mobile.

" I take the liberty of enclosing Dr. King's first report, which I have cut out of a bound volume of reports."

This report, whose leaves are brown with age, is of interest, not only as regarding Dr. King, but also as being an earnest, given so long ago, of what the Christian women of the present day, by God's blessing, are being privileged to undertake and accomplish.

CHAPTER IV.

GOING ABROAD, AND LIFE IN PARIS.

Studies Continued—Way opened to prosecute them in Paris—Appointment as Professor in Amherst College—Gospel Meetings held in Europe—Serious Illness—Letter from Pliny Fisk, calling him to Palestine—Acquaintance with Baron de Staël, and other men of note—Tracts and New Testaments distributed at Nôtre Dame, Malmaison, Versailles, and Mount Calvary—Preaching in Paris—First Observance there of the Monthly Concert.

THE following entry was made, May 30, 1821, in an early diary : "Decided to leave this country for Europe to study Arabic, under the celebrated De Sacy."

In order to a full understanding of the way in which Dr. King was led to this decision, and so onwards through France to his work in the East, it is necessary to notice in what direction his mind was turned during his last year in Andover.   He writes :

"From November, 1820, till the spring of 1821, I spent my time in reading the Hebrew Bible, Oriental Antiquities, by Jahn and Warnercroft in German, the Greek and Latin Fathers, Livy's History, Eichhorn's Extracts of History in Latin, the works of Massillon in French, Quintilian, and commenced a translation of Bellerman's Biblical Geography.   During this time, was put into my hands by Mrs. P. the Life of Henry Martyn, as she feared I was too much occupied with human science, and two little with divine. This I read with eagerness, but instead of abating my desire for study, it increased it. About the same time appeared a little pamphlet by Mr. Stuart, containing extracts from Jahn's dissertation on the Study of Languages, accompanied with notes by Mr. Stuart. The effect of this and of Martyn's Life was powerful, so that it was sometimes with difficulty that I could sleep. It seemed to me that something almost supernatural had possessed my breast. My desire was to go to Europe to acquire the Arabic language, and then enter whatever field of labor should be presented, perhaps a mission among the Arabians or Persians. It had been my plan for more than two years to take this course, if the way should ever be opened. I had often made it a subject of prayer, and had expressed my intentions to Mr. and Mrs. Russell and Mr. and Mrs. O'Neale, at Charleston.

"How to procure the means was now the question. What would support me at Andover or Princeton, could not do so at Paris or Göttingen. At length I concluded to address a benevolent and wealthy gentleman of my acquaintance, Col. I. C. Trask, of Springfield. After having written the letter, I spread it repeatedly before the Lord, and begged that if those feelings and desires that possessed my breast came of him, and if he would indeed go with me and preserve me from being led astray by human philosophy and the allurements of the world, that he would incline the heart of him to whom the letter was addressed to give me a favorable answer. After having sent it, I devoted a day to fasting and prayer; and thought that if I did not mistake my feelings, they were such as I had often observed previous to having my petitions granted.

"I soon received an answer from Col. T. requesting me to meet him at Boston, and to take lodgings there in the first hotel at his expense. I was on my way thither, when the letter was given me by a stagedriver. On arriving, he generously offered to furnish me with five hundred dollars. I at once decided to go to Europe, if I had to make my way back as a common sailor; and wrote to my Charleston friends on the subject. Without waiting for answer, I packed up my things at Andover, conveyed them to Boston, and had made every preparation to go on to New York to set sail for Havre, when I received from Mr. O'Neale the sorrowful tidings of his wife's death. I went back to Andover to spend a few days in mourning, and was by some circumstance led thence to Newburyport, where I unexpectedly received the offer from the Hon. W. B. Bannister, cousin of my father, of a passage in a vessel of his bound to Holland; also of provisions for the voyage."

The preceding year Jonas King had been able to procure for the Seminary at Andover, upwards of two thousand dollars. This may have influenced the Treasurer to make him now a loan of one hundred and sixty dollars, one of the trustees becoming security.

Letters from the South were received approving of his plans, and with fresh offers of service.

"Thus everything was favorable. The ship was ready, and I was only waiting for a fair wind to waft me over the ocean, when I received the information that I was appointed Professor of Oriental Languages in Amherst College."

This appointment was communicated to Dr. King by Noah Webster, LL D., then president of the Board of Trustees. While he appreciated the honor offered him, he was still somewhat doubtful what he ought to do. He feared the duties connected with it would shut him out of the direct work of the ministry ; but upon conference with the Rev. Dr. Storrs, Stuart, and other friends, he decided to accept this service for the Great Head of the Church, whose special guidance he was seeking as to his course in life.

Dr. Moses Stuart wrote :

" MY DEAR SIR : I have consulted my brethren on the subject of your office. We are unanimously of opinion that it will be a good thing both for you and for the college. It will give you advantages to go out as professor elect, and they may profit very much by your services in procuring books. In the mean time, as Oriental Literature in a college at present will hardly give you full scope, I presume they will superadd the Greek in due time, which will give you a chance to go to Göttingen. However, as Providence has opened the way for Oriental Literature, in conscience you are bound to make this the chief object of your attention.

" Yours in haste,

" M. STUART."

The Trustees of Amherst College were anxious to have their own professor well qualified for his position, and fully approved of having him still carry out his plan to study abroad.   Providence in every way favored this intention.   A passport was no idle form in those days, nor easy to obtain; yet just in time "a citizen from his own country" was sent to identify him as the law required.   A letter of introduction was given him by Mr. N. Carnes of Boston, to S. V. S. Wilder, an American merchant residing in Paris.   He sailed from Boston August 18, 1821, arriving in Holland in thirty-five days, and at Paris on October 9.

On his way he devoted some little time to objects of interest which were then especially attractive to one fresh from Massachusetts.   He formed acquaintances, afterwards of value, with some Protestant ministers and laymen in Amsterdam, Rotterdam, and other places; he also held religious services wherever practicable, both at sea and on land.   In proposing such meetings, there was a directness and simplicity in Dr. King's manner, such as implied expectation of success as a matter of course; it was not easy to refuse any appointment suggested by the earnest young American stranger, and he seems everywhere to have received a warm Christian welcome.

Once in Paris, he began study immediately, being at great disadvantage, however, because obliged to learn Arabic through the French language.   In about two months his health declined.   Change to other lodgings seemed of no avail.   "By the last of March," he writes, "I was taken ill of a high bilious fever, and was confined to my bed for nearly a month.   So little hope, at one time, was entertained of my recovery, that a place was selected for me in the Père-la-Chaise, where I might rest my weary head till the trumpet of the archangel should awake me.   The thought that my progress in study must now be interrupted, just as I had begun to pursue it with a little pleasure ; that I was spending upon physicians, and watchers, and nurses, and apothecaries, the little pittance of money that remained to me ; and that consequently I should be obliged soon to return to America without having accomplished the object of my coming— all this tended to sink my spirits still more, and add strength to my disease.   The thought of my poor parents distressed me, and such were the feelings of my heart, that I had little spiritual comfort.   Sometimes I was more resigned, and when the nurse would leave the room, I would lift up my voice and say, ‘ O Lord, continue thy chastisement if that be necessary to make me humble, and fit me for thy service.   Take away my health, keep me on this bed of sickness till I shall have gained spiritual strength to overcome the world.   Stop my progress in study, take away the little pittance of support I have, if I may but learn the heavenly art of living near to thee, and may be rich in faith towards the Lord Jesus Christ.’ ”   Thus like David he cried unto the Lord in his trouble, and was soon able to write, “ I can truly bless the Lord for this chastisement.   I have since had more comfort in prayer, more evidence of my union to Christ.”

It was not until the last of June, that he was able to take up study again with vigor ; and then suddenly, through the instrumentality of a letter received from the Rev. Pliny Fisk, his attention was fixed on a new object, a Mission to the Holy Land.

Before noting the circumstances that favored his acceptance of this missionary call, there is much to claim attention in Dr. King's life in Paris itself. Here he became acquainted not only with Mr. Wilder and family, but, at Mr. Wilder's house, with many Christian people from England and other parts of Europe, who afterwards proved friends indeed. Mr. Augustus H. Hillhouse of New Haven helped him in many ways necessary to a stranger in a strange city. Tuesday, November 4, 1821, Dr. King writes: "Was introduced to a large society of savants from all parts of the world at Mr. Langle's, Conservateur des Manuscrits Orientales. Conversed much with an American doctor. Met a Persian, a Dane, a Spaniard, etc.

"Monday, Jan. 14, 1822. Visited for the first time the Baron de Staël-Holstein, son of the celebrated Madame de Staël, and rejoiced exceedingly to find him much interested in the cause of religion. Said he found his mind fluctuating. Sometimes he thought he had some grace, at other times was almost disposed to say he had none. That he was in the practice of reading the Scriptures, which he would do if it were only for the beauty of the composition and the imagery. Said that he spent one year at Geneva, when about seventeen years of age, in attending lectures on theology; that this was the only year of his life that he should be willing to live over again, if it were left to him to choose; hoped that he should become more and more engaged in the good cause of extending the knowledge of Jesus Christ to fallen man. Said that it appeared to him that the grand truths taught by revelation seemed also to be graven on the heart of man: first, that he needed a Mediator, a Redeemer; and, second, that the operation of the Holy Spirit was necessary; that men absolutely find something that it is out of their power to obtain, and which must be given them. Made inquiries with regard to Arianism in America; said that unhappily in France, and on the Continent generally, Unitarian sentiments prevailed; that they were chilling; that he thought no man could read the Scriptures and not believe them, nor without at once admitting that Jesus Christ is truly divine and one with the Father. He thought also that the doctrine of the agency of God continually exerted upon man was evident. I related to him some things which were doing in America; he wished to know what sect was most engaged in doing good; thought exertions to do good were evidences of the purity of religion. Greeted me with much kindness, and said that he should be highly gratified to call on me often to converse on those interesting subjects."

Dr. King also notes interviews with Prof. Edward Everett, Dr. Spurzheim, Monod, father and son, Gen. Macaulay, Prof. Blumhartt, Rev. Lewis Way, F. André Michaux, Rev. Daniel Wilson, Soulier (pastor), Marron, President of the Consistoire, Rev. Gardner Spring, Olshausen, Van Lennep of Smyrna, Louis Mertens, Waddington, and other typical men of that day.

Dr. King makes special mention of the Rev. Mr. Tacey, because he was intimately acquainted with Henry Kirke White and Henry Martyn. "He showed me a letter in Martyn's own handwriting, and observed he had just paid a visit to the lady who was so dear to Martyn's heart. He spoke highly of our President Edwards and of David Brainerd, and remarked that he esteemed Martyn very highly; he thought Brainerd superior to him or to any other missionary whose life he had ever read."

But Dr. King had an opportunity in Paris to make acquaintance, not with persons only, but with places in and about the city which then, as now, was full of works of art and various collections of interest; among them some Egyptian antiquities were new indeed to the young American professor, who drew from his examination of them many lessons as to the past and present, little thinking he would himself so soon visit the actual places from which these relics had been taken.

He also went to Argenteuil, where Eloise was once abbess, and to the lunatic hospital at Salpetrière. Descriptions of these, as seen more than fifty-five years ago, are given, but must here be passed by.

At Malmaison, as elsewhere, Dr. King and his friends remembered the great commission, and talked to the porter, who had been in charge for twenty-two years, and to his family of the vanity of this world's glory, giving to his little girl, named Josephine, the tract entitled "The Dairyman's Daughter." At family prayers that evening it seemed most appropriate to sing Dr. Malan's hymn, just then published:

> "Que peut le monde
>   A mon bonheur?
> Car je le fonde
>   Sur mon Sauveur.
>
> "Il me l'acquit
>   Quand il suffit
> Pour mes péchés
>   Qu'il a portés."

In Paris, too, the actual sight of the mummeries of Roman-catholic worship, carried out there as was not the case at that time in the United States, still further prepared Dr. King for the war he was to wage for "the faith once delivered to the saints." To see the sacrilegious bowings to the images in the church of Nôtre Dame made his "blood fairly boil in his veins." At the same time the ceremonial was so imposing, he realized how easily the thoughtless or weakminded could be drawn away by it from the simplicity of the pure gospel.

An extract from his Journal of Aug. 15, 1822, gives Dr. King's impressions of Roman-catholicism, seen in its most favorable aspect.

"Called on Bishop Grégoire. Spent about two hours in conversing on the subject of religion and of my journey to Palestine. Asked him to tell me frankly if he thought that any out of the Catholic Roman church could be saved. His answer was very nearly that 'he thought not.' Said he was not in favor of persecution; *that* he condemned, and he only prayed for those who differed from him. I then stated to him my belief as nearly that of Massillon, except that I could not believe in images, etc.; that my Bible told me, 'Thou shalt not make thee any graven image—thou shalt not bow thy-self down unto them,' etc.; that I took the Bible for my guide, Jesus Christ for my Saviour, discarding entirely my own work as giving title to merit; that I believed in regeneration, and was willing to spend my life in doing good to the souls of my fellow-men. 'Now,' said I, 'you will pardon me for questioning you so closely, but I have a great desire to know your opinion, as in America we consider you as a distinguished and enlightened man. Do you think that if I die to-day or to-morrow with these feelings I shall be lost for ever?' He replied that he must say 'Yes;' and that I must be more culpable in the sight of God because I had had opportunity to know the truth, and ought to have been right by this time.

"After long conversation on various points I wished him a good-day. He took me by the hand very affec-tionately, invited me to call and see him, etc., and I came away.

"Saw the Feast of the Assumption of the Virgin. On this day the royal family walk around Nôtre Dame barefooted and bareheaded, in fulfilment of a vow made by Louis XIII. to the Virgin Mary.

"'There are some parts of our earth in which, al-though the sun shines ever so bright, it seems dark. Who could believe that a man so enlightened as Bishop Grégoire, a man who has such extensive acquaintance as he has in Germany, Italy, England, etc., who has made so great attainments in literature, has ventured to com-bat the high, the mighty pope, so that all good Catholics suppose that he aimed at deposing him—who, I say, could suppose that his views would be so narrow? And who could believe that in the nineteenth century the royal family of France would be seen walking barefooted and bareheaded in the streets of Paris, supposing this to be a most delightful sight to the Virgin Mary? Lord, what is man?"

Again, Sept. 17, 1822, on occasion of a visit paid to Versailles, and after reflections on the insufficiency of the prayers of all Catholic France to redeem the contaminated soul of Louis XIV. from the pains of purgatory—if purgatory could be supposed to exist—Dr. King writes: "While walking through the mighty hall of this immense palace, viewing its beautifully-gilded columns and splendid paintings, I stepped up to the officer who conducted us, and who was pointing out to us the most interesting objects, and said to him, 'Sir, what is all the glory of this world? Louis XIV., encircled with all this grandeur, could not help dying; and what is he the better for it? An interest in the Lord Jesus Christ is worth the whole of it, and infinitely transcends it.' 'I believe it,' replied he. I then asked him if he had ever read the Sacred Scriptures. The answer was, 'No, I have never seen them.' I then presented him with a New Testament, and charged him to read in it one chapter every day, with prayer to almighty God for the illumination of his Holy Spirit. This he promised to do, and said that he had a family of children, who should do it too. He thanked me repeatedly, and during my stay in the palace treated me with particular attention. On coming out he showed his precious treasure to another officer, who looked at me as though he wished one too, and I immediately returned and presented one to him, who seemed much delighted, and made like promises as his friend. After distributing a few tracts to some we met in the court, we made our way through the garden to the Grand Trianon, a house built by Louis XIV. for his mistress, Madame Maintenon. Here also we left a New Testament. Thence we went to the Petit Trianon, built by Louis XV. for his mistress, Madame Pompadour, and there we left another New Testament. Both were received with apparent gratitude and with many thanks.

"Met the Duke d'Angoulême and his suite; next, the king and his attendants. It was truly a brilliant sight. The king passed within two rods of me as I sat in my carriage. I had a full view of him, and he looked me full in the face. He is of a dark complexion, and looks like a man of greater talents than I had thought him to be. How many hundreds are put in motion by one man! The Marshal of France is answerable with his head for the safety of the king during his promenades. Had in the carriage with us a soldier who had made the campaign of Moscow, fought the Cossacks, and was taken prisoner. Began to talk with him about the spiritual combat which it was necessary to fight in order to gain heaven. At first he seemed disposed to make light of everything serious. But seeing we were in earnest, he began to be so too, and confessed that he often thought much of future things; that, when a child, he had been taught to read, and that he carried a New Testament with him into the army, and then lost it, but that he had always continued to pray, and that he believed in Jesus Christ. Mr. Wilder gave him some tracts and a New Testament, which he received with much gratitude."

Thus it appears that no scenes connected with the glory of this world were able to draw away the attention of the Christian soldier, Dr. King, from his appointed work. Like Paul, he said in practice if not in words, "This one thing I do."

Nor was the distribution of tracts, of which he made such a specialty, altogether unattended with personal danger, as may be seen in the account subjoined of two visits paid to Mt. Calvary, near Paris; the first one Sept. 15, 1822. After divine service, Dr. Spring, Mr. Wilder, myself, and some others, set out on a visit to Mt. Calvary, about a mile and a half distant from Nanterre, and which for nine days during the month of September is the resort of pilgrims, some of whom come sixty, eighty, or a hundred miles on foot, to pay their blind devotions there. Having filled our pockets with tracts, we began to ascend the mountain, distributing them on the right-hand and the left, to the thousands that were ascending and descending, After a walk of about three-quarters of an hour we reached the top of this eminence, on which stands a convent, and at a distance a large pile of stones and ragged rocks, beneath which is represented the tomb of our Saviour, and above which he hangs on the cross, between the two thieves. The representation is as large as life, and very striking. One of the thieves has marked in his countenance, horror, infidelity, and despair; the other, with eyes turned to the Saviour, expresses deep anguish, a sense of the justice of his suffering, mingled with hope. On a nearer approach I perceived a little cross, painted on the foot of the one on which hung our Saviour, and multitudes were climbing up to kiss it one after another. There was with us a young lady, who had lately turned from the Catholic faith to Protestant-ism. With her I entered the tomb, where men, women, and children were kneeling, and paying their adorations to the image of our Lord, which is lying wrapt in fine linen. By its side I observed a great quantity of sous and six-liard pieces, which were cast in by the worship-pers, and which, I suppose, are gathered up at night by the priests. Coming out of the tomb, I saw, at the foot of the cross, and back of it, a little place resembling a pulpit, in which stood a priest, and before him thousands singing with loud voice a sacred song. This was to me solemn, though the tune was an air from the opera. As the song ceased, the priest began to harangue the people on the subject of coming to this interesting moun-tain, and telling them when the royal family would come, and other things equally important. As I left the cross, my attention began to be arrested by the surrounding scenery. This mountain is a high elevation rising in the middle of an extensive vale, beyond which are seen, on the east, the domes and spires of Paris ; on the south, St. Cloud ; on the north, the villages of Nanterre and Chaton ; on the west, Marley and St. Germain. Between these, lie scattered along numerous clusters of houses, little villages and groves. At its foot on the east, the river Seine winds its slow and peaceful way through the midst of verdant fields, till it loses itself behind the village of Neuilly, and after a circuitous course appears again on the north near Chaton, moving onward towards St. Germain. In this vale, as far as the eye could reach, were seen pilgrims going and coming in all directions. The sides of the mountain, particularly towards the east, south, and north, are thinly covered with shrubbery and trees, among which wind about in various directions numerous footpaths leading to the convent on the summit. At different distances on the sides of these paths, stand little buildings, open in front, called stations. In them are images of Christ, the Virgin Mary, etc. Before these the pilgrims stop, kneel down on the ground and worship. One I observed was a station to pray for the dead. We visited several of these stations, and distributed the tract entitled 'Le Sermon de notre Sauveur sur la Montagne.' This was received with much avidity and gratitude. We even gave them to those who were on their knees, in the act of adoration, who would rise and come after us, to thank us. Frequently they would all leave their devotions, and flock round us to receive this precious gift; and when our tracts were all gone, some inquired when we should come again. We left them giving us thanks, and made our way back to Nanterre."

The second visit to this place of special superstitious observances, was made the following Thursday. "Went to Nanterre, where we arrived a little after midday. Mr. and Mrs. Wilder, and one or two others, had gone to Mt. Calvary, to distribute tracts and Testaments. Dr. Spring and myself having filled our pockets and hats and hands

with tracts and Testaments, set off with the hope of finding them. Just as we began to ascend the mountain, we
saw them coming at a distance. On meeting them, they
told us that they had been stopped by the commissary
of police, and that a policeman, by order of the priest
in authority, had taken away their tracts and Testaments,
and prohibited them in the name of the law to distribute
any more on Mount Calvary. Mr. W. advised us not to
proceed with the intention of distributing those which
we had. We, however, went on, giving to every one we
met, till we came in sight of the gens d'armes, when we
ceased giving, but occasionally let some fall from our
pockets, which the wind, which was very high, scattered
in all directions, so that they were gathered up by the
crowd. At length we arrived at the top of the mountain,
took our stand on the highest elevation near the cross,
and there in our own language offered up, each of us, a
prayer to the God of heaven for direction, and that he
would have mercy on those tens of thousands that we
saw around us, bowing before graven images. I then
felt in some degree strengthened to go on, and taking a
tract from my pocket, I presented it to a lady who stood
near me, and who appeared·to be a lady of some distinction. She received it with thanks, and I was not noticed
by the gens d'armes. Dr. Spring let some fall from his
pocket, and we made our way down to one of the stations. There he laid some on the charity box, while I
stood before him to hide what he did. We then went to
another station, and I gave ten or twelve to a lady, whom
I charged to distribute them. She was immediately sur-

rounded by a number, to whom she distributed, while we made our way to another station; and finally we took our way home, and distributed till we came to the foot of the mountain, when we found we had no more to give. Some took me for one of the Roman-catholic missionaries, and to these I gave a number, and charged them to go on to the top of the mountain and distribute, which they reverentially promised to do.

"The tracts we distributed were, 'Christ's Sermon on the Mount,' and 'St. Paul's Defence before Agrippa.' We gave about four hundred of these, and some New Testaments, which were received by nearly all with gratitude and joy. Occasionally we were refused. On the whole, we have distributed since last Sabbath, seventeen hundred tracts. I should judge there were on the mountain and around it twenty thousand people."

Dr. King preached more than once in the "Oratoire," and also at Mr. Wilder's house in Paris, and in Nanterre. Mr. Wilder, having special protection from Talleyrand, to whom he had brought letters of introduction from Dr. Jedediah Morse, father of the distinguished Morse brothers, was able to hold in his own house meetings, which under other circumstances were prohibited by law. Dr. King makes early record of a missionary-meeting held at Mr. Wilder's, in aid of three German missionaries on their way to Sierra Leone.

The following entry is of great interest, It tells of the first observance of the Monthly Concert in France, which was on Monday, Feb. 5, 1822. "At 7 o'clock Mr. S. V. S. Wilder, Mr. Hoshea Wilder, the Rev. J. Sohiear, and myself, held at my room the Monthly Concert of Prayer; the first ever held in this great city, and probably in France. Mr. Chaperon also came in and spent a part of the evening with us. Mr. S. read the 9th chapter of Daniel, and made the first prayer in French. This was offered principally for France, and the nations of Europe. After some remarks upon what is doing in the world to build up the Redeemer's kingdom, and what we had to expect from the promises of God, the second prayer was offered for the missionaries in different parts of the world. Then Mr. S. made some remarks in French, and Mr. H. Wilder offered the third prayer for the church generally. Then Mr. S. V. S. Wilder read a paper sent to him from England, ' Hints to Christians for unity in a general concert of prayer, for the outpouring of the Holy Spirit,' and concluded by offering the fourth prayer, in which he particularly gave thanks for what is now doing to spread the gospel. It was a delightful evening, and the Saviour seemed to be with us. May the Lord bless this first effort to set up here the Monthly Concert of Prayer; and may the time soon arrive when all the churches of Christ in the kingdom shall unite in it, and when the Spirit shall be poured from on high, and these waste places shall be glad, and this moral desert blossom as the rose."

CHAPTER V.

MISSION TO PALESTINE ACCEPTED.

Reasons for accepting Pliny Fiske's Invitation—Letters to the A. B. C. F. M. and to his Father and Mother—Means for Going to the East provided—Formation of the Paris Missionary Society, and Appointment as their First Missionary—Connection with Three Societies—Farewell Meetings for Prayer.

THESE visits and meetings and tract distributions, however, were but incidental. The study of Arabic had been kept up through them all, and the great question of Dr. King's life, that of his becoming a missionary, was under consideration. The turning-point of his life had come.

It greatly simplifies any decision a Christian may be called upon to make if first he has made a full consecration of himself to Christ. There is reason to believe that Jonas King had done this; for when that letter from Pliny Fiske, already mentioned, compelled his attention in a most unexpected way to the work of missions, he had but to ask, "Lord, what wilt thou have me to do?" Not, "Am I willing? am I ready? can I give up all prospect of literary distinction in America, and turn my knowledge of Arabic already acquired to immediate practical use in instructing the ignorant, far from my friends and native land?" There was indeed deep anxiety as to who should care for his aged father and mother, and a sense of his own incompetency for the great work to which he was invited; but there was no hesitation as to obeying the voice of the Lord whenever clearly understood.

Therefore his prayer was, "Make thy way plain before my face;" and it is most encouraging to trace in detail how God heard and answered by providences too marked to be lightly set aside.

Turn then to the Journal of Sunday, July 21, 1822.

"Went from the Oratoire with Mr. Wilder to his house, he having told me that he had something of importance to communicate. After conversing with him for some time, he said, 'I have some very joyful and some very distressing news to tell you. Mr. Parsons rests from his labors.' He then gave me a letter from Mr. Fiske, which contained another for me. I opened it with a heart agitated with joy and sorrow and anxiety: with joy that my beloved brother had reached another and brighter world than this; with sorrow, because another faithful missionary of the cross was taken from his labors, and because I had lost a friend, a brother in Christ; with anxiety, because it had been proposed to me by Mr. Wilder that, if Mr. Parsons should be removed by death (we had heard of his sickness), I should take his place for three or four years. In this letter Mr. Fiske expressed a wish that, if I could, I would join him. After a few moments I begged leave of Mr. Wilder that I might retire to the room where he and I had often bowed together before the throne of grace. I there fell down on my knees and spread my letter before the Lord,

and besought him to sanctify to me this dispensation of
his providence; next, that he would direct me in the path
of duty, feeling and confessing that I was not worthy to
have so great an honor as to go to that place where our
Lord suffered, and there proclaim his gospel.   I then in
a solemn manner besought the great Head of the church
to grant, if it was his will that a poor worm of the dust
should go and proclaim his precious word to dying souls
of Judea, he would incline the heart of Mr. Wilder to
give me that counsel and make some offer of aid, which
would be absolutely necessary in order to enable me to
go.   I then went out and sat down by Mr. Wilder near
his desk.   He immediately addressed me to the following
effect: 'Since it has pleased Him who governs all things
to throw you in my way, so that I should be acquainted
with you; since we have spent so many pleasant hours
together in prayer and in conversation; since it has been
proposed by me, I know not why, that you should take
Mr. Parsons' place should he be called out of the world;
and since also it has pleased God to send this letter to
you through my hands, I therefore offer, if you will go
and join Mr. Fiske for three years, to give you a hundred dollars a year; and furthermore, I will do what I
had offered to do when you were, to human appearance,
on the borders of the grave, give your honored parents
fifty dollars a year for three years to aid them during
your absence.'   After my prayer, and after hearing this,
I could not but reply that I had reason to believe that it
would be my duty to accept his offer and to leave all,
father, mother, sister, friends, and country, and go up to

Jerusalem, 'not knowing the things which should befall me there.'"

It was then made a question how I could procure the remaining four hundred dollars, which Mr. Fisk said would be necessary. After two or three plans had been suggested, I mentioned writing to Mr. Thomas Waddington of St. Remy. Mr. Wilder immediately approved of this, and advised me to write also to Mr. Louis Mertens of Brussels, Claude Cromlin and Wm. H. Nolthenius of Amsterdam, and John Venning of St. Petersburg."

The correspondence that followed shows the spirit that inspired all concerned. Dr. King, in the beginning of each letter, before explaining the object he had in view, asked the friend to whom he was writing to look to God for guidance before proceeding farther; and then goes on to say, "Nearly three years ago the American Board of Commissioners for Foreign Missions sent out two eminently pious young men (Messrs. Fisk and Parsons) for the purpose of establishing a missionary station in Judea..... They were men whose names were known and beloved in all the American churches. I had the pleasure of being for many years intimately acquainted with them. But it has pleased Him who makes darkness his pavilion to call the friends of Zion in America to mourn the loss of my dearly beloved Brother Parsons, who is now gone, as we confidently believe, to join those who, eighteen hundred years ago, labored in the same field and in the same glorious cause. Brother Fisk is now left alone. He has written to me to join him, if I can, for two or three years, and at the same time states that he thinks it doubtful whether the A. B. C. F. M. would be willing to employ me for so short a time (as they generally wish to employ missionaries for life), and especially as they are at this moment somewhat embarrassed in regard to funds, and are also fitting out a second mission to the Sandwich Islands. He says my expenses will not exceed five hundred dollars a year.

"The office which I hold as Professor of Oriental Languages in a college in New England forbids that I should engage in a mission for life. Besides, duty demands that I should return to America that I may teach others who are destined to missions in the East, for which I should be much better qualified could I spend two or three years in the Holy Land."

Dr. King then writes of what Mr. S. V. S. Wilder offered to do, and that if four other Christian friends were led to give the same amount for one year, and as the A. B. C. F. M., with Mr. Wilder, would probably supply what would be necessary for the remaining two years, he should feel it an indication that it was the will of God he should go to Palestine. He ought to go in September, that being the proper time of the year to embark, and this would not give him time to hear from the American Board. Also he adds, "If it be not the will of Him who suffered in Judea that I should go thither, I hope you will not contribute a single sou to aid me in this mission. If it be his will, I am confident he will incline your heart to do it. I leave the whole in his hands."

In answer, Mr. Louis Mertens wrote, offering five hundred francs, saying, "I received your kind and joy-inspiring letter.   My heart, or the voice in my heart, immediately answered, 'Yes.'"   Mr. Waddington returned the same prompt answer, saying, "Go, then, and may the God of Israel bless your journey to the promised land."

The friends at Amsterdam asked for further information in detail. Dr. King returns them a succinct account of Messrs. Fisk and Parsons' work in Asia Minor, where even the professors had received Greek tracts (extracts from Chrysostom) with avidity.   In the Holy Land, Mr. Parsons had spent several months in visiting the monasteries, conversing with the priests, distributing upwards of three thousand tracts, some of which were to pilgrims who lived more than a thousand miles from Jerusalem. These in *every instance* were received with gratitude.   In order to prepare more tracts in different languages to distribute, also on account of commotions between the Greeks and Turks, Mr. Parsons returned to Mr. Fisk at Smyrna.   There, in September or October, he was taken sick of a fever.   From this, however, he recovered, and intended to be in Jerusalem before the Passover, in order again to distribute tracts among the pilgrims; but it pleased the great Head of the church to send for him to go to the New Jerusalem.   He died at Alexandria, Feb., 1822.   Mr. Fisk, was now at Malta, expecting soon to go to Egypt.   Mr. Wilder, at the request of the American Board, had lately ordered to be cast in Paris a font of Greek types expressly for the Palestine mission.   This would be ready for Dr. King to take with him.

This report, when brought before the Dutch Missionary Society, proved satisfactory, and it agreed to furnish the remaining thousand francs necessary. Dr. King, in returning most grateful thanks to all these friends, asks most earnestly for remembrance in their prayers. In his final answer of acceptance to Rev. Pliny Fisk, he refers to a parting scene with him and Mr. Parsons and a Mr. Bascom, in an upper room at Rev. Dr. Porter's, Farmington, Conn.; when, after prayer together, Mr. Parsons came, and in a most affectionate manner said, " I shall expect that in three years from this time you will make up your mind to come to Palestine."

Thus the matter was now settled, but this "only son" has still a trying duty to perform, that of writing to his aged father and mother in America. In our day, when to go around the world is but a fashionable tour, it is difficult to realize how, in 1822, Palestine was indeed as the "ends of the earth ;" and to go there, like taking a leap into the past.

To his father, after many words of respect and affection, he writes in part, as follows : " I recollect you told me, when I was leaving college, that your heart had been much tried in reflecting that I might perhaps view it my duty to go on a foreign mission ; that you thought it would be the greatest trial of your life to lose the only prop of your infirm and declining years ; but that you had said within yourself, ' Did God so love the world that he gave his only Son to redeem it, and shall I be unwilling that my only son should go and proclaim salvation to a dying world, through my Lord and Saviour? No, as much as I love you, as much as I feel the need of your aid to comfort me the few remaining years I have to spend here, I say, "Go, my son, if you think it best. God has thus far taken care of me. He will no doubt give me in future what is best for me, and with this I ought to be contented." '" Then, telling his father what his new plans were, he writes : "Indulge not one anxious thought for your son. I am in the hands of Him who took me from the 'sheepcote, from following the sheep,' and placed me in the ministry ; who has brought me safely along through the sea and the wilderness, and who now, by the indications of His providence, bids me enter the 'promised land.' So clear to me are these indications, that I think I should go, were I sure that my earthly course would there be finished.

"And in what part of the globe would you be more willing that your son should breathe out his soul, than in that land where my Saviour suffered and died to redeem it ?—that land, whence so many prophets and holy men of old took their flights to glory ?—that land which has heard the songs of angels, and to which the eye of all heaven has been directed ?—that land, where the glory of the Most High was once visible, and which has been the scene of his wondrous works among men ?"

Dr. King tells his father of the friend who had promised him to be a son to his aged parents in America ; and how the money was to be sent to them through Gen. Longley. Rev. Wm. A. Hallock, Secretary of the American Tract Society, in his tract "The Only Son," gives an account of how the above promise was redeemed. See Chapter XXIV.

The letter to Dr. King's mother is of equally tender interest. He reminds her of her unparalleled devotion to him in order that he might acquire an education; speaks of his probable safety in Egypt, as the governor there was a liberal man and gave protection to strangers; and both there and at Jerusalem the great Governor of all would take care of his life, so long as there was anything for her son to do. Also, that he yet hoped to have a home in America, where his parents could be near him.

Dr. King wrote in full also to the American Board, explaining respectfully how, the means for one year being provided, he was taking the responsibility, by advice of Christian friends in Europe, of taking up Mr. Parsons' work; looking confidently to their endorsement of this venture, and to their furnishing his support for the second and third years proposed.

Friday, Sept. 6, 1822, was the birthday of the " Paris Missionary Society." " Dined at Paris, in company with the Rev. Daniel Wilson, from London (afterwards Bishop of Calcutta). In the evening attended a meeting at Mr. Wilder's, for the organization of the Paris Missionary Society. Mr. Wilder proposed that the society should grant me some aid, and employ me as their first missionary, to go out under their direction for the present year. The Rev. Mr. Wilson, after an animated speech, offered to contribute, expressly for this object, one hundred francs. Another gentleman said he would give fifty; another twenty; several ten. The society at once voted five hundred francs."

Thus this young missionary became connected more or less directly with three societies, the A. B. C. F. M., the Dutch Missionary Society, and that of Paris, besides having the advantage of personal interest felt in him by many English Christians.   There was an important object gained by this Christian alliance.   Missions were then a "new departure."   Regular reports from Dr. King were required by each society.   These were printed ; so that this special missionary information was soon very extensively circulated.   In this way too, Dr. King became better known in Europe than any other American missionary.

The Bible Society of Paris gave several boxes of Bibles and Testaments ; and the Paris Tract Society about one thousand French tracts.

It now remained but to secure suitable letters of introduction.   Here again God's hand was plainly seen. The Asiatic Society of Paris, of which Dr. King had been elected a member, while the Duc d'Orleans, afterwards Louis Philippe, was President, gave letters to consuls at Malta, Corfu, Aleppo, Beyrout, and Egypt. To this society he was to make regular literary contributions, to be published in its "Journal."   Sir Charles Stuart, then British ambassador at the Court of France, provided a passport into the Turkish dominions, with private letters to friends in the East.   One of the professors of the "École Royale," gave him an introduction to one of the sheikhs in Syria, with whom he was well acquainted ; also other letters, one to a bishop.   Through Miss Mary Elliott, a letter to Lady Hester Stanhope (a niece of William Pitt), who had for a long time resided on Mt. Lebanon, and acquired great influence there, was offered and obtained from William Wilberforce, who thought it would be of no use, as she refused to receive Englishmen, but still she might be willing to see an American. General Macaulay also (father of the historian), Sir Henry Lushington, Baron de Staël, and others, gave letters, and offered aid.

Thus, in ways truly providential, was this once New England farmer lad thoroughly furnished unto the good work before him.

Dr. King had encouragement in the example of Buchanan, who sailed for India when at the same age as he—which was the age when Martyn and Brainerd had entered into glory—and the same at which our Lord entered on his public ministry. He gave himself much unto prayer, and so was made "strong in the Lord, and in the power of his might." During the last few weeks before leaving France, frequent record is made of seasons of prayer at Mr. Wilder's, in Paris, or in the garden at Nanterre. Sunday eve, Sept. 22, 1822, was an especially affecting and interesting season. Mr. and Mrs. Wilder, Dr. Spring of New York, and Dr. King, celebrated together the Lord's Supper. "The time, the place, the occasion, the little company so dear to his heart," Dr. King always remembered with peculiar emotion. On Sunday, the 29th, he preached a farewell sermon to a large audience in the Oratoire. Books, and tracts, and the "font of type," had been sent on beforehand to Marseilles. The last night in Paris came. The evening

was spent in prayer. One after another, Mr. Waddington, Mrs. Wilder, Dr. King, left the room, the latter
not until 2 A. M., but his friend Mr. Wilder remained
all night, looking unto God. In the morning he accompanied his missionary friend to the diligence for Marseilles. There, after reading together from John 14,
they parted, commending each other unto God.

CHAPTER VI.

THROUGH FRANCE AND THE MEDITERRA-NEAN.

Distribution of Tracts and Preaching on the Journey through France—Nismes—Malta—Discussion on Missionary Topics with Rev. Pliny Fisk and Others.

"Why, on parting with your friend at Paris, did you point your hand towards heaven?" asked of Dr. King a gentleman in the same compartment of the diligence when a few miles only on their way. This gave opportunity, in literally the first stage of his missionary life, for Dr. King to preach Jesus Christ and him crucified—in this case, as it proved to be, to an avowed skeptic, but one who yet, after the conversation held, actually helped with much respect in the distribution of tracts in the little village of Essonne. This incident typified the whole character of the journey. At Fontainebleau, where the pen with which the Emperor Napoleon signed the act of abdication was even then on exhibition, there was some danger our missionary would be arrested by the gens d'armes as a disturber of the peace, the crowd, after receiving the tracts, loudly wishing him a safe journey and every blessing. At Nemours the same scene was repeated. The conducteur ordered the people away, as he could not drive on for them, they asking earnestly for

more of the books.   A lady of apparently high respecta-
bility living near, sent a servant for a tract, saying she
would use it in prayer night and morning.

At Fontenay, where a bridge and house remained
from the time of Julius Cæsar, Dr. King took special
pleasure in giving one of these messages of peace to a
military officer.   Also, after a woman with cross and
beads, asking for charity, had said she prayed to *all* the
saints, in answer to the question which of them she addressed, he said it was "very strange that none of these
would hear her and give her the few sous she wanted,"
which made all the bystanders laugh.   However, Dr.
King did give her a trifle, urging her to pray to God
alone.   At St. Pierre one of his fellow-passengers, whom
a woman had asked to get a tract for her, said, " You
have converted everybody since we left Paris."   At Ro-
anne the conducteur helped in the giving away of tracts,
driving off just in time to escape arrest, as two priests
were hastening to make complaint.   On going up the
steep hill of Fourvières, tracts were received by some of
the sisters belonging to a convent near.   From this
mountain the city of Lyons, of a hundred and twenty
thousand souls, appears as a little village.   Though as
connected with early Roman conquest, and the blood of
the martyrs shed there, crowded the traveller's mind, yet
he felt that, as an ambassador to Jerusalem from the
King of kings, he was a man more honored than Cæsar
or Hannibal.   In the cathedral he saw a bull of the pope,
recently put up, saying that " St. Peter had changed the
indulgences ; that they were now to be had in full every

day, both for the living and the dead, by coming to this church, and at the sound of the bell praying for the church, the state, the city, and the diocese." The church of St. Irenæus he approached as indeed a sacred place; for here hundreds, perhaps thousands, of martyrs had been slain. In the middle of it was a deep well into which their blood had run. The bones were piled up behind a grating to the height of fifteen or twenty feet. These bones may not all have been those of martyrs. Irenæus suffered martyrdom June 28, A. D. 202. In this church Dr. King, in·a formal manner, addressed the people crowding round on the nature of true faith and vital piety as not consisting in forms. Pothinus and Blandina also suffered in the prison here. The holes into which they were crowded before execution yet remain. Dr. King could not help joining in the prayer, recorded Rev. 6 : 10. In Lyons, while waiting at night for the stage for Nismes, Dr. King was struck with the temptations to which the traveller was exposed there, the same of which Solomon gave warning. Yet even here to the most degraded he preached the gospel, and was heard with attention.

At Tain, where was an ancient altar, Dr. King felt as if he would have to record " a day lost," for he had not spoken to any one on the subject nearest his heart; but towards night "a respectable-looking gentleman, who appeared quite intelligent, got into the stage with us. Some question was soon proposed which made it necessary for me to vindicate the authority of the Sacred Scriptures. The gentleman at once demanded if I believed in the passage of the Israelites through the Red Sea, the twelve plagues of Egypt, etc. I replied that I did firmly believe in *ten*. At this all in the stage burst out into a loud laugh. I told them they might laugh if they pleased; that did not do away with the fact that the Scriptures were true and given by inspiration of God; that I had read their Voltaire and their Jean Jaques Rousseau and our own infidel writers, and that I was ready to prove to them what I affirmed; that I did not wish them to believe blindly; that I only demanded that they should hold to maxims generally received. · I then went on to show them that if it were not beneath God to create a world consisting of many little things, it was not beneath him to take some care of it; that he that made their minds had access to them and could make communications to them, as certainly as we could communicate with words; that he who held the heavens and the earth in his hands could arrest the course of nature, and might be expected to do so if any great object were to be attained by it; but that they had commenced in the wrong place; they were trying to ascend a mountain on the perpendicular side; that is, to look at the miracles; that I would lead them round the other side of the mountain that was easier of ascent; that is, show them, by what passed within themselves and what they saw in others, that the doctrines of the gospel were true, that its precepts bore upon them the stamp of divinity, and that after they should see this they would easily believe in miracles. I then showed them that their hearts were naturally alienated from God; that they knew it and felt

it, if they would only compare their thoughts and feelings with what they acknowledged of God from the works
of nature; that from the very nature of things their souls
could not be happy after leaving their bodies and all
means of sensual gratification had ceased, without a ren-
ovation, a change of heart, of feeling; that if ever they
had tried to reform their lives in the least respect they
had found it difficult, if not impossible, without aid from
without themselves; that if all men followed the precepts of the gospel, this would be a happy world; that it
was by leaving these precepts, and adhering to forms
and ceremonies and superstitious rites, or by running
into infidelity, that they as a nation had drawn down
upon their heads the judgments of the Most High; and
that, if they did not repent, other vials of wrath were
ready to be poured out upon them. Thus I spent about
half an hour in reasoning, in making appeals to their
consciences, and in setting forth at last the beauty, the
simplicity, and the sublimity of the Bible, in comparison
with which all their boasted poetry sunk into insignifi-
cance; and that Voltaire, Rousseau, and all their infidel
writers, when put by the side of David, Job, and Isaiah,
looked like mere pigmies; that the only reason why they
rejected the Bible was because they did not love its
truths.

"When I had finished, four out of the five promised
to send to Paris and purchase each a Bible. The gentleman before mentioned then asked me if I knew a Mr.
Wilder, a merchant of Paris, with whom he was acquainted, and who often talked to him as I did. From this

moment I was treated with the utmost respect and politeness."

At Nismes it is strange to read of a Sunday-school
attended by about seventy women from fifteen to thirty
years of age. In 1815 some houses there had been razed
to the ground by some Catholics while persecuting the
Protestants, seventy of these being massacred that year,
some, like our Lord, being betrayed by a kiss. The Sabbath Dr. King stopped at Nismes he passed an amphitheatre where thousands were assembled to see a bull-
fight.

The ruins at Nismes are of great interest on account
of their antiquity and remarkable preservation. From
one of the altars, where once victims were sacrificed to
Diana, Dr. King discoursed of the Lamb offered once
for all.

Rev. Mr. Cook called on Dr. King on his arrival at
Nismes, and they had prayer together in the hotel.
Baron Castelnau invited him to a Bible society meeting ;
also a social missionary reunion of about thirty ladies
and gentlemen was held. At that meeting, after Dr.
King had been formally presented and asked to speak,
he insisted that prayer should first be offered. The Protestant ministers had before been consulted with regard
to this, and had deemed it imprudent, as spies might be
present, but it was finally concluded to ask a short blessing. Then followed statements from Dr. King and some
discussion, there being at least one pastor present opposed to foreign missions. After some time it was proposed that a subscription should be opened, and a society

organized auxiliary to that of Paris. When the vote was called almost every hand was raised. Some of the ladies lifted both hands. The subscription-paper was then laid on the table, and three hundred and four francs at once subscribed.

"This was as interesting a scene as I ever witnessed. So much joy seemed to pervade this little assembly. I also proposed to them to observe the Monthly Concert of Prayer, to which all seemed to assent with one heart. To the three hundred and four francs mentioned was added the donation of a poor woman, seventy-five years old, of seventy francs, which was her whole living. Having heard of the missionary society, she observed, 'I am going to die. I have neither parents nor children. I will give this money to spread the gospel of my Saviour before whom I am about to appear.' This interested my heart very much, and I determined to go and call on her immediately, which I did the next day. She is a poor widow, and has always labored hard, and by the strictest economy has amassed the sum above mentioned for the purpose of paying the rent of the house which she had hired; but as the gentleman who owned the house is a pious, benevolent man, he forgave her the debt, and told her to make what use she pleased of the little sum she had gained; and it gave him the highest pleasure to hear her say, 'I will give it to the Missionary Society at Paris!'

"Called on Madame Vizié to thank her for what she had done, and to comfort her heart by telling her what God is doing at the present day in our world. She is

now in the poorhouse, and lives by the charity of her
pious friends, who were all much delighted on hearing
what she had done for the missionary society. As I entered the room where she was, I saw a little, old woman
standing near the bed supporting herself by a staff, endeavoring to arrange some little articles of clothing, and
not noticing our approach. Her face was finely wrinkled,
and showed that age alone had triumphed over beauty
and a firm constitution. Her gray hairs were covered
with a neat white cap, and her arms were bare and withered like the husks of harvest. As my friend who was
with me addressed himself to her, she slowly raised her
light blue eyes, which seemed to me to bespeak an age
not more than fifty-five or sixty.

"Asking her if she put all her trust for salvation in
Jesus Christ, she instantly replied, 'To whom else shall
I go? He has the words of eternal life.' As I began
to speak of the donation she had made, she beckoned me
to speak in a low tone of voice, as there might be spies
present, who would make a bad use of what they
might hear. At this I was surprised, but lowering my
voice, told her that what she had done should be told in
France and England and America, as a memorial of her,
like the woman who broke the alabaster-box of ointment
to anoint the feet of Jesus. At this the tears came in her
eyes, and lifting up her withered hands she clasped them,
and devoutly raising her eyes towards heaven, exclaimed,
'I know my unworthiness. I am nothing but dust and
ashes.' On asking her if she feared to die, she once more
clasped her hands, and said with more than usual energy,

'We must die in order to see God. It is Christ who has increased my faith. Of myself I am nothing.' I asked her to give me a little history of her life, which she did in broken accents, and among other things informed me that she was born a Catholic, but that at the age of thirteen it had pleased God to touch her heart, as she hoped by Divine grace, and that since that time, she had been a Protestant, and had lived in the constant hope of immortal glory beyond the tomb. Giving her my benedictions, and receiving hers, I quitted this interesting spot."

Another missionary meeting was held near Nismes; after which Rev. Mr. Lusignol and a Mr. Porter accompanied Dr. King to Marseilles. Here there seemed a wide opening for work among seamen, which Mr. Porter was willing to undertake, as the Protestants there seemed to take but little interest in religious things. With Mr. Shaler, American consul at Algiers, just then at Marseilles, Dr. King had much serious conversation, and was warned by him against trying to convert Mohammedans, an Italian having just been executed at Tripoli for attempting it. In conversation with some Catholic ladies, one of them said she believed the commands of the church were to be obeyed, even though contrary in some respects to the Bible.

From Marseilles, Dr. King wrote to Amherst college, asking how he should expend in the East, for the benefit of that institution, a hundred dollars given him for that purpose, by Mr. S. V. S. Wilder; and speaking of the mission in which he himself was to engage as a

" new Crusade to drive out the infidels from the Holy Land, not by human power, but by the weapons of the Spirit."

After a storm, followed by a wind called the Mistral, had detained the ship for several days after the one appointed, Dr. King sailed Oct. 29., 1822. As France was fast receding from his view, he wrote as follows : " Land of science and of sin, of gayety and pleasure, I bid thee farewell ! The sun shines brightly on thy beautiful fields, the gales of Eden breathe gently on thy enchanting hills, and along the borders of thy streams, in the midst of vines and olives, lie scattered the cottages of peasants and the mansions of nobles. Thou hast within thy bosom all that can gratify genius, and taste, or sense. Thou art indeed lovely. But thou hast drunk the blood of martyrs, and God will visit thee ! He has visited thee, and given thee blood to drink. He has withdrawn His judgments, but thou hast not repented of thy sins. Thou hast here and there a little band, who fear God, and love the Saviour, but most of thy inhabitants are given to superstition, or infidelity, or never-ending scenes of gayety and pleasure. Oh, when shall the light of millennial glory dawn upon thee? When shall the spirit of Massilon rest upon thy priests and missionaries, who are erecting crosses at the corners of the streets of all thy villages ? With fervent prayers for thy salvation, I bid thee farewell."

On this voyage Dr. King commenced the study of Italian, thus beginning to acquire another of the several languages he was afterwards able to use with so much fluency. One of the captains spent most of his time praying for the soul of his father, which he supposed was in purgatory, and said that perhaps some day he would have a son who would do as much for him. The other captain, an Italian Catholic, laughed at this one for his devotion. After two or three days, the voyagers got a taste of the sirocco, putting a stop to every usual employment. This continuing longer than usual, the captain came, saying, "It is not God's will Dr. King should go to Palestine," yet asking him to pray for a fair wind, because, being a priest, God would sooner hear him than a sailor.

When in sight of Sicily, Dr. King was reminded of St. Paul there, 1800 years before. Now he himself was here, on his way to carry the gospel to that place from which the apostle had brought it. The same reflections filled his heart when Malta at last came in sight, after a passage of fourteen days.

Mr. Fisk was still here, having been detained by sickness in Rev. Mr. Temple's family, with whom he lodged. It can easily be imagined how these missionary friends spent the first evening together, drawing still nearer to each other around the mercy-seat. Often afterwards they talked to each other, perhaps too much, of their defects as missionaries; for Dr. King writes bitter things against himself, yet adds, "So long as I look at my own vileness, I am persuaded that I shall never attain much joy or peace in believing. If ever I have any, it is when I look away from myself towards Christ. I think I have erred, and that many Christians have erred on this point. God did not say to the darkness, 'Darkness, go away,' but 'Let there be light,' and the darkness instantly fled away as a matter of course. So with us; we may look at our own hearts, and dwell upon our vileness, and try to chase away sin and make ourselves better, and all to little or no purpose. But the moment we turn away from ourselves, and look at Jesus Christ, the soul feels itself transformed, quickened, invigorated, and rejoices with joy unspeakable. I feel more and more, that the best means of growing in grace is to look at Christ, and that the first thing to which a missionary should point a Jew, a Mohammedan, a pagan, or any sinner whatever, is Jesus Christ, and that every minister should preach Christ continually. This will not indeed give the world a very high idea of our wisdom or talents. We may appear simple and foolish, but God will be glorified, and our preaching will have effect, and souls will be saved. Jesus Christ is all and in all, and it pleases God 'by the foolishness of preaching to save them that believe.'" Again, when sick, and thinking how his constitution from infancy had been such as to need much care, Dr. King writes: "Silence, thou sinful body of mine, which would have ease and attention, and the kindness of friends, and would let the Jew and the Mohammedan and the pagan perish! Why dost thou so often shrink and tremble at the thought of perils and hardships, of persecutions and death? O God, grant me more of thy grace. Saviour of sinners, thou knowest that I would not go back if I could. If thou wilt grant me thy presence, then come life, come death, come what will, I shall be happy."

Rev. Mr. Jowett, of the Church Missionary Society of England, was in Malta at this time, also the Rev. Joseph Wolff, the converted Jew. An audience of about seventy to a hundred usually attended the Sunday services. On one occasion the friends celebrated the Lord's Supper, a time of special interest, because Christians from seven different nations were present.

The missionaries, while together, held prolonged friendly discussions, on points connected with the special work of each. Rev. Joseph Wolff asked how far he "should conform to Jewish customs, such as wearing a beard, and not eating swine's flesh," or not "lodging with Armenians, whom the Jews considered descendants of Amalek, whose name was to be blotted out." The conclusion was for Mr. Wolff to conform in things non-essential, but not to give in to prejudices against Amalek.

Mr. Wolff mentioned a fact confirming the truth of the New Testament, and not perhaps generally known. "In the Talmud of Babylon, which was compiled fifty years after Christ, the four gospels are mentioned under the name of Evangelion—Mattheus, Mordecai (which is Mark), Lukas and Johannen. This text is also quoted: 'Whosoever shall smite thee on the one cheek, turn the other also,' and is said to have been adopted as a practice by the disciples of Jesus. It is also said in the Baba Rama (one of the books of this Talmud), that Jacob, one of the disciples of Jesus, cured deadly sick persons by the name of Jesus."

Other subjects of importance were talked over by the little band, such as whether almsgiving in the East might be connected with preaching to the poor. Answer in short : "Relieve distress as far as possible. Preach to one's servants and household, as Christ did to his disciples, in a way that others would also have an opportunity to hear. Endeavor to form institutions for the poor and blind." Another question related to preaching to Mussulmans at the risk of life. Mr. Jowett advised, " Spend a considerable time (five years, or perhaps on the spot three years) in learning the language, customs, and prejudices of the people, before attempting publicly to combat their errors ; after which time it is a positive duty to gird ourselves with primitive courage and zeal, and openly combat Mohammedanism." Mr. Fisk thought it "perfectly consistent with Christian principles, and expedient, to talk about our mission, and feel as if it were for Jews, Greeks, and Armenians, and not for Mussulmans, quoting this passage, 'When ye are persecuted in one city, flee ye to another,' and saying the Mohammedans do persecute, and we must wait till God opens the way ; that should we attempt to preach to *them,* we should in all probability lose our lives, or at least be expelled from the country, and the mission would be stopped. 'Preach,' said he, 'among the Christians, and revive Christianity, and let Turks see what it is. Ask them about their religion, and tell them about ours ; give them the Bible, but not with the avowed object of converting them.' Others were of the same opinion, that there would be little danger among Arabs, but that among Turks we must be cautious. We need not tell them that they were in error, but show them the light.

God protected Henry Martyn when the Mohammedans talked of cutting out his tongue. We must go without dependence upon ourselves, but be mighty in Christ."

Dr. King adds: "This discussion was to me most impressive and solemn. I felt as though my own life was involved in it. I know not whether I have grace sufficient to carry me forward. But I have opened my mouth to the Lord, and cannot go back. I must gird up the loins of my mind, prepared to go forward to meet with persecution and death! This is a serious business, and I feel my utter weakness of myself. I can only cast myself upon the Saviour, and beg of him all that strength and faith and love and courage which I need."

A call of some interest was made by the missionaries upon the Chevalier de Greisches, the only knight of the Order of St. John remaining there. "He appeared like a withered stalk in the field after harvest." Thus passed away "one of the most illustrious Orders of men that perhaps ever existed, if we look at their military prowess." In the church of St. John, also in a convent of Franciscan monks, Dr. King spoke boldly against the worship of images. One priest admitted that it was forbidden in the Old Testament, but not in the New. He was reminded of the text, "Little children, keep yourselves from idols." Entering the outer door of another convent, and seeing several nuns who quietly retired, except one, who turned her face to the wall, Dr. King, with something of the humor of Mark Twain, asked a bystander, "What have these women done, what crimes have they committed, that they have to be shut up here?"

"Oh," was the answer, "they are not in prison. They pay 1,000 or 1,200 scudi in order to be permitted to come here."

While at Malta, in a packet of letters forwarded from Paris, came a welcome offer from the Netherlands Bible Society, to furnish Dr. King with as many copies of the Scriptures as he might wish.

Friday, Jan. 3, 1823, Dr. King, with Messrs. Fisk and Wolff, left the island of Malta, receiving substantial tokens of the best wishes of Messrs. Jowett and Temple.

While now again at sea, he wrote these lines:

Tossing, rolling on the ocean, when the winds and waves are high,
I 'll not fear their wild commotion, Jesus Christ my Lord is nigh;
At his bidding 't was I ventured to come down into the sea,
He will bring me to the haven where my spirit longs to be.

Earth is troubled like the ocean, man is tossed from wave to wave,
Finds no calm, no place of resting, till he finds it in the grave.
At thy bidding, Lord, I 'll venture upon death's dark, boisterous sea,
Thou wilt bring me to the haven where my spirit longs to be.

CHAPTER VII.

EGYPT.

Labors Among Jews and Roman-catholics—Preaching on the Top
of the Great Pyramid—Cairo—Thebes—Palace of Pasha—
Jewish Wedding—Traces of Work.

THE port of Alexandria was reached January 10,
being Friday, the day of Mussulman worship. Flags
accordingly were hoisted on twenty or thirty Turkish
ships-of-war then in the harbor. Before landing, Dr.
King asked the captain to call the crew together, "that
thanks might be returned to almighty God for his protection during the voyage." The mate offered to buy an
English Bible. The captain afterwards came to hear Dr.
King preach at the British Consulate, and also had religious services again on his own vessel. He expressed
the "new conviction he now had of the truth of the Bible
and of Jesus as the food of the soul."

Board was obtained by the missionaries in the family
of a Jew, some member of which was overheard by Mr.
Fisk to say "their lodgers were probably conjurers."

Descriptions of scenes in Alexandria agree with those
of more recent date.

One spot of sacred interest could not be forgotten—
the grave of Parsons. Upon the slab which covered it,
level with the pavement, Dr. King with his two friends
kneeled with uncovered heads, feeling as if he were indeed "baptized for the dead." After prayer Mr. Fisk

addressed him, saying, "Brother King, I welcome you with all my heart to the place rendered vacant by my brother Parsons' death."

And Parsons' work was immediately taken up by his successor, in season and out of season. Just now it was especially among the Jews, in company with Mr. Wolff. The two missionaries would sometimes seat themselves cross-legged on the divan, according to Eastern custom, and as the Jews came in would begin talking first of Old Testament facts, in believing which all were agreed; and thus securing attention, would go on to speak of the Messiah as already come. The conversation was usually in Italian. When a Hebrew word was used the Jews seemed much pleased. On one occasion a woman called out angrily to the most intelligent Jew present, "Thou cursed, why do you not answer him?" Some of the Jews avowed themselves skeptics, and proposed the same questions as other worshippers of human reason elsewhere do. Four rabbis from Galilee, when spoken to of the Messiah, answered, "My lord, we are come from a distant land, and at sea we were sick with great sickness, and therefore our mind is a little confused, and we cannot therefore speak to-day words of wisdom. But we will return unto you and open our mouth with wisdom, and speak about the Holy One, blessed be he and blessed be his name, and you will be astonished with great astonishment." Thus it may be seen that there is such a thing as true pharisaical succession.

Visits were paid in Alexandria to Roman-catholics also. With the superior of a Francisan convent Dr.

King had in some way before become acquainted. Calling to see him, Dr. King says, "Two of the monks met us at the door and said that he had gone out. I made some little conversation, and they invited us into their room. 'Do you devote yourselves,' said I, 'continually to prayer and fasting?' 'Yes, we pray to God the Father, Son, and Holy Ghost, and the Virgin and the saints.' 'Ah,' said I, 'to the Virgin and the saints? This is a thing that I have never seen in the Bible. We are commanded to pray to God and to Christ, but I have nowhere seen that we are commanded to pray to saints.' Quite a discussion followed, in the course of which the curate talked very loudly against the English, who, he said, were all excommunicated, were without a priesthood, were all going to the house of the devil, and would be damned. All that was said showed that these monks believed that the Word of God, without note and comment, was pernicious and destructive. The curate actually behaved like a madman, saying again, ' *We* are the true church. *We* are illuminated by the Holy Spirit. I can teach you, and not you me;' then stamping on the floor with all his might, 'When men go about vomiting poison I would crush them under my feet.' The monks who stood by seemed a little ashamed.

"It may be thought rash and imprudent by some to address the Roman-catholics with so much plainness as I did the curate, but I know not what else to do. They have perverted the Word of God and taken away the key of knowledge from the people, and introduced into the church as real an idolatry as the worship of Venus or of

Jupiter Ammon. They say they do not worship the images. Nor did the enlightened heathen worship images, except as representatives of some spirit, some overruling power, some great first cause."

Let no one think an acute mind, thoroughly trained and well-informed, was thrown away when called to meet the varieties of error into which the Oriental churches have lapsed. There were at this time one hundred Coptic convents in Alexandria, one of them claiming to have been founded by St. Mark. By the superior of one of them Dr. King was excommunicated, yet succeeded in selling a hundred Bibles and giving seventy away.

Mr. Gliddon, so well known as an Egyptian scholar, showed the missionaries much Christian hospitality, and his son accompanied them up the Nile.

Friday, January 17, appears the following entry: " Mr. Fisk and myself sold to-day, by way of exchange, four New Testaments for fifteen Egyptian gods. This seems to be a new kind of traffic. I would gladly buy all the gods of the heathen in the same manner."

The next Monday they left Alexandria for Cairo on board a large sailboat, called a maash. Soon a violent wind almost upset the boat, yet the Arabs in charge refused to furl the sails except on actual compulsion. The story of the whole voyage is but as an early edition of " Boat-Life on the Nile." In every place, wherever possible, religious conversation was held with the Copts and Mussulmans, and Bibles and tracts were sold and distributed. Fishermen's huts, built of reeds, reminded the travellers of Moses. Near Cairo immense heaps of wheat, supposed at first to be sand, and farther on buffaloes standing in water up to their heads then coming up out of the river, also took them back to the times of Joseph and Pharaoh. While stopping at a small village, an eclipse of the moon filled all the Mussulmans there with terror. "We could hear distinctly the cries and screams and howlings of men, women, and children, and their prayers: 'O God and his prophet! O God and his prophet! Most merciful God! O beneficent God! O Lord, O Lord! Waa, waa, waa! O God, have mercy upon us! O Mohammed!'" Such sounds filled the air while the eclipse lasted. The people did not seem to understand how those who believed on the Lord Jesus were not afraid as well as they.

Sometimes when the missionaries went on shore the captain of the maash would come, saying there was danger; that if anything happened to them he should be answerable for it with his head.

Arrived at Cairo, the missionaries called immediately on Henry Salt, Esq., consul-general, having letters to him from Sir Charles Stuart. In his courtyard, among other mummies, they saw one of a woman strangely described as "very beautiful." Mr. Salt himself was deeply interested in missions, and more than once gave warning when arrest threatened; for the Mussulmans often, with great excitement, accused these strangers of introducing infidelity. In encouraging contrast to this, Mr. Warton, a military man in the service of the king of Persia, spoke of the missionaries in India in the highest terms of respect; said his first serious impressions were made by

their preaching; that it was a current report among the
Mussulmans in Persia that their king once observed in
one of his assemblies, that "if *ten* such men as Henry
Martyn were to come into Persia, his kingdom would
soon become entirely Christian."

Dr. King preached here, not only at the English consulate, but on the top of the largest pyramid, reading
there 2 Peter, third chapter, and expounding it to a number of persons who were up there at the same time.
Thus this monument, recording, as is now conjectured,
mathematical and scientific, as well as historical, facts,
was used as a noble pulpit for a grander purpose.

The Koraite Jews at Cairo were peculiar in many
ways, having also long and very large noses, which easily
distinguished them.   They reject the Talmud, receive
only the written word of the Old Testament, and derive
their name from the Hebrew word קָרָא (kara), to read.
One of their rabbis gave Dr. King his benediction about
as follows: "O Lord, bless with a blessing Jonas King,
the son of King, and give him of the dew of heaven above
and of the fatness of the earth, and permit him to enter
Jerusalem."

The degradation and wickedness of the people here
and elsewhere in Egypt were beyond description, reminding one, both in its political aspect and as regards its citizens, of the prophecy, "It shall be the basest of kingdoms."   Ezek. 29 : 15.

In Cairo were sold or given away 256 Bibles.

Leaving this city on their onward journey, although
great excitement followed everywhere the arrival of the

missionaries, they went unarmed, trusting in the Lord. The Coptic patriarch at Cairo had given them a letter of general introduction to the convents, and Mr. Salt a firman, yet their situation was often a critical one. Duty to go on, however, seemed plain, for sometimes the Copts would follow on from a distance to buy a New Testament. "That people, in the midst of so much poverty and oppression and misery, are so earnest to *purchase* the Scriptures, shows that they *desire* them, and that the objections often brought by some of the Franks in this country against the distribution of the Word of God are futile." Occasionally a Coptic school was visited, and a premium promised to such children as should make the greatest improvement in Coptic and Arabic, to be given the next year, as at Beeădecăh, where Dr. King writes: "The first thing I saw as I entered the village was a boy sitting on the ground with a book in his hand reading. This was new to me in Egypt, but I was immediately still more surprised to find a man sitting at the door of a kind of mud-hovel, with a long reed or cane in his hand, which he was swinging over the heads of twenty-six children, all of whom were engaged in writing on tin-plates. The hovel in which they were was built of mud-bricks, and partly covered with the same and partly with reeds or cornstalks. It had only one door, and this so small and low that I was obliged to get down on my knees to look in. I endeavored to encourage both master and children."

Calling upon the Governor at Siout, the travellers saw his "hand and seal" applied in a decidedly literal way. They had asked for a passport. A writer (the Copts were usually employed as such) wrote it in their presence, and gave it to the governor, who "took from the pen of the writer a little ink on his little finger, on which he rubbed for some time the seal on his ring. This seal he then pressed upon the letter where the name is usually signed. This being done, the writer took the letter again, folded it, and delivered it to us."

Although schools have been mentioned above, so few of the people could read and write that it was most difficult to secure a competent instructor, and also to buy any Coptic books. One bishop, when asked for them, said he had a "very great number." This proved to be a library of six or seven volumes, and an Arabic copy of the Old Testament which he refused to sell at any price. This bishop invited the missionaries to dinner, after writing out for them the Coptic alphabet, which strange characters are preserved in the "Journal," with pronunciation affixed. "The dinner consisted of one plate of boiled eggs, with a little melted butter, two plates of cheese served up in a different manner, and one plate of date dessert, and nineteen cakes of bread. These were all placed in order upon a pewter server, which was placed upon a little stool about one foot and a half in height. Around this we gathered, six in number, and took our seat on the floor. Water was brought by the servant for us to wash our right-hand, as this was to serve us both as knife and fork. After washing, the bishop took one of the cakes and made some crosses over it, saying something in a low tone of voice which I did not understand.

Then he broke the cake and began to dip his hand in the different dishes, inviting us to follow his example. During our meal, which lasted perhaps half an hour, the conversation turned on various topics. We learned from him that the bishops and priests have no fixed salary, and live by the charities of the people; that the priests do not generally marry, but that some of them are married, and are generally more esteemed by the people than those who are not married."

Afterwards they dined with a koumus, an ecclesiastic between priest and bishop. "The first room was filled with smoke, and the floor was entirely covered with dirt, and appeared like a stable. At our approach the women drew their veils over their faces and retired into an adjoining room. In a few moments we were invited into the parlor and seated on the floor. The parlor was about twelve feet square, and but a little more decent than the other rooms. Presently raki was ordered. Of this I did not taste. The koumus drank very plentifully. After the raki, dinner was served. It consisted of soup, boiled meat, and bread. A candle was stuck in one of the loaves of bread to give us light. Such a scene I never witnessed before. The koumus was a large, brawny man, with a long white beard, and looked filthy as the swine in the streets. His eyes were sore, and this rendered him still more disgusting. His long bony fingers soon found their way to the bottom of the soup, and we dove after him. The boiled meat he tore in pieces and handed round to us. When his mouth was well filled with bread and meat and soup, he washed the whole down with a good dose of raki. After dinner I bought a Coptic manuscript of him, and sold six New Testaments in Arabic and eight of Genesis. ·Made him a present of a copy of each, and after mutual salutations he accompanied us down stairs through the two stables into the street and even to the entering in of the village. Some of the clergymen in America think their salary rather small, and so it is ; but there is not one, at least I never saw one, who does not live like a prince in comparison with most of the Coptic priests in Egypt."

Passing on up the Nile, the travellers meeting now boat-loads of black slaves for the market at Cairo, or seeing on the banks women wearing nose-rings, or anon some crocodiles, or having live scorpions brought to them for inspection, felt impelled to visit Thebes. No previous description in detail had prepared them to see ruins so vast and impressive, which brought, with comfort, to their minds the text, "They shall perish, but thou remainest." The tombs in the Necropolis had not been so utterly despoiled as at present. In one room were to be seen two or three thousand little wooden gods. Dr. King describes mummies and statues with exceeding particularity, also the grottoes in a mountain on the east side of the river, which were inhabited by Eremites in the fourth century, and where perhaps Antonius and Athanasius lived, and prayed for their persecutors. The views from some of these caves were of peculiar beauty, showing the good taste of the hermits in their selection of a retreat.

Soon a report having come of a general massacre of

the Franks at Constantinople, which would render life unsafe for them in all parts of the Turkish empire, and being two hundred miles away from an English consul, the missionaries hurried on their way back to Cairo. The alarm proved a false one, but had been none the less startling.

At Cairo Dr. King visited the pacha's palace, finding it truly an abode of sinful luxury; but it is amusing to read the full description of a camelopard in the court-yard there as of an animal almost unknown. On his way to this palace Dr. King met several young Arabs tied together, and followed by five or six hundred women, besides men and childen, weeping and wailing, and crying, "My liver! my liver!" These were young men whom the pasha had pressed into his service as soldiers. He had agents who went about in the villages, and whenever they saw a young man capable of bearing arms they took him from his parents and friends by force.

At Heliopolis, where Joseph found his bride, Dr. King attended a Jewish wedding. "At one end of the court was a kind of gallery, in which the bride was making preparation for the ceremony, and in front of which hung strips of different colored paper, red, pale red, and yellow, interspersed with gold leaves. Occasionally I saw the bride through the lattice, or wood network, which was in front of the lower part of the gallery. This brought to my mind Cant. 2 : 9. The bridegroom was a queer-looking young fellow, and seemed hardly to know what to do with himself. At about four o'clock the high priest, with five rabbis, came in and took their seats, and

the service commenced. The clerk and the rabbis repeated in Hebrew the eighteen blessings of the name of
God. Then the high priest arose and said, 'Blessed be
those who dwell in Thy house ; they shall praise Thee for
ever.' All the people responded, ' Blessed the people
whose God is the Lord.' After this the evening prayer
was said, in which the name of Jehovah occurs eighteen
times. Every time they repeated this name the rabbis
shook and trembled. After the prayer the nuptial torch
was lighted. It consisted of nine small wax candles tied
together at one end, and when lighted formed a branch
of lights. This was carried up into the gallery where the
bride was waiting, surrounded by married women and
young damsels. Boys below began to beat on cymbals,
and soon the bride descended, covered with a long white
veil, preceded by three women with cymbals, one on each
side holding her by the arms, and followed by several
others, one of whom now and then uttered a terrible
shriek, which I supposed was a shriek of sorrow, but I
was afterwards told it was an expression of joy. Being
led to the divan, the bridegroom took his place by her side
on the left. Both continued standing while Rabbi Mer-
cado and the people also repeated the forty-fifth psalm :
' My heart is inditing a good matter,' etc. The rabbi
then took a cup of wine, and said, ' Blessed art thou, O
Lord God, our God, King of the world, who hast created
the fruits of the vine.' The people responded, ' Blessed
be he, and blessed be his name.' *Rabbi.* ' Blessed be
thou, O God, who sanctifiest thy people by wedding and
by marriage.' *People.* ' Blessed be he, and blessed be

his name.' One of the rabbis then took a ring and put it on the finger of the bridegroom and then on that of the bride, and then gave it to the bridegroom, who put it on the forefinger of the bride, and said, ' Verily art thou espoused to me by this ring according to Moses.' A large camel's-hair shawl, called ' talis,' was then spread over the newly-married couple, and the rabbi twice gave them wine to drink, saying, ' Blessed art thou, O Lord our God, King of the world, who hast created all things for thy glory,' and repeating many other texts, the people responding, ' Blessed be he, and blessed be his name.' Then, after some drinking of wine and all the company repeating ' Semeantob' (good sign), the nuptial torch was extinguished, but immediately lighted again, and the bride was reconducted to her room by the women to the sound of cymbals."

While in Egypt the missionaries had sold or given away 900 Bibles and 3,700 tracts. God's word never returns unto him void. In 1866, Rev. W. C. Roberts, D. D., of Elizabeth, N. J., more than once found in Egypt old men, Christians, who well remembered Dr. King's work there, saying it had been blessed to their souls.

CHAPTER VIII.

THE DESERT AND JERUSALEM.

Emir Bushir—Kindness of Mr. Salt—Jerusalem—Gethsemane—
Scenes at Church of Holy Sepulchre—Deliverance from Ar-
rest—Bethany—Letters from Jerusalem—Visits to Ramah—
Jericho and the Dead Sea.

By this time, March 29, 1823, Dr. King had received
letters from the A. B. C. F. M., and from other friends
in America, approving the course he had taken.

Before leaving Egypt, Dr. King had an interview
with the Emir Bushir, prince of the Druses and Maronites on Mount Lebanon, who had been temporarily ban-
ished for attempting to make Syria free, but was now
about to return there. He treated the Americans with
great kindness, and said he should expect to see them at
Mount Lebanon. His attendants had much the appearance of New England men, one of them being almost
the fac-simile of Professor Stuart of Andover. Also the
missionaries saw Aboul Hassim, a Persian Sufi, whose
business it was to copy the Koran. His writing was
very beautiful, but it took him two and a half years to
make a single copy. A particular friend of his, Seid
Ali, had helped Henry Martyn to translate the New
Testament, and to him Aboul Hassim gave Dr. King a
note of introduction. Mr. Salt continued his efficient

kindness to the last, taking much pains to set the missionaries properly on their way.

During their last night in Egypt a death occurred in a house near by, and the loud crying and wailing called forcibly to mind scenes in this same land long ago, just before another departure from it.

The first night on their way, the Monthly Concert was observed by the missionaries, in strangely Oriental surroundings—a caravan, with camels and asses, of which there were about a hundred, and a noisy, incongruous crowd of persons from eight or ten nations.

To see barren sand far as the eye can reach, varied by appearances, now and then, of the mirage, was at this time not a wornout experience ; and Dr. King gives details of desert-life with a zest such as cannot be expected from a more recent traveller. He found it easy to sympathize with the Israelites in their murmurings for want of water, so offensive soon became that carried in the goatskins. He writes, " Oh, that my soul thirsted for the living God, as it does for the water-brooks ;" yet sometimes he went singing on his way, " Guide me, oh, thou great Jehovah, pilgrim through this barren land," and reading from day to day those parts of the Bible which seemed almost reproduced before their eyes.

Having passed the Isthmus, then undivided by Lessep's canal, and vexed on their way by thieving Bedouins, almost destitute of clothing, who would come to salute the sheikh of the caravan by butting heads in true Oriental style, and then insist on tribute, the travellers arrived in the land of the Philistines. Here it was something indeed new to see an actual shepherdess with crook in hand, with the skin of a lamb over her shoulders as a shawl, while women and children near by thrashed out barley on the ground with long sticks; then to pass metaphorically through the "gates of Gaza," into the public khan, its courtyard filled with merchandise, camels, horses, asses, and men, and where of course little rest could be secured. Here were sold or given away 38 Testaments, or copies of Genesis and the Psalms, some of them to Mussulmans. This distribution was continued at Esdud (Ashdod), and a prayer is recorded, that before the word of God the Dagon of Mohammedanism might fall, till not even his stump should be left.

At Yaffa (Joppa) the missionaries lodged in what is called the house of Simon the tanner, where upon the housetop they had prayer together, and Dr. King writes, "This is the city to which Jonah fled from the presence of the Lord; like him, may I, Jonas, not flee, but go and 'preach the preaching' that the Lord bids me." Here the sheikh was dismissed, receiving besides the backsheesh an Arabic Testament and Psalter. The road through the mountains of Judea proved to be worse than even the most rocky and uneven in New England, and was infested too by robbers.

"The country continued nearly the same as I have described, till we came within half an hour of Jerusalem, when all at once the Holy City opened on my view. Thus, thought I, is it often with the last hours of the Christian. He is obliged to pass over a rough and wearisome way, where he is continually exposed to the attacks of enemies, till near the close of life, when his feet are just about to stand within the gates of the New Jerusalem; then he is favored with some bright visions of the place he is soon to enter. The first I saw was the Mount of Olives, and supposed this to be a part of the Holy City; but I soon saw that Jerusalem lay lower down, between me and the Mount of Olives.

"As our Lord made his entrance into Jerusalem, riding on an ass, I alighted from mine, and went on foot. My feelings seemed to revolt at the idea of my entering Jerusalem in the same manner as he did, who was Lord of heaven and earth, and who came thither to make expiation for the sins of the world."

The sacred places in and about the Holy City are perhaps best unvisited, would one retain in full the charm with which a sanctified imagination cannot fail to invest them. Dr. King, however, in his journal, gives place to reflections, such as must after all crowd upon the mind and heart of every true believer. The scenes of four thousand years rushed upon him. Here God had rendered his glory visible; hither the tribes came up to worship; here David had tuned his harp to the praise of Jehovah. Here Jesus, our Lord and God, had poured out his soul unto death, and heaven and earth seemed to approach each other. It was fitting that special prayer should be offered, that the name of Christ should be here honored and the work of the Lord revived.

The missionaries found lodgings—Mr. Wolff among the Jews, the others in a small Greek convent looking out towards the Mount of Olives. Dr. King writes, "I looked all around on the Holy City, and could not help saying often, 'Is it possible that my feet stand within thy gates, O Jerusalem!'"

The next day it was impossible to visit the garden of Gethsemane, for a Turkish woman had just been murdered near there, which made it not safe to go where such an excited crowd of Mussulmans had collected. That day, however, they sold twenty New Testaments while walking about Zion, noting sadly the changes there since the time when David called it "the joy of the whole earth." The next day being Sunday, after a season of prayer with his friends, Dr. King was able to go to the garden of sorrow. Here, leaving the two guides to sit under an olive-tree, he went under the shadow of another of those eight old sentinels of the past, where, reading the New Testament account of the scene once witnessed there, he kneeled down, made confession of sins and renewed his covenant with his Saviour. There, too, he prayed for some of his dear friends and their children by name.

The account Dr. King gives further of Jerusálem in detail, is of interest, but the ground has now been visited so often that it is the more easy here to pass it over. The demand for Bibles was remarkable; thirty Greeks came for them the day of the missionaries' arrival. Also the sheikh Abou Ghoosh, who had two thousand Bedouins under his control, honored the missionaries with a call. "We were glad to form his acquaintance, and to ingratiate ourselves a little in his favor, though we should have preferred to have him call another day.

As soon as I was introduced to him, I took him by the hand (which is contrary to Eastern custom), and shook it, and he simultaneously squeezed mine, and shook it as cordially as if he had been an old friend from America. It seemed as if done by a kind of inspiration. He seemed much pleased, looked at me, and I sat down close to him, and looked at him, and conversed with him. All who were present laughed when they saw us shaking hands. He seemed friendly, offered us his services, and invited us to come and take lodgings at his house whenever we had occasion to pass by his village. After we had made him a present of a loaf of fine sugar, which we brought from Malta, and two boxes of phosphoric matches, with which he was highly pleased, having never seen any before, he went away."

The next day, when walking about Mount Zion again, and "marking well" the desolations there, a Mussulman Arab looked at the missionary with all the wildness of a man possessed of a devil, and endeavored by the distortions of his countenance to express the highest contempt possible. Many Mussulmans had come from Damascus and other places to visit the tomb of Moses, and it was really dangerous to go among them. "As we walked along and heard the wild noise and roar of the mixed multitude, feeling some little fear with regard to ourselves, Mr. Fisk repeated a verse from the 74th Psalm, which, had it been made for the occasion, could not have been more appropriate:

> "Where once thy churches prayed and sang,
>   Thy foes profanely war,' etc.

Dr. King had an interview at some length with Rabbi Mendel, the chief priest at Jerusalem, who, as might be expected, said he did not believe in the great sacrifice of Jesus Christ, but reciprocated every kind expression made as to Israel, saying, however, it was not good for Jews to enjoy so many privileges as they had in America, lest Jeshurun should "wax fat and kick."

In three days all the Arabic and Armenian Bibles and tracts on hand were disposed of.

Dr. King soon found his way to Bethlehem, and was met near there by many children, singing, " Pilgrims, go in peace; pilgrims, go in peace," as they went with him into the village. There, though he did not intend too much to regard time and place, he felt impelled to kneel in special prayer, not for himself alone, but for the children of his friends in Paris and the Netherlands and those of his sister in America. Bethlehem itself was a more rugged place than his own native town, yet he called its fields " happy ; they had heard the first news of salvation ; within its bounds had been born the God-man, the Saviour of the world." Here Dr. King gathered a few wild-flowers, which, sent to America, are yet treasured up, mute witnesses of this visit paid to Bethlehem more than fifty years ago.

May 1, 1823, was the anniversary of the Feast of the Passover, as observed by Greeks and Armenians. The three friends celebrated the Lord's Supper that same evening in Dr. King's room, "an upper chamber" in Jerusalem. Few modern Christians had then taken the "Communion" in a place so incomparably full of suggestive interest; yet Dr. King adds, after an account given, too long to be here transcribed, "It is not the place where we are that will cause us to have right feelings. A heart unsubdued by the grace of our Lord Jesus Christ would sin even before the throne of God and in the midst of the heavenly host.

"In the afternoon, the doors of the Holy Sepulchre being opened, I went to visit the place where it is said He suffered and died and was buried, in whom *alone* is my hope of freedom from sin and of eternal salvation. The new Turkish governor was sitting at the door with a crowd of attendants around him. Through these we made our way, and by showing a letter we had from the governor three days ago, were permitted to enter without paying the usual sum of twenty-five piastres ($2 63). I immediately found myself ushered into a large and splendid church capable of containing, I suppose, six or eight thousand persons, where, instead of solemnity, I found nothing but the noise and bustle of pilgrims who were flocking in crowds here and there, and among whom Turkish janizaries were walking to keep them in order. Having expressed my desire to see first the place of the crucifixion, I was led up a flight of stone steps unto the spot where, it is said, the cross was planted. But alas! I searched in vain for rude Golgotha, as it had always been presented to my mind when reading of our Saviour's sufferings. Not the least trace of nature was to be seen, and I felt disappointed."

Then follows a description of the whole interior, now made familiar to the ordinary reader. At the sepulchre, also, the same shock to one's feelings followed, the greater, of course, because more unexpected than to a visitor there now. Many of the pilgrims, women especially, showed signs of real grief, though in a place too artificial to resemble the tomb of Joseph of Arimathea. Yet here, though surrounded by marble walls adorned with pictures and pendant lamps, and though the sepulchre itself was represented by a mere hollowed-out slab, over which a priest was sprinkling rose-water, the missionary could not refrain from kneeling with other pilgrims present, and praying for himself and friends that they might indeed "be raised from the death of sin and walk with our risen Saviour in newness of life." Returning to the place said to be that of the crucifixion, he there asked of God that they "might all be crucified to the world, and their souls washed in that blood which flowed on Calvary." In this petition his own mother was especially remembered in memory of the mother of Jesus.

Saturday being the great Passover feast-day of the Greeks and Armenians, about four thousand of them met in the Church of the Sepulchre. "Never did I witness such abominable scenes in the house of God as in this place, which ought to be regarded as one of the most solemn and sacred places on earth. Hundreds of men and boys were dancing around the sepulchre and in different parts of the church, making all kinds of noises and antic gestures. Some almost without clothing were running about like madmen. Sometimes eight or ten would seize hold of one man and carry him, head or feet first, in a tumultuous manner around the tomb, singing,

' Kyrie, Eleeson ! Kyrie, Eleeson !' and yelling like Bac-
chanalians. Sometimes one man would stand erect on
the shoulders of another, and fifty or sixty would gather
around him, and then all would rush in procession, dancing and hopping, and screaming out, 'God is Sultan !
God is Sultan ! God bless the Greek convents ! God
bless the Greek convents !' In the midst of them Turkish janizaries with cat-o'-nine-tails would flog the pilgrims into order whenever they began to quarrel or to
crowd too near any place where they were not permitted
to come. This continued for the four or five hours I
was there.

"I should not have believed in such a scene had
I not witnessed it with my own eyes. We were told
that if such frantic sports were not permitted the holy
fire would not come down. I say the *holy fire;* for on
this day at a certain hour the Turkish governor enters to
give the command, and one of the metropolitan bishops
enters alone into the sepulchre, and fire comes down mi-
raculously, so the Greeks say, and begins to burn over
the tomb of Christ. From the sepulchre it is carried by
some one to the altar, where the bishops and priests
light their candles from it, and from them it is carried to
the people, who all stand prepared with wax-candles to
catch the sacred flame. As the time set for the fire to
come down approached the noise increased, although the
men and boys stopped dancing. At length it seemed
like the rushing of many waters, and all those around
the sepulchre pointed upward. We were now told that
the holy fire had come down, and that it began to burn

in a lamp which hung near the top of the dome over the
sepulchre, and we saw indeed a lamp burning, but whether
it had been burning all the morning, or how it had been
lighted up at this moment, we could not tell. From this
time for about half an hour the Turks had enough to do
in flogging the people into order. Finally came the
Turkish governor, and those who stood in his way were
flogged out of it, and then the bishops walked three
times around the tomb bearing seven standards on which
were painted Christ on the cross, the Virgin Mary, etc.
Then the head bishop of the Greeks entered the sepulchre. Soon a light was brought to the altar, and in five
minutes every man, woman, and child in this immense congregation had blazing torches or candles in their hands,
which made a very brilliant sight. This flame being
considered holy, some smoked their hands over it, then
rubbed their hands on their faces. Some held the candle under their chins, then moved it quickly about their
faces. I could not but fear that some of the hundreds of
women wearing long white robes, and some with infants
in their arms, would be burned to death. They say that
this fire will not burn like common fire, but Mr. Fisk
and myself both found that our fingers could not endure
it. Very soon some of the people began to extinguish
their candles carefully, saving all the snuff and as much
of the smoke as possible. Then commenced fraternal
salutations, such as kissing the cheek or the forehead or
the hand of some friend. After this the Greek bishops
proceeded to the ordination of some priests, and the Armenians, Syrians, and Copts formed a procession around

the tomb. All was tumult and confusion through the whole church, and I retired, wearied with standing and looking, and disgusted with such impious scenes. I felt as though Jerusalem was a place cursed of God and given over to iniquity."

Yet even now there are some who say the Greeks and Armenians need no purer gospel, no Protestant missionaries!

The evening after seeing the desecrations above mentioned was spent in special prayer for the polluted city, also that the messengers now come there might be more fully fitted for their work. They sang together, " Lord, what a wretched land is this!" "Truly it is a wretched land. The Jews hate the name of Christ, and when you mention it some of them will almost gnash on you with their teeth. The Turks exalt the name of the false prophet above His most glorious name, and are full of hypocrisy and iniquity. The Greeks and Armenians profane the temple of the Lord, and seem to know but little of the nature of Christianity. The Roman-catholics, who are as bad as the Turks and more intolerant, thunder their excommunications against all who receive the word of eternal life.

"In the morning, a little before we went to the Church of the Sepulchre, criers were sent by the new governor through the streets of the city to proclaim aloud that no Christian might wear anything of a red color, not even a cap or a pair of slippers. This order came, I was told, in consequence of his having demanded a tribute of money from the convents, which had not been paid.

Such orders are frequently given by Turkish governors in order to extort money from the Christians."

On the next day, Sunday, very suddenly a Turkish janizary cited the missionaries to appear.before the moollah, or judge, and on a singular indictment.

A Turkish dervish, to whom, being poor, provisions had been given on the journey, now requited the kindness shown, by entering a claim that a Persian Manuscript, purchased from him by the missionaries, had not been paid for. The new governor of Jerusalem when appealed to, soon discovered the falseness of the accusation, and ordered the dervish to be bastinadoed ; but the missionaries interfered, and saved him from this terrible punishment, and themselves, praying for the young and noble governor, rejoiced that what had threatened to give them much trouble, had rather "fallen out to the furtherance of the gospel."

The first Monthly Concert observed by Dr. King and his friends in the Holy Land was held on the Mount of Olives, where our Lord first commissioned his disciples to "go and preach the gospel to every creature," promising to be with them "even unto the end of the world." The occasion was indeed most suggestive.

At Bethany, the evident antiquity of a building encouraged the travellers to believe it to be, as reported, the home of Martha, Mary, and Lazarus. Flowers growing inside one of the rooms, also branches from an olive-tree near by, were gathered and sent to friends as visible tokens of the reality of a place so often honored by our Lord.

While in his lodging on Mount Calvary, Dr. King

did not forget his friends and their children. The following letter testified to the interest taken in the latter.

"Mount Calvary, 8th May, 1823.

"Dear Little Children: I write to you from this interesting place, so that when you are able to read what I write, you may know how much I loved you; and also that you may believe on Him who is the only-begotten Son of God, and who here hung on the cross, and bowed his head in agony, to make expiation for my sins, and yours, and for the sins of the whole world. Though you are little children, and innocent when compared with me, still you are sinners, and cannot be saved, except by the precious blood of the Lamb of God, slain on this spot.

"A few days ago I went to Bethlehem, the place where our Lord was born and laid in a manger. There I kneeled down and prayed earnestly for you, dear little children, that you might be born again, and become the true and humble followers of Him who was once a babe in Bethlehem, and whose birth was ushered in by a song of angels. I visited the plain where the angels sang, and there I prayed for you. I have remembered you too on Zion's Hill, on the Mount of Olives, and have plead for you in the sorrowful Garden of Gethsemane.

"Dear children, when you read the story of our Saviour's sufferings, you must love him and obey him and keep his commandments. The world around you is wicked, and unless you love Jesus Christ you will be led astray by the world, and fall into sin and lose your souls.

"You must not only love Jesus Christ, but you must

adore him. The angels adore him, and in heaven they sing with loud voice, 'Worthy is the Lamb, that was slain, to receive power, and riches, and wisdom, and strength, and honor, and glory, and blessing;' and all created beings who are holy, joyfully shout Amen to this song. Rev. 5 : 11, 12, 13, 14.

"If you love and adore Jesus Christ, you will have in your bosom such peace as the world can neither give nor take away; and when your bodies die, your souls will ascend to heaven, where you will never hunger, nor thirst, nor suffer any pain, 'For the Lamb, which is in the midst of the throne shall feed you, and shall lead you unto living fountains of water, and God shall wipe away all tears from your eyes.'

"Dear children, I love you and pray for you, and I hope you will not forget your friends at Jerusalem.

"J. KING.

"P. S. I send with this some olive-leaves, which I plucked with my own hands on the Mount of Olives. I have also some little flowers, which I brought from Bethlehem, which I cannot send in a letter, but if God will, I shall one day bring them to you."

To his father, he writes:

"JERUSALEM, May 18, 1823.

"MY DEAR FATHER : Last night in my sleep, I fancied I was with you, and that you began to converse as you used to do, about Jesus Christ and the things of another world. You said that Jesus Christ had ever been to you 'a *sure nail fastened into a living tree;* always *firm.* That you had taken him for your guide, now these many years, and had followed him through a great variety of scenes, and in the midst of tempests, and that he had never failed you.

"Now this was a dream of the night, but I doubt not you have followed him these many years, and ever found him faithful. How happy are you to have chosen such a guide. He will conduct you safely along, during your weary pilgrimage on earth; will comfort and support you when called to go down into the dark valley of the shadow of death, and in eternity he will lead you 'unto living fountains of water,' and all your sorrows and sighings shall be finished. I doubt not that you have followed Christ in the regeneration, and that your inheritance with him is sure.

"My dear father, can you believe me when I tell you that I am now in the Holy City, Jerusalem, and have my lodgings in a little upper room on Calvary, which stands within the walls of this present city, about a stone's cast from the place where it is said our Lord and Saviour was crucified ; and that here I am permitted to preach, and to distribute that holy word, which you taught me to read when I was a little child of four years of age, and when I thought Jerusalem must be somewhere almost out of the world!

"I am within a few minutes' walk of the place where Abraham went to offer up his son, his only son Isaac ! I know it must be painful to you to part with me, your son—your only son, whom you used to consider as the only prop of your declining years, and I often weep when I consider your situation. But think of the patriarch Abraham! When the Lord bids, we must sacrifice that which is most dear to us."

Again to his mother, after telling her of his prayer for her at the church on Calvary: "Do not regret, my dear mother, that I have come hither, but rather rejoice. Do you wish me to have honor? What higher honor than to be engaged as a herald of redeeming love? Do you wish me to have riches? The riches of this world are but *loss*, when compared with the excellency of the knowledge of Christ Jesus my Lord! Do you wish me to be happy? What higher happiness than to tread in the footsteps of prophets and apostles, and to wander over these sacred mountains, proclaiming glad tidings of good things to perishing souls?"

To his nephews he writes: "Here on Calvary, I charge you not to forget Him who died to redeem you. He is all in all. He is the Alpha and Omega, the beginning and the ending—the Almighty. Live near to him, love him, put your trust in him, devote yourselves to him and never be ashamed to be called his disciples."

One of these nephews, Daniel D. Wheeler, Esq., of South Adams, Mass., brother-in-law of General Plunkett, once Lieutenant Governor of Massachusetts, has no doubt often spoken of his missionary uncle, to children in the Sabbath-schools, in which he is so much interested.

To Rev. Dr. Spring of New York, Dr. King writes: "Jerusalem, 19th May, 1823. Oh, that you could be with me here on Calvary, where I am writing, and hear the roaring of the Turks from the minarets, and see the deep iniquity with which this Holy City is polluted!

Mine eyes run down with tears at the desolations of Zion! Everything around me seems blasted and withered by the curse of the Almighty. Before this curse shall be averted, there must be offered up many prayers and supplications, with strong crying and tears unto Him who has cast down from heaven to earth the beauty of Israel. I never felt, so much as I do now, the importance of praying that God would glorify his great name among all nations, and cause the name of his Son Jesus Christ to be adored throughout all the earth. I sometimes pray that he would arise, and shake terribly the earth, that the people may know that there is a God in heaven, and that Jesus Christ lives, and reigns over all, 'God blessed for ever.'

"The Jews here have generally all the blindness and stubbornness, and stiff-neckedness of their fathers. Some of them tell Mr. Wolff, that were they in power they would calmly judge him, and put him to death. The Catholics threaten with excommunication any one who shall receive from us the holy Scriptures, and pronounce a curse upon every one who in any way may aid us. The Mussulmans walk about in pride, and if any one of them should leave his religion, certain death would be his portion.

"So strict are they here, that I dare not even purchase a Koran, lest I should involve myself in difficulty. Any *native* Christian who should presume to purchase it and read it would instantly lose his life. The Greeks and Armenians have a name that they live, and that is nearly all. They are, however, more noble than the

other Christians, for they gladly receive the word of
God.　We have had sometimes thirty a day calling on
us to purchase the holy Scriptures."

After writing the above, however, Dr. King feared he
should be considered to be like the spies who brought up
an evil report of this very land long before ; and this he
wished to avoid, saying, " For although we are as grass-
hoppers in the sight of this people, and are indeed so in
our own sight, yet we hope to be of good courage, and
to go forward in the strength of the Lord ; and if he
delight in us, he will surely give us success."

To a friend in Paris, who had left the Roman-catholic
church quite recently, and who desired definite proofs as
to the authenticity of the Bible, Dr. King wrote:

" No one can say that Jesus is the Lord, but by the
Holy Ghost.　1 Cor. 12:3.　When once a soul is brought
by the influences of the Holy Spirit to see and to feel
its helplessness and entire pollution by nature, then it
begins to seek for aid from without itself, and as it looks
at the cross, and beholds the meek and lowly Jesus, and
hears him saying, ' Look unto me, and be saved,' it feels
that this is just such a Saviour as it needs, and ex-
claims in sincerity, ' My Lord and my God !'　It then
finds evidence *within itself*, that Jesus Christ is all
in all.

" Many a soul has found unspeakable joy in believing,
who never read a word of the evidences of the truth of
Christianity.　Do you need evidence to prove to you
that a rose is fragrant, that music is delightful, or that
bread will satisfy a man famishing with hunger ?　No

more does a soul, convinced of sin, and quickened by the lively influences of the Holy Spirit, demand evidence that Christ is precious, the one altogether lovely, the 'bread of life,' the fountain of joy. Its language then is, not 'read Volney,' nor 'search the writings of the fathers,' but 'oh, taste and see that the Lord is good;' 'I know that my Redeemer liveth—I feel that he is precious to me, and all those things which I once valued I now cheerfully resign for him, and count them but loss.' The infidel will smile at this, and the only reply I would make is found in John 14 : 17."

While at Jerusalem, Dr. King profited by some of his early acquirements in music in a way quite unexpected to him. "At the request of two of the principal singers in the Greek church, I have commenced giving them lessons in music, according to the English method. Mr. Fisk translates the rules, and I apply them to practice. This is to us an interesting occurrence, and it affords me much pleasure to be a teacher of music in the city of David."

At one of the convents, some curious books were to be seen, in Syriac, Ethiopic, Arabic, Greek, and Georgian; which latter resembles the Armenian, but no one there could understand it.

There were six Jewish synagogues in Jerusalem at this time, one belonging to the Koraites. One Sabbath two Jews, named Abraham and Isaac, attended the preaching services in Mr. Fisk's room. The one named Abraham came to Dr. King's room for further instruction. He was already satisfied that Jesus of Nazareth is the Messiah, and prayer was offered with and for him, that he might have courage to confess this fact, even at the risk of losing his life, either by poison or on some legal pretext obtained by bribery.

An excursion was made to Ramah. The prophet Samuel's house is said to have stood on a high elevation, from which is a very beautiful view. The visitors were allowed to buy the privilege of looking through a grated window, into a room said to be Samuel's sepulchre and that of his mother Hannah. About half way back to Jerusalem were shown tombs, seventy-two in number, said, by Jewish tradition, to be those of the last Sanhedrim. They professed to show also those of Haggai, Zachariah, Malachi, and Huldah the prophetess.

In the course of a detailed description of Jerusalem, Dr. King wrote: "I have viewed the city from many different stations, have walked around it and within it, have stood on the Mount of Olives, with Josephus' description of it in my hands, sometimes reading, sometimes looking, to see if I could discover any of those distinctive marks of the different parts of the city as laid down by him nearly 1,800 years ago; and after all my research, I compare it to a beautiful person, whom I have not seen for many years, and who has passed through a great variety of changes and misfortunes, which have caused the rose on her cheeks to fade, her flesh to consume away, and her skin to become dry and withered. Yet there are some general features remaining, by which I recognized her as the one who used to be the delight of the circle in which she moved. Such is the present appearance of this Holy City, which was once 'beautiful for situation, the joy of the whole earth.'"

After making an excursion together to the Dead Sea and the site of Jericho, Messrs. Fisk and King parted from Mr. Wolff, leaving him to pursue his work among his countrymen, the Jews, while they turned their faces toward Lebanon.

CHAPTER IX.

STUDY AND WORK IN PALESTINE.

Abou Ghoosh—Zidon—Lady Hester Stanhope—Rev. Lewis Way
—Studies Arabic at Deir el Kamar—Discussions with Roman-
catholics.

THE whole country north of Jerusalem seemed to
belong to Abou Ghoosh, whom our missionaries had
providentially met in Egypt, and there secured his
friendship.

Passing through the valley of Sharon, where a remarkable grapevine was seen covering a space of five
rods long by one rod wide, thus giving special force to
Scripture imagery, Messrs. Fisk and King came to Zidon.   Here they were glad to meet Rev. Mr. Lewis, an
English Episcopal missionary to the Jews, whom Dr.
King had met in Paris.   All three ministers took part in
the services held on the Sabbath.

From Zidon Dr. King forwarded his letters of introduction to Lady Hester Stanhope, who immediately sent
her dragoman, with her compliments, inviting him to
visit her at Dyhoon, three hours distant from Saide (Zidon).   On his arrival he was first taken into a piazza
enclosed with network all entwined with roses and jes-
samine.   Then an excellent dinner was served, after
which Lady Hester Stanhope received him very gra-
ciously, "saying that although she was very much occu-

pied at this time, yet she could not let an American pass without seeing him, and especially one who had come here with my motives, and who expected to stay in the country some time. I replied that it afforded me much pleasure to meet with one who belonged to that family, the name of which was known to every American, and repeated with respect by every child who knew how to read. She is the granddaughter of William Pitt, who plead the cause of America in the British Parliament. From this time our conversation was incessant for about three or four hours, after which she walked out with me and showed me her horses and garden." In the stables he found that curiously-deformed mare, having its back in shape of a natural saddle, which this singular woman kept for the use of the coming Messiah! The animal was no myth, as many suppose.

After surveying the establishment, Lady Hester left him for an hour, just when he really wished to be alone, it being the time appointed for the Monthly Concert, which Messrs. Fisk and Lewis had agreed to observe together. "After spending this hour alone, Lady Hester sent for me, and with the exception of about another hour spent at supper, our conversation was uninterrupted till near break of day. It turned on various subjects— America, England, France, Turkey, the present state of things in the world, the religion of Jesus Christ, of Mohammed, and of pagans, witchcraft, etc. She is really the most wonderful woman I ever saw. She believes in dreams as slight intimations of what is about to take place; believes that every person is born under some particular star," etc. This lady's strange views as to the Messiah and spiritual influences were due no doubt to the partial disorder of a naturally fine mind.

Dr. King writes: "There is not a single house on her mountain except her own, and here she can sit and see the Arab shepherds watching their flocks on the neighboring mountains, all of whom are at her command. Her influence here is very great, both among Turks and Arabs." The attention she paid Dr. King was quite remarkable. Her offers of assistance were afterwards redeemed by her securing for him a good lodging-place and teacher at Deir el Kamar.

The next point visited was that city whose name has been so variously spelled, which Dr. King writes Bairoot, stopping on the way "at an inn," where he could well claim "a warmest welcome," it being called "El Neby Yunas," or the tavern of the prophet Jonas. When just entering Beyrout, Dr. King's mule stumbled violently, and when a Druse Arab dexterously saved the rider from a fall, some Turk near said, "Why did you not let the Christian fall?"

The first thing necessary was to secure protection from the Emir Busher, who lived about ten and a half hours from Beyrout. The road there was a very rough one, but upon arrival the emir received the missionaries with great respect, and gave them a letter to visit different parts of the mountain, and to reside where they pleased to study Arabic. He also invited them to spend ten or fifteen days at his palace.

Another visit was made to Antoura, where that good

though very singular man, Rev. Lewis Way, had taken a house, intending to make it a sort of college. This plan, however, was soon given up, as Mr. Way's health failed, causing his return to England. Here Mr. Fisk and Dr. King assisted Mr. Way in the Church of England service. The next day the letters of introduction were delivered to the sheikh and the Maronite Bishop, who gave Dr. King a note that would be of use to him at Deir el Kamar, the place recommended for the study of Arabic by Lady Hester Stanhope. Arrived at this latter place, Dr. King records, July 29, 1823, "This day I am thirty-one years of age. Put on the Arab dress, and began to study Arabic in good earnest." The family in which he boarded was Roman-catholic. The women came into the family-room unveiled, and "conversed as freely as English ladies would do." One of them, after the baptism of a child, performed with superfluity of forms and with use of water, oil, and soap, said in Italian that women usually were more secluded; "but I was a better man than the curate and a great treasure in the place, so that they had no fear of me." This gave opportunity for a little talk about baptism and true regeneration. The women said they wished he was their curate. Dr. King replied, "Were I your curate, I could say nothing better to you than this: to love Jesus Christ with all your heart, trust in him for salvation, confess your sins before God, live a life of prayer, and do good to others. All were silent, and in this manner I addressed them for some time. While I was speaking the tears often came in my eyes. I felt that it was a wonderful thing that in this place, where a woman is seldom seen, I should be permitted to see them and preach to them Jesus Christ and him crucified. They then invited me to eat with them, and when they went away one of them invited me to visit at her house. These were some of the most respectable women in the place."

A few days were taken up by a journey in company with Hanna, his teacher, back to Beyrout, by request of Mr. Way, who wished to see him before leaving the country. He stayed over Sunday at a convent for nuns. It is sometimes denied that any changes are made by the Roman-catholics in the sacred text; but here in the Prayer-book of the Catholic Christians, printed in Arabic, Dr. King read the following heading: "'The ten Commandments as written by God on two tables of stone, and handed down to us, the Church.' Then followed *ten* commandments ; but the second, as in the law of Moses, was entirely left out, and the tenth divided into two, so as to make the number *ten*. The fourth commandment also said, 'Observe the first day and the feast-days.' Soon after I had read these the priest came in, and I remarked to him what I had read, and told him that these were not the ten commandments delivered to Moses ; that there was another, as I knew, for I had read them in the Hebrew. He seemed angry, and tried to make me believe that I was under a mistake. I told him it was in vain for him to speak in this manner, for everybody knew that there was another commandment, which was, 'Thou shalt not make unto thee any graven image, or any likeness of anything that is in heaven above, or that is in the earth beneath,' etc. : 'thou shalt not bow down thyself to them, nor serve them.'

"I really felt so indignant that any man should dare take away one of the commandments of God, that I told the priest plainly that it was an impious thing to make such a change.

"My teacher replied, 'If these are the commands of the church, they are the commands of God.' This I denied, and told him how one pope had said one thing and the succeeding pope had said another in direct contradiction to it; and asked him if he thought both were from God. 'God never acts in such a manner,' said I; 'it is man, erring man.'"

A servant of Mr. Way was lying very sick and died the night Dr. King spent at Saide, and it was almost impossible to keep the Roman-catholic priests from troubling his last hours with their sprinkling of holy water, that he might be reported a convert to their church.

When returned to Deir el Kamar, Dr. King writes: "When in a garden with my teacher some one knocked at the garden-gate, and we were told that the intended wife of my teacher had come to spend a little time in the garden. On hearing this he instantly arose, and said he must leave the garden, for it would be a very improper thing for him to stay there if his señora came in. I told him I had no idea of going with him; that I intended to stay there and see his girl, and all the company united in saying I must stay. He seemed to be in as great confusion as if there had been a cry of fire in the village, and immediately left the garden, and his spouse entered.

All pointed out to me the blushing damsel, and asked me before her if I thought her handsome.

"Here, when a young man wishes to marry, the parents make the agreement for him. My teacher told me he had not seen his spouse for nearly a year. He never goes to her father's house except with his father or mother.

"In the evening went to the house of Michael. Several Arabs were present. Soon came in a Catholic priest to hear the confessions of the family. The Arabs asked me if I confessed. 'To God the Father and the Son and the Holy Ghost,' replied I, 'and not to a sinful priest, who has need himself to confess.' 'But have you no need of a middle person between you and God ?' said one of the Arabs. 'Yes,' replied I, 'and Jesus Christ is the Mediator ; I wish for no other.'

"They then made further inquiries about my religion, and I told them how simple our forms of worship were, and how they were according to the examples of the apostles and the commands of Jesus Christ. All said, 'That is right, that is good,' and one man exclaimed, 'Henceforth I will be like you, and have nothing to do with these priests.' I replied that I thought the clerical office necessary, but that our priests should be such as Paul had described, 'not given to wine,' 'the husband of one wife,' etc. I then went on and proclaimed to them as well as I could Jesus Christ and him crucified, and the importance of relying wholly upon him for salvation."

The following gives some idea of missionary daily

life, and the difficulties in the way of acquiring the Arabic language. "I read Arabic every day, except Sundays, from morning till noon, and in the afternoon we converse. The effort I make in pronouncing the gutturals occasions pain in my breast, and I sometimes feel almost discouraged. At such times I go to my room and weep and pray, and in view of duty and of the shortness of life again make efforts to acquire this difficult language. I wish to be able to speak the Arabic like an Arab, so that I may be able to preach Jesus Christ to this dying people.

"In the afternoon visited at the house of Andrew Domani, called the father of Khalil. The father here takes the name of his first-born son, and the mother also. If the first-born be called Khalil, the father goes by the name of Abû Khalil, and the mother Im Khalil.

"Went to the house of Michael. While there, there came in a woman who made a long complaint against her husband, who had been beating her. She told of it in a laughing manner, and I said to her, 'I think he could not have beaten you very hard, for you laugh.' She is what is called a fellahh, and wears on her forehead a long horn. All the women here who are natives of the mountains wear horns, which give them a very odd appearance. They are generally made of silver, and are about a foot and a half long. I call them unicorns. After the woman had finished the story of her husband's beating her, I asked her if the women here did not sometimes *hook* their husbands. This set the whole company of Arabs present in a loud roar of laughter.

"My teacher would not believe that the priests had kept back the second command, and said he would bring a Jew to see me and ask him whether that command was in the Jewish books. I told him to bring him, for every Jew knew that this is the second command given by God to Moses. He had in the morning read this in my Arabic Bible; but, as it was printed in England, he doubted its authenticity. After a long discussion he sent for a Bible that he said was printed in Rome and must be true. I immediately opened to the twentieth chapter of Exodus, and told him to read, and he to his astonishment found that I had told him the truth.

"The mother of his spouse asked me why I did not make the sign of the cross. 'Because,' said I, 'that is nothing. Jesus Christ never told his disciples to make this sign, but to take up their cross and follow him,' and that if she attempted to follow Christ Jesus according to the gospel, she would find what that cross is; that if she had not the Holy Spirit in her heart, teaching her to deny all ungodliness and worldly lusts, she might make the sign of the cross every day of her life and then go to hell. My teacher said, 'You have reason, I have reason, every man has reason; let every one believe according to that and follow that.' 'Human reason,' replied I, 'is in the dark, you are in the dark, the priests are in the dark, and this book, the gospel, is the only sun which can dispel the darkness. Here is light; we must believe and act according to this rule, or there is no light in us.' All exclaimed, 'He is right; that is truth.' After three or four hours' conversation of this kind I retired to rest, but my feelings had been so much engaged that I could not sleep.

"A priest came in and several women also while I was reading to my teacher the twenty-second psalm : 'All the ends of the world shall remember and turn unto the Lord, and all the kindred of the nations shall worship before thee.' At this I stopped and asked the priest whether that time was past or whether it was to come. He hardly knew what to answer me, and I went on and proclaimed before all present how darkness covered the earth, and that a time was coming when Jesus Christ should reign on the earth; *i. e.*, when all should know his name and serve him.

"I then asked my teacher to read aloud the twentieth chapter of Revelation, and then the first three chapters of the same. As he read all were exceedingly solemn and the mother of my teacher wept, and I also could hardly refrain from weeping.

"A man noted as an astronomer said he thought 'if a man did what was right he would go to heaven, whether Moslem or Christian, Jew or pagan.'

"I replied, 'I am not the judge. God is the Judge of the whole earth, and he will save whom he pleases, and he may, for aught I know, reveal Jesus to a dying pagan. But without the blood of Jesus Christ there is no salvation, neither for you nor me, nor for any other son or daughter of Adam.

"'In a few years,' said I, 'all our knowledge of languages, of astronomy, of mathematics, chemistry, etc., will cease, and I value them only in so far as they tend to lead the mind to the great First Cause of all things, or fit it to make inquiries with regard to Him and the truths contained in his Holy Word.'   On his appearing to be a little confused at this, I said to him, ' If I am your friend and you love me, as you say you do, I must tell you the truth : there is no salvation for you out of Jesus Christ.'

" ' I have one question to ask you, Aboona, and then I have done : When Jesus Christ commissioned his disciples to go and preach, what did he tell them to preach, himself or his mother?   What did they preach?   Jesus Christ and him crucified ; salvation alone through his blood and intercession ; not one word about the Virgin Mary.   No.   Jesus Christ is all in all ; he was such to the disciples of Christ, he is such, I trust, to my own soul, and he is such to every Christian.'   All present listened attentively."

Another discussion related to purgatory.   " Aboo Troos spent the evening with me in conversing about purgatory, praying to the saints, etc.   I related to him the history of my forefathers, who fled from the storms of persecution in Europe, and told him for what reason we had left the church of Rome, and what enormities had been committed under its sanction.

" He seemed astonished, and listened to me with all the interest of a little chiid.   ' With regard to purgatory,' said he, ' suppose there is a man who has sinned a little, but is nearly pure, must he not go into purgatory to be purified ?'

" ' In the first place,' replied I, ' there are no such men as you mention, like white paper with here and there a little blot. We are all great sinners, altogether *blot*, and nothing but the blood of Christ can cleanse us. If you say it is necessary to go to purgatory, you take away from the merits of Christ's death and dishonor him. He bore our sins in the garden of Gethsemane and on the cross; and if his blood is applied to my soul, my sins are all forgiven, and I shall be clean, whiter than snow, purer than silver tried in the furnace, and I need no purification in purgatory. You make Him a half Mediator. His blood cleanses in part, and purgatory in part. No. He bore the sins of the whole world, and sweat as it were great drops of blood; and shall I now say his blood is not sufficient, but that I too must suffer in purgatory, and thus in part expiate my sins? No, never. ·Glory be to his name, his blood cleanses from all sin.

"'Thus,' said I, 'you see how the church of Christ, founded by the apostles themselves, turned away from the truth; no wonder, then, if there should be error and darkness now in the church of Christ, and all the churches and every Christian has need to read these words to the churches of Asia.'"

One Sunday evening "I remarked that all men were sinners, that every son and daughter of Adam, except Christ, were sinners, even the Virgin Mary. At this all started and exclaimed, 'The Virgin Mary, the mother of God, a sinner?' 'Yes,' said I, 'she was a sinner, and had need of the merits of her Son, and without his blood could not be saved. She was a good woman' ('A good virgin,' interrupted my teacher). 'Yes, a good virgin, and highly favored among women and blessed of the

Lord, but was saved only by the blood of Christ. Was not David a sinner, and Solomon, and Rehoboam? and yet Christ, as to the flesh, was of the seed of David. Christ was born without sin—you say his mother must have been without, because he was without sin. In the same manner you must say her father was without sin, and her father's father, and so on, till you trace the lineage back to David, and say he was without sin; but that you know is not true, for the word of God expressly says he sinned greatly, and he himself confessed it.' To this no one was able to give an answer."

After some discussion on the use of images, a priest said, "'The first commandment sufficed, and there was no need of the second.' My teacher said the same. I then raised my voice, and exclaimed, 'Where is the man who dare say to God Almighty, "Thou hast given more commandments than are necessary; one or two or three or nine suffice; I need not the whole"? Where is the man? If he says is a Christian, he is not.'

"One evening a very intelligent Arab came to my lodgings and spent three hours in reading the Scriptures with me, and in conversation about images, idols, praying to saints, and the importance of faith in Jesus Christ alone as our Redeemer. He said that God was great and to be feared, and men feel the need of some Mediator to speak to him for us, and for this reason they prayed to the saints. I replied, 'You have well said that we need a Mediator; and for this very reason Jesus Christ came down from heaven and took upon him our nature—was made in all respects like one of us, sin excepted. He is our Mediator, and there is no other.' I then read to him 1 John 1 : 1 : 'If any man sin, we have an Advocate with the Father, Jesus Christ the righteous.' 'There is not,' said I, 'a single word in the whole gospel about praying to saints and angels.' 'But,' replied he, 'would it be right to speak against the saints?' 'No,' said I; 'I honor their memory, for they loved Jesus Christ, and were heralds of salvation; but if you think to honor Jesus Christ by giving his glory to them, or by making them in part mediators between God and us, you are greatly mistaken. In thus doing, you dishonor him. He is the only Mediator between God and man. I fear there are many who put their trust more in the intercession of the Virgin Mary and Peter and Paul and the rest of the saints than in Jesus Christ, who is all in all to me, and must be all in all to you if you wish to be saved. Besides,' said I, 'how do you know that Paul hears you when you pray? Perhaps I am praying to him in America at the same time that you are praying to him here, six thousand miles away. Is Paul omnipresent? Certainly not. Jesus Christ is, and hears every prayer that is offered in every part of the world.' 'True,' said he.

"During the conversation he asked why many said this Arabic Bible printed in England ought not to be received. 'Because,' said I, 'there are many priests in the Roman-catholic church who say that the Word of God ought not to be put into the hands of all men, but only a few.' 'Why?' said he. 'Because,' replied I, 'there are many things in that church which the word of God condemns.'"

Dr. King seems ever to have had an answer at hand when any one questioned the doctrines of grace. His arguments against infidelity and error, many more of which might be gleaned from his Journals, are ever replete with good common sense, often quaintly expressed, and so well fitted to reach the mind and conscience. Of him, as of our Lord, it may be said, " the common people heard him gladly."

CHAPTER X.

MOUNT LEBANON AND THE SAMARITANS.

Convents—Druses—Mount Lebanon—Arrival of Messrs. Bird and Goodell—Beyrout—Missionary Tour—Tyre—Acre—Nazareth —Mount Tabor—Ebal and Gerizim—Samaritans—Second Visit to Jerusalem—Arabic Bible.

At every convent visited by Dr. King, he called attention to the truth held by the monks, rather than to the errors with which it was entangled. At the convent of Mar Antonius Kazhiah, it was sad to find about one hundred monks of most filthy appearance, only one-half of whom were able to read. One old man of venerable appearance listened with wonder to the simple story of a free salvation; and others privately expressed the opinion that they themselves were wrong, and wished they could follow the missionaries. A Maronite patriarch accepted an Arabic Bible and a Syriac Testament, and gave his address as "The vile Joseph Peter, patriarch of Antioch." He said there were eleven or twelve Bishops, and perhaps 150,000 Maronite Christians under his supervision. A question as to using leavened or unleavened bread had separated them from the Syrian church.

Of the Druses, Dr. King writes: "They believe in one God, and are supposed by many to worship a golden calf. They express a great deal of love for those they meet, but the Christians say they are hypocrites and deceivers, and worse than **the Bedouins** of the desert; for if you eat with a Bedouin, you are safe; or if he says to you, 'Peace be to you,' you have nothing to fear: whereas a Druse will welcome you, and eat with you, and perhaps be devising means to rob you or take your life.

"The Christians are many of them very punctilious as to saying their prayers and confessing, but there is very little good faith among them. On any occasion they will tell a lie. They say if they do not lie they cannot gain anything in trade. They regard the Sabbath as a day of sport, and are very profane.

"The women are kept in a state of ignorance. The mind of a woman is generally considered by the men as being on a level with that of an ass; and an ass, next to a hog, is considered as the most contemptible animal there is. At meals the men eat first, and then the women and servants eat together what is left."

Their way on this journey led over Mount Lebanon. After passing a lovely spot, "Eheden," called "Eden" by the English, our travellers came to the ancient cedars so long famed as the glory of Lebanon. "As you approach them, they appear like a little grove of spruce or pine-trees in America. They stand on six little hills in the arena of a vast amphitheatre formed by lofty barren mountains on the north, east, and south, the tops of which, I suppose, form the highest part of Lebanon. On the hill south are eighty trees, six of which are very large; one which I measured was twenty-nine feet in circumference, and another thirty-one feet. On the northeast are thirty-five trees; on the north are sixty-six; five very large—one being forty feet in circumference. On a hill toward the northwest are sixty-three trees. On the whole three hundred and twenty-one. Mr. Fiske counted some very small ones, and so made three hundred and eighty-nine. Of these trees, those of middling size are tolerably straight, eighty or ninety feet high, covered with limbs nearly to the ground. The large ones are very irregular in shape, and appear to be made up of several trees grown together, thus uniting their strength against the strong hand of time."

Further description in detail is given of these old settlers, under whose branches the Maronites hold a feast once a year, called the "Feast of Cedars." These cedars are called by the Arabs, Azek—almost the same word used by the Hebrews of old.

Dr. King visited the ruins of Baalbec, and made drawings and measurements which may still be of service to the more modern explorer. The Arabs account for the raising of such enormous stones more than thirty feet, by saying it was the work of the devil.

The journey on the whole was a rough and dangerous one; terrific rains quite demoralized the attendants; accommodations were most uncomfortable; at the convents opportunity was often given for serious talk with the inmates; patriarchs and superiors of highest rank were glad to converse with strangers so intelligent, notwithstanding their *heresy.*

At Antoura Dr. King's portrait was painted in his Oriental dress, by Reuben Costar, a Jew brought from France by Lewis Way.

Returning next to Beyrout, Dr. King made arrangements to continue his Arabic studies, receiving much kind attention from Mr. Abbott the English consul.

At the request of Rev. Mr. Jowett, Dr. King made a few notes in regard to a tract, which the former was about to publish, in order to stir up Christians to pray for "an outpouring of the Holy Spirit, upon themselves, their Jewish and Mohammedan neighbors, and also for pagans." They read, condensed, as follows:

"All men are our brethren; their souls are as precious as ours.

"Prayers are to be offered for all men everywhere.

"We are debtors to the Jews, for we have received all that we hold precious from them. They are to be ' grafted in again.'

"We should pray for Moslems, because they are the worst of men, and Christ came to save the lost.

"We should pray for pagans, for there is as much hope of their conversion as there was of that of our forefathers.

"' The ends of the earth' are promised to our Lord Christ.

"We should be followers of God, having the Spirit of Christ, who gave himself for the redemption of the world."

Then as encouragement to prayer, reference is made to numerous Bible illustrations of its power, and to our Saviour's direct promises concerning it; also to the "signs of the times," even then encouraging to watchmen upon Zion.

Dr. King did not stay at Beyrout very long, returning to Deir el Kamar, where advantages for study were much greater. Here he was received as a brother, with the utmost cordiality ; but his quiet studies were soon pleasantly interrupted again by letters from Rev. Isaac Bird, telling of his arrival with Mr. Goodell, and their wives at Beyrout. Dr. King felt at once much anxiety lest these friends should not take the right kind of lodgings, for a mistake here might compromise their character as missionaries. There had been a recent scandal concerning one man, on account of his allowing his daughter to marry a bishop who already had one wife ; so that the whole community was greatly incensed.

The local sheikh had impressed into his own service every horse, mule, and jackass, and it was with difficulty Dr. King made his way back to Beyrout, where, to his relief, he found Mr. Abbott had taken the new-comers into his own home. It is unnecessary to enlarge upon the delight with which Dr. King welcomed these fellow-laborers.

A house a little out of the city was soon taken at $36 for six months, and on Tuesday, Nov. 25, a service was held there, consecrating it to our Lord Jesus Christ ; and thus was begun a mission, which is still a power in the East. The story of Dr. Goodell's part in it has just been given to the public. Rev. Dr. Bird has himself written of " Bible Work in Bible Lands."

It was a little difficult for Dr. King to decide upon his own course. The new missionaries wished him to remain with them. He thought he could study to better

advantage by going, as before, right in among the Arabs.
Damascus might be a good place, but it was almost impossible to get there over the mountains at this season.
In the meantime, Arabic still engaged his attention,
while conversations were held by him as often as possible with Mussulmans and Jews, as well as with his own
teacher, Hanna Domani, who was constantly bringing
up quibbles of one kind or another as to the word of
God, and yet who soon allowed, that since knowing Dr.
King, he "could not rejoice as formerly in bowing to
images and pictures." This man believed in miracles
as performed in the convents, and offered twenty witnesses to them. Dr. King challenged him in vain to
produce even one or two.

When the question came up as to the best location
for a permanent missionary station, Nazareth and Tyre
were proposed; Dr. King gave his voice decidedly for
Beyrout, an opinion which an experience of now more
than fifty years fully justifies. He writes of Beyrout:
"It enjoys the advantage of consular protection; it is
the best place for a dépôt, having easy communication
with Malta; it is in the vicinity of all the Christians
of Mount Lebanon; there are several families of Franks
here, and the Turks are more civil than in most places
farther south. In case of any great commotion, flight to
the mountains or escape by sea would be easy."

Sometimes thoughts of parents and home for the
time overcame the stranger in a strange land. "Commended my dear parents to the care of Him who has
always been gracious to them and provided for them

'Why,' said I, 'should I wish to be with them in order to comfort them? If God is their friend, is not that enough? Is he not better to them than I could possibly be? If I had not left them for the sake of Christ, perhaps he would have taken me from them by sickness and death. O God, have mercy upon my soul and theirs; and if it be thy holy will, let me see them again in the land of the living; if not, let us be resigned, and may we meet in thy kingdom, where there is no separation of friends, no sorrow, no sin.'"

Study was now interrupted by a season of conference with other missionaries, Messrs. Jowett, Fisk, and Wolff; and by a missionary tour to Tripoli, or Trabloos. From El Kamar he wrote to his friend Mr. Wilder, "I am now alone, entirely surrounded by Arabs, in what may be called the capital of Mount Lebanon, as it is the place where the prince (the Emir Bushir) resides. Mr. Fisk and Mr. Wolff are two days' distance from us.

"My business is to read and talk Arabic from morning till night. I have put on the turban and the Arab dress, and my beard is so long that I am generally taken by strangers to be one of the sons of Ishmael. I sit on the floor like a native, and at dinner thrust my hand into the dishes of pillau as deep as any Arab of the country. Like the rest of the people, I get up in the morning and pick off the lice that are crawling on me, scrape away some of the biggest of the fleas, and sit down on my heels with the Arabs, who say they love me very much, and call me brother."

On the journey, as usual, he was engaged in selling

and giving away Bibles, and parts of the Bible published
as tracts; and he could have disposed of many more, had
they been on hand.

A letter now came from Mr. Fisk recalling his associate to Jerusalem.   It was thought expedient for Mr.
Bird to go there also.   As usual, special prayer was offered before these brethren set out on their way.   Dr King
writes, " In six hours and three quarters we arrived at a
place called Neby Yunas, the spot where it is affirmed
the prophet Jonas was 'vomited out upon dry land.'   His
name is revered by the Mussulmans, who believe that he
was buried here, and a tomb has been erected in which a
lamp is kept constantly burning."

A little time was given to the ruins at Tyre, the
missionaries taking a boat to examine the vast number
of columns lying "in the water and out of the water,"
just as the prophet Ezekiel had said would be the case,
and the position of which proved the great extent of the
ancient city.   In 1823 only three or four hundred mean-
looking houses occupied perhaps half the present island,
so that it may be said with truth, " Tyre is no more."

At Bosa and other places much direct religious conversation was had with the Mussulmans.   Acre was found
strongly fortified with walls, recalling many scenes connected with the Crusaders.   One reader of the Koran
said 'I can tell why the earth does not sink: it stands
upon a bull.'   'And what is under the bull?' said I.   Ans.
'A rock.'   'And what is under the rock?'   Ans. 'The
sea.'   'And what is under the sea?'   Ans. 'Smoke.'
'And what is under the smoke?'   Here he and the com-

pany burst into a laugh and he replied he did not know, but there was a learned sheikh in the city, and he wanted to bring us together, that we might dispute."

Nazareth of course was eloquent with thought of the Saviour's daily home-life. "There was a school of forty or fifty boys in a convent here. I asked one of them, who read Latin very fluently, whether they understood what they read. 'Oh, yes.' 'Tell me the meaning in Arabic.' This they could not do, not even a word. For any one who comes here and says one Pater Noster, and one Ave Maria, the pope promises seven years' and forty days' indulgence. To one of the Catholic Arabs present I said, 'What does this mean? seven years past or seven to come?' 'Seven to come,' said he. 'Then,' said I, 'I can say one Pater Noster, and one Ave Maria, and go away and sin as much as I please.' He did not know what to say to this, but another Arab Catholic came up and told him it was seven years past. 'But,' said he, 'if you do not repent, it is nothing!' 'But,' said I, 'the paper says nothing about repenting. It only says if you say one Pater Noster, and one Ave Maria you have indulgence ; and if I repent towards God He will forgive me for Christ's sake, and I have no need of this indulgence.' He seemed to feel the force of what I said, and made little reply."

At Mount Tabor, a bright rainbow so transfigured the mountain, just as the missionaries looked at it, that Mr. Bird said some men would have regarded the appearance as miraculous.

While waiting at the door of the church at Nazareth,

Dr. King being there alone, ten men came in ; and referring to some remarks Dr. King had made as to the sacredness of the place, he went on to say that our Lord Jesus is an ever-present Saviour, everywhere wherever his people worship him in spirit and in truth. A still larger number of people came together and listened for twenty minutes to a real Gospel sermon. One or more seemed deeply impressed.

Quite exact measurements were taken at Nablous of Mounts Ebal and Gerizim, and facts of interest obtained from the priest of the Samaritans, Salameh, who was acquainted with the Abbe Grégoire, whom Dr. King had known at Paris. This priest, in answer to inquiry, said, " The number of Samaritans is about two hundred, the number of males sixty, and the number of houses twenty ; there are three persons at Jaffa ; there were formerly many at Damascus, Aleppo, Tripoli, Gaza, and in Egypt ; but now there are none.'

" I asked him, ' When did your fathers separate from the Jews ?'

" PRIEST. Their separation commenced under Shilkiah, in the days of Saul. At that time four tribes revolted. The final separation was in the time of Ezra, after which, several of the tribes went to the east into India beyond a river, and wandered about and went to Russia.

" I. Do you know Hebrew ?

" PRIEST. Yes.

" I. Have you the Jewish books ? Do you believe in them ?

"PRIEST. We have the five books of Moses. This is our holy book. Moses commanded that nothing should be added. The Jews have changed the letters of the alphabet and added.

"I. Have you the book of Joshua?

"PRIEST. Yes. We consider it a good book, but not inspired by God like the books of Moses.

"I. Do you believe in the prophet Samuel?

"PRIEST. He was a great enemy to the Samaritans.

"I. Do you know anything about Jeroboam and Ahab who were kings here?

"PRIEST. No.

"I. Have you any sacrifices?

"PRIEST. Yes. Once a year, in commemoration of the passover, we offer six or seven lambs of a year old upon an altar of stone.

"I. Have you no daily sacrifices?

"PRIEST. No. There is no place to offer them. Gerizim is the place where we should worship.

"I. Had you a temple there formerly?

"PRIEST. Yes, but it is destroyed.

"I. Have you an altar?

"PRIEST. Yes, of stones on Mount Gerizim, where we offer the passover.

"I. Have you seen the Gospel?

"PRIEST. Yes, and read it much.

"I. What do you think of Jesus Christ?

"PRIEST. He was one of the first of infidels, because he said he was the Son of God.

"I. Were not his works good?

"Priest. I say nothing against his works, neither do I curse him. I only say he was an infidel, because he called himself the Son of God.

"I. Have you read his conversation with the woman of Samaria by the well of Sychar?

"Priest. Yes. It is all a lie. He came to the well, and all he said was, 'What is the name of this well?' and she replied 'Jacob's.'

"I. Do you believe in a Messiah to come?

"Priest. Yes.

"I. What will be his character? Who will he be, a man or God?

"Priest. The spirit of Moses will descend from heaven and take another body and reign over all nations.

"I. You believe, I presume, that I and you and all men are sinners.

"Priest. Yes, truly.

"I. What must a man do in order to inherit the kingdom of heaven?

"Priest. He must keep the law.

"I. But we have none of us kept the law, and Joshua said, 'Ye cannot serve the Lord, for he is a Holy God.' Your fathers were very rebellious and Moses called them stiff-necked, and the law says, 'Cursed is every one that continueth not in *all things* written in the book of the Law to do them.' We are all under the curse. How can we be saved?

"Priest. By repentance, that is enough.

"I. Moses sprinkled the book of the law with blood, and if a man sinned, he was to offer sacrifices, and without the shedding of blood there was no remission. Were you a king and I a subject, and had you issued a decree, that whosoever should kill or steal should be put to death, and I should commit either of these crimes, repentance would not atone for it. God, who cannot lie, has said, 'Cursed is every one who continueth not in all things written in the book of the law to do them.' We are all under the curse of God's holy law, which you and I believe; and there is no remission, but by the blood of Jesus Christ, to whom all the bloody sacrifices under the Mosaic dispensation had reference.

"PRIEST. I am not a sinner like you.

"I. Have you never sinned?

"PRIEST. Very little, very little, almost none.

"I. If you say this, you do not know your own heart. God told his covenant people they were ever inclined to go astray. Moses sinned and was not permitted to enter the promised land. Are you better than Moses?

"PRIEST. Yes, better.

"I. Is Moses in heaven?

"PRIEST. Yes.

"I. How was he saved?

"PRIEST. His sin was as nothing—small—small.

"I. But the Lord was angry with him and did not permit him to enter into Canaan.

"PRIEST. God commanded that you should not add to, or diminish from the law, or change a single letter. But you say the sacrifices are done away, and you keep the first day of the week. Why is this?

"I. The sacrifices all referred to the death of Christ,

the great sacrifice which was made to atone for the sins of the world, and they ceased, as a matter of course, when he suffered. All the ritual in the Law as it respects sacrifices was then fulfilled, and the work of redeeming man was so much greater than that of creating the world, that we keep the first day of the week instead of the seventh. You ask me, Why change the law? Why abolish sacrifices? You yourselves have left off the daily sacrifice.

"PRIEST. Why is circumcision abolished?

"I. That was a bloody seal of the covenant God made with Abraham, and like the blood of the sacrifices, probably had reference to him, the seed of Abraham, in whom all the nations of the earth were to be blessed : to his blood, which was to be shed that the covenant might be established. The covenant God made with Abraham was, 'I will multiply thee, etc., and in thy seed shall all the nations of the earth be blessed.' This seed was Christ; He said not seeds, as of many, but 'in thy seed.'

"PRIEST. No. The seed is all his posterity, and the promise or covenant was multiplication of them.

"I. Why then are you diminished to the number of two or three hundred, and the Jews to about seven millions, and scattered over the face of the earth?

"PRIEST. There are multitudes of Samaritans in the world.

"I. Where?

"PRIEST. I know not, but they exist somewhere.

"I. No. The promise made to Abraham had reference to those who should be of the like faith with him. Those who believe in Jesus Christ, and walk according to God's Holy Word, are his children according to the promise, and I trust there are many such in England and America, and among other nations, who are not his seed according to the flesh.

"Priest. The Mussulmans are the children of Abraham.

"I. Are all the nations of the world blessed by them?

"Priest. The blessing is with us Samaritans.

"I. Is this then the fulfilment of God's promise, 'I will multiply thee'? Here you are, pined away to the number of two hundred, without a temple. No, the promise is spiritual, and is fulfilling, and will be fulfilled: all the nations of the earth shall turn unto the Lord, and shall believe in Jesus Christ, and the seed of Abraham shall be like the stars of heaven for number, and as the sands upon the seashore, and I hope that you will be of that spiritual seed also.

"While I thus spoke he listened very attentively. Before leaving, I asked if he would permit me to see his manuscript of the Torah. He replied, 'Yes,' and asked how much I would give? I offered him two piastres. He then said the key to the synagogue, where the book was, was not with him.

"I answered, 'I know where the key is, sir; it is in my purse.' At this he smiled and said, 'Yes.'

"Afterwards showing this man a dollar, the roll was brought out and opened. He said it was 3,448 years old, and was written by the grandson of Aaron. He did not say a word against my touching it. I asked him to read the ten commandments of the Law, which he did from the 20th chapter of Exodus, and interpreted them to me in Arabic.   He called the first two one; and for the tenth, said it was written, 'Thou shalt make to thee an altar of stones upon Mount Gerizim.'

"The commandments were comprised in four sections. The Samaritan differs from the Hebrew in character, and in pronunciation. The priest charged the Jews with having changed the letters of the Hebrew language, and added to the word of God. Before closing the book, the priest remarked to me, 'You will now receive a blessing, on account of having seen this book.'"

On a shelf near the altar in the small neat synagogue, Dr. King saw many books written in Samaritan, but was not disposed to pay $2 00 for one of them. He went with the priest to his house, from which was a fine view of the Mounts Ebal and Gerizim.

The priest seemed really impressed, when Dr. King on leaving committed him to the care of God and of our Lord Jesus Christ.

The tomb of Joseph was shown here, also the well of Jacob, now partly filled with stones and earth. On Wednesday the missionaries received a most cordial welcome from Mr. Fisk at the Convent of the Archangel at Jerusalem. The expense from Beyrout, including servants, was thirty-four dollars.

Dr. King's second stay in Jerusalem was a short one. He still felt that in order to learn the Arabic quickly, he must be alone among the Arabs, entirely surrounded by them.   For this reason, after visiting the sacred localities with the new comer, Mr. Bird, and celebrating with him and Mr Fisk, the Lord's Supper and the Monthly Concert as before in an upper chamber. he resolutely left his friends for Jaffa.

On the way at Ramleh, a very venerable Arab, blind, and reminding one of Joseph of Arimathea, spoke highly of the word of God, and encouraged his countrymen to buy it.

The Arabic Bible circulated by Dr. King was a great improvement upon the one formerly used, which was full of errors, so that the Roman-catholics had indeed reason to complain of it ; but it was far inferior to the more recent translation made by Drs. Eli Smith and Van Dyke.

CHAPTER XI.

LIFE IN PALESTINE CONTINUED.

Jaffa—Discussion with Mussulmans and Catholics—The Koran—
Oriental Dress—Return to Beyrout—Damascus—Aleppo—
Antioch—Armenian Creed—Tyre—Third Visit to Jerusalem—
Letters written from Calvary—Journey towards Home—Asaad
El Shidiak, the Martyr of Lebanon—Farewell Letters.

DR. KING decided to remain for a time at Jaffa, and
engaged a teacher there at $4 a month, who, speaking of
the Koran, said it was the root of all knowledge, the
sum of perfection of all wisdom ; and that, in order to
know Arabic well, one must read it sixty times.

Mere human reason everywhere, east or west, among
the Arabs of Syria, the Brahmins of India, or the trans-
cendentalists of nominal Christianity, asserts itself, as regards the "mystery of godliness," in about the same terms.
One day Sheikh Khalil said to Dr. King, "I am willing
you should love Jesus Christ. I love him more than
all things in this world, more than my own life. All I
wish is that you should say he is the servant of God, and
not say God was in him, and he in God; and that they
are one." Dr. King replied, "O Sheikh, I have no
hope of salvation but by the blood of Jesus Christ. He
is God. He is my all." Dr. King said further of this
man, "He is very zealous in his endeavors to convert me
to the Mussulman faith ; says I am an infidel, in danger

of everlasting flames unless I give up the divinity of Christ. By the grace of a crucified Redeemer, I hope to be faithful to this deluded soul. My feelings are so shocked sometimes at hearing Gabriel called the Holy Spirit, and the name of the false prophet exalted above that of Jesus Christ, that I would gladly lay aside the Koran, and never read in it again, did I not think it my duty so to do, in order to enable me to be more useful."

Sheikh Khalil afterwards begged for a whole Bible, promising never to part with it, and some time after made no comment when Dr. King spoke of the Bible as far exceeding the Koran. Still he one day asked Dr. King to pull off his shoes while reading the Koran, who satisfied him by saying that among Englishmen (Americans went by that name) this was considered no mark of respect.

Khalil was exasperated at the conduct of a Catholic family who had ordered a Bible to be burnt. He said, " Do not let the Christians have any more of your books. We Mussulmans will take them. If I should see that Catholic priest I would kill him."

After some talk one day with a young man who became very vociferous about general councils and saints, Dr. King says, " The common people of this country are so noisy and impudent that one has need of much grace and humility in order to converse with them in a proper manner. They come at you like a mad bull, pawing and bellowing and throwing dust around them, and one is almost tempted sometimes to knock them down with weapons that are only carnal. We need to think much of Him 'who endured the contradiction of sinners,' that we be not wearied, neither faint in our minds."

A poor blind man called for books one day, which his younger brother could read to him, but soon came back saying the priests would not let him keep them. "I felt my indignation moved at this sinful act of taking away the light of heaven from one who will never more behold the light of the sun in this world."

Direct discussion was had with the superior of a Catholic convent, Terra Santa at Jerusalem, carried on with singular boldness on the part of Dr. King, considering how much he was really in this man's power.

Dr. King writes: "As I had seen him in Beyrout, I thought I would do him the honor to call on him. He immediately began to make remarks about my dress, and said, 'Aha! a white turban—all Mussulman. I must write to England and let the people know you have turned Mussulman. You missionaries have come out here—two at Jerusalem, two at Beyrout, with their wives—to turn men away from the true faith, and to make discords and divisions.'

"I interrupted him by saying, 'Christ said there would be divisions.' He continued, 'You come here and spread about your books, which are changed.' I replied, 'They are not changed, but are word for word according to the one printed at Rome, under the eye of the pope.'"

The next objection was that the Apocrypha was omitted, when Dr. King said, "The books composing it were not received by the early fathers of the church." "You are excommunicated," said he, "from the church." "It is a blessing so to be," replied Dr. King, "because the Roman-catholic church is in error, and no longer the true church." Some priests present could hardly restrain their rage.

"'What errors?' said he. Answer. 'Your images, your giving pardon for money. You have wholly taken away the second commandment. Why is there so much lying and iniquity here among the people and the priests? Because they have not the Word of God. If you would give the Word of God to the people yourselves, I would be glad.'

"The Austrian consul, who was present, started up and said, 'The Roman-catholic church is the oldest in the world.'

"'The Jews are before you,' said Dr. King. 'They were once the true church, but they have wandered.'"

The above is but a specimen of the conversation held with this superior, who, following Dr. King to the door, warned him to desist from speaking against their images and the worship of the holy Virgin, lest he should do him harm.

To show that Dr. King's studies of Arabic were not in vain, his teacher soon affirmed that he "was now fit to read the Koran in the Mosque of Omar or in the temple at Mecca;" that he read it with more propriety than Mussulmans who had been doing so for twenty years. Dr. King adds, "The beauties of the Koran consist principally in the language, in the fine jingle of words which it is utterly impossible to convey through the medium of any European language. But I cannot conceive that any

man of decent morals and of good understanding, who
admires thoughts rather than words, should ever leave
the Bible for the Koran.   This would be leaving a pure,
crystal fountain, to drink out of a dirty slough ; preferring tinsel to gold, or husks to bread.   I have often wondered how any man who had as much knowledge of the
awful truths of the Bible as Mohammed seems to have
had, could be so daring as to mix them with falsehoods,
and swear that he had received them from the Lord of
all worlds.

"The Bible is as much above the Koran, with regard
even to its precepts for the good order and happiness of
society in this world, as the heavens are higher than the
earth.   One conviction produced on my mind by reading
this book has been that a man, having a perfect knowledge of the Arabic language, possessing a strong mind
and fertile imagination, with the Bible in his hand and
the devil in his heart, would find no great difficulty in
writing the Koran."

Dr. King remained at Jaffa as long as he could study
there to advantage, and then returned by land to Beyrout.   Room cannot be given to his account of the journey, nor to a report of all the missionary work everywhere so persistently carried on, "in season," and often
no doubt apparently "out of season."   Yet one may imagine what a hearing the zealous stranger must have
gained even through the very incongruity of time and
place often chosen by him for religious conversation.

Dr. King's eyes were very weak at this period, and
he was obliged to use green glasses. ·He wore the Orien-

tal costume—for according to the example given in 1 Cor. 9:20, to the Arabs he became as an Arab—so that New England friends just now could scarcely have recognized him. Indeed, on one occasion he purposely quite mistified Dr. Goodell, who had just arrived, and passing up the street, supposed the figure which he saw seated on a stone by the wayside was a genuine son of the desert, until suddenly addressed by it in unmistakable American vernacular.

A long letter, sent to the Bible Society at Malta from Beyrout, reports with great particularity the sale within a short time of one hundred and seventy-five Bibles.

It was a great luxury at Beyrout to find there a true home with his missionary friends. Conferences were soon held on various topics; the first related to the spelling and pronunciation of Scripture and Mussulman names. A list of these is given, in which the name of their present abode appears as Beyroot, and Tripoli takes the place of Trabloos.

Discussion on the subject of fasting had the practical effect of leading the missionary band to observe the first Monday of every month in this special way.

The decision as to one's duty in the case of evil reports, was to "pay little attention to them. Christ did not. Preach the gospel; let your eyelids look right on ; commit your cause to God. If men think we are political spies or agents, denying it will do no good, etc."

While at Beyrout, Dr. King offered for the first time an extempore prayer in Arabic. Some of the Arabs kneeled, and while he was praying smote on their breasts, crying out, " Lord, have mercy upon us," but with what sincerity it was difficult to tell.

Upon returning for a time to Deir el Kamar, the personal greeting received by Dr. King was very satisfactory, but difficulties as to distributing the Bible had increased. The Roman-catholics had held a council at Jerusalem, and had ordered the convents not to receive the missionaries. Again, complaints were repeated as to the edition of the Bible circulated, because the Apocrypha was not in it. One of the priests, Abouna Yusuf, confessed that the opposition arose from fear that the Bible would be the means of bringing out those who read it from under the pope. Dr. King allowed there was danger of this, as it had had this effect on his own ancestors. This priest asked Dr. King why he did not go directly to the patriarch ; who answered, " I have no time to visit all who oppose the gospel. St. Paul kept about his own business, preaching the Word." Then Dr. King went on to tell how this very patriarch had received money from England and a press from America, five years before, in order to print and circulate the Bible, but had done nothing about it—was living on the funds and opposing the missionaries. When asked, " Why should you distribute the Bible, when an edition of it was published at Rome?" Dr. King answered, " Yes, but at a price no poor man could pay, thus virtually excluding it from the public. Those who profess to be built on Peter should observe his directions, and take heed to the Scriptures as to a light in a dark place."

Sometimes the priests became so much excited that the noise was deafening; especially was this the case when they were told there was no rule in Scripture "forbidding to marry," nor to abstain from meats. Again, they said that when Peter denied Christ, it was only with his mouth, not with his heart, and therefore not wrong; and that he never dissembled, as related in Galatians. These discussions were not useless. Sometimes a priest would say, "Sir, you are right. I think as you do. Go; you are right."

Sometimes the talk was with or about the dervishes. These men pretended to great self-abnegation, while in reality their lives were thoroughly wicked and impure.

When Dr. King visited Damascus he found it necessary to make some concession to Mussulman prejudice by not wearing his white turban nor riding into the city; but he refused to dismount until absolutely compelled to do so. Some of the smaller trials of life were here exceedingly numerous. Sleep sometimes could be secured only towards morning, and then in the open air, exposing one to cold and hoarseness.

Much kindness was shown to Dr. King and the friends with him by Hakeem (Dr.) Solomon. He told them that in Damascus there were about twelve thousand nominal Christians. Whatever may have been the purity of the Abana and Pharpar in the days of Naaman, in May, 1824, their waters were muddy and unwholesome.

About this time the superior of a Greek Catholic

convent, meeting Dr. King, said the discovery of America had been a great injury to the cause of religion, because the Indians were not men, not children of Adam. Dr. King asked that the conversation might be in Arabic, that all present might understand; but Abouna Saba chose to use Italian. Speaking of Protestants, he said, "You have protested against the true church."

DR. KING. "No, we have protested against the errors of the church."

ABOUNA SABA. "Errors in the church? No. There are no errors in the church. *Old* things are certainly better than *new.*"

DR. KING. "Surely; and for that very reason we protested against the errors of the Romish church, which were *new,* and returned to the ancient system, such as existed in the first ages of the church among the disciples of Christ, and we took the gospel and the Old Testament for our guide, which were of *old.*"

Abouna Saba went on asking about the course in America of collegiate and theological study, and seemed surprised to hear the Bible was received as ultimate authority.

With regard to the Druses, Abouna said that he had seen some of their books, and that they in reality worship the *light,* and have the image of an ox to represent power; that when one of them becomes of the number of those called Aakel, or Aakelin, there is an apparent change in his conduct for the better. He then leaves off smoking tobacco, swearing, and every vice, however abandoned he may have been before. This change he thought was merely external. Very little can be known of them. They have houses for worship, but no one can enter them except Druses.

The teacher whom Dr. King engaged at Damascus to give him lessons in Arabic did so in true ancient style. His scholars were obliged literally to sit at his feet, while he sat as if lord of the world. He was a firm believer in genii, some of which he said were under his control.

It was not possible for a stranger to remain in Damascus during July and August on account of fevers, so that Dr. King could not very long avail himself of the service of the above distinguished professor, and soon left for Aleppo—just before going having an interview with a very intelligent Jew, who claimed to be a lineal descendant of David, and to whom Dr. King enlarged on the story of Saul's conversion near the ancient city where they now were.

On the journey Dr. King had a talk with some well-informed Mussulmans, whom, however, it was difficult to convince that all Christians were not the idolaters which, from their personal knowledge of those so called, they believed them to be.

Hooms, now written Hums, and the seat of encouraging mission work, was passed on the way. Hamah, also, the ancient pass of Hamath, with its musical water-wheels, utilizing the waters of the Orontes, was a point of great interest. Here, too, were found priests who were great sticklers for the Apocrypha, while yet the missionary, like Lot, could not but be vexed with their filthy

conversation. Indeed, descriptions were given by them
of deeds so unlawful, so unmentionably wicked, as proved
to our traveller that he was indeed passing through some
of the dark places of the earth. There seemed little hope
of making impression on men so thoroughly defiled ; yet
to some of the early believers in Christ did the apostle
say, " But such were some of you."

The journey physically was a trying one, from sand
and heat and burning winds ; yet while thinking of rich
people in Boston and elsewhere, Dr. King writes of being
happy. " I would not change places with them. I would
indeed be willing to change for a little time, that they
might see that missionaries have something to suffer.
Many of our dear friends, could they see us here to-day,
would think that we could not live."

When arrived at Aleppo word was received that further distribution of the Bible was forbidden : copies already given out were to be collected and sent back to
England. Dr. King writes : " I have no doubt that the
Roman-catholics have caused this order." One of them
afterwards acknowledged that a communication on the
subject had been sent to the headquarters of the Greek
church, Constantinople. " Mr. Lesseps, the French consul," whose son Theodore is also mentioned, " called, and
in conversation said he would do all in his power to prevent anything which could in the least tend to injure the
Catholic church ; and avowed that it was according to
the principles of his church not to put the Bible into the
hands of the common people, and that they ought to
believe according to what the priests tell them. What a

disgrace to a man of his standing in the nineteenth century !"

Sept. 19, 1824. " The French consul read me a letter which he had just received from a captain of a French vessel at Alexandretta, stating that on his way from Cyprus he had fallen in with a Greek cruiser, who hailed him and ordered him to stop; that he did so about 5 P. M.; that the Greek cruiser told him he had many Turks on board, which he intended to massacre that night, but that he would sell them if the French captain would buy them. He bought five for fifty dollars. Twenty remained. While buying those five he heard some one from the Greek ship crying out in French, 'Au, nom de Dieu, achetez-moi et sauvez-moi.' The French captain demanded if he were French. He replied, ' No, but a Jew doctor well known at Aleppo.' It must have been Laybach. Upon this the French captain offered to buy him, but the Greek captain refused to sell, saying that he meant to kill him that night with the twenty Turks who remained. My heart was much pained at this intelligence. Dr. Laybach had bought of me, two or three days before leaving Aleppo, the Old and New Testaments in Hebrew and the New Testament also in French. This was about three weeks since."

Antioch was the next place visited. At this birthplace of the Christian name no Christian church remains. A few Greeks meet for worship in a grotto or hole in the rock. Here Dr. King learned, in regard to the late Firman of the Grand Seigneur, that the governor of Damascus had sent messengers after him in the wrong direction, and the order soon became a dead letter. Mr. Turner, British chargé at Constantinople, took a firm stand, claiming that the Turkish government had no right to destroy English Bibles any more than any other kind of British property. These were dangerous times in the East. Death by poison of men of high position was not unusual. Just after that of the Reverendissimo of Jerusalem, as strongly suspected in this manner, a French marquis, a Roman-catholic, was attacked by seventy Turks, who beat him, bruised him, and carried him by night, bareheaded, to Jaffa, not for having *made* any remarks implying this, but for having *heard* them.

Not far from Antioch, near Swedia, are " the ruins of a church on Mount Simeon, so called, I suppose, from Simeon the Stylite, who remained thirty-seven years on a pillar, and was the founder of that order of monks termed Stylites, or Pillar Saints. The pillar is still standing, I am told, in the midst of the ruins of the church."

From Beyrout Dr. King wrote immediately, through Colonel Greaves, to the trustees of Amherst College, recognizing his engagement to return to them, while he still wished to qualify himself further for his duties as their professor. As many otherwise intelligent Protestants doubt the need of sending the gospel to nominal Christians in the East, it may be well to insert here a synopsis, according to J. Agrarius, of the Armenian creed.

1. Christ is the Head of the church.
2. Gregorius is their principal saint.
3. They ask of the Virgin Mary and the saints that

they would intercede for them with Jesus Christ and with God.

4. They pray for the dead, and receive money for doing so.

They pray for those who die in India, in Russia, in Angora, in Constantinople, and other places, and send every three years to receive the money from the friends of the deceased. This money is for the poor priests at Jerusalem. They have twelve patriarchates, over whom the grand patriarch is like a pope. They do not profess to believe in purgatory, but their prayers for the dead imply it. They baptize infants by three immersions, like the Greeks; cross the child with oil in his face, his hands, his breast, his eyes, and his ears, then put in his mouth a little of the sacramental bread and wine and take it out again. They have secret confession; they believe in the Real Presence, but do not take money for pardons.

Dr. King writes with regard to one of the bishops, that towards the close of a conversation he seemed to comprehend what was meant by being born again and about salvation as wholly the gift of God. "I could not but be affected myself on thinking of the state of the Armenian church when I heard one of her most intelligent bishops asking me, like a little child, about some of the first and plainest doctrines taught in the gospel. He says that the only preaching they ever have is about abstaining from certain kinds of food on fast-days: 'Oh, my brethren, if you eat such and such things on such a day you will go to hell.'"

January, 1825, found our missionary studying at Tyre. Here he became acquainted with an old Greek priest named Antinous, one of the few who escaped the terrible massacre at Scio, from which a few Greek boys were also preserved and sent to America for education, one of whom, Dr. Alexander George Paspati, is well known at Constantinople.

It was common at this time for the Turks to go begging food from the Greeks, and then to ask pay for the use of their own teeth in chewing it.

Dr. King again attempted to establish a school for girls, but the priests and people said, "Women have small minds. If taught to read, they would be devils." Some young men said that they would put away their espoused wives, if taught to read. Reports that the missionaries bought converts, and took portraits of them to be shot at in case of retraction, and that this would cause death and earthquake, interfered with efforts made for the instruction of even the boys. Yet bright spots often cheered Dr. King's heart; as when, after a long talk, an Arab sheikh kneeled in prayer, and again when a warm welcome greeted him from some Greek priests upon his return to Jerusalem.

Here the influences of the place, ever fresh, led to a season of self-examination, during which Dr. King writes most bitter things against himself, acknowledging that every good thing in him was a gift from above, and writes: "Here, on Calvary, and at the foot of Thy cross, I wholly discard all right and title to merit or favor in Thy sight, by anything I ever have done, or ever can do." These heart-searchings seem to have led him on to more absolute dependence on our Lord, and consecration to his service.

Scenes connected with the taking of Jerusalem under Titus were forcibly recalled, as the day arrived, when the pasha of Damascus, with two or three thousand soldiers, made his yearly claim for tribute. Mussulmans and Christians all fled from the villages on his approach.

On March 31, 1825, the theatrical representations of our Saviour's crucifixion led the missionary to protest more strongly than ever against the errors of that religion which for popular effect turned the most sublime events of time into absurdity.

A bright sunbeam came now from Egypt, a letter from Mr. John Glidden, telling of his own and his wife's conversion by the influence of Dr. King and his fellow-laborers, together with the bereavement of a dear child. Sunday, January 3. Dr. King was privileged to preach on Calvary, from the specially appropriate text, "And when they were come to the place which is called Calvary, there they crucified Him," the first Protestant sermon probably ever delivered there in the current language of the country. The next day, the Monthly Concert was observed for the third time in this sacred spot. This, however, was not done without enduring some "contradiction of sinners," one of the Turks during the closing hymn even striking Mr. Fisk with his gun ; and at the convent of the Terra Santa, it was not safe to accept even a cup of coffee, for fear of its containing poison. The Jews also suffered greatly. Rabbi Mendel and forty others were bound with chains on their necks and legs, until some exorbitant demand was paid.

Jerusalem was just now literally in tears, as described by Jeremiah, the oppression of the modern Benhadad, Mustapha Pasha, was so crushing. The superior of one convent received five hundred blows on his feet, in order to make him give up treasures concealed under his care. Forty men were employed to beat him. After this he was left bareheaded on the ground, without any sustenance but water, for three days and three nights, with a rope about his neck.

Dr. King, knowing the interest that would be attached at that time to letters penned upon Mount Calvary, took especial pains to write to friends at home, and in Europe, thus strengthening greatly their missionary zeal, as well as their personal interest in himself. Among other things, he writes that he accounts for the extra wickedness of the people living near the sacred places in Syria, from the fact that they depend on these places, and not on Christ himself. Also that he becomes more and more convinced that the same divine Spirit is required to renew the hearts of men everywhere, whether among Greeks, "Cretes and Arabians," Americans or Englishmen. He also gives his plans for the immediate future, as the three years he had engaged to spend in these Oriental lands had about expired, which plans were to visit, before returning to America, some parts of Europe, everywhere preaching the gospel.

To a former classmate, Rev. Orville Dewey, who had

subsided into Unitarianism, after referring to early associations, and to fears long ago that his friend was inclined to speak "smooth things," Dr. King writes: "Judge then of my surprise, when I learned that you were doubting of the divinity of our Lord and Saviour Jesus Christ, who is the author and finisher of the Christian's hope, the alpha and omega of all things, the root and the offspring of David, the creator of the heavens and the earth, the brightness of the glory of the invisible God, the judge of the quick and the dead, the adoration of the angelic hosts, and the everlasting song of the redeemed in heaven.

"I said, 'this is only a temporary falling away; like Peter, he will presently weep bitterly! The great Shepherd will yet bring him back to his fold, and not suffer him to wander and perish.' But I hear that after so long a time you are still in doubt, or rather that you have entirely cast off your first faith as it respects Jesus Christ. You perhaps say that you still trust in him, although he be but a man. But remember that it is written, ' Cursed be he that trusteth in man, or maketh flesh his arm.' You will say, perhaps, that he is super-angelic. Be it so. But if he be not the everlasting God, you make him a liar, for he has said, ' He that hath seen me, hath seen the Father.' I will not here attempt, as it would probably be in vain, after all your advantages of study and research in theological subjects, to adduce proof of the Divinity, I mean the Godhead of Christ. With you, I deem it not so much the work of reason, but of the heart, to bring you back to the sinner's only hope.

"This from your friend and servant on Calvary, who knows and feels and acknowledges himself to be one of the greatest of sinners, and whose only hope is in that precious blood which was here shed for the redemption of man."

May 9, 1825, Dr. King turned his face homeward, leaving Jerusalem with some difficulty, on account of political troubles there. The journey was not made in a Pullman palace-car. One day, dry thistles and onions were the only food procurable. The same night the tents were attacked by robbers, who got off with a trunk belonging to the Englishman, Rev. Mr. Lewis, around which three men were sleeping. Attempts to regain this trunk led to difficulties with the Arabs, who soon after attacked the travellers with swords and clubs, and yelling like so many furies, riding upon their swift horses as they rushed upon the tents. Dr. King had heard the alarm, and galloped forward, but a sheikh came flying after him, and he called out, "Brother, do me no harm, I have not injured you." The Arab let down his sword. It seems that he had heard that Dr. King was a great man, travelling with a firman from Abdallah Pasha. No wonder the Journal of this day is full of praise. "He delivered me from my strong enemy." No lives were lost on this occasion.

The way now led through Cana of Galilee, to the Sea of Galilee, descriptions of which have now become familiar. A church at Tiberias was built in form of a boat, in memory of St. Peter's boat. The priest said that under the altar was the stone on which St. Peter was when

the Lord said, "On this rock will I build my church."
The people "were all praying with united vociferation,
beating their heads, jumping, weeping, stretching up
their hands towards heaven, as if to pull down mercies
thence, then suddenly bowing and crying aloud in the
most lamentable tones of voice; clasping their heads
with both hands, sobbing and smiting their breasts, reel-
ing to and fro, and in various ways making violent exer-
tion. Poor Jews! the veil is still upon their hearts! I
longed to tell them of Jesus Christ, and call on them to
believe in him whom their fathers crucified."

Passing through Safed and Tyre, Dr. King came again
to Beyrout, and says: "The more I see of Palestine, the
more I see that it is a goodly land, and capable of sus-
taining an immense population." Letters here from his
aged parents greatly cheered his heart, telling as they
did of the faithful kindness of his friend and their son,
S. V. S. Wilder, who had well redeemed the pledge made
by him in Paris nearly three years before. There were
letters also from Mr. Wilder and Dr. Heman Humphrey,
president of Amherst College, expressing willingness to
have their professor of Oriental Literature remain away
still longer, if thus better able to promote the cause of
Christ; while yet they felt that his presence would be of
essential help in making Amherst College what Dr.
Humphrey writes it would be, 'and must be, one of the
first colleges in New England.'"

Simple incidents alone of the homeward journey can
be given. At Beyrout he was not satisfied to rest in the
enjoyment of the society of his friends, the American

missionaries, but sought to acquaint himself still more fully with the customs of the Turks, having in all an eye to the great object of his life; and he began also to write a grammar in Syriac. His teacher, the priest Asaad el Shidiak, afterwards better known as the Martyr of Lebanon, now appears on the scene, and is soon forbidden by one who signs himself, Aug. 12, 1825, "the contemptible Joseph Peter, patriarch of Antioch," to have any intercourse with "these men," viz., the missionaries. Another firman was soon issued by the Grand Seignior, warning every one against these books. Dr. King sent out a reply, defending, by testimony from the early Fathers, the Canon of Scripture as issued by the British and Foreign Bible Society, as free from the apocryphal writings so much insisted on by the Greek church.

As rejoinder to Dr. King's reply, came another manifesto, commencing in a style proving that pure transcendentalism is not indigenous to Boston or New England soil: "In the name of the Eternal Being, the Necessary of Existence, the Almighty; the Contemptible Ignatius Peter, patriarch of Antioch and of the Syrians." The paper sought to justify the patriarch in his failure to carry out an agreement made with some English Christians, which has already been noticed, and it still more positively forbade the people to receive the Bible or any books from the missionaries.

These special efforts of the priesthood were overruled for good in a way which time alone has helped to bring to view, for they led to the writing by Dr. King of his now celebrated "Farewell letter to his friends in Palestine and Syria," which through all these years has proved a shaft of wonderful power, and which our modern missionaries still retain in their armory, not as a relic of the past, but rather as a weapon well fitted for the present conflict.

A letter, very sad, as showing determinate enmity to our blessed Lord, just now came from Lady Hester Stanhope, from Djaun Lebanon, in answer to one of sympathy from Dr. King, on occasion of the death of her brother. She says: "I should have liked your letter better, had you not talked of Jesus Christ, in whom I shall never believe, and that you know; therefore never *preach* to me any more upon that subject, for it will be perfectly useless. The future will prove who is right; till then let the matter rest, with me at least. Your own book, the Bible, gives no mathematical proof of what you wish to inculcate."

In contrast to this, came a visit paid to a Christian emir and his father, who had had their eyes burnt out and their tongues cut off the winter before, by the Emir Bushir. As in the case of Milton, so much the more the true light shone in them, and strange to say, their articulation was still almost perfect.

A record here appears in detail of Bibles and tracts distributed in the East by Messrs. Wolff, Fisk, Goodell, Bird, and King, from 1822 to 1825, amounting to 3,329 Bibles or parts of Bibles, and 13,800 tracts, making with those already given out by Messrs. Fisk and Parsons, 4,000 copies of the Bible, and 20,000 tracts, besides those

circulated by Mr. Temple. We now begin to see the
harvest from this seed sown fifty years ago.

Dr. King closes Vol. IV. of his journal, "Let not
missionaries or missionary societies be discouraged, because they see no present fruits of their labor. They
shall reap in due season, if they faint not."

CHAPTER XII.

HOMEWARD THROUGH EUROPE.

Asia Minor—Death of Pliny Fisk—Smyrna—Spain—Nismes—
Paris—Duke de Broglie—Louis Philippe—Lafayette—Count
Verhuell—Countess of St. Aulaire—Visits in England—Hannah
More.

Dr. King left Beyrout for Smyrna, Sept. 26, 1825, in
company with an English nobleman and his suite, some
of whom, infidel as to religion, sought to entangle the
missionary in his talk. One of them died within a few
days, of malignant fever, without apparent knowledge of
his danger. He had asked that no clergyman should ever
be sent for to visit him, if sick. Reason was taken away
almost from the first. All that Dr. King could do, at
the funeral, was to seek to impress the truth upon the
rest of the hitherto gay company.

A stop was made at Tarsus, and a visit paid to the falls
of the Cydnus, so full of association with the brief and
brilliant career of Alexander the Great, and the early
aspirations of the boy Saul of Tarsus. The journey was
pressed onward through Asia Minor. One can well imagine the many points of interest: old volcanoes and ruins
of places now scarcely known. Danger of attack by robbers supplied a dash of excitement. In one place the
travellers passed about a hundred and fifty graves of men
who had been murdered quite recently. Lord St. A.

said that in case of difficulty, he was ready to turn Mussulman ; but neither this willingness, nor the better resolution of the missionary to trust in God, was brought to the test.

At Buluwaden, the party "took lodgings in a khan, which had one tolerable room, but it was so full of Turks and Rayahs, that we concluded to sleep in the stable where our horses were. Indeed, one part of the stable was intended for men, and had six or seven chimneys or fireplaces. At our feet as we lay down horses might have been fed. This came nearer to what I used to suppose an oriental khan to be, than any I have seen before in this country. I could not but think of Him who was ' wrapped in swaddling clothes, and laid in a manger.'"

A curious superstition was found attached to a spring about three feet in diameter, which bubbled and whirled at the top of a mound, as if from intense heat, but still was cold. The Turks consult it when about to buy a horse. In such a case they "pile up three stones, one upon another, then hold a cloth or the corner of a handkerchief in the water for one or two minutes. On taking out the cloth they find a small hair attached to it, and the color of this hair shows them, they say, what color the horse ought to be."

The name of Philadelphia was found most appropriately to be "Allah Shahein," "the city of God, for he that dwelleth in love dwelleth in God." And in its ruins was a striking fulfilment of the prophecy relating to the church there. Rev. 3 : 12.

Upon arriving at Smyrna, eighty-nine days after

leaving Beyrout, sad news met the homeward bound missionary. The vessel of Lord St. A. which, after landing the passengers at Tarsus, was to make its way round to meet them at Smyrna, had been taken by the Greeks, and stripped of everything, including Dr. King's books, manuscripts, minerals and clothing. Making the journey by land had been the means of preserving their lives. Some of the boxes were afterwards recovered. Upon opening them, Dr. King writes, " Many of my beautiful Korans and Arabic manuscripts, and Syriac and Persian books were gone, or torn in pieces, and the greater part of my letters, I believe. I however found the most important of my journals and private writings." But there was a greater trial. Pliny Fisk was gone ; the dear friend, whom Dr. King had left in perfect health, had finished his work on earth. At the grave of Parsons the two had sung, " Brother, thou art gone before us." Now the survivor was left to sing alone, " Brethren, ye have gone before me." The fact was one difficult to realize. Here at hand were freshly written letters from Pliny Fisk, full of love to the dear friend who had come for three years to his aid in mission work. But one of those insidious eastern fevers, at first scarcely threatening danger, had suddenly done its office, giving however this servant of God time to write a second letter as follows :

" MY BELOVED BROTHER KING: Little did we think when we parted, that the first, or nearly the first intelligence concerning me, would be the news of my death ; yet this is likely to be the case. I write you as from my dying bed. The Saviour, whom I have so imperfectly

16*

served, I trust now grants me his aid, and to his faithful care I commit my immortal spirit. May *your* life be prolonged and be made abundantly useful. Live a life of prayer. Let your conversation be in heaven. Labor abundantly for Christ. Whatever treatment you meet with, whatever difficulties you encounter, whatever vexations fall to your lot, and from whatever source, possess your soul in patience, yea, let patience have her perfect work.

"I think of you now with my dying breath, and remember many happy hours we have spent together. And I die in the 'glorious hope of meeting you, where we shall be freed from all sin. Till that happy meeting, *dear* brother, farewell.

"P. FISK."

Dr. King's long term of service is in accordance with the above dying prayer.

At Smyrna, Jan. 19, 1826, a Greek family named Mengous, knowing of Dr. King's great desire to speak the Greek language not only with correctness but with elegance, consented to receive him under their roof, wishing in return to perfect themselves in English. This removal is important only in relation to ensuing events. If the young American learned things other than Greek in this hospitable mansion, it is not to be wondered at by those who knew of the extreme attractiveness of the daughter of the house.

Notwithstanding Dr. King's acquaintance thus with one of the best families in the place, his name was by order of the bishop, read out in the French and Italian churches, as "an American who distributed bad books, contrary to church and religion, and that it was a sin to read them."

In a different spirit came a letter, written, the day after Dr. King had preached on board the United States corvette Erie, by Dorotheos Papa Michael, who was present with other Greeks on that occasion.

"ELOQUENT AND VENERABLE MAN, Mr. King, all hail! Many times before, my friend, and especially yesterday, I could not but wonder at the zeal which you have in preaching the word of God; nor less could I help praising the density of your ideas; from thence auguring concerning the gigantic steps which your mission has made, is making, and will make.

"The fear of God, my friend, united with upright words, and with sincere searching for the truth, are truly those energetic means by which everything may be accomplished. Want of time does not permit to praise also the zeal, which yesterday I witnessed in the great attention of the sons of America to your words, sure and incontestable signs of internal worship and of a continued returning of the heart [towards God].

"My friend, may the grace of our Lord Jesus Christ, and the love of God the Father, and the communion of the Holy Spirit, be with us all. So let it be. Farewell.

"DOROTHEOS PAPA MICHAEL."

To Smyrna, Dr. Wolff also soon came, and the work of distributing tracts was carried on as before in Egypt and Syria.

M.·J. Van Lennep's name now appears, representing a family planted in Eastern Asia Minor, and owned of God for the furtherance of the Gospel.

After about five months stay in Smyrna, Dr. King saw the way clear to continue his journey, passing Magnesia, now a mission station, on his way to Constantinople. At Thyatira, he was told that tracts left there by Messrs. Fisk and Parsons had been read by more than two hundred persons.

Dr. King arrived at Constantinople, taking lodgings in Pera, just after the surprising stroke by which the Sultan had relieved himself of the Janizaries. Over 7,000 of them perished in a single massacre, on occasion of some too extortionate demand made by them.

Turkish law was so stringent in regard to the Greeks, that Dr. King could not pursue his Greek studies in Constantinople to advantage, and consequently returned to Smyrna—glad to leave a place which, although he was treated there with great kindness by the English residents, he yet found to be a city "full of oppression, deceit, and false religion, of confusion, plague, and death."

"Fuit Ilium" seemed the most appropriate passing remark, as a few tumuli were seen in the distance on the plains of Troy.

Smyrna friends gave him a most cordial welcome, and mission work was resumed there for a time, soon interrupted by the arrival of the "Erie," whose officers pressed Dr. King to join their mess, either to Mahon, or to America. This invitation it seemed wise to accept, and Dr. King bade farewell to the lands of the East.

August 9, 1826. Visits were made to Tripoli, where Decatur burned the frigate "Philadelphia," which had run aground and been taken by the Tripolitans. It was commanded by Commodore Bainbridge, whose war-cloak has been made historical by his nephew Dr. McLean, late President of Princeton College; and also to Algiers, where Dr. King renewed acquaintance with Mr. William Shaler, consul, whom he had met in Paris. At Mahon, on invitation, Dr. King held a friendly discussion with two Roman-catholic friends, who, as usual, denied the right of private interpretation of the Scriptures.

The establishment of the Circumlocution Office was not left to the present day. It cost him a world of trouble to obtain a passport for Marseilles or Barcelona, but it was finally secured through the interposition of Commodore Rodgers and other officers of the United States government vessels, for whose kindness in many emergencies Dr. King was deeply grateful.

Expenses at the best hotel in Barcelona at this time were $1 a day. The inhabitants were a singular mixture of Spanish and Arab types, having many customs peculiar to the East. In drinking, they would hold the vessel a little distance above the mouth, inclining the head back, and would thus pour the water into it in a stream. The original coat-of-arms of the Bonaparte family was to be seen there, showing, as the name implies, what is called a noble origin : on one side a lion, on the other six stars ; above them an eagle and a casque with feathers.

The archives of the Count of Aragon were also of interest, containing a treaty with the Moors, dated in the

year 86 of the Hegira. An old papal bull, issued in the
tenth century, was also on exhibition. At this time the
dust caused by the demolishing of the walls of the Inqui-
sition had hardly settled. A Jew had been hung only
three months before, simply because he was a Jew. Poi-
soning was of frequent occurrence. Over fifteen hundred had been assassinated in the province of Catalonia
within three years, and no note made of it, except here
and there by the erection of crosses. Did not such a
land call for a pure gospel?

It was a delight to cross the line between Spain and
France, and to join at Nismes in observing the Monthly
Concert with true Christian friends, whose first exclama-
tion was, " We have been praying for you for four years!"

A letter from Jeremiah Evarts, Secretary of the
American Board, was received here, having been forwarded from Smyrna. It refers to Mr. Gregory Perdi-
cari and two other Greeks, who had come to America for
education by Dr. King's advice, recommending that although these young men were now provided for, no others should be sent, unless funds should be secured in
advance for their support. Dr. Evarts expressed great
interest in the cause of Greece. Missolonghi had just
fallen. He said the American Board were ready to employ Dr. King as agent to arouse the church, hoping he
himself, after a time, might return to Greece ; for from
the engagement made with Amherst he might no doubt
be honorably released, as it was the common opinion
that there was no need to teach Arabic in our colleges,
and Amherst just now had no funds to spare. The let-

ter closes with words of touching sympathy in regard to Mr. Fisk, on whose help in various ways the Board had been depending. Such a letter could not fail to produce some excitement on Dr. King's part. On its proposals might hinge his whole future life. Dr. King says, " All sinful as I am, still I feel as if there was an invisible hand guiding me." To this letter Dr. King returned a glowing appeal in behalf of the Greeks, defending them on every point.

To Nismes came also at this time Rev. H. G. O. Dwight, since so well known as missionary at Constantinople. It was pleasant, too, to receive letters of greeting from that true Christian gentleman, Baron de Staël, from Prof. Kieffer, Thomas Waddington, and the well-known philanthropist, John Venning, who was indeed a light set in a dark place, St. Petersburg, and from Count Admiral Verhuell, peer of France, and president of the Evangelical Missionary Society at Paris. The latter writes in behalf of the society, and also of some young missionary students in training for the foreign work, asking Dr. King to visit them, also to prepare in detail such facts and fruits of his experience in the East as would prove useful to any future laborers there. Offers of further assistance as to funds were also made in a very considerate way, and were peculiarly acceptable on account of the loss of clothing through Greek pirates, which has been before mentioned. Mr. Wilder had written that 1,000 francs were placed to Dr. King's credit in Paris; and now through these Paris Christians the Lord provided for every temporal want.

Several missionary meetings were attended by Dr. King in the vicinity of Nismes. At one Monthly Concert at Anduze about four hundred persons were present.

Letters now came from Rev. Daniel Temple and Rev. Eli Smith, then his associate at Malta, and also from Rev. Josiah Brewer. Mr. Temple wrote, "I am sorry to say that Government refuses to give me permission to print your valedictory letter, assigning as a reason that it is 'an overt attack upon the dominant religion of these possessions.' You will be gratified to hear that Asaad Shidiak, your teacher in Arabic, mentions your letter to his friends as the means of his conversion to the truth as it in Jesus."

Leaving Nismes, a visit was paid to Montauban. Here Dr. King addressed the students on Missions, and made note of their course of study.

Monday, April 2, Dr. King writes: "At 6 P. M. arrived at the place which I left four years and seven months before to go up to Jerusalem, not knowing the things which might befall me there. I will not attempt to describe the emotions which I felt when I first came in sight of this city. In silence I praised the God of heaven, all whose ways are mercy, sought of him forgiveness through Christ for all my unfaithfulness, and begged of him to order all my future ways in kindness, to keep me from falling into sin, to enable me to walk in humility, and as becomes a poor sinner who hopes for pardon alone through the blood of Christ."

The following note shows into what a circle Dr. King was at once received at Paris: "Dined at the Duke de Broglie's in company with the Countess de St. Aulaire and Madame R., who was formerly much in company with Madame de Staël. After dinner General Lafayette came in. Conversed with all on the subject of religion. When speaking to the children of the Duke de Broglie and of the Count de St. Aulaire (who is Roman-catholic), all came round me to listen. I spoke of regeneration, love to Christ, the sinfulness of man, etc. General Lafayette himself seemed to listen with pleasure, and invited me to come and spend a little time with him and his family at La Grange. The Countess of St. Aulaire invited me to call and see her the next day, saying that she was a Roman-catholic, and that she had something in particular to communicate to me.

"At 1 P. M. I called on the Countess de St. Aulaire, who began immediately to open her mind to me with regard to her religious views and feelings, the difficulties she had to encounter, etc. She is one of the most interesting women I have met with in France. Her New Testament is marked from one end to the other, and I think she is truly born of God. She introduced me to all her daughters, and I spoke to them on the subject of religion. I spent with her nearly two hours and a half.

"Dined with Mr. Porter and spent the evening at General Lafayette's. He introduced me to all his family. Madame Lafayette said she had desired much to see me. The General again invited me into the country."

Dr. King also called on Count Verhuell, Baron de Sacy, and by invitation on Madame Lasteyrie, the daughter of Gen. Lafayette. A proposal came from Dr. Thayer

of Amherst that Dr. King should join him in charge of
an institution there, afterwards called Mount Pleasant.

A Greek princess was a refugee in Paris at this time
under circumstances of great trial. Her husband had
been killed by the Turks, and four of her children had
recently died. The Duchess de Broglie and the Countess
of St. Aulaire took Dr. King to see this lady; and the
truths of the New Testament, a copy of which he left
with her after the visit, proved, as ever to those who receive them, of unspeakable comfort to her.

After giving an account of a missionary meeting, Dr.
King writes: "At six, dined with the Duchess de Broglie, who had invited me the Thursday before, in order to
read the Scriptures and explain them to her family and
others that might be present. There were present, besides the duke and his family, his sister Madame Randall, Madame de St. Aulaire and all her children, the
brother of the Baron de Staël, and others. There were
perhaps ten of these Roman-catholics. After dinner I
conversed with the children on religion, and at 8 read
and explained the fifth chapter of second Corinthians,
and concluded with prayer. How interesting to have
such a meeting at the Duke de Broglie's! Really it is
of the Lord, and all glory be to his name."

The next day appears the following entry: "At half
past two went to call on Madame Scherer, Rue St. Ho-
nore, No. 362, who received me in the most cordial manner, though an entire stranger. Soon after I began to
converse she and all her family wept; and here also I
proposed having prayer, in which we united. At quarter

before six went to dine with his excellency, Mr. Brown, the American ambassador. Spent the evening at his house, where I met some persons of distinction.

"Tuesday, 24. At half past two went by invitation to Madame Jules Mallet's, Rue Montblanc, No. 13, to meet a number of ladies, for the purpose of reading to them the Scriptures, with explanations and prayer. Among those present was the daughter of Baron Cuvier. There were twelve or fourteen present, and all ladies of high rank. How interesting to be invited to hold religious meetings among this class of people—at Paris, where a few years ago one was almost ashamed to own that he believed in Christ."

Meetings were held also in the interests of the Tract Cause and that of Christian morals. One day while conversing with the Countess St. Aulaire, "Mademoiselle Randall came in, and in speaking of the dismission of the National Guards, and of the Duke of Orleans (afterwards Louis Philippe), 'Ah,' said the Countess of St. Aulaire to me, 'you would be delighted to see the duke;' and I said, 'Yes, certainly, if I could be introduced to him.' Upon this, Mademoiselle Randall, who is very intimate with him, at once offered to introduce me." This promise was not forgotten. A note came, saying that the duke would receive Dr. King at Neuilly, the next day at 12:30. "He received me in his room alone, and we spent about one hour in conversation with regard to America, France, Greeks, Turks, and evangelical missions. He seems to be very liberal in his views, is a warm friend of the Greeks, and wishes that the European powers would unite to put down the pride of the Turks, and to give liberty to the Oriental Christians, who should have a government of their own establishment in Constantinople. He spoke against slavery, and seems to be a friend of man. On his asking me whether it was true that the Sandwich Islands and Otaheite had become Christian, I gave an account of our mission to Hawaii; and on his asking what religion we introduced, I told him the doctrines which we preach—man lost by nature, Christ his only Saviour, regeneration by the Holy Spirit, and the fruits of it the spirit and temper of Christ. I told him that these were the doctrines God had blessed to the conversion of Greece, Rome, and all pagan Europe, and that we believed these doctrines would be blessed in these last days. I then related to him the conversion of Jews at Constantinople by the preaching of these doctrines. 'The end of the world is then approaching,' said the duke. I also spoke of some of my labors among the Mussulmans. 'We have a number of them here,' said he, 'and I do not see that anything is done for them.' 'It is prohibited by the director of the institution where they are,' said I. 'But,' said he, 'we see no conversions among Mussulmans.' 'No,' said I, 'for nobody makes any effort to save them, and the Christians who are among them avoid speaking on religion; but when an apostolical spirit shall revive in the Eastern churches, and men are willing to lay down their lives for the name of the Lord Jesus, we may then expect to see some conversions. It is nothing,' said I, 'but the grace of God through Christ that can change our own hearts, and nothing else that can soften the heart of Jews and Mussulmans and civilize pagans.'

"At length I told him that our missionaries endeavored to preach as much as possible as St. Paul and St. John and the early disciples of Christ preached—in a word, to know nothing else but 'Jesus Christ and him crucified.' 'If they continue to limit themselves to this,' said he, 'they will do well.'

"On my rising to leave, he followed me to the door of his apartment, and stood conversing for ten or fifteen minutes. I then begged pardon of him for taking so much of his time. He said he was most happy to have formed my acquaintance, and should be happy to see me again.

"Blessed be God that I have thus had opportunity to speak a word to him for Christ and His holy gospel, and in favor of evangelical missions. Much of the morning before I went to call on him I spent in prayer to the Prince of princes and the King of kings that He would prepare our hearts and open the way for me to say something for Christ. Blessed be his name, he heard my poor prayer offered in the name of Jesus Christ."

Dr. King's irrepressible work among the Catholic nobility excited fears lest his staying at the Mission House might lead to difficulties with the government. May 5, 1827, it was thought expedient by his friends that he should take lodgings elsewhere. "'Is it your design,' inquired I, 'that I should be silent, and not speak the truths of the gospel as I may have opportunity at Paris among Roman-catholics?'

"'Not in the least,' said Count Verhuell, with emphasis; 'who on earth can stop your mouth that you should not be faithful and speak for Christ? But as you are drawing the attention of many towards you, it is better that you should not remain in the Mission House. If you stay six days more, take another lodging. If your funds are short, I will pay for your lodging myself.'"

After visits paid elsewhere, everywhere preaching Christ and him crucified, both in the diligence and in the homes of luxury, where he was always welcome, Dr. King accepted General Lafayette's invitation to visit him at La Grange. "Soon after I entered the saloon the general and all his family came in to welcome me to La Grange. To the general, who took me by the hand with both of his, I said, 'May the peace of our Lord Jesus Christ ever be with this house, so dear to my dear country.' Soon after I entered the house the rain fell in torrents, mingled with hail and attended by lightning and peals of thunder. I thought of the storm that hung over my country when Lafayette came to her assistance. I thought of the liberty so dear, those privileges so precious, which I had enjoyed, and of which the Old World knows so little. I felt that I wished to reflect and not to converse. I retired to my chamber, and there I spent some time in prayer. At a little past six we sat down to dinner. The general placed me between him and his daughter Madame Lasteyrie.

"The evening was spent in conversing about the American war, Major André, Major Ales, Arnold the traitor, the system of slavery, the best way to eradicate it, the Colonization Society, etc."

In Dr. King's Journal are found autographs of Lafayette and his family ; of "Charles Carroll of Carrollton, far advanced in the ninety-first year of his age ;" also those of the Duke de Broglie and his family. The duchess, upon giving these names, said, " I trust that not one of these will be forgotten in your prayers." With her name as one of the "transplanted flowers," whose record was preserved by Rev. Dr. Robert Baird, is connected that of Mademoiselle Clementine Cuvier, daughter of Baron Cuvier. Dr. King writes of her as "very serious," and "a person of great distinction in Paris, with a mind highly cultivated." Of the Countess of St. Aulaire he says, "She is a person of great attainments in learning, of exquisite taste, and has left all the principal errors of the Roman-catholic church. The Bible is now her study and her delight. She is of a distinguished family, from which three popes have been chosen. She corresponds with the king of Prussia, and has a numerous literary acquaintance."

A plan now appears for an institution foreshadowing Lincoln University, which Dr. King suggested should bear the conjoint names of Washington and Lafayette.

Dr. King's time, during his stay in Paris, was much taken up in translating into French some of his manuscripts, a work which the friends of missions had asked him to do. The East was then almost a *terra incognita.* Information as to every point was called for. Again, Armenian type was needed at Malta, and books of reference for the missionaries there, all of which he was able to secure. But through it all we learn, by frequent reference to hours of prayer, whence came the power that made this plain, earnest American missionary so acceptable a guest in the first society of Paris. As he left some of these homes, all, even the servants, were in tears.

Passing over the Channel, the same warm welcome was accorded to our missionary in many of "the stately homes of England," where further contributions were made to the font of Arabic type. After a meeting at Miss Farrar's, conducted by Miss Stevens, a lady of the Church of England, of eminent piety, who in her reading and explaining of the Scriptures to large circles anticipated the work done by many Christian women at the present day, Dr. King was asked to speak of the work in Palestine. When through with his remarks, "a little boy of eight years, Master T. H. Farrar, stepped up to me, and said, 'Here is one pound towards the types.' This seemed to give an impulse to others, who came also and contributed, and I got more than six pounds. This I considered a large sum."

The pages of the Journal are brilliant just now with the names of persons well known beyond their own country for their interest in the cause of Christ's kingdom: Drummond, Lord Calthorpe, Mr. Pratt, the biographer of Richard Cecil, Rev. Mr. Saunders, Mr. Symes—who showed Dr. King no little kindness, Rev. Baptist Noel, Lord and Lady Teignmouth, Marquis of Cholmondely, Mr. and Mrs. Hawley, Mr. Harford of Blaise Castle, and others. Rev. Robert Hall asked Dr. King to preach for him, and after this service introduced a captain from

Beyrout, who confirmed from his own observation every word that had been said in regard to certain matters in Syria. The coming in of this captain just then, Dr. Hall said, was one of the most remarkable events he had ever known.

July 19, 1827, Dr. King writes: "Went to Barley Wood, the residence of the celebrated Mrs. Hannah More, about twelve miles from Bristol. I arrived about 10 A. M., and met with a most cordial reception. Mrs. More is now in her eighty-third year, and converses with I might almost say the vivacity of youth. Her eye, though a little dimmed with age, still speaks in conversation, and animates what her tongue eloquently utters.

"I remained with her till about 5 P. M., and it was then with much difficulty that I could get away, she was so urgent, and so often repeated her solicitations to have me stay another day at her house. She took great interest in the accounts I gave her of Palestine; said, 'I want no more of Italy and France, nothing but Palestine.' She gave me one of her books, the Life of St. Paul, and some little pamphlets, and also £5 for the Arabic type. I afterwards sent to her from Bristol an olive-branch from Bethany. I would gladly have remained a few days at Barley Wood, and also at Bristol with Rev. Robert Hall, and a little longer at Blaise Castle, but I have for a long time past made it a rule not to go to any place, nor to remain there, unless there is hope of doing some good, or unless circumstances evidently point it out as a duty either to go or stay."

CHAPTER XIII.

MISSIONARY AGENCY IN AMERICA.

Arrival in New York—Visits to Friends—Agency with A. B. C. F. M. in New York and the South—Dr. Kirk—Washington—Letter from Ladies' Greek Committee of New York—Becomes their Missionary—Sails from New York—Kind Reception at Paris.

AUGUST 2, 1827, Dr. King took leave of England, sailing by packet Pacific for New York, and September 4 he was able to write: "At thirty-eight minutes past ten my feet pressed the soil to which they have so long been a stranger." Here, upon landing, he was immediately greeted and made welcome by S. F. B. Morse, Rev. W. A. Hallock, W. W. Chester, Pelatiah Perit, Mr. William Williams of Norwich, Dr. Rice, Rev. Matthias Bruen, and others, while a letter awaited him from Mr. Wilder; a constellation of names, all but one now passed onward into the heavens.

Parents and friends in New England were first to be visited. At Ware village he soon found Mr. and Mrs. Wilder, then went on to meet an appointment made by Colonel Trask at Springfield; then reporting himself to Dr. Humphrey at Amherst, where he preached on Sunday, he passed on to Northampton and Hawley. Here were his now aged parents, feeble in health, yet truly resigned in regard to his long absence. After a few days' visit, when another parting seemed doubly hard to bear, while yet Dr. King was both affected and strengthened by his father's fervent prayers, he went with Col. Longley to Shelburne, to visit the father of Pliny Fisk. "As I entered the house," he says, "my heart was full. All the scenes of the East came fresh to my mind. And the wounds that had been made by the death of Mr. Fisk seemed to be opened afresh. His father had gone out, so I sat down and wept in silence. He soon came in, and with weeping took my hand and exclaimed, 'Oh, that I have lived to see any one who has seen my son!' All the afternoon he sat close by me, and seemed to feel as if I were all that was left him of his deceased Pliny. He is now seventy-nine years old, and expects soon to go home to his rest. At half-past six in the evening went with him and his son about two miles to the meeting-house, to attend the monthly prayer-meeting."

Passing on again towards New York, where the American Board was to meet, an offer was made Dr. King of a professorship in Yale College, $15,000 being already raised for an endowment.

At the first meeting of the American Board Dr. King was called to speak, and special interest was felt in his report as to Asaad el Shidiak. The Board still wished him to undertake an agency, and though the compensation was of necessity small, he said there was a call to it in his own bosom louder than the Board could give, and more tempting than to settle down as professor on an assured salary. He felt impelled to urge upon the Board itself more earnest, onward movement, so many places in the East were opening to the gospel. Dr. Beecher, Dr. Porter, and Dr. Proudfit, also spoke on the subject, and then followed one of those supreme seasons, when God was indeed shedding down upon every heart the blessing of the Holy Spirit. A subscription of $25,000 was made on the spot, $20,000 of which was annual for five years ; a large sum at that time.

Dr. King also addressed a meeting of 250 ladies in Dr. Mathew's vestryroom, besides one or two others of the same kind in other churches. Mr. Abeel, afterwards so useful in China, was in New York just now, and conferred with Dr. King as to his going on a foreign mission, praying together in reference to this. Rev. Sutherland Douglas invited Dr. King to speak on missions to a convention of Episcopal clergy at Washington.

Other names now appear in New York as friends of the same great cause. Col. Rutgers, Col. Crosby, Mr. Gilman of Norwich, Rev. Dr. Ferris, Rev, Edward N. Kirk, Dr. Henry G. Ludlow, Mr. Joseph S. James, Moses Allen, and Mrs. Bethune, in whose infant-school he told of Bethlehem ; visiting also Mr. Seaton's Sunday-school of three hundred and fifty scholars.

News now came of the death of Dr. Payson at Portland, and Dr. King copied in full the letter, now so celebrated, dictated to his sister just before he entered the gates of heaven.

Arrangements being completed with a Committee on Extra Efforts, now appointed by the American Board, it was thought best to attempt securing $500,000, payable within five years, and a meeting was called in order to begin this effort. Gen. Van Rensselaer presided, Dr. Chester, Mr. Ludlow, and Mr. Bissell, urged the object, and $14,000 were obtained. Special subscriptions were also gained towards the education of Greek youth then in this country. The new missionary agent was directed first to go up the Hudson river, which he did, preaching at Troy, Albany, and Schenectady, as the way opened; and the tour proved quite a successful one. On his returning to New York, we find in one case the same objections were made at that time as in this, to the work of missions abroad. "Nov. 23, 1827. Called on Col. V. and presented my subscription paper. On looking at it he began to say that he should not subscribe anything; that Col. R. and Gen. V. R., who had subscribed so largely, received large estates from their fathers, but that he had received nothing, began the world poor, had many nephews, etc., to provide for, had been building a house and could hardly get funds to meet the demands of carpenters, etc. On hearing this my heart was moved within me with pity for the man, and real sorrow to hear one so rich (without a child on earth to provide for, one who professed to love the Saviour who became poor for our sakes) pleading his poverty. Besides, he said, he thought we had enough to do at home in the cause of missions. I replied, 'This is in part to establish missions among our Indians.' 'We ought to take care,' said he, 'of the white Indians before the yellow ones.'

"I replied, 'This is a thing that I do not wish to urge at all. As I had the names of two of your friends, I thought I would present the paper to you. But I do not

wish any one to subscribe, unless he thinks the object a
good one, and I hope you will excuse me for calling. I
would never have called were it not in the cause of Jesus
Christ, who came down from heaven and died for our
ruined world; and I have been much struck with the
fact that there is wealth enough in this city to send the
gospel to the world without making any man a beggar,
or depriving a single individual of a single comfort of
life; that one theatre here, as I am told, receives three
hundred thousand dollars in one year and no one thinks
anything of it; but when one thousand a year is needed
in the cause of Christ, it is thought a great thing! Is
this a Christian city? Do men believe the gospel? Are
the souls of men of any consequence? Was the cause
of missions worthy the sacrifice made by the Son of God
in coming from heaven to earth? Was it worthy the
sacrifices which the apostles made in laboring and laying
down their lives? or that missionaries should have come
to proclaim the gospel to our forefathers, without which
we might have been sacrificed to idols, instead of enjoying civilization and all the comforts we now possess?'
In this manner I addressed him a few minutes, and again
with tears in my eyes begged him to excuse me for having called. He seemed moved, and said, 'I do not say
that I will give nothing. I will think of it.' 'Then I
will report to the committee that it is not a refusal, and
if they choose to call on you they can.' 'Yes,' replied
he, and I went away with a sorrowful heart." Better
success attended a series of parlor-meetings, of which
Dr. King says: "A much greater effect can usually be

produced on a small number assembled in a private house, than on a large assembly in a church. Each man of a small party feels as if he had a part in all that is said."

It was now proposed by Mr. Evarts, Secretary of the American Board, that Dr. King should make the tour of South Carolina and Georgia, meeting the Synod there, then visit the Choctaw and Cherokee Missions, also Natchez and New Orleans. This would take six months; afterwards the northern cities were to be visited, and then perhaps in two years, Europe was again to be the scene of his labors. The matter of compensation he was willing to leave to the Board, but he did not see the way clear to make an engagement for so long a time as proposed, nor was he sure that to go to the Indian stations was the best way to use his time. The committee in New York were divided on the subject, and special conference was held with Mr. A. G. Phelps, Mr. Arthur Tappan, and some members of Dr. Spring's church, when $1,600 were added to the funds. Another letter came from Mr. Evarts, expressing great satisfaction at the report Dr. Kirk had made of the meetings in Albany, and taking this as a proof that Dr. King ought to continue very closely connected with missionary, rather than collegiate life, for the engagement with Amherst was not yet cancelled, to say nothing of the offers made by Yale. In case Dr. King consented to spend a few weeks among the Indians, Mr. Evarts urged the importance of his trying, by such suggestions as his own reflections, aided by the Scriptures and the Holy Spirit, might enable him to do, to increase the piety, zeal, and self-denial of the missionaries. Time given to the Indians, Mr. Evarts thought, would not be lost, for the facts gained respecting them would be exceedingly interesting to the religious literati of France and Germany.

Everything now pointed to Dr. King's return after a while to Europe: his parents were willing, friends were in favor of it, and he felt that all had come about in answer to prayer. Dr. Cox said, at a dinner at Mr. Guy Richards', that Dr. King could not consistently sit down as professor in a college, when the whole world was before him as his diocese. Mr. Evarts consented to let Dr. King work yet for a time under the New York Committee, and Rev. Edward N. Kirk was appointed to labor with him.

Names, still familiar, occur in Dr. King's Journal from day to day. Col. Crosby, Shepherd Knapp, Mr. Hedges, Moses Allen, Rev. Mr. Nettleton, Mr. Woolsey, Rev. Mr. Mortimer of the Moravian church, Rev. Mr. Eastburn of the Episcopal church, Dr. Milnor, Zechariah Lewis, Prof. Halsey of Princeton, Rev. Absalom Peters, Rev. Henry G. Ludlow, Mr. Thomas Chester, Mrs. Codwise, Joseph Brewster, Rev. Mr. Schroider, Rev. Wm. B. Sprague, Theodore Frelinghuysen, and others, with all of whom Dr. King was variously brought in contact, and whose interest in missions seemed in consequence to be greatly increased. Mr. Wilder came from his country-home in Massachusetts, and the two friends, meeting at the Tract House, prayed together in reference to the building of the Hillside church at Bolton. Mr. Wilder favored decidedly Dr. King's going back to Europe before very long. He had seen there for himself openings at points usually almost inaccessible to the pure gospel.

A short visit was made to Princeton, and a warm welcome given by Drs. Alexander, Miller, Carnahan, and Halsey. Soon after which, Jan. 4, 1828, arrangements for the southern trip being complete, Drs. King and Kirk took passage for Charleston, South Carolina, where, on his arrival, he was soon welcomed by his old friends, Mr. O'Neill and Dr. Palmer, and his brother Rev. Edward Palmer.

The Journal teems with memories of eight or nine years before; the people crowded to hear what their own city missionary had seen in the Orient, and were attracted also by the eloquence of Mr. Kirk. Miss Angelina Grimké made a special contribution of $60 for four years, to establish a school on some Eastern mission ground.

Beaufort, Augusta, Savannah, Columbia, and other southern points were successively visited, and meetings held in each. At Fayetteville, Dr. King became much interested in Moreau, a slave belonging to Gen. Owen. This man was able to write and speak Arabic, and was indeed a monument to that grace, which out of bondage had brought a soul into the full liberty of the gospel of Christ. At Washington, D. C., Gen. Van Rensselaer of Albany introduced Dr. King to the White House, where the simplicity of the republican court made a marked impression on one who had witnessed the elaborate ceremonial connected with those of Europe. At a reception here Dr. King met Daniel Webster, Henry Clay, Southard, Rives, Varnum, Wirt, and others. He writes: "I had opportunity to speak most fully on the worth of redeeming love. Returned to my lodgings, feeling almost as if I had been on missionary ground, and prayed for those with whom I had been conversing. I could not but feel that the Saviour had in some degree been with me, and given me strength to speak in his cause." On Sunday, April 6, 1828, by invitation Dr. King preached on Missions, in the hall of the House of Representatives. In Baltimore, also, the same great cause was presented in Dr. Nevins' church, and Dr. King called on Charles Carroll of Carrollton, then in his ninety-first year. Here, too, Dr. King met Rev. Mr. Robertson, an Episcopal minister, then in feeble health, yet thinking of going on a mission. He afterwards did go to Africa and Greece.

While in Washington a letter of importance was received, proposing Dr. King's almost immediate return to Europe as missionary to Greece. This letter was signed by Frances Tappan, Mary Murray, Hannah L. Murray, Anne Innis, Sarah P. Doremus, Catherine M. Hurd, A. M. Boyd, M. Perit, and H. M. Chester, who at this time constituted the Ladies' Greek Committee of New York. The hearts and hands of these ladies had become stirred up to relieve in some measure the poor Greeks, now suffering terribly from Turkish despotism. A ship was to be despatched without delay, to carry the food and clothing collected in New York, Baltimore, and other places. But these Christian ladies thought of the soul as well as of the body, and determined to raise funds among themselves to support a missionary in Greece, at least for a year or two. They wrote to Dr. King that his own recitals as to the state of that country had been the principal means of leading them into this effort, and urgently invited him to become their missionary, believing that the very fact of his arrival in this vessel bearing much needed supplies, would at once disarm prejudice, and be most favorable to his success.

To this letter Dr. King answered he should be willing to go to Greece, after present engagements with the Committee on Special Efforts were fulfilled, and after he had again seen his father and mother. Secretary Evarts approved of this course, and soon after in New York Dr. King met the Ladies' Committee at Mr. A. Tappan's, and the arrangement was concluded.

In view of this work for Greece, Dr. King sent to Amherst College a letter of resignation of his office as professor there, and also definitely declined Rev. Mr. Thayer's proposals as to the Mount Pleasant Academy, and those made to him from New Haven.

In Philadelphia, Drs. King and Kirk spoke in five churches. Great sympathy for Greece was felt here as elsewhere, and Dr. King was encouraged by his friends in his plans to go there.

New York was reached by easy stages: steamboat at noon for Trenton, then stagecoach to Princeton, where the night was passed; coach the next day at noon for New York, and arrival there the same evening. Such arrangements would have been very inconvenient for day-visitors to the Centennial in 1876.

A parting visit was again paid to his parents, to whom

he did not go empty-handed.   Friends in Northampton
and Hartford also claimed attention; among others, Dr.
King mentions Dr. Coggswell and his daughter, who
was deaf and dumb, and through this very disability was
used of God to the blessing of hundreds thus afflicted.

Rev. Mr. Gallaudet, her teacher, well-known as the
father in this country of efforts for the deaf and dumb,
sent Dr. King the following lines:

"FAREWELL.

"Stranger and pilgrim here below,
    Again attend thy Master's call;
Yet unsolicitous to know
    What trials may thy steps befall.

"Go, in His strength who conquering rose
    Over the power of death and hell,
And let new captives of his foes
    The splendors of his triumph swell.

"Go, in His strength who reigns on high
    Joint partner of the Eternal's throne,
Whom all the armies of the sky
    Their sovereign Lord with reverence own,

"Go, in His strength, who strength can yield
    Constant and equal to thy day,
Securely sheltered by His shield
    From all that can thy soul dismay.

"Go, and leave all to thee most dear,
    Thy country, kindred, friends, and home;
O'er stormy seas and deserts drear,
    In foreign climes again to roam.

"Go, for thy Maker bids thee go
    And preach His gospel to the poor;
Enough for thee His will to know,
    And that his promises are sure.

> " Go to the battle-field once more,
>   And put thy heavenly armor on ;
> The fight of faith will soon be o'er,
>   And soon thy crown of glory won."

Some difficulty arose as to the best way to go to Greece. Mr. John Tappan offered to bear all the expense, should the route be through England, Holland, France, and Switzerland ; but the ladies and Greek Committee decided upon a Greek vessel going direct. Dr. King's own judgment was for this. He says : " It is always better to pursue an original plan, if there be no very obvious reasons for changing." By mutual understanding with the Greek Committee and the ladies, Dr. King was not to superintend the distribution of stores alone, but was also to establish schools among the Greeks, preach as he might be able, and distribute Bibles and Tracts. The Bible Society immediately voted $500 towards this object, and the American Tract Society $300, for Greek tracts already printed at Malta, and for new translations.

A final meeting for farewell was held May 25, at Mr. W. W. Chester's—about eighty present—which served to strengthen the bands uniting these New York Christian philanthropists and the messenger who was to bear for them to Greece food for both body and soul.

Parting letters too were written and received. His father wrote : " In order to determine our willingness to have you go to France and Greece, we need only to know whether it is God's will. If it is God's will we say Amen to it ; for we would rather have you die in the way

of your duty, than live in the neglect of it." All the
colleges seemed ready to receive Greek youth, if sent
to this country for education. Rev. Mr. Cornelius offered to be responsible for twelve of these. All this made
the last days just before sailing, very busy ones. Many
friends accompanied him to the ship.

A short stop was made at Malta, where Messrs. Temple, Goodell, and Bird, were just then together. Monday,
July 28, 1828, Dr. King landed at Poros, a good point
for his work, being the residence of the President of
Greece. He was away from home, but his brother,
Count A. Capodistria, received the American Christian
envoy with great politeness ; as did also other persons
connected with the government. A public magazine or
storehouse was at once offered, wherein to bestow his
goods, which were to be free from all government supervision in regard to the distribution of them.

Volume VI. of his Journal closes with the copy of a
hymn then new, " From Greenland's Icy Mountains."
Its true ring as a missionary battle-cry was at once
recognized by this soldier of the cross, now again on
foreign soil, ready for what the great Leader had for him
to do there.

CHAPTER XIV.

POROS—GREECE.

Poros—Count Capodistria—Greece open to the Gospel—Sufferings of the People—Egina—Smyrna—Syra Marriage—Tenos.

DIFFICULTIES attend every enterprise. There was much sickness at this time at Poros. Objections were made by some of the foreigners there, that the Greeks deserved no help from America. But Dr. King went on quietly with his work. The first application made to him was for books. A visit was paid, on his return, by appointment, to Count Capodistria, the President, who received the letters of introduction from Mr. Gallatin and the Duchesse de Broglie and Madame St. Aulaire with brightened interest. A long conversation followed, on the state of Greece and the best methods for her relief and elevation. The President showed great common sense, not wishing to have the stores of food and clothing distributed in a way to foster the idleness into which the Greeks, through the effect of a serene climate, an oppressive government, war, and Oriental habits, had more than ever subsided. He told Dr. King to go first to see the destitution, and he himself would furnish guards; advised him not to let it be known he had brought supplies. After personal information was thus obtained, the President said, "Do not give away your

stores, but sell them, even on bonds due in three years.
In that time, if the money is collected, expend it in establishing schools, or building schoolhouses." The President himself was about to found a school for about five
hundred children, and would buy and pay for clothing for
them immediately. Thus did God answer the prayers of
his children in America, opening the way for a proper use
of their gifts. By means of this President, the whole of
the Morea was at once open to receive, not temporal
relief alone, but the gospel itself. Every day persons,
sometimes a hundred and fifty or more, came begging
for the New Testament. Before breakfast sometimes, a
school of boys, with their teacher, would come for this
purpose. One of these teachers made a most touching
little address, thanking American Christians for their
great benevolence. Everywhere the same gratitude was
expressed. The President told Dr. King if he, Dr.
King, had $50,000 to expend in the establishment of
schools, it could be used without difficulty. It was a
time of high tide now in Greece for evangelic and educational effort. Who is to answer for the neglect of it?
for the church did not take advantage of it to any great
extent.

Dr. King did not content himself with merely visiting the schools and distributing books, but took every
opportunity to give the gospel *vivâ voce* in the public
streets, or "under a fig-tree," or in almost any place.
The poor, sick, and suffering would soon collect to the
number of over fifty or sixty, and eagerly drink in the
glad tidings of One "mighty to save." Even the priests

would listen and give attention and approval to the preaching. A bishop asked for New Testaments for the priests under his care, that they might be able properly to instruct the people.

Egina was the first point visited after Poros. The general suffering there was distressing. In a population of not over one thousand, in a place opposite Poros, three or four hundred were ill with fever. The tattered garments of many seemed but a collection of shreds. Pages of the Journal are filled with descriptions of cases of special destitution. A blind woman of one hundred and ten years, emaciated, withered, was still the sole dependence of three or four little ragged great-grandchildren. Many of the poor were living in caves. About two-thirds were widows and orphans, " made so by the sword of the Moslem." At Egina young girls were employed by the government to transport stones, found in the rubbish of an ancient temple of Venus, to put into an orphan asylum. Tickets for food and clothing were given out with as much discrimination as possible; but as thousands crowded to receive the flour and clothing, and Dr. King could not fully control the arrangements, more or less friction attended the distribution.

The letter sent by the women of America to the women of Greece was published in the local papers, and received with tearful interest, and a response was written by one of the women of Ipsara. Another was sent from Athens, and signed by 2,047 widows and orphans, imploring a portion of the American stores for their relief. Beyond even this demand came that for books and education, so that Dr. King wrote to Miss Angelina Grimké, and other friends at home, urging further help, in order that forty or fifty schools might be established at once.

Napoli and other places were visited also, and the same welcome to the American envoy everywhere tendered. It was striking to see the energy which a prospect of political freedom had infused into the schools, and into the printing of new books for them. Properly speaking, there were but three Greek presses in Greece at this time. Mr. Skoufas, a lawyer, said that "the first National Assembly of the Greeks adopted as the *Civil* code the Justinian code; for their *Marine* (and, as Col. Pisa said afterwards, their Military code), the Code Napoleon; and for the *Criminal* code, a few articles were drawn up and printed by the Greeks themselves; that at present it may be said that they have no fixed code of laws."

Near Argos, at Mycenæ, the tomb of Agamemnon, a large structure on the apex of a hill, and lighted by a triangular window at the top, claimed his attention for a few hours even from the pressing wants of the present.

At Argos, Dr. King had opportunity to witness the varied and singular ceremonies connected with a Greek wedding of that time, his minute description of which occupies several pages of the Journal, bringing the whole scene to view—the motionless bride, decorated fancifully with gold-leaf, the patient bridegroom submitting to all arrangements thought necessary by his noisy attendants, the cry, "The bridegroom cometh," and the final throwing of a silken band about the necks of bride and groom as they enter their new home.

At Tripolitza Dr. King felt that he was indeed in a land desolated by a barbarous enemy. The ruins were new, complete, and prosaic. It had been destroyed by Ibrahim Pasha just after the battle of Navarino, in February, 1828. From here the way to Demitzana was but a series of steep ascents and descents, stones, rocks, and precipices, which, passed by night, seemed doubly dangerous and appalling. The village itself was perched on the top of a mountain, built out as wide as it could be made, and around it were craggy ravines and jutting rocks, from which even daylight could not dispel the terror. On Sunday, Dr. King, after the usual church services, was able to address a number of persons who came to his room, giving them the messages sent from America, all of which moved many here as elsewhere to tears.

An excellent school was in existence here, having been established seventy years, and which was now under the care of Niketopoulos, a liberal-minded, intelligent man. It had had a library of over two thousand volumes, but most of these had been used for cartridges the first year of the revolution. Dr. King was here also invited to a wedding supper, and when the health of the American ladies was proposed, for eight or ten minutes nothing was heard but prolonged cheers, "Long live the American ladies! Long live the American ladies!" It was strange to hear this cry in Arcadia, in the heart of the Peloponnesus.

Amid many small hardships, for want of suitable clothing and lodging, things which affect one's comfort more than we are wont to allow, the tour was continued into Sparta, where the words once uttered by a mother of ancient time in giving her son his shield, "Either this, or upon it," came to mind with full force, in relation to the commission given to the Christian missionary. The shield of faith—or rather the Lord God himself, a sun and shield—is indeed invincible; therefore in life or death the soldier of the cross will be upborne in safety unto victory.

Associations less suggestive of good were also called to mind. A very ancient stone platform was shown by the guide, on which those used to sit who gave instruction to the Spartan children in various arts and sports; among others, that of stealing without being discovered. In some of the villages not a single modern Greek Testament was found, and copies of it, and also of tracts, were most gladly received.

At Marathonisé, the soldiers, who were called by order of the governor to pay respect to one whose name and whose mission they had read about in the public prints, quite came up to one's ideal of the Spartans of old. "Their countenances were those of men bold and daring, and their eyes bespoke souls ready to kindle at the slightest offence, and to pounce upon their adversary with all the swiftness of the eagle. In short, they looked like men who had lived in freedom, and who would sooner die than wear the yoke of oppression. And such indeed is their character."

There is ever danger that new-born liberty may run into license. The captain of these Spartan soldiers told Dr. King of a "delegation assembled at Marathonisé from all parts of Mani, to decide upon the question whether they should submit to pay tithes to the government, and that they had decided in the negative ; that they had not retired to the mountains, and lived in hunger, and submitted to every hardship, for the sake of freedom, now to be brought into bondage to a *Greek* government." Dr. King replied, " In America, where we are free, we do not consider it bondage to pay taxes for the support of a government which we choose, and which cannot be administered without expense." These men really prided themselves upon their readiness to take offence "for a word only ;" but when told of the spirit of meekness the Prince of Peace had come to establish, one man said, "You turn my head. What you say is true. This is what we need to hear, and what we never heard before."

The priests at Marathonisé were obtaining money from the people on a strange pretence. The bodies of the dead were examined a year after death, in order to judge of the present state of the soul, and the bones finally were left unburied, if friends did not secure a favorable verdict.

The patriotism, expecially of some of the mountain districts that had never been subdued by the Turks, seemed identical with that of ancient Greece. Among many distinguished families, whom Dr. King compared to broken columns of the Doric order, that of the Mavromichaelis was recognized as leader. All the Morea looked to them for guidance during the late revolution. "The time to raise the standard being arrived, the head of this family pronounced these words, which the Greeks will never forget: 'When the liberty of a whole nation is concerned, every feeling of family must be extinguished.' On leaving Tchimova, an old lady, who had shown great heroism in the recent war, brought me a loaf of bread, and presenting it to me, asked me for some books for two or three little girls who wished to learn to read, and begged me, if possible, to establish there a school for the instruction of females. 'We will all go to it,' said she, 'young and old, married and unmarried.' I told her that I would write to America, and, if possible, the school should be established. There is now scarcely a female in the whole country that knows Alpha from Omega."

Descending now towards Coran, amid continual discomfort through wretched roads and want of accustomed food, Dr. King found the spiritual and educational destitution greater even than that which was merely temporal. The governor of Upper Missinia seemed quite sensible of this. He said that among ten thousand souls, not a single school existed. In one district, Ibrahim destroyed two hundred and ninety thousand olive-trees, and only ten thousand now remained. "The governor took truly correct views of the needs of his countrymen. 'The Americans have done much for us,' said he, 'and we owe them everlasting gratitude; but if they could establish schools for us, the benefit conferred would be far greater than that of food and clothing, which are soon gone, and we are left in the same situation in which we were before; but the effect of these schools would be without end.'"

At Navarino, fifty or sixty ships lay at anchor, and as the fire of a salute roared among the hills, it was easy to imagine the scene of Oct., 20, 1827, the day of deliverance for Greece.

Corinth reminded Dr. King of the nobler conflict carried on there long ago by the apostle Paul, the echo of which is still sounding round the world. The politarch and his secretary here received the gospel and tracts with much feeling. Everywhere in fact, the way seemed open for the truth.

At the end of fifty-two days, Dr King came again to Egina, finding there Dr. Howe, since so well known as a Philhellenist. Lengthened reports of his journey Dr. King now sent to the Ladies' Committee, whose almoner he was, and his advice as to the best mode of sending and distributing such charities is most valuable.

From Egina where Dr. King now again took up his abode for a season, he wrote to the Greek Committee in New York, giving his impressions as to what could be done for a people who seemed to have "nothing left but rocks and liberty." One of the priests, speaking of the thieves, said, "They are holy men. Go and see how they live, and you will pardon them." Dr. King was anxious that men and means should at once be employed to secure the "House thus swept and garnished." He urged Mr. Chauncey Colton to come to Mani or Sparta, and establish a school similar to the one at Amherst. Four such, he thought greatly needed.   But the church then, as now, was slow to take advantage of such calls for help.

Wednesday, Jan. 28, 1829, appears the following entry: "At 2 P. M., went to the house of Madame Macri, where I joined in holy wedlock Mr. William Black of Yarmouth, county of Norfolk, England, and Miss Teresa Macri, youngest daughter of Madame Macri, and the one addressed by Lord Byron in his poem, 'Maid of Athens, ere we part, Give, oh give me back my heart.' etc.   Application having been made a few days since by her mother and Mr. B. to the Bishop of Talanti to marry them, he refused even to give them permission to be married ; and the especial Ecclesiastical Commission, appointed by the President, also refused this permission, on account of Mr. Black's being an Englishman and not of the Greek Church.   So Mr. Black applied to me, and having no such scruples as the Greek bishop, I very cheerfully consented to perform the ceremony."

About the middle of February, Dr. King sailed in an Austrian Brig, "Onion," for Smyrna, where he met a welcome reception in the family of Mr. Mengous, and the question long pending between him and Miss Annetta Aspasia Mengous was definitely settled.   The journal records his gratitude, in view of these new prospects which he believed were ordained to promote the usefulness of both himself and the beautiful Greek lady, a prize which it may be said, as of Maguori's Indian bride, "He bore from a hundred lovers."   Dr. King's next move was to Syra, where an American school had been established by Mr. Brewer, and thence to Tenos with Dr. Korck of

Syra. It was difficult to decide upon plans. No letters had been received from America for six or seven months; yet the promises that God would direct as to duty were felt to be sure, and our missionary stayed himself upon them. Tenos contained about sixty villages and 25,000 inhabitants. It was a stronghold of Roman-catholicism. A church, called Evangelistica, had been built here on account of directions which an old nun said she had received in a dream. Other islands of the Cyclades were also visited, the schools examined, and addresses made to the scholars, where the same current of religious conversation went on as ever, "in season and out of season." Eternity alone will reveal the fruit of such continual seed-dropping.

At Egina, which seemed headquarters for the time being, Dr. King found his friends, Dr. Anderson, secretary of the American Board, and Rev. Eli Smith, long known as a most useful missionary at Beyrout.

May 20, came the news of the fall of Missolonghi into the hands of the Greeks and public rejoicing followed. The President made proclamation that the people should render public thanks to God for this favor. He also treated the offer of help in establishing schools, made by Dr. Anderson of A. B. C. F. M., very respectfully, sanctioning the reading in such schools of the New Testament and the Psalms; but he wished to establish no precedent which should hamper him in case persons in whom he had less confidence should desire to do the same work. He disliked gifts, and had already refused them from the King of France, and the Emperor of Russia ; but if Dr. King and his friends chose to establish schools, no obstacle from the government should be placed in their way. He wished, however, that the aid offered by the society should be placed in the Greek bank by way of loan. Drs. Anderson and Smith soon left Egina, but the seasons of prayer held together were of unspeakable comfort to the one still left in charge of the work that Christian America sought to do for Greece. By request of the Ladies' New York Committee, he decided to remain their almoner for another year. He urged upon these ladies to establish a school for girls, where they might learn to be the teachers so much needed in a land "not yet divested of Turkish ideas." He wrote on the same subject to Miss Margaret Carswell Ely of Philadelphia, who was interested in forming a missionary society about the time when Dr. King was there. Such being Dr. King's views, it was indeed inspiriting to receive from Miss Angelina Grimké and her brother a timely gift of $60 for the above purpose. Miss Grimké writes, "Thou inquirest whether the females of America will not furnish the means necessary for the establishment of forty or fifty schools. This question I cannot answer, but that they *can* do it is very certain. I fully believe that professors spend at least fifty dollars annually on *superfluous* dress ; and as long as the ministers of the gospel do not disapprove of this waste of money, this sinful conformity to the vain fashions of the world, of course their people will follow their misguided policy-conformity to the world, so as not to render themselves conspicuous, forgetting the declaration of the great Head of the church, 'Ye are the light of the world. A city that is set on a hill *cannot* be hid;' and the injunction of the apostle, 'Be not conformed to this world.' Perhaps thou mayest feel surprised to hear such sentiments from me. But often when I attended the meetings thou heldest last winter in our city, my heart was filled with shame and sorrow, as I looked at the extravagant dress of multitudes of professors who flocked to them, and I often thought, if primitive Christianity existed among us, how different it would be, and how much more would conveniently be spared and cheerfully given to send the Bible to the heathen and to establish schools for their ignorant children."

In 1879, would fifty dollars a year cover the unnecessary expenditure for dress of Christian women ?

All this time the work of Bible and tract distribution was going on. One man gladly exchanged a pack of cards for a Testament, which he was more than once seen reading to his companions.

July 22, 1829, Dr. King was married at Tenos to Miss Annetta Aspasia Mengous. The ceremony was performed by Rev. Rufus Anderson, secretary of A. B. C. F. M. with Rev. Eli Smith as bridesman ; also reading the Scriptures. A house was taken at Tenos, and arrangements made for a school for girls ; and Dr. King writes to New York of the interest his wife was taking in its establishment and superintendence. The Greeks seemed much pleased at this event. It brought one who had come to them a stranger into identity of interest with themselves. The school soon increased in numbers. Other encouragement was given. In one of the villages about twenty women met every Lord's day when one would read aloud to the others from a Testament which Dr. King had given her.

While it is essential to make record of Dr, King's marriage, an event of such importance in every one's history, the public are little concerned to know the details of a missionary's domestic life. Suffice it to say, that in the hope Dr. King cherished, that an alliance with the Greek nation would be of advantage to his work, he was not disappointed. More than once in his after-history, his wife's influence was so strong, as probably to save his life, and secure him from ultra-persecution. A family of six daughters and one son was given them. Five of these daughters, with Mrs. King, yet survive in 1879. Three of the daughters are settled in homes of their own in America ; one is married to a gentleman living in Constantinople, and another to an Englishman well-known as in high position in diplomatic circles.

Much interest continued to be felt in the United States in regard to Greece. Rev. Matthias Bruen wrote at much length to Dr. King, as to what might be done for its elevation, by promoting common-school education, and the following gentlemen living in New York were suggested as a Greek School Committee : " The Hon. Albert Gallatin, Mr. Arthur Tappan, Rev. Mr. Bruen, Mr. Knowles Taylor, Seth P. Staples, Esq., Eleazer Lord, Esq., Dr. Samuel Akerly, Mr. Richard T. Haines."

Rev. Mr. Bruen writes, " Your letters have done and will do immense good."

To show the need of enlightenment in Greece, it is only necessary to speak of a strange custom observed by the priests, of baptizing not merely the people and their houses, but the sea. Dr. King describes the scene: " After we had waited some time at the shore, the bishop came and threw a cross into the sea. Six men stood ready to plunge in to find it, and the one who was so fortunate as to seize it received from the bishop a present of money, and then went about from house to house to receive it from others. After this ceremony, the bishop went also from house to house, to sprinkle holy water, and to receive money from those he visited. At one of these visits, I and my wife happened to be present, but he did not even speak to us, nor make the least sign of recognition. It is most evident that he is by no means friendly to us."

In January, 1830, Mr. J. Evarts wrote to Mrs. Pelatiah Perit, urging the desire of the American Board that Dr. King should become their missionary in Greece, in case the Ladies' Committee in New York would release him ; and Dr. King was eminently qualified to carry out their plans at the same time, of going largely into the business of providing school-books for Greece.

The Board would also provide an assistant. Mrs. Hurd, secretary, answered that the Ladies' Committee were pledged to support Dr. King another year, but that they had no right or desire to control his inclinations farther, although willing to continue their efforts through him. All seemed to desire that Dr. King should be employed in a way to be most useful. His friend S. V. S.

Wilder saw he was now at disadvantage from having it supposed that he had ample funds at his command, which he had not, and the letter from him proposed that $5,000 should at once be raised. Mr. Chester approving this, yet urged that such funds be placed in the treasury of the American Board, that there should thus be one head, unifying efforts for Greece—which experience proved it was important to do.

It may well be seen that Dr. King was in a somewhat trying position. He says, " If I know my own heart, I wish to labor in such connection and such manner, as may best forward the interests of the cause of Christ in this country. I laid the subject before Him who has hitherto dealt wonderfully with me, and who alone can give wisdom, and direct me in that way which shall be for the best." After friendly correspondence, Dr. King left the subject to the decision of the Ladies' Committee, expressing full confidence as to the large-hearted views they would be enabled to take. Dr. King's first knowledge of the issue was ten months after, March, 1831, in the Missionary Herald of December, 1830, which stated that his connection with the American Board was again resumed. Special contributions made by Ezra M. Ely and family of Philadelphia, and others, were most opportune, and no time was lost to the cause in general; for while Dr. King's relations to workers at home were being settled, the work practically was not disturbed. Now and then some opposition was shown by the bishop, which usually proved to be of advantage, as when Prince Vlachoutsa of Russia with his son visited the school on account of reports against it; but he examined the catechisms, and said that, so far from finding anything bad in them, he was so highly delighted as to ask for a copy to use in his own family. Sometimes it was whispered that Dr. King was a Jesuit. To this his friends replied that he and his ancestors had suffered so much from Roman-catholics, that it was not likely that he had come to preach their doctrines.

As to Dr. King's daily life, every hour seems to have had its allotted duty, systematized in a way most worthy of imitation. He thought it important that he should understand thoroughly the past history of the Greek Church, and so spent much time in examining the Apostolical canons, and the records of different councils, and others of the writings of the fathers which were received by the priests as of authority. Thus he became qualified, as after-years proved, to answer from the mouth of their own standards the errors which in these modern times prevailed among them.

It was encouraging to Dr. King to notice the attention with which his scholars listened to the exposition of the word of God. A poor ignorant woman whose mother and brother had been killed by the Turks, and her sister carried into captivity, was determined to become a nun. Dr. King persuaded her first to learn to read, then to study the Gospels before deciding the matter. He gave her a home in his house for six months, also other assistance, until money was raised to send her to her native place.

CHAPTER XV.

ATHENS.

Persecutions of Asaad el Shidiak in Syria—Drs. Anderson and Eli
Smith—Death of Dr. King's Father—Doctorate Conferred.

EARLY in September, 1830, Dr. King visited Athens
for the first time. So much property had been confiscated there, that in view of the best interests of his family and his probable removal there, he thought it wise to
secure some lots then offered for sale. A bargain was
made, when Dr. King found the lock of his trunk had
been broken and the money was gone. The thief was
soon found; the police required him to write a confession. This done, the young thief threw himself down
from the tower where he was confined, full forty-eight
feet. Life still remained. The government ordered a
sheep to be killed, in the skin of which he was placed,
and given into the physician's hands. The man finally
recovered, and called on Dr. and Mrs. King about six
months after, expressing great penitence, and the government of Lebadra, in returning the money, minus expenses, sent a strong letter of acknowledgment " to the
most noble Philhellen, Mr. Jonas King, for his forbear-
ance, saying all sensible Greeks admired the greatness
of his soul in not prosecuting the offender further." The
government was grateful for the continued assistance
received from America through the American Board and

other channels. An invoice of slates and pencils sent in 1831 was particularly welcome.

Yet when the truth, which as a Christian missionary Dr. King took pains to scatter everywhere and at all times, took effect in the heart, persecution only less severe than that meted out to Asaad el Shidiak, whose death occurred about this time, very often followed. A Cretan Meledon had been introduced to Dr. King by Dr. Korck. This man had read Dr. King's Farewell Letter, and desired to see the writer and learn the word of God more perfectly. Upon his return to Crete he began . there the distribution of the Bible and other books. Many opposed and tried to silence him, but in vain. "At length one night several men came to his house and called to him to come with them to administer medicine (as he professed to know something of medicine) to a member of the Council, one of the principal men of the place. This, he told them, he could not do, as he was unwell and in his bed, and besides, he had no medicines. They then began to speak in a different manner and to revile him, and at length dragged him out of his house and beat him most severely, and led him to the brow of a steep place and cast him down headlong. Afterwards one took out a knife in order to cut his throat, but his companions said this was going too far, and prevented him from being killed, and left him. In consequence of his bruises he was confined to his bed for about three months."

The story of Asaad el Shidiak has been given in full by Dr. Isaac Bird in his little book, "The Martyr of Lebanon," and also by Rev. Rufus Anderson, D. D., in his history of the missions of the American Board. Yet the experience and fate of this man were as a baptism of blood to Dr. King's evangelistic labors, and therefore must not be passed over. Suffice it to say, Asaad el Shidiak was a very intelligent Maronite, highly esteemed in Syria as a teacher and public lecturer. When the patriarch issued a proclamation against the missionaries, Asaad wished to answer their reply to it, but for some reason was not suffered to do so by the patriarch. He soon afterwards, in 1825, became Dr. King's teacher in Arabic, and as such assisted him in preparing his celebrated " Farewell Letter," holding with him at the same time many discussions as to the truth. After Dr. King had gone, Asaad was asked by the missionaries at Beyrout to teach an Arabic grammar-school for native boys. This he did, but gave his leisure to attempting a refutation of the doctrines in Dr. King's " Letter." While doing this he was led to read the twenty-ninth chapter of Isaiah, and the rest of that prophecy, and then to the study of the New Testament. This was the means of his conversion. He was now thoroughly convinced of the errors in which he had been trained; and although threatened by the patriarch, engaged himself to Mr. Bird for a year, and protection was obtained for him from Mr. Abbott the English consul at Beyrout.

Asaad was confiding in disposition, and therefore too easily taken in when, through his relatives, the priests contrived to get him into their power. He was taken to the Convent of St. Alma, where he had daily controversy with the patriarch, bishop, and others. Three things were before him, either to be regarded as mad, to commit sin, or offer up his life. Sometimes promotion was offered him if he would recant his so-called heretical opinions. But his answer ever was, "I will hold fast the religion of Jesus Christ, and I am ready for the sake of it to shed my blood; and though you all should become infidels, yet will not I." Asaad escaped for a time from his persecutors, but was recaptured by them and thrown into prison. Here he was put in chains and beaten a certain number of stripes daily. His allowance for food each day was six thin cakes of bread and a cup of water. Sometimes the thin flat mat used as a bed was taken from him, and a heavy chain fastened his neck to the wall. The door to his dungeon was walled up, so that there was no access to it except through a small loophole. Its state cannot be described. His death is supposed to have occurred in October, 1830. In one respect it was like that of Moses, no one among his friends knows of his sepulchre; but the Lord is faithful, and precious in his sight is the dust now somewhere awaiting the resurrection. His record is on high, as well as in the annals of a true Christianity now reviving in the East.

In December, 1830, Dr. and Mrs. Hill, missionaries of the Episcopal church of America, arrived at Tenos, also Dr. and Mrs. Robertson. Dr. King writes: "I had the pleasure of giving them a most hearty welcome to my house."

In April, 1831, Dr. King revisited Athens, as yet occupied by the Turks, and secured the premises for a school which had been recommended to him by M. Constantine, and also engaged an agent to sell Bibles. The first boy who entered the school when opened was named "Saviour," and the first girl, "Peace."

Dr. King also opened a preaching service at this time, and records, May 8, 1831, "God has blessed me in all I have as yet undertaken in Athens;" and amid subsequent discouragements, sometimes through coldness or misapprehension of friends, even of some coming from America, he was able to work on, "as seeing Him who is invisible." Such feeling found expression in several Greek hymns written by him about this time.

At times a hundred would be present in the schoolroom Sunday mornings, and forty or fifty in his own house in the afternoon. Nor were home efforts without fruit. "One day Sophia, our servant-girl, said that when she went a few days since to confess to the priest, she told him that she no longer worshipped pictures, and explained to him what I teach in my house, and that the reason why she did not often go to church was because she heard the Scriptures morning and evening at my house, whereas in church she heard whispering and talking that she could not understand. The priest said that Mr. King must know better than he did, because he had been to Jerusalem and had seen the holy places. He remarked to her, however, that he had heard or supposed that we bought some of the old idols (antiquities) for the purpose of worshipping them. She told him that it was not so, for she had been long in my house and had never seen any such thing."

Dr. King's own house needed so much rebuilding that the coming of his family there was quite delayed, and this the longer as the Greek artisans observed so many saints' days as to interfere very much with their labor.

While in Smyrna, in October, 1831, Dr. King received from Dr. Rufus Anderson a letter of importance, telling of movements in New York to have him transferred from Greece to France and other countries where the French language is spoken, in case he should think it expedient to leave Athens. Other missionaries had come to Athens, and were beginning schools there. Dr. Anderson himself hesitated as to whether his friend ought to leave. He writes : " Since I have read your last communications my doubts are greatly increased. Where is there the missionary whom the government of the country has been more forward to honor in view of the people than yourself in Greece ? If you leave, who shall circulate our books in Greece ? We are looking for a man to send to your aid..... Travel occasionally. Keep your eyes and ears always open and write constantly, and with the blessing of God you may yet.again excite a great interest in Greece as a field of missions."

The possibilities opened in this letter were most unexpected to our missionary. Strong ties drew him to both fields. Times calling for immediate and important decisions come into every life. As one marks the events in a Christian's earthly career, particularly if now finished, he almost wonders at the anxieties felt ; for above all and through all, from such an outside stand-point the guiding hand of an all-wise, loving Father is distinctly seen, disentangling every difficulty and bringing good out of seeming evil. Yet in the heat of the conflict how hard to practise at all times the lesson, "Rest in the Lord," "Wait also on him." This, Dr. King was at this time able to do. He says: "I want to be enlightened on the subject by the providences of Him who governs all things in an inscrutable and marvellous manner."

The death of Jeremiah Evarts, secretary, with other causes, delayed the decision. We know the result: Dr. King remained in Athens.

The cholera was now raging. Guns were fired to purify the air. The priests of Cooklegah walked about the village in procession with their images, and gave permission to all to come and partake of the communion, even without confession; so great was the consternation with regard to the cholera, and the feeling that all ought to be ready for a sudden exit from this world. This step was enough to show that the priests did not consider confession as necessary to salvation.

The missionaries were all obliged for a while to leave the city.

A treaty had been made about this time between the Grand Seigneur and the United States. Dr. King says: "Like the contract made by the prophet Jeremiah with Hanameel, his uncle's son, for his field in Anathoth, there were two writings—the one sealed, and the other open. I only saw the one which was sealed, and which I understood from M. H. was not to be opened at all, but that there was another which contained the same articles.   See Jer. 32 : 6–12."

These pages cannot give any history of Greek affairs, yet the assassination of the president, Capodistria, in October, 1831, by Constantine and George Mavromichaelis, should be noticed.   One of these men was killed on the spot, and the other was soon given up by the French—laws of equity ruling, rather than those of technical extradition.   This event helps one understand how the unsettled state of the country made persistent Christian work there doubly difficult.

There was much suffering.   When in Smyrna, Mrs. King collected money for the poor, and was asked to superintend the distribution of it, which was of advantage to missionary effort among them.   The ignorance of many of the people about equalled their destitution. A monk attending one of the schools said one day he had heard Dr. King pray that God would enlighten idolaters, and he wished to know if there were any such in the world now.   A certain bishop also wrote to Dr. King in a way that called forth from him the following answer :

"To the Bishop of T. and Deputy-bishop of A.: Yesterday I received your friendly letter, dated June 21, 1833, in which you say you have often observed little books printed at Malta and from other presses, which are not suitable to be given as presents or rewards, according to my custom, to youth ; and you beg me that this may henceforth cease, as the Greek youth are mortally injured.

"I beg therefore that you will send me a catalogue of the above-mentioned books by which in your opinion 'the Greek youth are mortally injured,' that I may examine them carefully, and if I find in them anything contrary to the Holy Scriptures, cease immediately from distributing them, and I remain, yours,

"JONAS KING.

"ATHENS, July 6, 1833."

No immediate reply was sent, but about three months after these objections were virtually withdrawn. One book alone was complained of, and this Dr. King had not distributed at Athens, though a copy of it might have been lent from his own library. "Peter Parley's Geography" was suffered to pass, though it said something in regard to feasts appointed by the pope, which might as truly apply to those in the Greek church, and which the missionaries of the Episcopal Board cut out from the copies used by them.

On an excursion made near Syra, a boy came asking for a tract ; but after retiring to a little distance, held it up and tore it to pieces. It was a copy of the Ten Commandments, and it was found out afterwards that the priests had supposed that Dr. King had printed the words of the preface, "I am the Lord thy God, who brought thee out of the house of bondage," in reference to *himself*.

On the other hand, light appeared in other directions. Dr. King speaks of calling "on Pharmakides, who read to me a piece which he had written on the subject of church dignities, to show that the primitive church government was democratic. He is undoubtedly the most intelligent priest and most learned theologian now in Greece. I trust the time is coming when the church generally will rise to the simplicity of the first century, and when bishops shall lose that temporal power which they received from men, and seek for nothing more than that equality which the gospel teaches."

The above gentleman was not in favor, however, of outside influence in the work of purifying the church from error, preferring to wait until men of intelligence connected with it should unite in throwing away the idols.

Intercourse with Dr. and Mrs. Korck and Mr. and Mrs. Benjamin, the latter of whom Dr. King once received into his house after shipwreck, and also with Greek gentlemen of large views with regard to the interests of their country, was a source of real comfort. In July, 1832, the national newspaper, published at Napoli, gave a very fair statement of the work undertaken by our missionary, which may be found in the closing chapter.

In whatever arrangements Dr. King made at any time, the care of his parents was considered by him a paramount duty; and with regard to them, and indeed as to all his affairs, he often wrote at great length to his faithful friend, Rev. Wm. A. Hallock, D. D., sometimes saying, "Your word is as good as your bond." Memories of Dr. King's early home were constantly brought back to him by the scenes of the present.

"September 1, 1832. Near sunset I walked in my

garden and stood by the side of a little mulberry-tree, the only tree in my garden, and thought of the little sprout, now a large elm, by my father's house, near which the light of heaven first broke in upon my soul. Shall I live, thought I, to see this mulberry increase in size as the elm had increased when I last saw it? Twenty-five years more will bring me near to the term of life allotted to man. How soon will it pass away, even should I live so long! Am I ready?"

In January, 1833, Dr. Riggs arriving in Athens, brought news that Dr. King's beloved and venerated father was beyond the need of any further care. "He told me he died in a most happy manner. I could not but weep, though I felt assured that my dear father was now in the joy of his Lord. Among the last words my father uttered when I last bade him farewell, and I asked, 'Have you anything to say to me?' were, 'Nothing but that God may be glorified in you.' I often think of it. What can I desire more or better?

"On arriving at my house I welcomed Mr. and Mrs. Riggs to it, introduced them to my family, and then we united in prayer. Afterwards I retired for a few moments to my chamber to weep and pray alone. I blessed the Father of all mercies for having given such grace to my father as to triumph over death, which he had formerly so much feared, and that He had glorified His great name in showing to all who were acquainted with my father that He is a God of mercy and truth, and will never leave the humble and contrite man who trembleth at His word."

A letter soon came from his bereaved mother, saying, "Ah, my dear son, if I could see you I could talk more in one hour than I could write in a great while. My son, I never expect to see you again in this world. Do n't you go one step out of the path of duty for me. Your father said a great deal about the love of God, and his soul was full of that love."

Dr. Riggs brought him twenty-eight letters from America, a list of the writers of which appears in the diary. This private express brings vividly to mind the changes made in postal service all over the world, even during the past few years.

A monument, yet to be seen by any visitor to Hawley, Mass., bears the following inscription :

"𝕾𝖆𝖈𝖗𝖊𝖉

TO THE MEMORY OP

MR. JONAS KING,

THE VENERABLE FATHER

OF THE DISTINGUISHED

REV. JONAS KING, D. D.,

MISSIONARY TO PALESTINE AND GREECE."

On being asked by a friend if he felt any regret in parting with his son as a missionary to the heathen, this father in Israel replied, " 'God so loved the world, that he gave his only begotten Son, that whosoever believeth in him should not perish, but have everlasting life,' and shall I withhold my only son from obeying the commandment of our ascending Saviour, who said, 'Go ye

into all the world and preach the gospel to every creature'?"

Mr. King was one of the first settlers in Hawley. He
lived, in example and precept, a life of holiness.

He died September 20, 1832, aged 78 years, having a
blissful faith in Jesus Christ and an unshaken hope of a
glorious immortality.

His last words were,

> "How often shall my pulses beat
>   Before my bliss shall be complete?
> Come, Lord Jesus, oh, come quickly."
>
> "Ask you my name? 't is Jonas King.
>   Beneath these clods I lie.
> In life I suffered much from sin,
>   And sin caused me to die.
> But by the blessed Jesus, I
>   Do hope to rise again;
> I then shall live, and never die,
>   And praise the Lord.   Amen."

Another of these letters was from Dr. Carnahan of
Princeton, announcing the conferring of a title, not so
common then as now, and of which Dr. King says: "I
suppose that it is considered by my friends that it will
give me some influence and be the means of promoting
the cause of Christ, but I doubt whether such means
should be employed." His visiting-card always still read
simply "Jonas King."

In April, 1834, Dr. A. G. Paspati came as special
messenger in a vessel, chartered for the purpose, from
the missionaries at Constantinople, proposing that Dr.

Riggs should go to Persia with Mr. Perkins. Just before receiving this message he and Dr. King had been
speaking of the strong attachment they were beginning
to feel for Athens and the work there; so this new
question was trying, as well as sudden. On the whole,
Dr. Riggs decided not to leave Greece at present. Dr.
King himself was invited before long to come to Napoli,
but he also declined making a "change of base."

CHAPTER XVI.

MISSIONARY WORK NEEDED IN THE EAST.

Indulgences—Infidelity—Errors and Superstitions—Worship of Virgin Mary—Relics—Bones of St. Antipas—Image-worship —Letter to Society of Inquiry, Princeton.

EXAMPLES have already been given, showing clearly how far the Papal and Oriental churches have lapsed from the simplicity of the gospel.   Many others are found scattered here and there in Dr. King's Journals.   Let a few of these speak more loudly than words can do, of the necessity of such work as that in which he was engaged.

"Tuesday, Oct. 29, 1832. Mr. Venthylos showed me a curious document which he found some years since on Mt. Athos; a letter signed by the patriarch of Constantinople, and twelve bishops (the whole Synod), and given to a monk on Mount Athos, in March, 1816, stating that by the power given unto them to bind or loose, his sins were all pardoned, of whatever nature or kind they might have been ; if he had disobeyed God, broken his commandments, despised Jesus Christ, and been an atheist, etc., they were all pardoned, both for this world and that which is to come, and that, even should he be under the censure or excommunication of any priest, bishop, etc. I wished to take a copy of it, but he was not willing to give it.

"March 6, 1834. This is what is-called by the Greeks,

Tcheknepefti, which I should translate Singe-Thursday—as on this day they are accustomed to kill a fowl or turkey, and pick it, and then singe the small feathers as we do usually in the fire—in other words, to prepare it for Saturday and Sunday next, after which the feast begins.

"Went with my wife to call on Prince Karagin. His wife expressed herself in a shocking manner against God and his government; expressed a doubt with regard to revealed religion, and the prince talked like an infidel. The captain of the Guards also was present, and took part with them. By the grace of God I was enabled to speak boldly for Christ and God's holy word.

"April 20, 1834. After the service at my house in the afternoon, several of the scholars asked me questions about the Scriptures, such as 'Did John the Baptist have wings?' and 'Why was he thus painted in our churches?' I told them that if he was a bird he must have had wings; but if a man, not. Another asked if he had not two heads; if one did not grow out immediately when the other was cut off. For this I referred them to the Scriptures, which say, his disciples took up his body and buried it. Another asked about angels' wings, etc. To all these questions I gave such answers as I thought true and proper."

The following lets one in behind the scenes as to the motives that led even some enlightened men to oppose Dr. King's mission:

"July 12, 1835. Mr. K. called and wished to speak with me alone. Taken with me into my study, he said:

'Whatever may be your object in Greece, I rejoice that you are here and wish you success in your work, for my views are like yours; and being such, I thought it my duty to come and tell you what I have heard from certain learned men who were speaking in regard to you and your labors here. They said that you have in your employ and pay at Syra four hundred and fifty Sciots to disseminate your doctrines, and that the son of a shoe-maker (who, I think he said had been in my gymnasium) spoke about the Virgin Mary, etc., according to your doctrine, and that the people were in danger of getting into a civil war on the subject of religion, which of all wars was most to be dreaded, and therefore it was expedient to prevent you from proceeding; that though your doctrines might be true, still the people were not prepared for such a change as those doctrines would bring in. I consider your mission,' added he, 'as a new mission for preaching the gospel, similar to that of the primitive age of Christianity, and you must expect to suffer what the first preachers were called to suffer; but be of good courage, for God will not leave you to suffer anything.'

"Some priest also told Meletius, a student whom I had employed to sell the New Testament in the market-place, that it was wicked for common people to touch that book! Meletius and another boy sold, however, in three days, between 90 and 100 copies.

"Sept. 28, 1836. The Greeks appear to depend more upon external forms than upon the religion of the heart; they believe all the truth and something *more*, and the additions that have been made by man to their religion seem to be of more consequence in their eyes, than what God himself has taught.

"Sunday, March 7, 1839. Preached from John 1:29. I was led to take this text from seeing the lambs that were brought to be slain at the Passover, as it is still a custom among the Greeks for every family, however poor, to kill a lamb on this occasion.

"Sunday, April 21, 1844. Two deacons called in the morning. Conversed plainly, seriously, and pointedly; endeavored to convince them of the error of worshipping images and praying to saints. They seemed convinced; I found them exceedingly ignorant of God's word. I verily believe that an ordinary child in New England, eight or ten years old, knows far more of theology and of the Bible than they.

"May 16, 1844. Narcissus, a priest, called. Spent two or three hours in conversation on religion. He has gained much, recognizing as the only rule of faith the word of God, rejecting from the fathers everything which does not agree with that; also rejecting, as contrary to the word of God the monkish system; also the abstaining from different kinds of food, which is called fasting; while at the same time he approves, as I do, of what is true fasting: and on the subject of images he is not far from the truth, and also in regard to despotism in the church. This he says will most surely cease. Gave him a New Testament in ancient Greek, and a copy of my 'Farewell letter.' He is to me the most interesting man among the clergy in all Greece, on account of his

·efforts to preach the gospel here.   He is the only man I know of who preaches the gospel.

"May 18, 1844.   Called on Madame Covoqui.   Conversed about prayer to saints and the virgin.   After showing her several passages of Scripture, she said she was convinced of the truth of what I said, and that she should no more offer her prayers to the virgin, but to God alone.

"Thursday, July 31, 1845.   Mr. Pheovater said that an old nun at the monastery, 102 or 104 years old, on seeing the Old Testament which he gave to the church, seemed delighted with it, and begged him to ask the man who gave it to him to let her have one; and remarked that she had never till then heard that such a book existed as the Old Testament!"

March, 1847, Dr. King describes a miraculous medal ordered by the Virgin Mary to be made, after three appearances, and by which one might enjoy the particular protection of the "mother of God."   The prayer to be read from the medal was in the usual wording of the Roman-catholic prayer-book.

In February, 1848, Dr. King makes note at Malta of a Roman-catholic procession in honor, or rather *dis*honor, of St. Paul, whose image was paraded about the street, borne on the shoulders of eight or ten men, who evidently found the wooden god a heavy load.   They were preceded by perhaps five hundred priests and monks of the clerical order.

In a letter written from Athens in January, 1849, Dr. King writes, that " Protestants are considered by the

Greek church as *heretics*, it is sufficient to say, that all who do not call Mary the 'mother of God,' and who condemn the use of images (pictures), and the worship of the cross and relics (bones of the saints), are condemned as heretics by the several councils, which the Greek church universally considers as inspired and of undoubted authority. I may add, that acording to some of those councils, baptism, as performed by Protestants of any denomination whatever, is condemned as heretical."

"February, 1849. Having some business at the Notary's, and having occasion to state where I was born, as I wrote, ' Hawley, America,' he said, ' Write, Happy America.' This led to some conversation on the subject of religion, and he avowed that the cause of the wretchedness here, of the bad state of society, is the priesthood ! Mr. P. was formerly governor in Mani.

"November 8, 1849. I conversed with two Italians on the subject of Transubstantiation, and the worship of the Virgin Mary. One of them said that he was convinced that the Roman-catholic religion is erroneous; but that before he came here, had an angel from heaven told him so, he would not have believed it. That since he had seen the Bible and heard my conversation, and read some copies of the " Catholico Romano " which I gave him, he is convinced. But still I think he clings in some degree to the worship of Mary. She is the *actual* god of the people in these regions."

On one occasion, when in Naples, Dr. King was shown

1. A bone of the arm of St. Paul.
2. A tooth of St. James.
3. A lock of the Virgin Mary's hair.
4. Two hairs of the Virgin Mary.
5. A bit of Mary's robe.
6. A piece of Christ's garment.
7. Some of Mary's milk on a bit of cotton.
8. A copy of an original letter of the Virgin Mary in Syriac, from which the Latin was made.

"But after the priest assured me that this was a true copy of the original in Syriac, I said to him, 'I have studied Syriac, and this is not Syriac, but Chinese; at least so it appears to me.' It seemed to me to be nothing but a bit of wormeaten Chinese paper, with Chinese characters here and there, which very probably is a bit of a Chinese passport, or a bit of paper taken from a chest of tea."

"March 17, 1851. Had a long talk with the abbot of the convent at Ipsara on the subject of religion and the errors of his church. Among other things he said that whosoever went to the Old Testament was an adulterer. On asking me what were the commands of Christ, I began to repeat the Ten Commandments ; but he said these were in the Old Testament, and would not listen to them. He finally asked me if I did not believe the miracle of St. Spiridion, when he took the tile and squeezed out blood. I said, 'No, it is a fable.' At this he became quite angry, and threatened to tear my eyes out.

"June 16, 1851. Mrs. K. S. brought me two images or pictures which have long been objects of devotion in her family. The smallest one is St. Athanasius, which, she thinks, was used by her grandmother. This is on wood. The other, which is on brass or copper (and is the largest), represents the flagellation of our Saviour by the Jews. This, she says, is three hundred years old. Both came down to her as a parental inheritance; but she no longer values them, and will not permit them in her room, and has given them to me to dispose of as I choose.

"April 6, 1853. Mr. A. told me that the indulgence which the pope gave him was *plenary* for him and his parents and family to the third generation, and that the pope signed it with his own hand.

"August 26, 1853. I have to-day received from a Greek female what I never before received from any one—holy relics, saints' bones. One is said to be of St. Antipas, the same, I suppose, who is mentioned in • Rev. 2 : 13 ; another of St. Mercurius. They are set in silver, and have been handed down from one generation to another for I know not how long. The female who sent them to me received them from her mother, and she from her mother, and they were considered very precious. When any of the children were ill these bones were put in water, which was given to the patient for his recovery. After taking them into my hands I felt almost as if I were defiled, and I went and washed them in water, and then again with soap and water! How strange that men should be so deluded as to have hope in dead men's bones, and worship them! It is a device of the devil to keep men from God.

"January 3, 1854. Was called to see a dying woman. She was most anxious to live another year, promising to follow my directions, and even to kneel in prayer. To kneel in prayer, except once in the year, is considered by the Greeks as amounting almost to a renunciation of their religion."

March 10, 1857. Of some pictures Dr. King says, "One was the picture of the Virgin Mary, which has long been the object of worship, and which was supposed on some perilous occasion to have saved life in shipwreck; and sometimes it was supposed to creak—when displeased! The board on which it is painted is so thick and large that it might well keep a man from drowning, and in hot weather it might creak."

The question of images was an important one. A priest of much intelligence calling, Dr. King says, "I conversed much about the errors of the Greek church, particularly in the use of images or pictures. He said the fathers were from the Eastern church, and had taught all this. I told him that the first fathers in the church were Jews, and that they taught the Greeks. He said the Eastern church had preserved the doctrines entire. I told him that this assertion, so often in the mouths of the Greeks, showed their ignorance of ecclesiastical history. He said that images were received by the fathers, and that St. Luke made them, etc. I told him that was not true, and that images began to be introduced about the fourth century, not earlier, and that it was against the command of God, the second command. He said he believed the traditions of the fathers. 'So did the Pharisces,' said I, 'and our Saviour condemned them for it. The Greeks do the same, and do wrong.' He said that the Catechism taught the proper use of images, and that the common people did not use them aright. I said, ' The proper use of them is to let them be hung up, without having any reverence whatever paid to them, just as I have the plan of Athens,' pointing to it in my room. He said if they were in error he did not care, he would remain where they were, or something to that effect. I said, ' I wish for the truth,' etc. I spoke as plainly as possible, but I know not that any good will result."

Strange ceremonies were observed on occasion of the burial of a bishop, the President of the Synod. " He was not placed in a coffin, as other people are, but seated on a throne, with all his priestly robes as bishop, with his crozier in his right hand, the gospels in his left, with his mitre on his head. Multitudes went to the house to kiss his hand ; and thus he was carried to the church on his throne, and placed in the centre, with his face towards the altar during the prayers and funeral service. When Barnabas delivered the oration, the corpse was turned with the face towards the pulpit, in an opposite direction from the altar. After the service and oration, all crowded to take their last look, and he was borne through the streets on his throne, by the palace and to the grave, where he was buried in the same position."

Extract from a letter to the Society of Inquiry, Princeton, October 29, 1850 : " The longer I remain among the Greeks, the more I perceive that in all things they are ' too superstitious,' and that the true God is little known among them. And though they may not 'think the Godhead is like unto gold, or silver, or stone graven by art or man's device,' yet he is represented in this church as an old man with a long beard, with the inscription in Greek, 'I AM,' and on the throne of this great I AM they seem to have placed a woman, whom they call his mother, 'Mary, the All-Holy, the Mother of God.' The faith which Paul once preached in this city has become so sadly shipwrecked (1 Tim. 1 : 19), that one can hardly find a board or bit of the ship big enough to keep a man from sinking. The very essence of Christianity, the doctrine of salvation by faith alone, has been perverted into a doctrine of salvation by works, fastings, penances, almsgiving, etc., so that if a man has not money to leave to buy prayers for him after he is dead, he is afraid that his soul will go to the place of torment. I speak now of the mass of the common people, and not of the learned in this city, many of whom, I have reason to believe, have rejected not only their superstitions, but the truth also as it is in Christ, and like the Sadducees of old, believe nothing, though they profess to be orthodox members of the Eastern church. So that on the one hand I have to combat the deep-rooted superstitions and errors of the ignorant, and on the other the infidelity of men called enlightened."

On one occasion Dr. King writes : " Last Sunday I went with my wife and her mother to the church of the Evangelistria to see a poor deranged woman brought here from Smyrna to be healed. She has a husband and one child, both, I believe, at Smyrna. Her hands were tied very tight behind her back, and a young man, her relative, stood by, often beating her and tying the cords which she endeavored to loosen. She stood looking out at a window and constantly crying, 'O thou Holy Trinity, save me and help me!' Her relatives said she was possessed of the devil, and was crying to him to help her, and when she said, 'O Holy Trinity,' she meant the three sisters, the Nereides. Many of the Greeks suppose that the Nereides come to people in the night-time, and take them and walk and dance with them, and that, in consequence of this, they become deranged."

Again. "Heard that the body of a saint had been found, and that the people were running to pay their adoration. Supposing it to be some trick of the wonder-working church here, I had the curiosity to go also, and found that a priest from Athens had, when he fled from that place, brought with him the body of a female who died about two hundred and fifty years ago, as he said, and he was now exhibiting it to the people, who came and kissed the relics with great veneration."

Of the Greek church Dr. King says, " Multitudes of the people have a thousand times more fear of eating meat on Wednesdays and Fridays than they have of uttering a falsehood ; and the Virgin Mary and the saints really seem to be more reverenced and more fervently adored than the God of heaven ; and the traditions of men are more honored than the commandments of God. Still this church is far from being plunged in the superstition and ignorance and wickedness of the Papal church. The Greek church receives the gospel, and a spirit of refor-

22*

mation has begun to operate. The monkish system is going by, and the priests have lost much of the influence which they possessed ten years ago. Many begin to see and believe that true religion does not consist in abstaining from meat and eggs two days in the week. In short, the Greeks as a body are inclined to think for themselves, and to express their opinion, though it should be contrary to that of their priests. They cling to their images and relics and crosses and prayers to the saints with great tenacity, nor can I expect that it will be otherwise with them till the gospel is more extensively distributed and read, and till some of their own preachers shall receive the influences of the Spirit from on high, and call their attention to the truth as it is in Jesus.

"The sister of Mr. C. called September 3, 1848, and asked for a leaf from each tree in my garden. I asked why, and found that she wished them for a woman whose child was ill, and she thought, with some magical words said over the leaves, the child might recover."

CHAPTER XVII,

LIFE-WORK AT ATHENS.

1. Schools and Religious Services—Bible in Schools—Notice of Students in Gymnasiums and Seminaries—Testimony from Napoli Newspaper. 2. Direct Mission-Work—Reasoning out of the Scriptures—Publishing of Bible with Notes from the Fathers Proposed—Letters to several Societies of Inquiry— Qualifications needed for a Missionary—Delight in Christian Union — Letter to Dr. Goodell — "Greece as a Missionary Field." 3. Bible and Tract Distribution. 4. Efforts in the Temperance Cause. 5. Visits to Prisons.

DR. KING being now fairly identified with Greece by his marriage, by the ownership of property, and by other providences, it would not interest the public to follow his history at Athens in detail from year to year. It is better to treat it topically, even could space allow a different method.

SCHOOLS AND SUNDAY SERVICES.

In 1836 Dr. King began to build a schoolhouse at Athens, which, by the aid of private friends, he was enabled to finish in 1839. In this work he received no aid whatever from the American Board. He had planned this building long before he came into connection with that Society as missionary to Greece, and before that time had also secured the greater part of the means necessary. In order to finish it, he was obliged to rent it for one or two years, after which time he had regular services there

in Greek every Lord's day till the year 1860, when he
was prevented by illness from continuing them. When
we remember the attention which Dr. King in his early
manhood gave to sacred music, we need not wonder at
the enthusiasm with which he writes on occasion of a
small choir "first singing in Greek" as "truly delightful." He wrote several Greek hymns himself, besides
making translations of many from the English.

But beyond even the above pleasure, he notes more
than once how greatly he was comforted and strengthened by his little Greek prayer-meeting, even though the
attendance upon it was small. The help thus given was
especially realized during times of persecution.

The establishment of schools seemed ever a prominent object with Dr. King. Mention has been made of
those at Tenos, Menido, and Eleusis ; and now at Athens
he sought still to give his work permanent form in this
direction. The "Evangelical Gymnasium," which ranked
well with others of the kind, he hoped would be the germ
of a future college or university, to be built up by Phil-
hellenists in America, ten or twelve of whom had given
him some encouragement in regard to such an enterprise
before he left New York ; among these was General Van
Rensselaer of Albany ; and for several years his friend
S. V. S. Wilder pleasantly gave Dr. King in advance the
title of Professor in Mars' Hill College. But the germ,
though never developing in this way, has borne rich fruit,
well repaying our missionary for the religious instruction
given by him in this Gymnasium "six or eight times a
week to sixty or seventy pupils, varying in age from ten

to thirty-five years." One of these, a priest, afterwards became Professor of Theology in the University of Athens, another is a Professor of Law, and a third became the head of a gymnasium. Others are teaching in schools in various parts of the kingdom and in Turkey. Some are military officers, or otherwise in the employ of the government. At one time a college was proposed in Smyrna also.

In 1835 a regular theological class was commenced, composed of Greeks and Italians. Some of these young men were sent from Constantinople. Dr. King gave instruction in this class seven or eight times a week, and for want of suitable books at hand, was obliged to prepare for it his own course of theological study. Nor were these labors vain. The work of some of the students is telling now in Greece. The name of M. D. Kalopothakes cannot be passed by. It appears in Dr. King's Journal as early as December 2, 1846, when the young man called to show an ancient writing obtained from a friend who had been to Jerusalem on a pilgrimage; and his name after this finds frequent mention, in a way showing how the light of the gospel, finding entrance, shone clearer still as time passed on, fitting the young man to take up the work laid down by his loved and venerated father in Christ. A Spartan by birth, in his uncompromising determination he shows many traits of that remarkable race. Dr. Kalopothakes is now laboring under the auspices of the Southern Presbyterian Board. He is editor of the " Star in the East " and a " Child's Paper," and is pastor of the Greek Protestant church

lately established at Athens, which he represented at the
Evangelical Alliance of 1873.   His missionary policy is
to favor a growth from within, in opposition to having
an American mission chapel planted from without.   He
and his lovely American wife were privileged to be with
their beloved friend Dr. King during his last days on
earth, ministering to his comfort quite down to the river.
M. Constantine, another of Dr. King's pupils, has been
able to interest many in the cause of Greece and true
religion, and by his eloquence promises to do a great
work for his countrymen.   Sakelarios has gone into the
Baptist church, and may be able to serve the Master well
in that connection.

Young men for some years were sent from Greece to
America for education.   A few of these have remained
in this country ; and thus has there been an interchange
and commingling of interests and civilization not otherwise secured.   Drs. Riggs and King, in March, 1834,
wrote a long letter to Rev. Dr. John Codman of Dorches-
ter, Mass., recommending two members of the Gymnasium at Athens to his special care, and four more were
consigned subsequently to Mrs. Cornelius.

About the same time Dr. King wrote to Miss E. Stuart, Secretary of a Ladies' Society at Andover, Mass., in
regard to the school supported by them at Eleusis, near
the ancient temple of Ceres.   He said, " May you, by
your exertions, be the means of revealing to them in a
spiritual sense ' the mystery which was kept secret since
the world began, but now is made manifest.'   Romans
17 : 25, 26.   The study of the Scriptures I make one of

the conditions of their receiving your aid.... Little articles of presents to the girls would be likely to have a good effect, inducing their parents to send them."

While in this Christian land of America many are found willing to exclude the Bible from our public schools, it is truly refreshing to read the following entry, made February 10, 1855 : "To-day I received a communication from the Minister of Education and Religion, Mr. George Psyllas, in answer to my communication to him last September, concerning Chrysostom on 'Reading the Scriptures,' thanking me for my donation of a thousand copies, and enclosing a circular from him to all the teachers in Greece, calling upon them to recommend to the scholars the reading of it, and also the reading of the Scriptures themselves in their houses. This is admirable. This is just what I desired. Blessed be God, who is wonderful in working." The circular reads as follows :

"To the Schoolmasters and Schoolmistresses of the District Schools :

"That nothing tends so much to the regulation of morals, to the knowledge of the duties of man both to God and his neighbor, as the reading of the Sacred Scriptures, St. Chrysostom has shown in many parts of his numerous sacred writings.

"These passages of the divine father, collected with care, and simplified by a translation, are distributed gratis for the use of those who read.

"The reading of this collection, of which a sufficient number of copies has been already sent to the Nomarchs, that they may be distributed in the district schools in proportion to the number of scholars, we recommend to you, both for the perspicuity of the style and the wholesomeness of the sense, not doubting that you will, by applying practice to theory, render operative the injunction of this divine father, by inspiring the youth who attend your schools with a ready mind to read the Sacred Scriptures, so that they may resume at home, in the hearing of those about them, the sacred lessons they are taught, and the advantage they derive from them be thus multiplied, and the Scripture fulfilled, which saith, 'The entrance of Thy word giveth light; it giveth understanding to the simple.'

"THE MINISTER, G. PSYLLAS.

"ATHENS, 19th January, 1855."

In October 1853, the Napoli paper gave the curiculum of study in the Evangelical gymnasium, appending the following note : "The superintendents, Drs. King and Riggs being persuaded, that, in order for any one to acquire a truly useful education, the cultivation of the mind alone is not sufficient, but that the cultivation of the heart is also necessary, so as to excite in him a desire for things truly good, and induce him to shape his conduct according to unchangeable principles ; being persuaded also that there exists no other book, the study of which has so much influence in attracting the heart to that which is right and good as the Word of God; on this account, while they recommend in this institution the study of Homer, Plato, Demosthenes, Plutarch, and other celebrated writers of Greece, they wished also to bring the attention of the young to the study of Moses,

Job, Daniel, Solomon, the Prophets, the Apostles of Christ, and of Him who spake as never man spake. We revere the classics because they were written by men of splendid minds and contain many things useful, as it respects morals and politics ; but we revere much more those books which proceeded from the Fountain of wisdom, from Him who created all that was ever brilliant and glorious in the world.

" By means of the Sacred Scriptures, we hope that the youth will acquire principles for their conduct and an accurate knowledge of the true religion which they profess, and that they will one day show themselves to be not only enlightened men, but also virtuous and good citizens and true Christians, loving not only their country, but also the whole human race ; and while they enjoy earthly happiness, be prepared for everlasting blessedness in heaven."

The teachers in these schools often spoke of what the Americans had done for Greece in giving them food, knowledge, and instruction. Many strangers took interest in visiting the schools. When in 1834 Rev. Charles Stewart, then chaplain of a United States frigate, stopped at Athens, Dr. King availed himself of this opportunity to commission one so much interested in evangelistic work to procure more funds for the gymnasium, also philosophical apparatus and a press. This gymnasium was finally closed in July, 1837. In the more primary schools, the question of using the Greek catechism was one of some difficulty, though in Dr. King's opinion, duty seemed plain, not to use it at all. At Mani, at one time, the minister of religion and instruction compelled the missionaries to teach the catechism or dismiss their schools ; but this was an arbitrary act, not according to their own laws. Objections were made to the use of the Old Testament also. One bishop said, "You will make the children Hebrews," but he would give no direct answer to the question, "Does your catechism contain things contrary to the word of God ?"

MISSION WORK.

Dr. King's plans of work, as has been seen, were of the most simple and direct character. He seemed to take advantage of every opportunity to speak a word for the Master, whose commissioner he was. Some of the more intelligent Greeks sometimes came to him, Nicodemus-like, at night. By his familiarity with their own religious classics, he was ready to meet every argument, gladly recognizing the points of agreement, and proving his own position from the Bible and those fathers whose authority is recognized by the Greek church. Such a course of argument was of course unanswerable, and his reasoning, like that of Paul, was made in many cases, a power for good.

April 4, 1842. "Called on Œconomos and gave him Gallaudet's 'Natural Theology,' and 'Child's Book on the Soul' in modern Greek, and the 'Greek Reader.' Conversed, I should think an hour and a half, on the subject of translations, creeds, doing good in Greece, etc. Proposed to him that the Scriptures should be printed in a separate volume, and the notes of the fathers in another to accompany it, so that we might get help from abroad to print the Word of God, and from subscriptions among ourselves for the notes to accompany it. This after awhile he assented to. He acknowledged that the Word of God ought to be placed in every family, but with some notes from the fathers. I see no objection to this, and I have always been of the opinion that the Translation of the *Seventy* should be given to the Greeks."

As to the qualifications needed for a missionary, Dr. King's standard was rightly a high one. The following extract is taken from a letter to the Society of Inquiry at Williams College in 1838 :

"The qualifications of a missionary to Greece, as well as to any other part of the world, should be good common sense, such a degree of intelligence at least as is thought necessary for a clergyman in America, a heart deeply humbled before God under a sense of its own sinfulness, still rejoicing in the love of God to man through Christ, who in going on his mission seeks no honor except that which comes from God only." In a letter of similar character to Amherst college he wrote, "It does not seem to me so important that the *number* of missionaries should be increased, as that those who go should be of the right spirit, and properly qualified." "Study much the Sacred Scriptures, and as much as possible in the language in. which they are written. This is of the highest importance."

In a letter to the Missionary Society at Oakland, Mississippi, Dr. King writes, "The questions you ask

me are of the greatest importance. If the missionary
have a truly apostolical spirit he will surely find, as the
apostles did, his comforts increasing in proportion as he
is called to meet with trials. Outward afflictions are but
very light when the heart within has peace with God,
through Christ ; and when he has a lively hope of being
clothed upon with his spiritual house when the earthly
shall be dissolved. My greatest trials, I think I may say,
are those which I meet with from my own heart. Revi-
lings from men, having my name cast out as evil on account of Christ and his Gospel, generally produce in my
heart much joy. At the same time I must confess that
these afflictions are not in themselves joyous but griev-
ous."

To the Society at Andover, Oct. 26, 1850: "I fully
agree with you in the belief that efforts to do good
abroad produce happy effects at home. Light cannot be
shed on far-distant objects without illuminating those
that are near."

As to the establishment of missions by different sects
on the same ground, Dr. King's views were very decided.
He felt it was a great pity that they did not choose their
stations at different places. "I cannot feel it right for
missionaries of another society to come in to disturb
those who have been endeavoring to labor faithfully for
the conversion of souls." Yet, while regretting any friction ever arising from such causes, Christian union and
coöperation were near his heart, and it delighted him to
make note of the fact that when first sent out to Palestine by the French Missionary Society of Paris, "which,"

he says, "was formed at the house of one of my friends (a dissenter also), one of the first who arose and proffered aid to send me, was Rev. D. Wilson, now bishop of Calcutta; and some of my principal supporters were of the Church of England." No one could enjoy more than he reunions of Christians of various names, as on the occasion of a missionary meeting of the United Brethren at Basle, in June, 1843, at which Dr. Barth, Professor Stein, Pastor La Roche, and Mr. Pilet took part, when all hearts seemed melted together and gave outward expression of this in a hymn commencing, "Hallelujah," with its chorus of "Holy, holy, holy is God."

To his loved and congenial friend, Dr. Goodell of Constantinople, Dr. King in 1854 gives a succinct idea of the Greek field after twenty-five years' experience.

Allow first a few words of friendly preface. "You say you are changing, growing gray, that your voice shakes, and that 'the native grinders are reduced to four.' All this may be, but the man Goodell never changes. And I am happy to see, from the spirit of your letter, that your friendship for me has not grown old or gray, or been shaken or reduced because you did not receive my answer to your letter, nor any acknowledgment of the receipt of your interesting book.

"You ask me whether I am growing older or younger. As a man's testimony in regard to himself, especially when in his favor, is liable to be considered doubtful, I think it better to adduce what some others have said with regard to me. When I returned to the United States after an absence of about seven years, Mr. Jere-

23*

miah Evarts, Secretary, said he thought I had not changed at all during that time.

"My wife has often remarked that I never change, or but very little, and attributes it to her kindness. She says it is because I have so good a wife; and really when I think how long I have lived, and what varied scenes I have passed through, it seems to me strange that I should be so little changed as I think I am. Still I have many gray hairs, and those 'that look out at the windows' do not distinguish objects as clearly as formerly, especially fine print, without the aid of glasses, of which, however, I do not generally make any use. My heart feels as warm towards my old friends as ever.

"Now as to the report of the state of evangelical religion in Greece, which you wish me to give, so as to be incorporated with yours of Turkey, for the 'great meeting at the opening of the Crystal Palace in Paris next spring,' and with regard to which you say, 'the shorter and sweeter I can make it the better,' here it is, in about as few words as I can make it.

"GREECE AS A MISSIONARY FIELD.

"Greece covered with the thorns and briers and thistles of superstition for ages, is a difficult field to cultivate; I have been laboring in it for about twenty-seven years, ploughing and sowing in tears, yet with hope, and still feel sure that the time of harvest will come and that sheaves will be brought in with rejoicing. Prejudices are giving way; a great victory with regard to religious liberty has been gained within the last few years. I distribute thousands and hundreds of thousands of religious tracts unhindered. The word of God, the Scriptures of the Old and New Testament, is received in all the schools of the kingdom, has 'free course' among all the people, and will be 'glorified.' A few only appear to have received the truth in the love of it, but many are convinced of the folly of their superstitions, and the importance of receiving the word of God as the only rule of faith and practice. The restraint already put upon the influence of Gog and Magog has had a happy effect, and should that influence be wholly restrained, a still happier may be expected. I have never had more reason to hope for success in my labors than at present.

"With affectionate remembrance to Mrs. Goodell and your family, and to all the brethren and sisters of your mission, I am, as I have been for thirty years past, your sincere friend and brother in Christ,

"JONAS KING."

BIBLE AND TRACT DISTRIBUTION.

Dr. Isaac Bird has called his book on Eastern Missions, very appropriately "Bible Work in Bible Lands." Missionaries there were called Bible-men, so emphatically was the distribution of the pure word of God their special work. To none could the above title be applied more truly than to Dr. Jonas King. The word of God was not only the man of his counsel, but the sword which he used, knowing its power through the Holy Ghost.

When possible he would employ an agent to assist in thus spreading the truth, securing, if possible, the scr-vices of a priest, for "a priest could go into the churches and preach on the importance of having the word of God in the language they understand."

In the year 1835, Dr. King sold or distributed gratuitously 2,656 copies of the Sacred Scriptures, or parts of them, and 25,893 schoolbooks and religious tracts ; in 1838, 6,275 New Testaments, and books in all, 32,410. The average was 30,400 a year.

Such work was not carried on without opposition. In 1836, a boy who had bought some Psalters and New Testaments, and received some tracts, asked the bishop of Talanti if he might keep them. The bishop replied, " The tracts leave with me to examine. The Psalters and New Testaments bury." Still, as a people, the Greeks were enlightened enough to know that it was contrary to the injunction of Christ for the Synod or others to prohibit the common people from reading the Word of God.

In 1834 a letter was sent to Rev. John C. Brigham, Secretary, giving some criticisms asked for by the Bible Society as to their new edition of the New Testament in modern Greek, which was an improvement, he found, upon that put forth by the London Society, though still containing words that were falling into disuse among the more intelligent people of Greece. There was a great demand for these Bibles. One day forty or fifty called for them, coming from different parts of the country, although the priests often opposed this work.

With regard to tracts, Dr. King's early acquaintance with Dr. W. A. Hallock, ripening as years passed on into

full and appreciative Christian friendship, would naturally lead him to use those weapons of attack and defence which his friend so earnestly and successfully was
preparing. But their own adaptation to the end in view
was a sufficient motive for Dr. King to keep his armory
supplied with them, not only from New York, but from
London, Paris, and Brussels. The average number of
pages distributed was about 400,000 yearly, more than
half of which were provided by the American Tract Society. Close correspondence as to every detail was kept
up with his friend, the Secretary of this Society, which
no doubt is to be found in its archives. The influence
of efforts in this direction was far-reaching.

In 1857 Dr. King writes: "A son of the chaplain of
the King of Prussia, who was here last summer, and who
is himself assistant chaplain to the king, informed me
that a copy of the 'Prayers of the Saints,' which I sent
to his father several years before, had been the means of
the publication of many thousands of copies of the same
in the kingdom of Prussia, with the difference, I believe,
that they were accompanied with remarks as to the occasion of the prayers; whereas I published the prayers as
they are found in the Bible, without any remarks, except
what are contained in the caption or summary of their
contents."

Dr. King, during his last years of active service, gave
more and more time to translating and revising books
and tracts, finding from experience that a pure religious
literature was greatly needed in Greece, also a better
style of schoolbook. Thus does his work remain more

permanent in effect than was possible in any other form, which yet at the time might have attracted more attention. A list of books and tracts, prepared and supervised by Dr. King, is given in Chapter XXIV. In eleven years 281,399 books had been distributed.

TEMPERANCE.

In these days of revival in the temperance cause, it is pleasant to trace footprints in the past in the same direction, and Dr. King found reason indeed for effort of this kind. Of one school of eighty boys in Greece he says : "The teacher told me that it is so customary here for people to drink wine and to give it to their children, that very often he has been obliged to send home these little boys on account of their having drunk so much wine with their dinner as to be stupid and unfit for study. At parties, I am told, they make the children drink in their turn, as if they were men grown! After hearing of this, I reproved some of the people I saw for such an unchristian usage. In one school I found a copy of the ancient Greek New Testament, printed at Boston, which I suppose I brought with me eleven years ago, or which was sent to me for distribution."

In 1842 Dr. King drew up a temperance pledge in Greek, and persuaded ten or more persons of different grades and employments to sign it. One gentleman said that he had left off wine since some conversation had with Dr. King on the subject. A physician at Megara was delighted to join in the effort to obtain names there. One man wanted the privilege of taking a little now and then, but Dr. King said, " Keep your feet wholly out of the devil's trap."

Six years before this time, however, the first step was taken to form a society at Athens for the diffusion of knowledge and promotion of temperance and sobriety, and opposed to card-playing, duelling, intemperance in eating and drinking, and luxury in dress and furniture, that the mind and body may be kept in a proper state for acquiring knowledge and improving in virtue. The first meeting was held at Dr. King's house. Reports of the temperance work in America were translated and read aloud, together with a letter from Dr. King to Dr. Justin Edwards, in answer to a notice received of his own appointment as Corresponding Member of the American Temperance Society. Thus was the tidal wave of reform in America felt upon the shores of Greece. Dr. King in his letter compares the manufacturers, sellers, and drinkers of ardent-spirits to the hosts of Midian, and said that to overcome them lights must be put " within the pitchers." He contradicts the assertion as to the little evil that comes from wine-drinking, for on the feast-days the people would drink it at the taverns until their faces were inflamed, and they would sit and sing nearly the whole night. Still there were in Greece very few sots, or habitual drunkards. The influence of Europeans, however, had been unfortunate. Rum was used more than formerly, and was often mixed with the wine. Soon after Dr. King came to Athens a Turkish bey, under the influence of rum, caused a poor man to be beaten on the back in such a horrible way that he died a few hours after, and for no other reason than that the poor man would not purchase his beans at more than the market price. Dr. King says, "I saw him carried to the grave, followed by many mourners. The weeping widow and several little children can tell something of the suffering occasioned by the use of ardent spirits."

In 1843 steps were taken in Athens for the formation of a society having reference to temperance alone, and which was favored by Dr. Roeser and other Greek friends. In one year Dr. King distributed over a thousand copies of a translation into modern Greek of the American Tract Society's tract on the " Effects of Intemperance." In August, 1848, there appears in the Journal the following note : " Went to the Piræus with my family to take the baths. A man there asked me if I remembered speaking with him on the subject of intemperance when riding up to Athens in a carriage in 1845, and said that that conversation had been the means of saving him ; that he had left drinking rum, which he before used in large doses ; that he then was ill, but was now in good health ; that he owed this to me, and that he had spoken to many others, and had been the means of turning them from their intemperance." He seemed grateful.

The editor of the " Athena" once said that by means of a piece prepared by Dr. King for reading at a meeting of the Temperance Society, and which had been printed in parts in his paper, he believed about one thousand persons had been reclaimed from drinking.

In 1854 Dr. King wrote to Commodore Stringham in

regard to a young man left by him at Athens who greatly needed Christian aid and encouragement. This Dr. King was enabled to give. The young man, upon recovery to usual health, signed the temperance pledge.

These selections in regard to temperance may close fittingly with a fact much to the honor of Governor Wright, U. S. minister at Berlin at the time of the meeting of the Evangelical Alliance there in 1857. In connection with a nine days' meeting held at that time, of which Dr. King made record, he adds: "Dined, in company with other Americans, with our minister, who had no wine on his table, and whose health we drank with bumpers of water."

VISITS TO PRISONS.

Dr. King did not forget the prisoner. He sought particular permission from the king's attorney to visit the prison at Athens, and was referred to the minister of justice, and then to the Synod. About a year after he was still unable to get an order allowing the New Testament to be given to the prisoners, even those condemned to death being thus deprived of the gospel. The minister of justice remarked, however, that owing to what Dr. King had said, religious books had been put in the prison, and the Catechism of Plato, and a priest had been ordered to go every Sunday and teach the prisoners. Dr. King asked, "Of what account is this so long as the gospel of our Lord is excluded?" He answered, "But the Synod, whose authority is respected in Greece, has so ordered it." Dr. King. "Well, we all, synods and rulers and kings, shall soon appear before a higher tribunal, before Jesus Christ, to give an account."

In 1843, when at Ratisbon, a visit to the dungeons there, and a sight of the instruments of torture used by those in old times, weighed heavily on Dr. King's heart. The details are too shocking to repeat. The terrible appliances used in the rack-chamber haunted the visitor's mind night and day. He said, "Thank God for the light which has now driven away such darkness of iniquity."

CHAPTER XVIII.

LIFE-WORK AT ATHENS CONTINUED.

Home, Hospitality, Correspondence, and Personal Religious Experience.

THE most cursory view of Dr. King's life and influence in Greece would recognize the warm-hearted hospitality which made his home a centre, not only to the missionary traveller, but to every American and Englishman passing through Athens. Frequent excursions were made to the seaport, the Piræus, to " welcome the coming or to speed the parting guest." Mr. and Mrs. Buel of the Baptist Board were stationed there, and many pleasant hours were passed under their roof while waiting for tide or steamer.

It were an impossible task to give the names of all the friends thus received. Gov. Cass, Dr. Willett, Dr. Calhoun of Mount Lebanon, Dr. Geo. B. Cheever, Mr. Littlefield, Miss Susan Holmes, Dr. Van Rensselaer, Rev. Mr. Lawrence of Marblehead, Rev. Arthur Mitchell, Charles A. Stoddard, Thurlow Weed, and Dr. Duffield, Brooks of Boston, Rev. W. C. Roberts, and many others, were of the number. A Mr. Allen was sick at the house for weeks of typhus fever, and Rev. Francis Parker of Boston spent his last hours there, both of them receiving attention as in a brother's house. Dr. Leyburn

came, a welcome assistant in the work, and the Arnolds
of the Baptist church gave loving sympathy on occasion
of the death of Dr. King's youngest daughter, Aspasia,
after a severe illness of seven weeks.   This affliction
was the more trying, because just then Mrs. King was
with her daughters in America, and the cholera was literally raging through the city.   Intercourse with Dr. and
Mrs. Korck, and Mr. and Mrs. Benjamin, was also of
pleasant character.

Rev. S. I. Prime, D. D., and a son of Henry Hill, Esq,
visited Athens in 1853.   There seemed a comedy of errors as regards their experiences in a rainstorm, but all
was forgotten in the delight of a communion service together, administered by Dr. Prime, who also preached in
the evening. "A good audience and an admirable sermon.   I do not know that I have heard such a sermon
for many years.   His text was Colos. 3 : 3 : 'For ye are
dead, and your life is hid with Christ in God.'"

Dr. King's acquaintance with Dr. and Mrs. Robert
Baird was particularly intimate.   Meeting Dr. King first
during his first visit to America, Dr. Baird afterwards
said that Dr. King had been the means of his going himself to Europe.   This, on account of its results, Dr. King
considered an item of considerable importance.   The
friends met afterwards in Switzerland, and the union was
still further cemented by the long stay in Athens of one
of Dr. Baird's sons, who by his studies there in 1851 still
further prepared himself to fill most honorably a chair in
the New York University.   By his prayers and Christian
sympathy he greatly cheered his venerated host, and his

book on "Modern Greece" is a valuable contribution in regard to that country.

Saturday, March 16, 1853, Dr. King writes: "The celebrated poet, William Cullen Bryant, called to see me with three other Americans. When a boy I was acquainted with Mr. Bryant, and visited at his father's house. That was about fifty years ago." Again on the 18th inst.: "Mr Bryant and Mr. Durand spent the evening with us. I was much pleased with Mr. Bryant, a man of merit, with great simplicity of manner. This is what I like—a man of first-rate talent without seeming to be aware of it."

In 1854 Washington's birthday was observed by the Americans in Athens with much ceremony. Hon. Hugh Maxwell of New York, "in a brief but lucid and happy manner, portrayed the noble character of the man whose name is honored by every freeman in the world. Others besides Americans were present, and many eyes were filled with tears." The following notice appeared in the "Panhellenium" soon after:

" Thanks and gratitude to the American orator, Maxwell, for the noble and truly most Christian sentiments of himself and of the illustrious American nation, which he expressed in his speech at Athens, the 10th of February (22d, N. S.), 1854, in the house of the most Reverend Mr. King, the representative of this evangelical nation of the New World, at the celebration of the birthday of its glorious and ever-memorable reformer, George Washington. These truly divine and golden words which he uttered will remain ineffaceable in the hearts of the

Greeks everywhere, exultant with enthusiastic joy and gratitude.

"Such was the sympathy which the people of the United States felt and expressed for those who were struggling for liberty when Greece sought to throw off the Mussulman yoke. Nor will this sympathy be less fervent, nor the manifestation of it less speedy and decided, in any similar future struggle of any other part of the Greek race.

"Eternal, eternal be the memory of the glorious and celebrated George Washington!

"Live for ever! Live for ever, the glorious and most Christian American nation!

"COUNT WINCHESEY."

Prof. Blackie of Scotland, Dr. Raffles of Liverpool, and other European Christians, helped brighten the house where they themselves were refreshed. Lady Franklin also here received sympathy and greeting.

Greeks and even Mussulmans took refuge in Dr. King's house in time of trouble. Sometimes ten or eleven strangers would be there; nor let us wonder that sometimes his kind heart was imposed upon by strangers whom he could not bear to think of as less honest and sincere than himself.

Hon. Geo. P. Marsh and Commodore Stringham were privileged to do a great work in defence of the right, as appears in the account of Dr. King's persecutions. His acquaintance became in time a very large one, and his correspondence consequently extensive. In his travels we find mention of C. Edwards Lester, Powers the sculptor, Count Cavour, who called and walked out with Dr. King to show him the city of Turin, and of whom he speaks as a very liberal-minded, intelligent man. Charles Tilt at Florence showed Dr. King no little kindness, as did also Rev. Mr. Hare, Henry Innis, Esq., and Rev. Mr. Loundes at Malta, where also he met the reformers Achilli and De Sanctis. A sister of Kossuth, "a very interesting person," Dr. and Mrs. King called to see at the Piræus, who said her brother and all the family were Protestants, which brought the cause of Hungary very near his heart.

At Rome in 1847, Dr. King had a most interesting conversation with the Padre Ventura, said to be the principal mover in all the reforms about that time instituted by the pope, Pio Nono, and the eulogist of Daniel O'Connel. Padre Ventura wrote under his own likeness, which he gave to Dr. King, these words: "L'unico mezzo evangelico de propagare il Cristianismo é la predicazione da parola del Vangelo"—"The only evangelical means of propagating Christianity is the preaching of the word of the gospel." More than one friendly discussion was held by these two representative men, who finally parted with a friendly embrace and with mutual good wishes.

Dr. King was presented to the pope, but says he did not bow the knee before him nor kiss his hand, though he witnessed the adoration that he received from the populace.

After conversing with Cardinal Mezzofanti in five or six of the fifty different languages which he could use, but principally in Arabic, which Mezzofanti spoke very fluently, he gave Dr. King, at his request, his autograph, writing the subjoined lines :

> "Great many tongues resound among mankind,
> Their number overwhelms the power of mind;
> Here under English lines I write my name;
> I like this noble language, dear to fame.
> "J. MEZZOFANTI."

"ROME, Oct. 18, 1847."

Dr. King himself had studied, more or less, ten or eleven languages.

Very probably a part of the conversation between the two linguists turned on the proper pronunciation of Greek in our schools and universities, for Dr. King often expressed the opinion very decidedly that that of modern Greek should be the exemplar. Many words are the same in the ancient language and the present. The new dialect among the more intelligent Greeks is constantly drawing from the old ; and if a student in the United States or in Europe were taught to pronounce the words as they are pronounced at Athens, he would be able to hold conversation with the learned there in a very short time, and very soon with the common people. Dr. King thought Homer and Demosthenes would hardly recognize their own productions as read in our colleges, the sound of which "has been evolved from modern inner consciousness."

Many letters were interchanged by him with Mr. J. C. Symmes of London, whose liberal spirit devised and carried out many things in aid of his friend's work and personal comfort.

In November, 1852, we find mention of the name of Howard Crosby, Esq., who has since proved himself, as a divine as well as a layman, a warm and efficient friend to the Greek mission, and whose house in New York has been a home indeed to some connected with that mission.

Letters passed also between Dr. King and Fisher Howe, Esq., of Brooklyn, whose work on "Oriental Scenes" was much enjoyed by one so familiar with these subjects as was Dr. King. Other names also appear of men distinguished in the world of literature, science, or Christian benevolence, such as Dr. Edward D. Atwater, Nathaniel Hawthorne, Rev. Edward Robinson, D. D., Prof. C. C. Felton, and O. E. Wood. Official correspondence was had with Daniel Webster, B. F. Butler, Secretary of State under Van Buren, and other well-known statesmen, who seemed to take personal interest in vindicating the rights of an American citizen and missionary abroad. To Edward Everett Dr. King sent a fragment of marble from the Acropolis ; and through Dr. King also a larger block was consigned by the Greek government, to become a part of the Washington Monument.

In 1844 Rev. Dr. Anderson made a second official visit to the East, accompanied at this time by Rev. Dr. Joel Hawes of Hartford, at which time free conference was had with Drs. King and Benjamin. It was decided that Dr. Benjamin should go among the Armenians in Turkey,* while Dr. King remained until his death the only

* Dr. Anderson's Oriental Churches, p. 160.

missionary of the American Board in Greece. During nearly the whole of Dr. King's life in Athens, Dr. Hill, an American Episcopal missionary, whose coming to Greece has been mentioned, was resident there also.

Athens was by no means as quiet a place as its age might lead one to expect. On one occasion Dr. King, returning from Smyrna with his family, found his house occupied by Bavarian soldiers, and several days passed before the Nomarch and Demagerontes succeeded in dislodging them. At another time, a house used for his Lancastrian school was claimed for use by the Government party just then in power for the accommodation of some officers, and the furniture and benches were turned out into the streets. These were troublous times. Further facts will be given in the account of Dr. King's persecutions.

His personal relations with the kings of Greece were always pleasant and satisfactory. A Bavarian prince, named Otho, was put at the head of affairs in 1833, after the murder of President Capodistria. The Acropolis was then given up by the Turks, and Athens became the seat of government.

King Otho proved friendly to the American residents there. Dr. and Mrs. King were invited a number of times to the palace. When the notes of invitation came, it was sometimes pleasantly said, that Otho, king of Greece, wished to confer with Jonas, king of America. When a ball was proposed, special word would come that there would be rooms where there would be no dancing, and that Dr. King might retire when he chose. In 1834, the king and the bishop of the city attended the examination in Greek, geometry, algebra, and the philosophy of language, held for three days, of the students of the gymnasium.

In February, 1835, at a public reception of Count Armansberg, King Otho asked Dr. King many questions as to his work, and a few days after sent for his American compeer. The Journal states: " At half-past six I was received by the king with much urbanity and kindness, who asked me many questions about my work, my country, and the colleges in America. I told him that it was the students of my gymnasium that presented to him a crown on a book, as he came from Eleusis to Athens the first time, and how many difficulties they had to encounter for want of a lexicon and other books. On his asking me why the United States had no debt, how they managed to arrive to such a state of independence as to debt, I replied that we pay but little to those in office, except to our judges, have but few soldiers, and many husbandmen. In speaking of Greece, I said, 'Your majesty has a great task to perform.' Toward the close I mentioned to him that I had a friend, Mr. Riggs, who would like to pay his respects to his majesty, and he said, 'To-morrow evening at half-past six, I will see you with your friend,' and I retired much gratified with my reception, and also with the apparent good disposition of the king. At the time appointed I presented Mr. Riggs to the king, who received us very kindly."

Of one evening, on occasion of a visit of the king of Bavaria to his son, King Otho, Dr. King says: " About two hundred and fifty were present, nearly all the foreign ambassadors with their families, the ministers of state, and many others. At about nine o'clock the two kings came in, bowed to the party, and took their seats in two great chairs placed nearly in the middle of the hall, and the concert commenced. The most of the time was spent in singing and playing on the piano by ladies present. An interval of perhaps half an hour was spent in conversation, during which time cakes and lemonade were handed to the company." In 1853, when under sentence of exile, Dr. King was still invited to the court as before. The queen too proved very friendly. She once gave to Dr. King's little daughter, Elizabeth, a pretty little basket, long treasured in remembrance of her visit to the palace. When Dr. King at one time had just returned from Germany, the queen asked many questions about the journey, and told him what he did not know before, that the archduchess of Austria, and the margrave of Baden, whom he had met, were her relatives.

The frigate "Constitution" coming to the Piræus in 1835, Dr. King entertained the officers at his own house, and went with them when introduced to the king and ministers. Commodore Elliott proposed that Dr. King should be made a consul, which he at this time declined ; he was used, however, more than once as an informal medium of communication between the government of Greece and that of the United States, and seemingly to the satisfaction of both parties, even before he became, in 1851, assistant consul for America. It will be seen that during subsequent persecutions, this official position was one of the orderings of Providence in his behalf.

Dr. King's relations with the Duke de Broglie were such as to enable him to aid the cause of Greece with France also. In 1843 M. Colletti, coming to Athens as special messenger, told Dr. King that what he had written about Greece had prepared the way for the recognition of the new order of things there by the French government, and that his representations had had influence in England also, for Dr. King's statements had been received, when those of others were more than doubted.

Dr. King's health was ever frail; yet his constitution must have been excellent, to allow of such persistent effort for so many years.

As many false reports have been made of the wealth acquired by him in Athens, suffice it to say, that upon his first going there, purchase of land was necessary, for no place could be hired for school or dwelling. Much property had been confiscated. The market was over-flooded. Dr. King bought some lots on most advantageous terms. Afterwards the Greek government wished to use about an acre of this ground for a public park, and it was not until after twenty years that Dr. King's claims were adjusted, through the intervention of Hon. George P. Marsh, who also secured his rights as an American citizen. The facts as to these purchases and the rise of property in Athens, have been much exaggerated. Dr. King's salary was small, barely sufficient with economy to meet the current expenses of his hospitable home and growing family. Twice he kept a horse on account of his health, but sold it again after a few months, to save expense to the Board. Does any one regret that a missionary, as well as any other man, should be able to leave his wife and children in comfortable circumstances?

As to this family, what joy came to the father's heart as from time to time he heard of the hoped-for conversion of his children while absent from him in America! His letters to them on these occasions are epitomes of parental gospel instruction. A code of maxims, written by him in June, 1842, is herewith subjoined.

"1. Forget not to pray in secret every day. If possible, two or three times a day.

"2. Read a portion of God's Holy Word both morning and evening.

"3. In the morning, think, 'What can I do to-day to glorify my God and Saviour?' and at night ask yourself, 'What have I done to-day to glorify him?'

"4. Remember that our home is in heaven; that your father hopes to meet you there one day, and to remain there together through eternity; that to go there, we must love God with all the heart, must repent of all sin, believe in Jesus Christ and obey all his commands. These commands you will find in his Holy Word, the Bible.

"5. Devote every Lord's day to the Lord, to reading his Holy Word, to prayer, to hearing the gospel preached, and to meditation on the things that are above, where Christ is.

"6. Speak the truth at all times. Never dissemble. Never tell a lie.

" 7. Choose for your friends and playmates those who love the Lord Jesus Christ and his Holy Word.

" 8. Keep yourselves from idols.

"9. Do not keep company with those who lie, who trifle with the truth, who disregard God's holy day, who neglect his Holy Word, and who seem not to reverence the name of God, the Creator of all things.

" 10. If any one laughs at you for being devoted to God, for praying to God, for loving prayer, for keeping his day holy, for reading his Word, for being religious, do not be angry with them, and do not be sorrowful; rather rejoice that you should suffer shame for Christ's sake. All good people are more or less despised by the wicked people of this world.

" 11. Never go to a ball or a theatre, however much your young friends or old friends may solicit you and urge you.

" 12. Remember your father and his instructions, and pray for him every day."

Of Dr. King's own inner life, it may be said that he was well aware of his besetting imperfections ; and that he often wrote about as follows : " I desire a meek and humble and quiet spirit, that will submit to anything that God sends." Under the influence of early training, he, for some years, probably spent more time in fasting and in searchings of his own heart for tokens of his acceptance with God, than was profitable; but it is to the glory of our God to note that as life passed on, and was

more and more given to the service of Christ, this dear
servant of his learned to look upon him as a Saviour all-
sufficient to deliver from all evil ; so that he found out
the secret of casting anchor, not in one's own experience
or feelings, but in the finished work of our blessed Redeemer.　In June, 1840, Dr. King writes : " God would
never have given me such a spirit of prayer and suppli-
cation and of dependence on him, if he did not intend
finally to give me the victory."　Again in 1843 : " I think
I have more joy in believing than I used to have, perhaps
than I ever had before, and I feel a degree of *certainty*
that I love the Saviour and that I am born of God, which
I perhaps never felt before ; and I can speak differently
now from what I used to speak.　Oh, I am so happy in
Christ ; have such a hope of a crown, a kingdom, an inheritance in heaven, that all the grandeur of this earth
seems vain.　To love Christ, serve Christ, live for Christ,
to glorify Christ, whether by life or by death, seems so
great, so wonderful, so glorious.

" As I walk the streets of this joyous city [Vienna], I
sometimes weep to think that I am permitted to do
something for Christ ; to say a word for him to those
whom I meet with !　Glorious service, happy service, the
service of Christ !　I long to do much for him ; I beg of
him to give me much to do in his vineyard.　Lord Jesus,
help me to glorify thee."

" Jan. 24, 1849.　This has been to me a happy day.
I have had opportunity to converse with ten or twelve
different persons, Greeks, seriously on the subject of religion."

"Jan. 18, 1852. Almost the only thing which greatly interests me now on earth is the work of my mission. The world seems to have lost its charms. Intercourse with those who have nothing to speak of but the things of this world seems wearisome. In conversing with people in regard to the concerns of their souls, and in preparing my sermons, I am happy."

Amid all his trials and anxieties, facts like the following, which came to him through Rev. David Stoddard of Ooroomiah, more than once brought "comfort and joy and strength" to his soul.

Sometime since as one of the Secretaries of the Board was travelling in Vermont, he went into a house where he was unknown, and commenced conversing with the inmates. He soon found that the mother of the family was deeply interested in missions. Said she, " I have read the 'Missionary Herald' for thirty years straight through, and there is not a single missionary that I have not known something about." She then went on to enumerate different individuals who have been at times in circumstances of peculiar trial, and for whom she had been accustomed to pray by name. "There," said she, "is Dr. King, at Athens. I have long prayed for him. Sometimes when I have waked up in the night, and begun to pray for him, I have felt impelled to get up and pray on my knees. 'No,' said I, 'it will do just as well in my bed;' but nothing would answer till I got up and poured out an earnest prayer for him on my knees, and then I went to bed and slept quietly." When she was through, the Secretary said, " Well, I 'm extremely interested in all this.   I know Dr. King very well myself.   I have been with him at Athens, in the midst of his troubles."   The woman looked at him with surprise and incredulity for a moment, and then said, "Go right out of my house, this minute.   There is not a word of truth in it."   Her faith, strong as it was, did not extend to this. She could not believe that any one who had actually seen him in Athens, could ever see her in Vermont.

Of the above account in a letter from Dr. Anderson, Dr. King says, "I read it with tears; and when I read it to my wife, she seemed affected even to tears."   Upon his return to this country, though making many inquiries, Dr. King was never able to find out the name of his Vermont friend.

CHAPTER XIX.

FRUITS OF LABOR.

Yusuf Aga—Various Testimonies—Luigi Bianchi—Dr. Anderson's
View of Dr. King's Missionary Work.

THE promise reads, "My word shall not return unto
me void," and Dr. King's distribution of the Bible, and
his expositions of it, so plain and simple in opposition to
the technicalities of the priests, the instruction given by
him in the schools, his preaching in the chapel and by the
wayside everywhere, could not fail of good results, for in
all and through all it is plain to see that he ever looked
above for a blessing upon every effort. Although Dr.
King's was eminently a work of subsoiling and preparation, still he was permitted himself to see, here and there,
the promise and even the first fruits of a rich harvest.

Incidental instances of this have been given, and also
of the way in which the hearts of men in political power
were sometimes turned in favor of the gospel.

In 1841, the Greek ambassador to England expressed
deep interest in regard to having the Septuagint repub-
lished in Modern Greek, and thus adapted to popular
use. A colonel in the army said he often sent people to
Dr. King for books and that he approved of his teaching.
The story of Yusuf Aga is an interesting one. When a
boy of twelve years, he was treated so cruelly at home
by his step-brothers, that he jumped from a window and

went to the cadi at Tripolizza, and became a Mussulman.
Being of a distinguished Greek family he rose to power
and wealth. About 1841, he came to Greece and took
on him some expenses for his nephews and nieces there.
Dr. King sought his acquaintance and soon commended
to him the study of the New Testament, and Yusuf came
to the next Sunday service. With the uncle of this man
Dr. King held spirited discussions also. After a while
Yusuf was dangerously sick. There was a suspicion of
poison, never proven. Afterwards this man took refuge
in Dr. King's own house, bearing all his own expenses ;
coming there at first at night with all the importunity
of the man desiring three loaves and which could not be
resisted. His stay continued for over two months. Every day some time was given to the religious instruction
of himself and his followers ; and his Greek relatives
came often to hear Dr. King preach. There was danger
that Dr. King would be accused of the terrible crime of
proselytism. One thing was true, that the teaching of
the Gospel was of more use to Yusuf's bodily health than
all the prescriptions of the physicians, who yet were intelligent and excellent men.

Sometimes a young Greek would come and say that
he owed to Dr. King's instructions at Athens his safety
from evils to which he was exposed, that he should oth-
wise have been ruined ; or a lady would send for Scott's
"Force of Truth" and then tell Dr. King she had left
all her images and prayers to saints, and prayed only to
God through Jesus Christ, taking the Scriptures as her
only rule and making them now her constant study.

Others are mentioned as also coming to the light and saying they could not conscientiously remain believing one thing and practising the other. One man said that if he made his true belief known he should be destroyed. A Greek lady present confirmed this, saying that he would be torn to pieces—that he could not live three days. Another young man, a teacher, said that he owed everything to Dr. King and to that Word of God he put in his hands. Without it he would have been a wild beast; that it had been his comfort in trouble; that he recommended it to all his scholars, so that, as some of them were now quite enlightened, suspicions of heresy were excited with regard to himself. Another said that when, twenty years before, he heard of Dr. King's school at Tenos, he had said, " Why do you suffer him ? why do you not kill him ?" and that he would himself at that time have killed him, but now he considered his presence a benediction."

June 5, 1844. " N. M. T., a Hydriote, 42 years old, called; said he had formerly been in my service; that he was at first very superstitious and opposed to us; wished to kill us; that he led on men to attack the schoolhouse in Syra. But on reading the New Testament his eyes were opened, and now he wished to support us."

Once, attending the funeral of one of the students, the father said, " Ever since your visit to him a few days ago he talked constantly of Christ; said the world was worth nothing. When told to pray to the saints to help him, he said, ' First look to Christ.' His talk was all of Christ."

July 30, 1834. "To-day two of the students belonging to the third class in the gymnasium called and told me of their conversation with their uncle, a priest, who asked them if I made the sign of the cross. They said, 'He teaches us the gospel and to do what Christ says, and what signifies the sign of the cross?' He told them they must pray to saints and worship them; they said they did not find anything of this in the gospel, but simply that they must worship God. He said the saints would tear their eyes out if they did not; they said, if Christ was their friend they did not fear, and that if the saints would tear their eyes out, they were not saints, but devils."

March 18, 1849. "Mr. Whiting's letter from Constantinople informed me of the hopeful conversion of M. M. and others, and that M. M.'s first impressions in favor of truth were made on his mind by me some twenty-five years ago."

August 15, 1856. "Three young men called, asking to be admitted to the communion. One attributes the change in his feelings to reading 'The Dairyman's Daughter,' which I gave him perhaps a fortnight ago. Another to 'Alleine's Alarm,' which I published in modern Greek several years ago. The third dates his conversion several months back."

In 1859 there appeared in London a book called "Incidents in the Life of an Italian : Priest, Soldier, Refugee. By Luigi Bianchi," which bears testimony to the blessing attending one of Dr. King's various efforts. About thirty pages of this volume are given to an account of Dr. King's kindness to the author when a stranger in Athens. He says :

"Some days after my arrival, Mr. King, a missionary, called, and the progress of the acquaintance clearly demonstrated the benevolent purpose with which it was sought. His questions were not only put with the most delicate discretion, but were themselves so intelligent, that I became much interested. My obstinacy only seemed to inspire Mr. King with fervor, and from a pious zeal for my soul he began to prove that all essentially Roman-catholic doctrines are in direct opposition to the gospel. He strove to enlighten me with double earnestness when he became aware that I had been a priest. I knew no arguments for his refutation. I defended a cause that I knew to be lost, from the inveterate habit of priestly life, which teaches a man that he must inculcate certain dogmas, though he has already rejected them. This truly Christian teacher would not leave me to my blindness, but with nobleness of mind, softened by brotherly love, unveiled to my view doctrines not as yet understood, without allowing my pertinacity to discourage him. He led me at last to doubt myself ; to look at the truth in humility of spirit, confiding no longer in myself, but in God. Soon I began to perceive that salvation could not be wrought by works, but only by a lively faith in Him who had already saved me. Mr. King read me many passages ; he watched over me with the anxiety of a father or brother. He often prayed with me. The Lord led the good Mr. King to me in Athens, who, besides inexpressible and much more important spiritual benefits, shared with me from his own large heart his temporal good things also, procuring me employment as a translator at a generous compensation, thus giving me, like a true gentleman, substantial assistance without humiliation."

The above scattered specimens of good work accomplished, in the case of individuals here and there, give, after all, but an imperfect idea of Dr. King's success as a missionary. From the heavenly heights alone can a satisfactory bird's-eye view be obtained of the life of any Christian. There we may see plainly the difficulties of the way, and study to all eternity the wondrous grace that out of the very weakness of the instruments used, reveals the more strikingly the power and glory of Christ.

The church accepts in theory the fact that one soul is of more value than the whole world, but seems practically to feel a minister's work is almost in vain unless crowned with many conversions. God judges with more "equal eyes;" nor can any unprejudiced person look at the results of Dr. King's labors, even in Europe alone, without being satisfied that he was a shaft both strong and polished, fit for the Master's use, and that few have been privileged to do so much as he for the honor of our Lord.

The history of Greece is not yet finished, but it is even now conceded that the labor of American missionaries there has not been fruitless. In 1873, Dr. Rufus Anderson, after long observation, was able to say of the Greek government, that it was not what it would have been had not so much good seed been sown in that country. "And the same may be said of the social state. Nor were the same ideas prevalent among the people as to the authority of councils and of the ancient fathers, and the authority of God's Word stood higher than before; nor were there the same impressions concerning Protestantism. The Word of God, printed in the spoken language, was in very many of the habitations of the people."

Of Dr. King he says: "He was evidently designed by Providence to be a reformer; and though he lived not to witness anything that could be called a reformation among the Greek people, the battle he fought, through so many years, with the bigotry and intolerance of the Greek hierarchy, will be held in perpetual remembrance. A reformation has begun, and Dr. King, more than any other Protestant, was the instrument of Providence in bringing it about. To him is it owing preëminently that the Scriptures, since the year 1831, have been so extensively used in the schools, and that in Greece 'the Word of God is not bound.' It is not forgotten that others labored with him, and not in vain; but it is mainly to the preaching of Dr. King, during his protracted residence in Greece, in connection with his persistent and triumphant struggle with the Greek hierarchy, that we owe, under God, the visible decline there of prejudice against evangelical truth and religious liberty."

CHAPTER XX.

PERSECUTIONS.

Excommunications—Accusations in Newspapers and before the Courts—"Defence of Jonas King"—Conspiracies—Temporary Exile—Power of the American Flag.

GREECE, as Dr. King himself said in his letter to Dr. Goodell, was a difficult field. After the people there became free from Turkish rule, old ambition for political power in Europe was stealthily kept up by Russian agency, and national pride was aroused against the influence of every foreigner, and a reaction followed the gush of intense gratitude at first felt for kindness shown during the time of their struggle for liberty.

Again, the Greek church is in some respects even more exclusive than the Papal church. It claims to have the only true apostolical succession and right baptism. Protestants, Episcopal or Non-episcopal, are all considered unbaptized heretics. It holds to transubstantiation, worshipping the Virgin Mary, baptismal regeneration, and the power of ordinances to save the soul. Excommunication is regarded with extreme dread. An amusing instance of the ignorance of the common people in regard to such an edict is as follows: Early in Dr. King's missionary experience, a paper of excommunication against him had been read one Sunday in one of the

Greek churches. Some person was overheard asking another what it was all about. No doubt the word "Jonah" had caught the ear, and the answer was, "I think it was an excommunication of any one who should eat of the fish that swallowed Jonah."

Before any persecutions of Dr. King actually commenced, mutterings of a coming storm had long been heard. The messenger who came from America in 1828 with supplies of food and clothing had indeed received a grateful welcome, and many listened to his words with respect through the years succeeding. But as time passed on it is certain that the ecclesiastical authorities became alarmed.

In 1835 the bishop, formerly of Talenti, a member of the holy synod, preached for several weeks against the American schools, threatening excommunication, and saying, "The curse of the three hundred and eighteen fathers will be upon all who shall send their children to them." But Dr. King was still able to say, "The feelings of the *people* generally, I think, are with me; and the Minister of the Interior said to me some time since, 'Go on with your work; it is good; do not be afraid.' I had told him what I teach in the gymnasium, and that the bishop was threatening curses, and I said to him, 'If the three hundred and eighteen fathers were in heaven, I presume they would obey Christ, who said, "Curse not;" and that I, in teaching His gospel, was not afraid of curses coming upon my head from heaven.'"

He also writes: "The work in which I profess to be engaged is the *Lord's*, and not *mine;* and if the way in

which I thought to perform it is not the way he chooses,
I hope to be led by his providence clearly to perceive
it."

Dr. King's preaching of the pure doctrines of the
cross *must* have had some effect, since it attracted attention from both synod and government. The secret of
the opposition aroused on the part of the priests may
have been that "their craft was in danger."

Be this as it may, the fact remains that "in 1844,
being accused in some of the Greek newspapers in Athens of reviling the images, the Virgin Mary, and the doctrine of transubstantiation, he replied through the same
papers, giving extracts from the writings of Chrysostom,
Basil, Epiphanius, and others, showing that his opinions
on these subjects were the same as those entertained by
some of the most distinguished fathers in the Oriental
church; and in 1845 he collected these accusations and
answers and published them, with some additions, in a
small book in Greek, entitled the 'Defence of Jonas
King.'" This book contained, for instance, the following from Epiphanius, one of the fathers of the Eastern
church: "Let the Father, the Son, and the Holy Ghost
be worshipped; Mary, let no one worship," and being
sent to the most prominent men, civil and ecclesiastical,
in Greece and Turkey, produced a great excitement
through these countries; and in August of the same
year, 1845, "the Greek synod at Athens issued against
him what was called in the public papers an excommunication, and such as was considered by the Jews the
highest kind of excommunication, namely: not an ex-

communication from a particular church, but from the whole community ; and soon after a similar excommunication was hurled against him by the so-called 'Great Church' of the Greeks at Constantinople. These excommunications were sent to churches throughout Greece and Turkey ; and in one of the churches at Athens the little book was burned publicly in the midst of anathemas and execrations against the writer of it. A prosecution was commenced against him by the Greek government, at the instigation of the Greek synod, and in April, 1846, he was brought before the Areopagus, the highest court in Athens, and condemned to be sent to Syra, to be tried before the criminal court in that place, before which felons of the lowest order are tried."

Dr. King in these official papers was characterized as a "hypocrite, deceiver, impostor, impious, abominable, and a vessel of Satan." In September, about one hundred copies of this book, the "Defence," which he had on hand, were seized by the government, but nine hundred copies were already abroad, each blazing with the light of truth. Dr. King gives a characteristic account of his examination before the Areopagus.

"QUESTION. What is your name?

"ANSWER. Jonas King.

"Q. Your country?

"A. The United States of America.

"Q. Of what city?

"A. Hawley, a country town.

"Q. What is your age?

"A. Fifty-three.

"Q. What is your profession?

"A. I am an evangelist; that is, a preacher of the word of God.

"Q. What is your religion?

"A. What God teaches in his Word; I am a Christian most orthodox.

"Q. Did you publish this book, entitled 'Jonas King's Defence, etc.'?

"A. I did, and distributed it here and elsewhere. I gave it to all the professors in the University and to others.

"The judge then read to me my accusation as follows: 'You are accused of having in your book reviled the mother of God, the holy images, the liturgy of Chrysostom and Basil, the seven œcumenical councils, and the transformation of the bread and wine into the body and blood of our Lord Jesus Christ in the fearful mystery of the communion.'

"Q. Have you any defence to make?

"A. Those things in my book with regard to Mary, with regard to transubstantiation, and with regard to images, *I* did not say; but the most brilliant luminaries of the Eastern church, St. Epiphanius, St. Chrysostom, the great St. Basil, St. Irenæus, Clemens, and Eusebius Pamphyli say them.

"Q. Have you anything to add?

"A. Nothing.

"I was then directed to subscribe my name to the examination, which I did, and went away."

The fact that Dr. King was summoned to appear,

July 22, 1846, before the criminal court at Syra, proved that the offences against him were declared criminal in law. The penalty was imprisonment. An inflammatory pamphlet, secretly printed, was circulated in advance among judges, jurors, and the populace, with the avowed sanction of a high priest. Great excitement followed. The governor of the island, Syra, "declared that he should not be able to protect him, and all Dr. King's lawyers whom he had employed, five in number, advised him not to set his foot on shore, but to return to Athens in the same steamer (Austrian) in which he came. This advice he followed, but was insulted on the way by Greeks who were on board with him, and even his life was seriously threatened. Towards evening the same day he was back again in Athens, and here learned from a credible source that there was a conspiracy of fifty persons to take his life. This was communicated to his wife by a Greek female, who was friendly to her and did not wish to see her a widow; and so his life was preserved, but he was obliged for some time to remain in his house." There were threats made of stoning him should he appear abroad, but the Lord stirred up the minds of some persons connected with the police to offer to defend him in case of need.

"By the more intelligent in the community, whether native or foreign, and by several of the ablest journals, the proceedings of the court were strongly condemned. Twelve Greek lawyers, several of whom had held the highest offices in Greece, and were among the most distinguished of their profession, signed their names to a letter declaring their entire dissent from its proceedings."

In 1847 he was again cited to appear before the criminal court in Syra. On receiving this citation he went to the Minister of Foreign Affairs, and remonstrated, telling him that he might as well send him to the guillotine as to send him to Syra. He also went with his lawyers to the Minister of Justice and made a verbal remonstrance against being sent to Syra, where his life would be in jeopardy, instead of being tried at Athens, where the offence, if any, had been committed.

The Minister of Foreign Affairs being the friend of Dr. King, and the Minister of Justice seeing the reasonableness of his demand, the citation was recalled.

Soon after this, in July, 1847, there appeared in one of the first Greek newspapers in Athens, certain articles, called "The Orgies of King," and signed by a man named "Konstantine Simonides," which produced such an excitement against Dr. King that the government was obliged to send soldiers to guard his house; and he was at length induced by the advice of the king and his ministers, amounting to little less than an order, to leave the country for a while till the excitement should abate; and so he fled to Geneva in Switzerland, where he remained for a time, then visited Sardinia, Tuscany, Rome, Naples, Sicily and Malta.

Soon after his departure from Athens, an order for his imprisonment was issued by one of the king's attorneys at Athens, and a new prosecution commenced on the accusation of proselytism brought against him in the

"Orgies," and a great number of persons, perhaps two hundred, as he was informed, were examined by the king's attorney at the criminal court, in order to find evidence to establish the charge.

The "Orgies" purported to be a description by an eye-witness of shameless scenes and ceremonies, such as the very name suggests, and carried on at night in Dr. King's house, under the guise of religious observances. Of Simonides it should be said, he seems to have been an unprincipled adventurer, used as a tool by the Archdeacon Leontius E. of Constantinople, the real author of the "Orgies." Simonides himself was set aside as a witness in one of the courts, as being "a servant dismissed by his master for stealing." In 1849 this same man brought forward some parchments which he said he had found in a monastery, and which he tried to palm off as writings of Homer, Hesiod, and Anacreon, more ancient than any others extant. These manuscripts attracted much attention. A committee of Greek scholars was appointed to examine them. This committee pronounced them to be forgeries, executed with great skill. Although masterpieces of calligraphy, the writer had failed, in some cases, to preserve the distinctive spelling or the form of letters peculiar to each epoch, and thus the deception was discovered. Thus too, did God still further vindicate the cause of Dr. King. The testimony of a man, proved to be a forger of ancient writings, could not be received concerning modern events.

Dr. King's enforced absence from home gave him opportunity to witness for Jesus in Italy and Rome it-

self; so that the truth was the "more abundantly scattered abroad." His name was already known; for this
persecution, though a "thing done in a corner" of Europe, could not be hid, and attention everywhere was
called to it.

Mr. and Mrs. W. W. Chester of New York, Dr.
Riggs and the Count de Gasparin all wrote, suggesting a
visit to America: but this idea, though a tempting one,
was after a few months abandoned.

In 1848, in consequence of the great revolution in
France, the ministry at Athens was changed, and the
new Minister of the Interior being friendly to Dr. King
he ventured to return to Athens, where he arrived from
Malta in June, and again resumed his missionary labors.
Not wishing that there should be any appearance of his
being in Athens in a clandestine way, he called on the
ministers of state, and was received by them very cordially. By advice of friends however, he did not hold public services until September.

March, 1851, Dr. King was appointed United States
consular agent. The hand of God appears in this, just
in time of need; for popular excitement had again been
aroused in regard to the preaching of pure Bible doctrines.

Saturday, March 22, the journal has this simple entry: "Opened a tin-box, which was sealed, and took out
the American flag, which at the request of Mr. Dioma-
tari, consul, had been sent from Washington for the
American Consulate at Athens."

The same evening Dr. King learned that some members of the House of Representatives, perhaps even its president or vice-president, would probably attend his service the next day, that they might judge themselves as to his teachings; but he told his informant that would make no difference, his sermon was prepared and he should make no changes.

The next morning, Sunday, he says, "I felt calm, and committing all my concerns for time and eternity into the hands of my Creator, feeling that if my life should be taken, I should go to be with Christ which is better than to be here, I went down to my service. On entering the room I found it crowded to overflowing. More than a hundred, perhaps a hundred and fifty, were present. All arose. I bowed to them and took my seat as usual. At my right hand, and close to me, I observed a soldier with a short sword, and the thought entered my mind for a moment, that perhaps he had come to do me harm. Near him was a secretary from the House of Representatives. In the room there was no place for the females, not even for my wife." After two or three minutes, Dr. King arose, offered prayer and went on with the usual services. As soon as the benediction was pronounced, a student in the university, who was a nephew of the late patriarch of Constantinople, came forward, and said he wished to make one remark. Dr. King answered, "If it is with regard to my discourse to-day, and nothing that will bring on a discussion, well; if not, I do not wish it." "He said, 'Yes, with regard to what was said to-day,' and began by saying, that I had remarked that Cain killed Abel, because his own works

were evil, and his brother's righteous; and that all that
persecute and kill their brethren because they believe in
Christ and are good people, are actuated by the same
spirit by which Cain was actuated; that in this remark
I had intimated that they were such because they persecute me.

"Here I interrupted him and said, 'I spoke of no
one in particular, but in general ; but if what I had said
fitted any one here, of course he might receive it.'

"He then began to speak of what I had said on other
Sundays contrary to the dogmas of the Holy Eastern
Apostolical Church ; but I again interrupted him, saying,
that if his remarks were not confined to my discourse this
day, I did not wish them: that if he wished, I would ap-
point some other day when all might come, and hear
what he had to say.

"At this, different voices were heard saying, 'Now,
now, let him speak ! We wish it now ! We are all concerned in this business; it is an affair of religion,' etc.,
and many became somewhat noisy.

"At this juncture my wife made her way through the
crowd to the table at which I was standing, and told the
priest, or deacon, or monk, that she would not have him
talking here in this manner; that this was our house,
and not a theatre or public place in which he could take
such liberty. I finally thought it would be best, perhaps, to let him speak, and said so to my wife; but she
said 'No ;' and then I said to the audience that as my wife
did not wish it he must desist; that this was a private
house, and not only so, but the Consulate of the United

States. Then one N. G. rather insulted my wife, and told her that the woman did not rule; and she said to him that he must go somewhere else to talk ; and he said, ' Where ?' and she said, ' Where you like ;' and he said, ' To the temple of Olympian Jupiter,' and then pressed along through the crowd as if to go out, crying, ' Let us go ! let us go !' But seeing not many ready to go he returned, and now the vociferation of those who were for and against became so great that the voice of my wife was drowned, and some of her female friends were frightened. Some beckoned to give me a beating, some beckoned to me to retire, and the tumult at last became so great, that telling them again that this was not only my private house, but the Consulate of the United States, I went up stairs and took the United States flag and gave it to my man Constantine, with whose aid I had it unfurled at the upper door of my house, and at the sight of this the crowd immediately dispersed.

" It seemed to me to be by a peculiar providence that the flag arrived just at this time, and that I had been led to take it out of the case the day previous, so that it was in readiness.

" I noticed another peculiar providence. The soldier who sat at my right-hand armed with a short sword, called on me afterwards, with Mr. Katachana, and told me that two or three days since he had heard that some fifteen persons were coming to my service, with intentions of using personal violence, and that he and another took a seat close by me, for my defence, but that many motions were made that they should begin to beat me."

To the credit of the Greek police, let it be said, that when they heard of the disturbance, they came and took the names of two or three of the ringleaders; and a military officer also called, and expressed regret at what had taken place.

Dr. King adds: "During all this time I felt perfectly tranquil, and should not have left the room, were it not that others beckoned for me to leave, and that I saw no other way to still the tumult but to go up and unfurl the American flag. Blessed be God, who has preserved me and given me such perfect peace of mind and joy in my work."

The effect of Dr. King's own glowing description of the power of the "Stars and Stripes" to protect an American citizen, cannot be reproduced here. During his last visit to America, as he told the story before the United States Senate, one may well imagine the thrill felt all through the audience. Every one, forgetting himself for a moment in thoughts of what our country's flag is everywhere able to do, gave loud vent to loyal enthusiasm.

But to return to Greece. On the Monday following the above demonstrations, Dr. King, by advice of his friends, sent to the Minister of Foreign Affairs a statement of the disturbance.

Petitions were soon made against him to the Greek synod, also to the Senate and House of Representatives, signed by forty or fifty names, and a new prosecution at law was commenced against him; and after the examination of many witnesses, an indictment was made out against him, "for reviling the God of the universe and the Greek religion."

In March, 1852, he was brought to trial, and "condemned to fifteen days' imprisonment, to pay the cost of the court, and then to be exiled from the country." In prison he appealed from this decision to the Areopagus, the highest court in Greece, which confirmed the sentence in all respects, except that the term of imprisonment was reduced from fifteen days to fourteen. On receiving the decision of the Areopagus, he sent to the Greek government a protest in the name of the United States government, against the unjust decision of the courts, and against the execution of it. This brought the Greek government to a stand, and the sentence of exile was not executed, though the Minister of the Interior, as Dr. King was told, declared that it should be; and Dr. King, in expectation of this, had all his effects packed ready for departure.

In the summer of 1852, the Hon. George P. Marsh, minister resident at Constantinople, came to Greece, by order of the United States government, "to investigate the whole affair of Dr. King's trial and condemnation," and also the affair of a lot of land, of which Dr. King had been deprived the free use for about twenty years by the Greek government, and to make report to the United States government relative to both cases. This investigation he made in the most splendid manner, and as very few men would have been capable of doing, and that on account of his knowledge of various languages, especially Greek, German, and French ; and he trusted

to no interpreter, but examined all the documents himself, as well as the laws which were intended to be applied to Dr. King. Having done this, he went to Italy
and made his report in the case to the United States
government, and in 1853, by the order of that government, returned to Athens, entered into correspondence
with the Greek government with regard to the settlement of the case; but as his presence was required at
Constantinople, he went away without bringing the ne-
gotiations to a close.

In March, 1854, the king of Greece, at the proposition of Pellicas, the Minister of Justice, who was one of
the distinguished lawyers who pleaded Dr. King's cause
before the courts of justice which condemned him, issued
an order, a copy of which was communicated to him by
the criminal courts, freeing him from the penalty of exile imposed upon him by that court, and confirmed by
the Areopagus in 1852.

So he remained in Greece and continued his labors
there, in the same way as previous to his prosecutions
and condemnation.

The above account is necessarily much condensed.
The full record is on file at the rooms of the A. B. C. F.
M., and no doubt open to examination.

The whole history is to the honor of our country, and
to that of the noble men called of God just then to guide
our ship of state—Daniel Webster, Edward Everett, Benjamin F. Butler, Secretary Marcy, President Fillmore,
Geo. P. Marsh, and Commodores Porter and Stringham,
and others. On one occasion, Commodore Stringham

sending for Dr. King to take tea on the "Cumberland," ordered a salute of nine guns, to give loud testimony of how the persecuted American missionary was regarded by his own countrymen.

The real point at issue all through the contest between Dr. King and the Greek hierarchy, was freedom to worship God. A precedent has been established not soon to be forgotten, and to God be all the glory.

CHAPTER XXI.

TOURS, TRAVELS, AND EVANGELICAL ALLI-ANCE.

Corinth—Smyrna—Thebes—Experience with Robbers—Constan-
tinople—Pesth—Maria Dorothea, Archduchess of Austria—
Jewish Converts—Vienna—Baron de Rothschild—Munich—
Reiche Kapelle—Paris—Geneva—Zurich—Italy—Rome—Sici-
ly—Malta—Evangelical Alliance at Berlin—King of Prussia—
Berlin.

THE tours, longer or shorter, which, undertaken in
the prosecution of family and missionary duties, or rendered necessary by persecution, varied Dr. King's life
in Greece, always afforded him many opportunities for
preaching the truth, besides proving sources of rest and
refreshment to himself. Near Corinth, on one occasion,
he writes, "On seeing some persons sitting by the side
of a hut, I asked them if they had no school in the place.
They said, 'Neither school nor priest.' 'What, have you
no priest?' 'No.' 'Well, then,' said I, 'after I have
taken something to eat, come to the place where I am
staying, and I will read to you from the words of our
Saviour.' In the course of an hour many assembled,
men, women, and children, and I took the Scriptures,
arose, and began to read from Christ's Sermon on the
Mount, and to expound. All listened with the greatest
attention. Mr. Riggs also made remarks, and when I
proposed to unite in prayer, several voices responded,

'Yes, yes.' So I offered a prayer with them, and gave the benediction. It did not occur to me at the time that it was the first Monday of the month, and the hour of prayer for many who love Zion."

Going to Syria in 1834, he says, "There were about fifty passengers on board. Read the Scriptures with them, and conversed much on a variety of religious subjects."

In March, 1836, Dr. King, taking his eldest daughter to Smyrna, on her way to America, met ten or more ministerial brethren who were holding meetings there for prayer and conference. It is only necessary to say that Messrs. Bird, Goodell, and Temple, were of the number—to prove how much all must have enjoyed such an interview. A sincere vote of thanks was passed to Mr. Van Lennep of Smyrna for his numberless attentions, not to those present alone, but to all the missionaries about the Mediterranean and in the East. It is but just to make note of this. The Lord has work for all his children. The Christian merchant as well as the preacher can do much in his own line to promote the cause of Christ on the earth.

A gathering of the missionaries was held again at Smyrna, in October, 1837, when Drs. Eli Smith, Dwight, Riggs, Benjamin, Calhoun, Messrs. Adger and Hallock, and Miss Danforth, still further swelled the number present. After the convention had closed, Dr. King, remaining to help settle up the estate of his father-in-law, who had died recently, preached in the Dutch church. A few days after, he received warning from the bishops, through the United States consul, that he could not preach again in Smyrna, except at the peril of his life, for there was great indignation against him.   He was particularly struck by this, for his text had been Acts 3 : 4 : "Being grieved that they taught the people, and preached through Jesus the resurrection of the dead."   The eighteenth verse reads, "And they called them and commanded them not to speak at all, nor teach in the name of Jesus."   The consul had been told that Dr. King called on Turks, Jews, and Greeks to renounce their religion ; but Dr. King told him this was not so, but that he had prayed for them all, and warned them to examine their faith by the Word of God.   The Patriarch had issued a strong letter just before this time against the Bible, and Dr. King thought it only right to preach in this manner.   His business in Smyrna was soon closed satisfactorily, so that he returned to Athens, and of course there was no further difficulty.

In 1838, on his way to another conference of missionaries, we find Dr. King stopping to comfort some wretched Sciotes by reading from the book of Job.

At Thalamic, a soldier who had once received books from him at Athens, took much pleasure in showing him around this supposed birthplace of the celebrated Helen.

In 1839, being in Thebes, the chief officer of police called and reminded Dr. King that he was formerly a scholar in his gymnasium, and said he was indebted to him for all he knew.   This led to Dr. King's being treated there with great attention.

From the highest peak of Mount Parnassus Dr. King

counted eight or ten other heights. Each Muse could thus have one to herself without interference from her sisters. At the Castilian fount Dr. King not only drank deeply *a* himself, but his groom talked of watering the horse also, until deterred by the laughter his master could not repress.

The way to Chalcis was infested with robbers. Still, Dr. King deciding to keep on his journey, the governor furnished him with a guard of soldiers. To one of the officers Dr. King had once given a trifle when he was in want, and this officer ordered one of his men to accompany him as far as Dadi. To him and another soldier of the phalanx Dr. King felt that, under God, he owed his subsequent safe journey, and in connection with this fact was reminded of the text, "Cast thy bread upon the waters," etc. It turned out that these very men were connected with the robbers, but their honor was pledged to defend Dr. King. One of these men confided to him that the members of the band were sworn to each other, that they have their own laws, and that they generally consecrate a part of their gains to some church or some saint. For instance, if there were ten robbers, they would make eleven shares, of which one was to be the Virgin Mary's, and this they were very careful to pay over; that the robbers with whom he was associated generally had the Panagia of Tenos as a partner, and that when they went out to rob, with her as a partner, they were always successful. This man also said that, by mistake, he and another had once killed a poor man having a wife and six children, instead of a rich man expected to pass on the road, and in the poor man's pocket they had found sixteen piastres only. He said he had repented of this a hundred times, and for ten years would not partake of the Lord's Supper. Dr. King talked to him very plainly, telling him to get a New Testament, and learn there what he must do in order to be saved. The man answered that if anything would do Greece good it was the gospel; that a soldier at Larnica had a New Testament, and was always reading it, and that it had kept him from much wickedness; that he himself had been much affected by reading a little book about a man that was sold, and put in prison, and interpreted some dreams, and he would give almost anything for a copy of it.

The impression made by the above journey was that Greece at that time was desolate and poor. One could ride for hours without seeing a single house or person. A great desire existed in the villages for education. Books were already exerting a very salutary influence.

In 1843, on account of ill-health, Dr. King made a journey to Smyrna and Constantinople, and thence over the Black Sea and up the Danube, and visited Hungary, Austria, Bavaria, Switzerland, France, and Italy, and returned to Athens in September of the same year.

At Constantinople games in honor of Easter were being celebrated over the graves in the burying-ground. The sultan's procession in honor of Mohammed's birthday, with the carriages for the women drawn by oxen, the sultan's dwarf, and the barbaric splendor, was a display of this world's pomp not often to be seen. But it was a richer treat to meet at Dr. Goodell's house some of the true aristocracy of earth, Dr. and Mrs. Perkins, Miss Fidelia Fiske, Miss Catherine Myers, Drs. Eli Smith, Dwight, Schauffler, and Hamlin, and Rev. Messrs. Bliss and David Stoddard. Mar Yohannan also was present, on his way back to Persia from the United States.

At Pesth, Dr. King received a hearty welcome from Messrs. Wingate and Smith, Scotch missionaries, who took him to their own lodgings. Having a letter of introduction from Mr. Schauffler to her imperial highness Maria Dorothea, Archduchess of Austria, he called upon her by appointment, and found her indeed a "nursing mother" to the cause of evangelical religion. "Conversed about an hour and a half on the great things of the kingdom of Christ. While with her, her little son came in, ten or eleven years of age, and I spoke to him on the subject of religion. I spoke in French, and the archduchess translated to him in German, as he knew but little French. I said about as follows : 'If one is the son of a king or emperor, he is thought to be happy, because he is heir to a throne or to a piece of earth which is called a kingdom ; but when one is born of God he is an heir of heaven, a joint heir with Christ to an inheritance which fadeth not away. A crown, a sceptre, riches, honors, a kingdom, cannot alleviate one pain of the body, not even of a tooth ; but the love of Christ can alleviate even the pains of death. My father was not a king, but he taught me in my childhood to read God's holy Word, and I owe everything to this. It taught me what was better than all the crowns, sceptres, and kingdoms of the whole world. Come to Christ, and you will be happy ;

live for Christ while you live, and you will be happy for ever.' The duchess thanked me for what I had said, and brought out her album, and wished me to write something in it with my name. So I wrote the forty-second verse of the tenth chapter of Luke, ' One thing is needful,' etc. Her little daughter also came in. Her name is Maria. I said only a word or two to her, and mentioned to the archduchess that I came from Constantinople to Kustandy in the steamer which bears her name, and in which I went with my daughter Mary to Smyrna seven years ago, when I sent her to America. At this she seemed delighted, and said, ' The day it was launched was my birthday, and I prayed to God that many missionaries might be conveyed in that boat.'

" She asked me if I was acquainted with the Countess de St. Aulaire; spoke of her in the highest terms, and said she should write to her that she had seen me. When I got up to come away, I said, ' I am happy to have had the pleasure of seeing you.' She replied, ' It is a friendship formed for life.'

" My heart was much affected by this visit and seeing her so devoted to the Saviour. From the palace had a beautiful view of the city of Pesth, which is the capital of Hungary, and contains about a hundred thousand inhabitants. On my way back I learned from Messrs. Wingate and Smith that the establishment of their mission was in consequence of Dr. Keith's having been detained here by illness. The archduchess, in consequence of a dream, was led to seek him out, and to administer aid to him with her own hand, and in return received spiritual comfort with regard to the loss of a beloved child. Dr. Keith told her she was violating the eighth commandment by wishing to take from God what he had claimed as his own. This had an effect on her heart. She had mourned excessively. She was converted by means of her mother, her royal highness the Duchess Hen‚ riette of Wurtemberg, who is also an eminent Christian."

With the *grand maîtresse* of the palace Dr. King had much serious conversation, and was treated by her with marked respect. He visited with her and the Countess of Brunswick, whom he calls "a lovely Christian sister who had never formally left the Roman-catholic church," an infant school, also a hospital for poor, aged females, which had been founded by the archduchess. There were thirty-seven inmates. One of them, the daughter of a Protestant minister at Wurtemburg, had been bed-ridden for fifty-six years, but still seemed very happy. Upon occasion of a second visit to the archduchess, one of the first men of the nation, the leader of the Roman-catholics, came in, and Dr. King found opportunity to preach him quite a little sermon.

At Pesth a most interesting work was going on among the Jews. Dr. King writes that he heard of and saw here wonderful things, as may be seen from the following extracts:

"Dr. Keith and Dr. Black (Professor at Aberdeen) had arrived at Pesth in 1839, having parted from the Rev. Mr. McCheyne and Bonar at Constantinople. At Pesth Dr. Keith was taken ill, and obliged to remain there several months. The archduchess, who had long been praying that some one might be sent to preach the gospel at Pesth, hearing that he was ill, said, ' This is in answer to my prayers ; this is the man !' and went to see him, and attended to him in person. While here, Dr. Keith was much exercised in his mind for Hungary, and often prayed for it. The archduchess said that he spent at one time three hours in prayer in pleading for this people. He went to Scotland afterwards, and made a report, and proposed to the Church of Scotland the establishment of a mission at Pesth, and the Rev. Dr. Duncan of the Scotch church, who had previously devoted himself to the Jews, was selected for this station, and sent, with his family, accompanied by Mr. Allen and Mr. Smith, in the year 1841. After meeting with some difficulties, he succeeded in establishing a service for the English, a few of whom were providentially residing in this city. At first very few attended ; but the congregation gradually increased, till finally it amounted, of all nations, to forty or fifty. It was soon known to the Jewish community that Dr. Duncan was a good Hebrew and Arabic scholar, and this induced some of the more learned Jews to visit him. For a considerable time not much fruit appeared. Still they labored as they had opportunity. Mr. Allen taught English. Gradually their influence increased. The Jews began to speak of the manner in which Dr. Duncan's household was conducted, according to the Word of God, and different in many respects from all around him. Many of the Jews who knew English came and attended his English service. The first who was impressed, or showed some signs of life, was old Mr. Saphir, whom Dr. Keith had known, and with whom he corresponded. Mr. Saphir had projected the principal Jewish school in Hungary, a model school, after which others were formed. In this school about three hundred boys were taught. He was esteemed one of the most learned Jews in Hungary. When he was fifty-four years of age he studied English for the purpose of reading English literature ; and this became in the providence of God one of the means of his conversion, followed by that of his family and of a number of other Jews. Persecution ensued. Mr. Saphir lost his position, but was accepted as missionary by one of the churches of Scotland at Edinburgh. The secret of the wonderful change is found in the following fact : " There is in Edinburgh a society composed of ladies, and another in Glasgow, for the purpose of sending the gospel to Jewish females by means of schools or otherwise. In Glasgow the wives of thirty-six ministers are in the direction of the society. They meet every Wednesday, from twelve till two, for prayer." There are similar meetings in other parts of Scotland, to pray particularly for the Jews. Money was also raised. One of the converts at Pesth was a young man whom the Jews had begged to write against Christianity, and he had actually arranged the heads for a book when he resolved to study the New Testament with prayer. He came to hear Dr. King preach, and seemed much affected—said he believed the New Testament was the Word of God. All those who were converted had been subjects of individual prayer, some of them by the Archduchess Maria Dorothea. A servant-girl was brought in through seeing the change of conduct produced in her employer's family through the gospel.

When Dr. King left Pesth many friends "accompanied him to the ship," or rather steamer. His heart was very much affected by the kindness received there, and he stood looking toward the palace and city until the Palatine Island hid them from view. He afterwards kept up some correspondence with the archduchess and other friends in Hungary. On the steamer one of the passengers, about thirty years of age, and having his wife and child on board, expressed much surprise on hearing Dr. King was an American, for he thought they were black and were all cannibals.

At Vienna Dr. King was invited to dinner twice by the Baron de Rothschild, who seemed inclined to be very sociable with him ; called the Van Lenneps " Les braves gens," and listened with earnest attention to what Dr. King told him of Palestine and the needs of the Jews there.

Dr. King met here the Metropolitan of all the Greeks in Austria, having ten bishops under him, and had a long conversation with him on the importance of having the Holy Scriptures taught to all the people. He replied that the Roman-catholics consider it a crime for young persons to read the Scriptures, but that he considered them necessary, and that he was about to issue an order that all students who are to be priests should study the Hebrew and Greek, because the Bible was written in those languages.

At Munich Dr. King was again introduced into royal

circles. He had become acquainted in Athens with the Count Saporte, who was court marshal. Going to the palace to find him, he met him in one of the courts. "He took me by the hand like a brother; took me to his own house, and made arrangements to have me presented to the queen; then he went with me to the palace, got me presented to the two younger sisters of King Otho, Hildegarde and Alexandra, and to his young brother Adelbert." They visited the palace and the curiosities together. "With the sisters of Otho I had a good deal of conversation, and was enchanted with them— amiable, intelligent, and easy in manner. Spoke with them on the importance of Christians of all denominations uniting to do good; told them how the first crown their brother received at Athens was given him by the scholars of my gymnasium." In the queen's reception-room Dr. King was first introduced to the Duchess of Leuchtenberg, aunt to King Otho, also to the princess royal, a niece of the king of Prussia. "The queen soon came out to see me. We spoke of Greece and Palestine, my mission there, of her Imperial Highness Maria Dorothea, etc., and she expressed her pleasure at seeing me, and said, 'I shall write to my son Otho that I have seen you.' She is just twenty-one days younger than I am, and very sweet and mild in her appearance. Count Saporte showed me the 'argenterie' of the king. The quantity of gold and silver vessels is immense. Next he sent a man to open the Reiche Kapelle, which is indeed properly so called, for I doubt whether there are greater riches in so small a compass in any part of Europe. The

floor is of precious stones, its walls of mosaic, its altar
with all the images of solid silver, as also the pipes of
the organ, the ceiling inlaid with gold, several closets
full of vases and crucifixes of gold and precious stones.
Though I have seen of late so many precious things, yet
I was astonished at the riches of this chapel, which is
perhaps not more than twelve or fifteen feet square. In
different vases were relics, so called: the hands of St.
Dionysius, St. Chrysostom, St. John the Baptist, the finger of St. Peter, the thigh-bone of St. Matthias, the jaw-
bone of some saint whose name I have forgotten. In
one vase I saw some earth which was said to be stained
with the blood of our Saviour when he was crucified.
Among other things was a small portable altar which
belonged to Mary Queen of Scots, who performed her
devotions before it when in prison, and at the moment
she laid her head on the block she gave it to an attend-
ant. I was told there had been offered for this a million
of florins. I took it in my hand. It doubles up in a
very small compass, and can easily be carried in the
pocket, being, say, three inches long, two and a half
wide, and half an inch thick.

"King Ludwig of Bavaria, though he has a small
kingdom, has seventy-five palaces. The University
building is the most splendid thing of the kind I ever
saw."

Leaving Munich, Dr. King took his seat for the first
time in a railroad car; in fact he had never seen a railroad
before. Continuing on his way he arrived in Paris in
July, 1843, and felt quite overcome there by the associa-

tions and recollections of his stay there twenty years before, but of his early friends "some were scattered, some were dead." Of those remaining, the Duke de Broglie and the Countess of St. Aulaire were out of town. Mr. Adolphe Monod, however, and Pastor Grandpierre, received him with open arms, and at a prayer meeting held at the house of the former, Dr. King soon found himself at home, and before long other of his friends returning gave him the warm greeting always so much prized by the stranger. On his return through Switzerland Dr. King notes, with peculiar interest, interviews held with the Count and Countess de Gasparin, with the sentiments of whose books he had in general fully sympathized. The close tie which laborers in the mission field, both East and West, feel for each other, was shown by the pains which Dr. King took to visit the little Swiss village of Orbes, from which Madame Feller had gone to her work at Grande Ligne, Canada.

At Geneva Dr. King met Mrs. Dr. Baird, Col. Tronchin, and Drs. Malan and Gaussen. The widow of his friend, the Baron De Staël, was also there, and sent for him to come to her home at Coppet. Dr. King writes that "she said that the ten months of her union with the baron were months of unmingled pleasure, without a cloud, and when he was taken away she would not be comforted Then her child, two years after, was taken away, then her sister-in-law, the Duchess de Broglie, but now she feels that all is well." Of her home, Dr. King writes: "It is a fit place for study, meditation and prayer. Here Madame De Staël wrote in former times when the world was full of noise, and revolution and terror; here her daughter, the Duchess de Broglie, meditated sublimer themes, and spoke of things far more interesting than philosophy and politics. It seems as if some age long gone by had returned, as if the dial had turned back a hundred years; and how soon I too shall go the way of all the earth and be silent as those whose shades now pass before me."

While in Geneva, Dr. King took the opportunity of buying the watch he afterwards carried, with money given him for the purpose by l'Admiral Count Verhuell.

In 1847, during his time of persecution, Dr. King was urged, indeed almost commanded by the king, and some personal friends, as has before been stated, to leave Athens for a while, and he decided to go first into Germany and Switzerland. At a parting service held at Mr. Buel's, at the Piræus, Dr. King was much comforted by means of a prayer offered by Miss Waldo, as also by singing with his friends the hymn, "Jesus, I my cross have taken." Landing at Patmos, some men in a restaurant were overheard saying, "There is King. Let us stone him." Another said, "He has doubtless been sent here to be tried, and we shall then have the opportunity." To this an old man replied, "It is better to take a knife and go to his door, and watch him as he comes out some evening." At Corfu, Lord Seaton received Dr. King very kindly, inviting him to breakfast at his palace. Passing through Venice and Vicenza by car, Dr. King came to Trent, famous for its council; and in the record-book, kept there for travellers, he inscribed the following words, as a sort of protest against the errors once endorsed there : "'The counsel of the Lord, that shall stand.' Jonas King, Aug. 12, 1847."

Through the "beautiful country" of Bulgaria, yet "defiled by idols set up for worship by the sides of the road," our refugee went on to Innspruck, crossing the Alps, missing his baggage, comforted as a stranger in a hotel by overhearing some unknown fellow-traveller at prayer, who, while enjoying communion with his Saviour, knew not he was being used as a means of blessing to another. At Constance was to be seen a statue of Abraham, much defaced, which the people took for one of Huss, or perhaps Jerome of Prague. Zurich, the home of Zwingle, next claimed attention. Here Dr. King called on Prof. Langé, since so well known, and whom he speaks of as "friendly to missions." All this change of scene and this Christian intercourse was the very medicine needed by Dr. King. At Berne he attended one or more sessions of the Diet, and tells of the quaint customs as to dress, handed down from olden time. Lauzanne and Geneva he was glad to revisit, finding there friends old and new—Baptist Noël, Merle d'Aubigné, Prof. Tholuck, and others. Conversation turned often upon the Evangelical Christian Alliance, formed the year before at London. Dr. King was made at home at the house of Mr. Rivier, one of whose daughters was Madame G. de Félice.

Dr. King next spent a part of his exile in Italy.

Sir Culling Eardley had given him a letter of introduction to the Count Pietro Guicciardini at Florence, who in a private conversation said that he was convinced of the errors of his church, and that this change came from reading some passages of Scripture. He said also, that a law still existed condemning to the galleys a man guilty of heresy, though he doubted whether it would now be put in execution.

At St. Peter's Dr. King was struck with the suggestive arrangement by which the throne of the Pope was supported by statues of St. Chrysostom on the right and St. Athanasius on the left, Greek saints, and St. Ambrose and St. Augustine, Latin Saints. He was glad to know of this from personal observation, because he could now appeal with more effect to certain portions of the works of these fathers against the worship of the Virgin Mary, and in regard to the importance of reading the Sacred Scriptures. Of all the objects he saw at Rome, the Coliseum affected him the most. There multitudes of Christians had formerly been put to death. As he walked over the arena he could almost hear the cry, " How long, O Lord, dost thou not judge and avenge our blood on them that dwell on the earth."

Descriptions are given by Dr. King of Pompeii, Herculaneum, of Virgil's tomb, &c., with all the delicate appreciation of a Christian scholar ; but all through Italy it was trying to see the grand facts of our religion scandalized by puerile representations. Thus, however, was he still better prepared to testify against such perversions.

At Messina, Sicily, he found the Cyclops still existed in the form of police officers, who, with four eyes instead of one, looked at everything and suspected everything

as much as if he had come from the moon. Visiting the
Cathedral there, he had a ladder brought so as to read for
himself a letter set high up above the altar, purporting to
be written to the city by the Virgin Mary, daughter of
James.   Dr. King next spent a few weeks at Malta.
Here he was able to watch more closely the course of
events at home, and was soon gladdened by a visit from
his wife and son.   The welcome given to a new missionary, Mr. Johnson, brought to mind his own arrival there
twenty-six years before.   His present stay at Malta,
while waiting, "like a bird on a bush, with one wing up
and ready to fly at any moment back to Athens," was
not ill spent.   The "Farewell Letter" was revised, and
editions of it put through the press, and into circulation;
and other missionary work was accomplished, especial
efforts being made to give the Gospel to Italy, Even at
this time a call came for three thousand Italian Bibles.
Copies of the "Farewell Letter" were sent into Tuscany,
and found their way to Constantinople, and into Egypt.
Has the sowing of such seed no relation to the progress
of liberty and Protestantism, as now seen in the kingdom
of Italy?

Dr. King made no further journey in Europe until
1857, when the desires of his heart were indeed fulfilled,
for he was then present at the meeting of the Evangelical Alliance, held that year at Berlin. A more impressive
scene he never witnessed, than when English and American Episcopalians, Methodists, Baptists and Presbyterians, Congregationalists, French, Swiss, Spanish and
Germans, all, as one in Christ, communed with each other

around His one table. The Dean of Canterbury and Dr.
Wm. Patton of New York took direction of the service.
Next comes mention of Bishop Simpson, beloved in all
all the churches, who delivered, says Dr. King, "one of
the most impressive discourses I ever heard. It was admirable, and I felt how much I had lost in personal enjoyment by being absent so long from my native country."

Friday, September 11, the members of the Alliance,
as a nucleus, and others, in all about nine hundred persons, went by a special train, ordered by the king, to visit
him at Potsdam. "On arriving at the palace we found
a suite of splendid rooms, with tables covered with re-
freshments, of which all partook. We walked through
several of the rooms, which were open, and among them
was the one that Voltaire occupied in the time of Frederick the Great, and who said that twelve foolish men
had invented Christianity, and that one man would destroy it. Here the king, a successor of Frederick, received us in the kindest manner, using all his influence to
promote Christianity and Christian union. At about five
P. M. the king and queen and suite arrived, and received
us in front of the palace, in companies, according to our
respective nations.

"The first he met, on coming out of the palace, was
the German Committee, a member of which addressed a
few words to the king, saying that we had come, an army,
but not with swords to fight, or with earthly armor, but
to pray for his majesty, etc. The king replied that he
hoped the Spirit would be poured out upon us, as on the
day of Pentecost. He then came to the Americans, some

forty in number, at the head of whom was our worthy minister, Governor Wright, to whom the king gave his hand in the most cordial manner, and also to Dr. Baird, and said, 'Oh, I am so glad to see you.' I was then presented, and then Dr. Dwight, Bishop Simpson, and others. Dr. Dwight addressed a few words to his majesty, expressing his gratitude for what the Prussian ambassador had done at Constantinople in aiding the missionaries, and mentioned a school at Smyrna in which, Dr. Dwight told me, the king took a particular interest. The king seemed affected even to tears. He then went to the English, at the head of whom stood Sir Culling Eardley, who addressed him, and then introduced several of his distinguished countrymen. The delegates from other nations were presented also. The king spent with us, I should think, an hour and a half. The queen was present all the time with her maids of honor, and I and several others were presented to her, and she received us with the greatest simplicity. As the king and queen were retiring into the palace, the multitude who had been presented sang a hymn, and shouts of joy, 'Long live the king,' in various languages, were heard from the whole assembly, like the roaring of the waves of the sea. We were then, by the same train that brought us, conveyed to Berlin, where we arrived about eight or nine in the evening. All hearts were glad, and all praised God for having inclined the heart of the king thus to favor the meeting of the Evangelical Alliance."

For nine days the meetings continued. "The king attended three or four times, and sat each time for an

hour and a half or two hours, and gave the strictest attention.   On the eighth day, Dr. Dwight was called upon to
speak, and I followed.   The king was present, and perhaps four thousand people.   As I turned to go away, Dr.
Krummacher took me by the hand most cordially, and so
did Dr. Barth and others."

Dr. King was one of a committee sent the next day
to wait on the Emperor Alexander of Russia, and present
a certain document, which had been drawn up in English,
French, and German, to solicit his interposition in favor
of the distribution of the Bible in his dominions in the
Russ language.   The emperor had been reviewing about
forty thousand troops, and was about to leave Berlin;
but the king of Prussia, notwithstanding his extra fatigue,
received the deputation, and expressed himself as much
pleased with the addresses, one of which was made by
Dr. King.

An occasion of peculiar interest, as foreshadowing
that true Christian union of which the grand gathering
in New York in 1873 was a glorious exemplification, was a
dinner given by Sir Culling Eardly at his hotel, to which
Dr. and Mrs. King and daughter were invited.   After
speeches made in various languages, Rev. Mr. Alford,
Dean of Canterbury, closed with an extemporaneous
prayer, "most beautifully appropriate in every respect."

Going on to Paris, Dr. King met there his old friend
Sidney E. Morse and M. de Tassy.   He made at this
time a very short stay in Paris, returning by as direct
a route as possible to his home and work at Athens.

CHAPTER XXII.

LAST VISIT TO AMERICA.

Many Changes—Warm Welcomes—Dr. W. A. Hallock—Hawley and Plainfield, Mass.—Old Elm-tree—Chicago—Rochester—Clifton Springs—New Haven—Meeting with Dr. Goodell at Elizabeth, N. J.

DR. KING remained at his post until 1864, when, his health being much impaired, he came, in July, with his wife, to the United States, remaining about three years.

While received everywhere with warm and respectful attention, he could yet realize with Wordsworth, that there are some advantages connected with " Yarrow unvisited." Dr. Hallock had given him warning of many changes, especially in his native place. But Dr. King's daughters, who were in this country, vied with each other in securing his presence and their mother's at their several homes.

A few of his old friends still survived. His meeting at Elizabeth, N. J., with S. V. S. Wilder, now in his eighty-fourth year, was indeed one of peculiar interest. As Dr. King, his own head now touched with silver, entered the room, he said, " I once had a friend ; when I asked him, 'What shall I do ?' he said to me, 'Go.' 'But what will become of my aged father and mother in America ?' " I will be a son to them.' 'Then,' said I, 'I will go up to Jerusalem, not knowing the things that shall

befall me there.'" The whole scene was in keeping with
the touch of romance that had ever attended intercourse
between these two honored servants of our Lord; and
when, the following year, the older friend was called to
his home above, no one took more interest than Dr. King
in doing honor to his memory, aiding by most valuable
contributions in preparing the Records published by the
American Tract Society concerning him. Long before,
in 1836, Dr. King, on occasion of his own birthday, had
written to Mr. Wilder: "Is it possible that eight years
have elapsed since I saw you? With what rapid pace
are we travelling on toward the eternal world! We shall
soon meet, if we are in Christ, never to separate. There
we shall, I trust, spend hours more happy than those at
Nanterre, or in the little boudoir at Paris. All the comforts we receive here in our souls are but an earnest of
the Spirit—a near foretaste of the joys which shall be
hereafter revealed. May your path be like that of the
shining light which shineth more and more unto the perfect day. Yours in the best of bonds, JONAS KING." The
time of separation was short; Dr. King followed his
friend to heaven in a little more than four years.

Hawley, his native place, and Plainfield, Mass., too,
were points of interest to the returned wanderer from foreign lands. One can hardly imagine the old elm-tree as
quite devoid of feeling, as came again under its now wide-
sheltering arms the worn missionary, who in his boyhood
had consecrated himself to Christ under its young shadow.
The hills, the woods, the landscape were there as of old-
en time. Few changes had come into the quiet country

town of Hawley; yet "its sound had gone out into all the earth," had been repeated in the courts of the Areopagus, and with its neighbor, Plainfield (where had been educated in a school taught by the Rev. Moses Hallock fifty ministers of the gospel, of whom ten were missionaries), it stands in silent testimony of what God can do, using for his own glory and the good of souls places so obscure that but little is expected from them.

Dr. King visited many parts of this country, spending some time at Chicago, where he received much kindness from Gov. Bross and others; also at Rochester.

By invitation of Dr. Henry Foster, Dr. King spent three weeks at Clifton Springs, N. Y., and found his stay there of decided benefit to his health, enjoying at the same time the society of the many Christian friends always to be found at this modern Bethesda.

At New Haven it was pleasant to meet again Mrs. Pelatiah Perit, as also at New York Mrs. T. C. Doremus, with her home ever open to the missionary.

At Bible, Tract, and Missionary meetings, in city or in country places, Dr. King's marked and venerable countenance was, during this last visit, ever most welcome. To younger members of our churches his presence was almost as if one rose from the dead. He often afterwards referred to one evening as of special interest. His old friends, Dr. and Mrs. Goodell of Constantinople, and daughters, had come for a few days on a visit to Elizabeth, N. J. Dr. King also was there at the same time. Other Christian friends living in the neighborhood were invited in to share in the pleasure of meeting these two veteran soldiers of the cross.   It was an occasion for prayer and praise.   The pastor of the family, Rev. Dr. William C. Roberts, who had become acquainted with these missionaries in their Eastern homes, and whose church Dr. King, while visiting one of his daughters and other friends, attended for several months, led in the services, and was able, in his own native Welsh, to join in the chorus of the favorite hymn of Dr. Goodell. Can we doubt that the Master of Assemblies heard, as in Arabic, Armenian, French, English, and Welsh, the invitation, " Come to Jesus just now," was given in such various as well as heartfelt tones ?

But time passed on, and although enjoying the many welcomes given them to the homes of their children and of Christian friends, Dr. and Mrs. King felt that their steps must turn homeward to the East.

A few friends, Mr. E. C. Benedict, Amos Clark, Jr., William E. Dodge, E. A. Saxton, Mahlon Mulford, W. W. Chester, J. B. Sheffield, Theodore Dwight, R. T. Haines, Mrs. Thomas C. Doremus, and Mrs. Alling of Rochester, together with Mr. King's sons-in-law, made strenuous efforts to retain him in this country by securing for him a home here ; but strong ties drew both himself and Mrs. King to Athens : and " so it came," as John Bunyan says, and as is recorded of the apostles, "they were let go in peace."   It was a parting such as that of Paul from Miletus.   Of the long-known and beloved missionary, also, it may be said, his friends " sorrowed most of all " that in this world they would probably "see his face no more."

CHAPTER XXIII.

RETURN TO GREECE—DEATH IN 1869.

Paris Revisited—Missionary Reunion—The Past and Present of Palestine—Rev. Mr. Jessup—Athens—Letter to Mrs. Doremus, Wilder, and Perit—His Sickness, and Death—Dr. King's Manner and Character, in Letters from Mrs. Kalopothakes—His own Review of his Missionary Life.

DR. AND MRS. KING returned to Greece in the autumn of 1867.

In Paris, which Dr. King found "much improved and beautiful, but not so dear" to his heart after all as some of the cities of his native land, a pleasant incident met him at the Greek consulate. On entering the office, the consul rose to meet him, and said, "Are you not Dr. King?" and added, "Why, I used to attend your service on the Sabbath;" and then gave him the most cordial welcome possible, and showed him every mark of respect before the other Greeks present. Thus did Greece meet her returning missionary halfway, on his return for the last time to her ancient shores.

Of the Paris Exposition, then open, Dr. King writes as one might now the better do of the more elaborate display by which America celebrated her centennial: "It is splendid. On entering, one feels as if he were in a fairy wilderness of beauty, where, as if by magic, everything most exquisite of nature and of art has been assembled from every part of the globe."

But the "heights of Zion" afford a wider scope of vision than "all the kingdoms of this world, and the glory of them," in their relations to the present alone, can ever do. A glimpse of such does a correspondent of the New York "Observer," A. C. P., give, under the heading, "Dr. Jonas King in Paris," in the following account of services singularly appropriate held during his last visit there:

"PARIS, November 17, 1867.

"I have just had the pleasure of attending a very interesting meeting of welcome to Dr. Jonas King, held by the Evangelical Missionary Society, under which he went out as a missionary forty-five years ago.

"Dr. King was requested to give some account of the condition of Palestine, and of his work while there, and was introduced to the audience by the Rev. Dr. Grand-pierre, who presided. Dr. King spoke nearly an hour to an audience intensely interested, and moved to smiles and tears at his simple history.

"Especially were they affected by the story of the 'Martyr of Lebanon, Asaad El-Shidiak.' When Dr. King mentioned how, being called to choose between kissing an image of the Virgin and a coal of fire, he pressed the burning coal to his lips, an audible murmur was heard in the assembly.

"The speaker, being urged to continue his address, gave a brief account of his work in Greece during nearly half a century. He spoke in French, and it was a marvel to all how he could speak so fluently and correctly, after being so long unused to the language.

"At the conclusion of Dr. King's address, Dr. Grand-pierre arose and grasped his hand, bidding him God-speed in his work, and expressing his pleasure at being permitted to meet him again in Paris.

"Rev. Dr. Casalis, Director of the Mission House, followed with a short address of welcome and thanks in the name of all present. He spoke of Dr. King's assistance in the organization of the Society, and of his influence in causing himself to become a missionary in South Africa. Dr. Casalis read part of a letter from Dr. King to the Society in 1823, which was very pertinent to the object of the meeting.

"The Rev. Mr. Jessup, who was in the city a few days, on his way home from Syria, was then introduced as one able to give information of Palestine as it *now* is. He spoke in English, and Rev. Mr. Fisch interpreted it admirably. Mr. Jessup alluded to the work done by the pioneer missionaries, Revs. Dr. King, Pliny Fisk, and Levi Parsons, and said that, overlooking the grave of Mr. Fisk at Beyrout, were now established steam-presses, turning out copies of that gospel for which he had laid down his life, and for which Asaad El Shidiak suffered and died. He stated that in all that region every priest, every man, woman, and child knows the story of Asaad, and why he died. So he by his death yet speaks, and to a class difficult of access by the truth. It was beautiful, this mingling of the past and the present of France and America. There sat Dr. King, the modern Paul of Athens, the representative of the fearless and faithful laborers who forty years ago broke up the ground for the seed to spring up afterwards ;

and here stood Mr. Jessup, the no less earnest worker, who is gathering in its fruits to-day. The work of one is nearly completed, that of the other we will pray may be continued yet many years. And the little band of French Protestants, whose lot has been so hard in this great Catholic country, must have been encouraged by the friendly words of their American brothers. Many came forward to shake hands with the two missionaries, and one of the French pastors remarked : ' These Americans are made of granite, we of dough.' Dr. King replied, ' It is you who say it, not I.' This Society, whose first missionary was Dr. King, was established in 1822. In 1821, when Dr. King came to Paris, there was but one evangelical preacher, the Rev. Frederic Monod, then just entering upon his career of usefulness. Adolphe Monod, whose name is familiar to Americans, and his brother William (or Guillaume) followed after. The last of these gifted brothers, a lonely old man, still remains. He it was who made the impressive prayer at our good meeting. He often alludes to a conversation with Dr. King nearly half a century ago, as being the means of turning him from Unitarianism to orthodoxy. He spoke of it to Mrs. King at his own house this week.

"It was exceedingly gratifying to Dr. King to be so cordially welcomed among the French Protestants of Paris. I think the meeting did us all good. As Rev. Mr. Fisch said, it was quite a remarkable and beautiful incident that Mr. Jessup should have been present to follow up Dr. King's account with a statement of the present condition of the country in which he had labored. The contrast between then and now was very striking; as also in Paris, where forty evangelical ministers now stand up in the place of one! May the good work progress continually."

When arrived at home, Dr. King never had strength to undertake much missionary labor. Dr. Kalopothakes, Mr. Constantine, and M. Sakellarius each had established Bible classes and Sunday-schools; and Dr. King wisely refrained from holding a separate service of his own.

Dr. Anderson states that "in April, 1868, a distinguished professor in the University arranged for an interview between Dr. King and the President of the ' Holy Synod.' This man, in 1863, signed the accusation against Dr. King, in consequence of which, after his return to Greece, he was a third time cited before the criminal court, though without any result. The interview was altogether pleasant, and was a striking illustration of the progress of public opinion. 'A considerable degree of religious liberty has been gained,' writes the missionary, 'and a foundation has been laid on which, I trust, will one day arise a beautiful superstructure.'"

Dr. King employed a part of his time in revising plans he had already drawn up in view of the organization of a distinctively Protestant Greek Church.

Such a candlestick has now been lighted in Athens. A neat and beautiful church building, since 1874, witnesses for Jesus, a true altar to the "Unknown God," once worshipped there.

In this waiting time, Dr. King's thoughts turned

warmly to his early friends, as a letter from Athens, bearing date January 26, 1869, best testifies.

"To Mrs. T. C. Doremus, Mrs. S. V. S. Wilder, Mrs. Peletiah Perit:

"My very dear friends: I often think of you, the only remaining three of the nine of whom the Ladies' Greek Committee consisted; by whose invitation, and under whose auspices I came out to Greece, nearly forty-one years ago, and in connection with whom I labored with so much pleasure for two years or more, before I received from the American Board my appointment as its missionary in this country.

"Six of the nine have gone to their rest, as I doubt not, in the world above, and are now in those mansions which our Saviour long ago went to prepare for his followers, that they might be with him where he is, and behold his glory, the glory of the only begotten of the Father, full of grace and truth.

"I think of you, who remain, as probably approaching the time of your departure, as I am that of mine, from this world, in which you have so long labored for the good of many, and my prayer to God is often that when that time shall come, which I hope may not be till after many more useful and happy years, you may have grace given you from on high, so as to overcome all fears of death, and rejoice in the prospect of having a better and happier life than we can have here in the body exposed to so many trials, encompassed by so many infirmities; and in this world where sin and death reign, rejoice in the prospect of life without sorrow, pain, or sin, life eternal.

"I often think of your great generosity, and the kindness you showed me more than forty years ago, and during the time of my late visit to my native land: and from one of your number nearly half a century ago, when I was a stranger in a foreign land, and who, when I was a sick and nigh unto death, visited me and administered to my wants; and who, with her beloved husband, who now rests from his labors, when I began to recover, received me into their house, and by their Christian kindness contributed much toward my restoration to health, so that I was enabled to go out as a missionary to the land where patriarchs and prophets once lived, the apostles of our Lord and Saviour labored, and where he poured out his soul unto death for our sins, and the sins of the world.

"To your generosity and kindness, my dear friends, I owe much, and shall remember you with gratitude, esteem, and affection, as long as I live.

"I am now nearly seventy-seven years old, and have been absent from my country for the greater part of half a century; but I feel that my heart is as warm as ever; and that my love for my country and my friends, time and distance can never abate.

"With affectionate remembrance to the members of your respective families, with whom I have the pleasure to be acquainted, I remain,

"Yours truly,
"JONAS KING."

The "last of earth" was soon at hand. Dr. King "passed away" May 22, 1869.

Of his last hours, his death, and the funeral services, Mrs. Kalopothakes, at request of Mrs. King, wrote to friends in America, as follows:

"We are all overwhelmed with the suddeness of the event, for although he has been very feeble this spring, and has had several attacks of his old complaint, yet it is only within two days that any serious symptom appeared. You could not have been more surprised, I think, than we who are on the ground, and as it was a complaint from which he had suffered occasionally for years, we did not apprehend danger till the very last. The pain was so great during the last two days that he could not converse; and it was only in the cessation which usually precedes death, that my husband, seeing him sinking, approached, and asked him whether there was anything he wished to say. He found his mind at peace, resting upon Jesus as his only hope, and clear to the very last. He gave parting counsel to those about him, and sent messages to his son, to the little band of Greek converts about us, etc., and gave directions as to his burial, which was to be without pomp.

"A consultation of physicians was called on Friday evening, and again at ten o'clock in the evening; but his agony was great, and at a little after one at midnight, his spirit was released from the poor suffering body. I can only say that we feel that our father is taken from us; that a prince in Israel has fallen. He is lying there in the parlor, looking so sweet and calm, as if in a peaceful sleep. For him we cannot weep, for he is now in the presence of that Saviour whom he loved, and so faithfully served; but for ourselves, and the work here, we may well say that our 'Master is taken from our head to-day.' May a double portion of his spirit rest on those who are left to carry it on."

At a little later date, Mrs. Kalopothakes again writes:

"Not only at the funeral, but the next day (the Sabbath), at our preaching servive, my husband delivered an address, giving an account of Dr. King's life and character, the sacrifices he had made, and the service done for Greece, which drew tears from many eyes. His day of honor here will come, if it has not already: not even his enemies could deny the simplicity and uprightness of his conduct and character. Generous, loving, kind and forgiving, he was a friend to all.

"To the missionary work here his death will be a great loss; for although since his return from America he has not been able to do a great deal of active work, yet his mind and heart were ever busy devising plans, suggesting, counselling and encouraging those whom he was to leave to carry them on. He brought forward the Nicene Creed as the basis of union for the Evangelical Greeks, and had lately had it printed in a large and attractive form, and hung in our places of worship. He hoped to live to see the building of an Evangelical Greek church in Athens, and even the prospect of this did much to gladden the last year of his life. His heart was full of hope for this nation, as it was also full of love."

In view of the coming end, Dr. King had left the subjoined directions as to his burial: "In case of my death here in Athens, I wish to be buried near the wall in the

cemetery where I purchased, some years since, of the
Rev. John H. Hill, D. D., a burying-place, and where I
buried my little daughter, Anna Aspasia; leaving between me and her a space for my wife, should she die in
this place.

"On my tombstone I wish for no inscription, except

JONAS KING.

BORN JULY 29TH, 1792.

DIED

"My tombstone I wish to be perfectly simple without
any carving on it.

"JONAS KING."

His wishes were carried out. There was a large attendance at the funeral, although Grecian skies were
weeping heavily at the time, as if in sympathy.

Mrs. Kalopothakes, just before leaving this country,
after a visit here in 1871, wrote by special request some
of her impressions of the venerated friend, whom she was
allowed to follow so soon to a heavenly home. Her note
is not alone discriminating as to his character, but so
descriptive of the courtly simplicity of Dr. King's manner, as to bring him vividly before us.

"I have not forgotten my promise to give you some
of my personal impressions of dear Dr. King, and now,
on the eve of going back to the land and the work so
associated with him, many memories cluster around me
of my first arrival there, the warm welcome I received
from him, and the pleasant friendship which lasted
through the fourteen years of our acquaintance there.

" Having heard from childhood of Dr. King, I had expected to see a venerable-looking patriarch, so old and so grave as to have no sympathies in common with me. What then was my surprise at his almost youthful face and his erect figure, the vivacity and courteousness of his manner, combining the dignity of the gentleman with the warmth of the Christian heart.

" His character, too, was transparent in its purity and simplicity. He seemed the very soul of truth and uprightness; indeed, I have often thought that the real source of the hatred of his enemies arose from this, that it was impossible for him to dissemble, and they saw as in a glass his inward disapproval of all that was wrong in them or their doctrines.

" He has been represented as bitter and severe, always ready to attack and provoke opposition. He was, on the contrary, almost effeminately fond of good-will and praise. It must have been a trial to him to incur anything else; but his moral sense was so high and strong, that he could not smile at evil nor wink at sin ; he could not but stand up for the truth, like his Master, even though the whole world should frown upon him. He could not compromise with error even by silence.

" But his large, warm heart shone from his eyes, and beamed from a countenance peculiarly sweet and winning. The smile with which he would greet a guest, whoever he might be, and the style he had acquired, perhaps by living so long among Orientals, of placing his right hand over his heart, as he bowed low, was a true index of his Christian love and humility.

"With such a nature, the cross which he had continually to bear in his forty years of missionary labor, of being misunderstood, abused, and reviled, must have been the very hardest that could have been laid upon him. How keenly he felt any word of sympathy or praise, was shown by the way in which he would repeat it to his friends, and so often, that it was by some ascribed to a foolish boasting. I always felt that it was because his nature craved that appreciation, which had been so long withheld, that when it came it was like water to a thirsty traveller.

"Dear, holy man of God! His life was a perpetual crucifixion; few sympathies or joys were allowed him, his children being nearly all sent away at an early age to be educated; and his cultivated mind, that could have found such congeniality among friends and pursuits opened to him in his native land, was confined to presenting the truths of the gospel in the plainest manner to men who came to mock and to turn them into shafts against him. Yet he was very patient; he made me think of of 'the man Moses who was so meek,' and of 'the meekness and gentleness of Christ' that Paul inculcates.

"But he labored faithfully; he bore the heat and burden of the day, he toiled on when others would have fainted, and he took possession of the soil for Jesus. We to whom, when the Master called, he relinquished his labors, see what he accomplished, and rejoice in the springing seed.

"Oh, how we mourned when he died! We felt as if we could not give up that warm sympathy, that ready and sound counsel, that interest ever planning and praying for the good of Greece and the extension of Christ's kingdom there. We felt that both we and the work needed him still. Yet God knew best. His dust is there as an incitement to labor on, and the day will come when Greece will honor it as that of the greatest of her benefactors."

A few lines from his own pen give a little idea of Dr. King's own feelings as to his life's work: "In all my missionary labors I have ever sought wisdom and direction from on high, feeling that I could not trust to my own wisdom and understanding. In many trying scenes and difficult circumstances the hand of God has been most manifest in my deliverance. The wrath of man has been made to praise Him, and the remainder of wrath has he restrained." "I have been endeavoring to declare those great truths contained in the word of God necessary for men to know and believe in order to be saved." "In my missionary labors in my native country, in France, in Palestine and Syria, and in Greece, my great object has been to build up the cause of the Lord Jesus Christ. To this I have sacrificed my own private interests and my personal reputation and comfort, and God has been faithful to his promise and has provided for me. 'Seek first the kingdom of God and his righteousness,' he has said, 'and all these things shall be added unto you.' With a constitution naturally feeble, and with frequent bodily infirmities, I have been enabled, by strict temperance in eating and drinking, and in all the enjoyments of life, to perform more labors than I could at first

have thought possible. God strengthened me, he supported me, he healed my diseases, he delivered me in
times of danger ; he who led Israel through the deep as
on dry land, and fed them in the wilderness, and cast out
their enemies, and gave them possession of the promised
land—he who sent his angel and saved Daniel from the
mouth of the lions, and the three children from the power
of the heat in the fiery furnace—has stood by me, and in
him alone has been my hope. If I have done anything
in his cause, to him I ascribe the glory. For my short-
comings in duty, and for any errors I may have committed while engaged in his work, from him I hope for pardon, through **Jesus** Christ our Lord."

CHAPTER XXIV.

CONCLUSION.

1. List of Texts heading Volumes of Journals.—2. List of Books Written and those Revised.—3. Articles from Napoli Newspapers relative to Dr. King's Work.—4. Letter regarding Confession of Faith for Greek Church.—5. Letter to Professor Hopkins about Williams College Revival.—6. The Only Son.

BIBLE TEXTS, which in Greek, Hebrew, Arabic, and other languages, head the volumes of memoranda kept by Dr. King for forty years, and which, in fact, give a synopsis of his history:

MOUNT CALVARY, February 1, 1824.

"For my brethren and companions' sake, I will now say, Peace be within thee." Psa. 122 : 8; Isa. 62 : 1 ; Rev. 22 : 20.

"And he hath on his vesture and on his thigh a name written, King of kings and Lord of lords." Rev. 19 : 16.

MOUNT CALVARY, March 31, 1825.

"There they crucified him." Luke 23 : 33 ; Isa. 53 : 4 ; Luke 22 : 44.

"All we like sheep have gone astray, and the Lord hath laid on him the iniquity of us all." Isa. 53 : 6.

"For God so loved the world, that he gave his only-begotten Son, that *whosoever* believeth in him should not perish, but have everlasting life." John 3 : 16.

"This is the work of God, that ye believe on him whom he hath sent." John 6 : 29.

"He that believeth in me, though he were dead, yet shall he live : and whosoever liveth and believeth in me, shall never die." John 11 : 25, 26.

"Lord, I believe ; help thou mine unbelief." Mark 9 : 24.

TARSUS, October 25, 1825.

" But Paul said, I am a man which am a Jew of Tarsus, a city in Cilicia, a citizen of no mean city : and, I beseech thee, suffer me to speak unto the people."   Acts 21 : 39.

MARSEILLES, October 30, 1826.

" Of making many books there is no end ; and much study is a weariness of the flesh."   Eccles. 12 : 12.

EGINA, January 13, 1829.

" The Lord is nigh unto all them that call upon him, to all that call upon him in truth.   He will fulfil the desire of them that fear him : he also will hear their cry, and will save them."   Psalm 145 : 18, 19.

" Humble yourselves therefore under the mighty hand of God, that he may exalt you in due time : casting all your care upon him ; for he careth for you."   1 Pet. 5 : 7.

ISLAND OF TENOS, GREECE, July 5, 1830.

" And the king said unto Zadok, Carry back the ark of God into the city : if I shall find favor in the eyes of the Lord, he may bring me again, and show me both it and his habitation : but if he thus say, I have no delight in thee ; behold, here am I, let him do to me as seemeth good unto him."   2 Sam. 15 : 25, 26.

" . . . Let him alone, and let him curse ; for the Lord hath bidden him.   It may be that the Lord will look on mine affliction, and that the Lord will requite me good for his cursing this day."   2 Sam. 16 : 11, 12.

" And when ye stand praying, forgive, if ye have aught against any : that your Father also which is in heaven may forgive you your trespasses.   But if ye do not forgive, neither will your Father which is in heaven forgive your trespasses."   Mark 11 : 25, 26.

ATHENS, January 1, 1837.

" That like as Christ was raised up from the dead by the glory of the Father, even so we also should walk in newness of life." Rom. 6 : 4.

ATHENS, May 20, 1840.

" Not rendering evil for evil, or railing for railing: but contrariwise blessing ; knowing that ye are thereunto called, that ye should inherit a blessing. For he that will love life, and see good days, let him refrain his tongue from evil, and his lips that they speak no guile; let him eschew evil, and do good; let him seek peace, and ensue it. For the eyes of the Lord are over the righteous, and his ears are open unto their prayers: but the face of the Lord is against them that do evil." 1 Pet. 3 : 9–12.

" Peace I leave with you, my peace I give unto you : not as the world giveth, give I unto you. Let not your heart be troubled, neither let it be afraid." John 14 : 27.

ATHENS, September 1, 1842.

" Which were born, not of blood, nor of the will of the flesh, nor of the will of man, but of God." John 1 : 13.

" But as he which hath called you is holy, so be ye holy in all manner of conversation." 1 Pet. 1 : 15.

" Be ye therefore followers of God as dear children." Ephes. 5 : 1.

ATHENS, October 5, 1843.

" Then Samuel took a stone, and set it between Mizpeh and Shen, and called the name of it Eben-ezer, saying, Hitherto hath the Lord helped us." 1 Sam. 7 : 12.

" My help cometh from the Lord, which made heaven and earth." Psa. 121 : 2.

" He giveth power to the faint; and to them that have no might he increaseth strength. Even the youth shall faint and be weary, and the young men shall utterly fall : but they that wait upon the Lord shall renew their strength ; they shall mount up with wings as eagles ; they shall run, and not be weary; and they shall walk, and not faint." Isa. 40 : 29–31.

" He doeth according to his will in the army of heaven, and among the inhabitants of the earth : and none can stay his hand, or say unto him, What doest thou ?" Dan. 4 : 35.

" And those that walk in pride he is able to abate." Dan. 4 : 37.

ATHENS, September 20, 1845.

" Blessed are ye, when men shall hate you, and when they shall separate you from their company, and shall reproach you, and cast out your name as evil, for the Son of man's sake. Rejoice ye in that day, and leap for joy : for, behold, your reward is great in heaven : for in the like manner did their fathers unto the prophets." Luke 6 : 22, 23.

" And ye shall be brought before governors and kings for my sake, for a testimony against them and the Gentiles." Matt. 10 : 18.

" The disciple is not above his master, nor the servant above his lord. It is enough for the disciple that he be as his master, and the servant as his lord. If they have called the master of the house Beelzebub, how much more shall they call them of his household !" Matt. 10 : 24, 25.

" And fear not them which kill the body, but are not able to kill the soul : but rather fear him which is able to destroy both soul and body in hell." Matt. 10 : 28.

" But if ye suffer for righteousness' sake, happy are ye : and be not afraid of their terror, neither be troubled." 1 Pet. 3 : 14.

ATHENS, May 1, 1847.

" He sent from above, he took me, he drew me out of many waters. He delivered me from my strong enemy, and from them which hated me. He brought me forth also into a large place. As for God, his way is perfect : the word of the Lord is tried : he is a buckler to all those that trust in him." Psa. 18 : 16–30.

" Trust ye in the Lord for ever : for in the Lord Jehovah is everlasting strength." Isa. 26 : 4.

" It is better to trust in the Lord than to put confidence in princes." Psa. 118 : 9.

" And he answered, Fear not : for they that be with us are more than they that be with them." 2 Kings 6 : 16.

GENEVA, September 6, 1847.

" The Lord thy keeper." Psa. 121 : 5.

" Thou wilt keep him in perfect peace whose mind is stayed on thee." Isa. 26 : 3.

ATHENS, October 2, 1848.

" When the Lord turned again the captivity of Zion, we were like them that dream. Then was our mouth filled with laughter, and our tongue with singing: then said they among the heathen, The Lord hath done great things for them. The Lord hath done great things for us; whereof we are glad. Turn again our captiv ity, O Lord, as the streams in the south. They that sow in tears shall reap in joy. He that goeth forth and weepeth, bearing precious seed, shall doubtless come again with rejoicing, bringing his sheaves with him." Psa. 126.

ATHENS, November 12, 1850.

" And all thy children shall be taught of the Lord: and great shall be the peace of thy children." Isa. 54 : 13.

" Mary hath chosen that good part, which shall not be taken away from her." Luke 10 : 42.

" He giveth power to the faint; and to them that have no might he increaseth strength. Even the youths shall faint and be weary, and the young men shall utterly fall: but they that wait upon the Lord shall renew their strength; they shall mount up on wings as eagles; they shall run, and not be weary; and they shall walk, and not faint." Isa. 40 : 29–31.

ATHENS, August 1, 1851.

" Weeping may endure for a night, but joy cometh in the morning." Psa. 30 : 5.

" Fear not: for I am with thee: I will bring thy seed from the east, and gather thee from the west." Isa. 43 : 5.

ATHENS, November 1, 1852.

" But David encouraged himself in the Lord his God." 1 Sam. 30 : 6.

" In God is my salvation and my glory: the rock of my strength, and my refuge, is in God. Trust in him at all times; ye people, pour out your heart before him: God is a refuge for us." Psalm 62 : 7, 8.

" Notwithstanding the Lord stood with me, and strengthened me; . . . and I was delivered out of the mouth of the lion. And

the Lord shall deliver me from every evil work, and will preserve
me unto his heavenly kingdom: to whom be glory for ever and
ever.   Amen."   2 Tim. 4: 17, 18.

ATHENS, July 12, 1855.

" Why art thou cast down, O my soul? and why art thou disqui-
eted within me? hope thou in God: for I shall yet praise him, who
is the health of my countenance, and my God."   Psa. 42:11.

List of Books published by Dr. King:

1. His " Farewell Letter " to his friends in Palestine and Syria,
in 1825, written in Arabic, and published in that language afterwards by the Church Missionary Society of England, and which has
been translated into various other languages, and printed in Modern Greek, in French, in Italian, etc.   It was put in the Index at
Rome, and prohibited by Pope Gregory XVI. and by Pope Pius
IX., and a volume in answer to it was printed in Arabic by the *De
Propaganda Fide.*   Of the effect produced on the Armenians at
Constantinople by a copy of it in manuscript, sent by an Armenian
bishop from Beyroot, Rev. H. G. O. Dwight, D. D., writes in his
book, " Christianity Revived in the East."   He says that the letter
was translated by Bishop Dionysius.   " And soon a meeting was
called in the Armenian Patriarchal church, at which, it is said, the
letter was read, and the references to Scripture examined ; and, as
if by common consent, it was agreed that the church needs reform.
Out of this grew immediately the famous school of Peshtima Gian.
It was established within the precincts of the Patriarchate at Constantinople, and one particular object was the education of the
clergy ; the rule being adopted that no individual should thereafter
be ordained to the priest's office in the capital who had not completed a regular course of study at this school."   This " Farewell Letter " was distributed extensively among the Greeks and Italians in
Sardinia and Egypt, and is still used by our missionaries in the
East.   An English officer printed at his own expense about three
thousand copies, and in two nights distributed sixteen hundred of
them in Sicily.

2. His " Defence," written in Greek, and published in that
language at Athens in 1845, produced uncommon excitement in the

whole Oriental church, not only in free Greece, but throughout Turkey.

3. "Exposition of an Apostolical Church," written in Greek, and printed in Cambridge, Mass., U. S. A., in 1851 and 1857. This has been translated into French and Italian, and printed in those languages at Malta.

4. "Religious Rites of an Apostolical Church," written in Greek, and printed at Athens in 1851.

5. His "Speech before the Areopagus" at Athens, written in Greek, and partly delivered April 23, 1846 (the President of the Court did not permit him to finish it), and printed in New York in 1847, and at Cambridge, Mass., in 1857.

6. "Hermeneutics of the Sacred Scriptures," written in Greek, and printed at Athens in 1857.

7. Two volumes of "Sermons" in Greek, printed at Athens in 1859.

8. "Synoptical View of Palestine and Syria, with Additions," etc., written and printed in French, and translated into Modern Greek, and published at Athens in 1859.

9. His "Miscellaneous Works" in Modern Greek, one volume octavo, pages 840, and containing all the above-mentioned except the "Sermons," and in addition a "Letter to a Unitarian Minister," and all the Documents with regard to his various Trials before the Courts in Athens, the Examination of the Witnesses, all the Accusations brought against him and the Decisions of the Courts; the Communication of the Hon. George P. Marsh, United States Minister to the Greek Government, relative to the same; and the King's Order revoking the Sentence of Exile. Printed at Athens in 1859 and 1860.

10. His Answer to a Pamphlet entitled "The Two Clergymen," by the Bishop of Karystia, Macarius, Kaliarchus, 1863.

The books printed under his direction and revised by him in Modern Greek at Athens are:

1. "Mother at Home."
2. "Baxter's Saints' Rest."
3. "Dr. Lyman Beecher's Sermons on Intemperance."
4. "Alleine's Alarm to the Unconverted."

5. "Extracts from Chrysostom."

6. "History of the Church of Christ by Dr. Barth," printed at Smyrna.

7. Four Tracts, written by the Countess Agenor de Gasparin.

8. "The Sisters."

9. Lessons taken from the Sacred Scriptures on various subjects.

10. "The Prayers of the Saints." (Prayers found in the Old and New Testaments.) This book is published in English by the American Tract Society.

11. Five volumes, entitled, "A Collection of Various Works and Religious Tracts," and published from 1853 to 1856. These had already been printed in Modern Greek, but in a style quite unsuitable for the present time. The above works in all are fifteen volumes.

The number of the Scriptures of the Old and New Testaments, or parts of them, of school books and religious tracts, which he has distributed among the Greeks in free Greece and in Turkey (not including those circulated in Egypt, Palestine, and Syria), will probably amount to not less than four hundred thousand copies.

Eighty schools received books from him in one year. From the 1st of January, 1842, to the 30th of November, 1843, one hundred and eight schools were furnished with books from his shop at Athens. Of these schools, 20 were in the Peloponnesus, 60 in Continental Greece, 7 in the Cyclades, and 21 in Turkey.

Translation of an article from the national newspaper printed at Napoli, July 23, 1832, concerning the literary institutions in Athens under the superintendence of Mr. Jonas King, American:

1. One school of mutual instruction, under the direction of Mr. N. Niketoplos, containing ninety-four scholars.

2. Another school of mutual instruction, under the direction of Mr. P. Skepesos, containing sixty-eight scholars.

3. A school for girls, under the direction of Miss Anastasia Kapenaki, containing sixty-three scholars.

4. A school for the study of the ancient Greek writers, under the direction of Mr. D. Sonomales, containing thirty-seven scholars. It is expected also that higher branches will be afterwards taught. This Philhellen, Mr. J. King, is one of the apostles of one of the apostolic churches of the Presbyterians (meaning those who have not bishops in the present sense of the word), sent by it with large expenses and every kind of means for establishing such schools for the instruction of youth in the renowned Athens.

He has also bought a place, where he is building an institution simply for females, in which shall be taught such branches necessary for the instruction of females as are taught in similar institutions in Europe. We learn also that the female friends of Greece in Philadelphia, America, contribute in a particular manner to this institution, and for this reason there has been inscribed over the gate, " Philadelphia."

Mr. J. King, in 1828, established at Tenos a school for girls, containing about eighty girls. It continued till 1831, when he removed to Athens.

This American Society contributed to the school for girls in Syra under the direction of Mr. Korck. It made a present also to the government, in 1830, of about thirty-five hundred slates and seventy-five thousand pencils, for the use of schools of mutual instruction in Greece.

It established also, in 1822, a printing-press in Malta, at which are printed elementary books in different languages, for the most part Eastern. Thousands of such little books have been given gratis to the schools in Greece.

The Philhellen Americans have ever shown kindness to our nation, giving, in 1826, much food and clothing, but now they contribute for the education of our youth.

The Athenians, seeing the progress of their children in learning, tender, together with the other Greeks, their gratitude to the Philhellen Americans.

In 1824 the Philo-muse (literary) Society first established in Athens a school for girls, having for teacher Mr. N. Niketoplos ;

but in 1831, the 10th of April (old style), Mr. J. King, having the same N. Niketoplos as teacher, established a school of mutual instruction, containing a sufficient number of pupils, both males and females, which last, the 3d of June (old style), he ordered to be in a separate school for girls.

Afterwards, the 6th of July (old style), the wife of Mr. Hill, American, established a school for girls.

The reverend priest, Mr. Jonas King, full of zeal, and a preacher of the gospel, sent by the same Society, for nearly two years preached the gospel in France and in other parts of Europe, and four years in Egypt, Syria, and Palestine, and other parts of Asia, and in Constantinople.

A plan of the gymnasium sent to be published in the " Minerva," September 9, 1831, was prefaced by the editor with these remarks :

The Rev. Mr. Jonas King, known for his charities and beneficence to almost all the wretched in the time of our struggle, and since the settlement of the affairs of our nation, devoted to the work of enlightening it, has sent us the new organization of his gymnasium at Athens, which we hasten to publish in our paper, that the public may see how well the sincere friends of humanity know what are the best means of benefiting it and bringing it to its true happiness.

Far from attributing to the venerable King or others any designs of proselytism, which designs, did they exist, would in the nineteenth century be rather ridiculous than worthy of regard, we cannot but express the gratitude of our nation to the Americans who have set such a worthy example, while we would also proclaim the virtues of the venerable King, especially the diligence and assiduity which he as well as his colleagues exhibit for our illumination.

Copy of a letter to the Rev. Rufus Anderson with regard to a confession of faith for the Greek church :

ATHENS, February 7, 1850.

REV. RUFUS ANDERSON, D. D.—My Dear Brother : I am not certain whether I mentioned to you or not, some months since, that I had been occupied for a while in writing a small work in Greek, entitled " Exposition of an Apostolic Church," with a " Confession of Faith " and a " Covenant," all founded entirely on the Word of God, from which, in proof of what I have said, passages are quoted in full. The " Exposition " consists of thirty-one articles and the " Confession of Faith " of twelve.

The object of the whole is to show in what a truly apostolical church consists, on what foundation it is built, by what rule it is guided, what doctrines it believes, what powers it possesses, in what manner its officers are to be chosen, what their character ought to be, what are their peculiar duties, and how they are to be supported; its relation to other churches, as also the relation of its officers to those of other churches; to whom baptism is to be administered, in what manner, and for what object; who are to partake of the Lord's Supper, in what manner, and how often, the nature and object of the elements used in that supper; how the discipline of the church is to be administered, and with what spirit, and what punishment it may inflict on disorderly members; in what manner prayers are to be offered, and to whom and through what mediation; what kind of fasting is permitted, and when; under what circumstances divorce is permitted; what kind of worldly diversions are condemned; in what manner the Lord's day is to be consecrated; that feasts are not to be kept in honor of saints and angels; that certain Jewish and heathen customs are not to be permitted in religious rites, such as the use of lighted lamps and candles during the day, incense, offerings for the dead, the worship of images of whatever kind, servile reverence of religious teachers, theatrical representations of the sufferings and death of Christ at Easter, the worship of dead men's bones, the kissing of crosses, the making the sign of the cross as a preservative against evil or the evil influences of the devil, or in the room of prayer, the use of amulets, prayers, and ceremonies for the souls of the dead; that the so-called mysteries are to be rejected; that the object of baptism and the Lord's Supper is manifest, and not to be called mysteries; that the ceremony of marriage and of inducting a pastor into office contain no mystery whatever; that no miracles are now wrought by anointing with oil; that secret confession is not enjoined, but that confession, in case of public scandal, should be public and in presence of the whole church; and in case of sin, to whom we are ever to apply for pardon, and in what way it can be obtained.

To the whole I have written a short preface, bringing into view certain principles and traits of the human mind which lead men to err on the subject of religion, and showing why I reject all traditions and commandments of men, and take for my guide the Word of God alone.

The work is intended principally for the Eastern and Western churches, but also for all others which have in any degree wandered from the purity and simplicity of the gospel either in faith or practice, either in internal organization or in outward ceremonies.

And as the people in the East are lamentably ignorant of the Sacred Scriptures, and as multitudes do not possess them, I have thought it important to quote in full the passages of Scripture to which, in other circumstances, I should need perhaps only to refer. But even where the Sacred Scriptures are in the hands of all, many probably prefer to see a text quoted rather than to be sent to another book in search of it.

The whole will not make, I think, more than eighty or a hundred pages 12mo, and of course can be read by almost any one without much fatigue. Large books on religious subjects most men are not fond of, and only a few will read.

I was moved to write this in part by the impression on my mind that such a kind of guide is necessary for those who perhaps begin to see the light, but from never having been taught the way in which they should go, are in danger of wandering every time they see a path that turns to the right or to the left, and that it would be especially necessary should there ever be in these regions, as I doubt not there will be, any considerable excitement on the subject of religion, or any great movement towards a change.

I have not only prepared it in Greek, but have also had it translated into French and Italian, in each of which languages I wish to print, if possible, a thousand copies.

Will you allow me to do this at the expense of the Board? It must, of course, be printed *out of Greece,* for if printed here I should be subject to prosecution, imprisonment, and perhaps exile.

The expense of printing a thousand copies in the three above-mentioned languages would not exceed, I think, *two hundred dollars.*   Yours, truly,

JONAS KING.

THE ONLY SON.

TRACT NO. 530, A. T. S.

SOON after the Rev. Pliny Fisk and Rev. Levi Parsons left their mountain homes in Western Massachusetts, near the close of 1819, as the first American missionaries to Palestine, their young friend JONAS KING, from the same neighborhood, was elected professor in Amherst college, and proceeded to Paris to pursue the study of Arabic with the celebrated De Sacy. He there became familiar with an American gentleman, then at the head of one of the first commercial houses in Paris, to whose care his correspondence was addressed.

In February, 1822, the lamented Parsons died, and Rev. Mr. Fisk without delay addressed a letter to Mr. King, requesting that he would meet him at Malta, and, in place of Rev. Mr. Parsons, accompany him as a missionary to Palestine ; and fearing delay by waiting the action of the American Board of Missions, he in the same enclosure requested Mr. King's mercantile friend not only to second his invitation, but, if possible, to raise the sum of $1,500, requisite for his support for three years.

Mr. King, receiving the letter in the merchant's counting-room, retired to his private office to read it. Oppressed with the weight of the proposition it contained, he spent an hour in prayer for divine direction ; and hoping to gain further light as to the path of duty, sought the merchant's advice. He returned to the counting-room, and asked with deep solicitude, "What shall I do?" Said his friend, "Go." "But," said he, "what will become of my aged and infirm parents in America?" "I will be a son to them in your stead," replied his friend. "Then," said Mr. King, "I go up to Jerusalem, 'not knowing the things that shall befall me there.'"

"Now," said the merchant, "sit down at this desk and write to my friends Thomas Waddington of St. Remy, France, Louis Mertens of Brussels, Claude Cromlin of Amsterdam, and John Venning of St. Petersburg : state to them the circumstances, and that you are willing to go ; tell them I will give one-fifth of the $1,500, and leave it to their decision whether they will join me in filling up the amount." By the return of the mails it appeared that God had put it into the hearts of these gentlemen cheerfully to respond to the appeal by enclosing each $300, making the sum required; and Mr. King lost no time in preparing for his departure.

A few months previous to this, Mr. King had established the monthly concert of prayer in his own hired upper chamber in Paris, which had been attended with increasing interest; a large concourse assembled in the church of the Oratoire to listen to his farewell address and join in commending him to the God of all grace; he was cheered in a similar manner on his way by Christian assemblies at Lyons, Nismes, Montpelier, and Marseilles. where he embarked for Malta and Jerusalem. He is now the well-known, persecuted, but laborious and successful missionary at Athens.

His friend the merchant, from time to time, wrote to the solitary parents, enclosing some tokens of regard "from their affectionate son;" the next year he returned to America, and early in the spring of 1824 he was at Northampton, about twenty-five miles from the parents, meditating a visit to their humble abode. He applied to the landlord, who furnished him a wagon with *his little son* for a driver; and freighted with a bag of groceries which extended the whole length of the wagon, they set off early in the morning, and after encountering snowdrifts and other obstacles by the way, arrived at the cottage about two in the afternoon.

Leaving the lad with the wagon in the street, the gentleman knocked, saying as he entered, "It is a chill, uncomfortable day, friends; would you be so kind as to allow a stranger to warm himself a little by your fire?" He was welcomed and seated between the aged couple, in whom he distinctly recognized the features of their son Jonas, and they in turn fixed on him a scrutinizing eye. After a short pause he said deliberately,

"I once had a friend who said to me, 'What shall I do?' Said I, 'Go.' 'But what,' said he, 'will become of my aged and infirm parents in America?' I replied, 'I will be a son to them in your stead.' 'Then,' said he, 'I go up to Jerusalem, "not knowing the things that shall befall me there."'"

Instantly the aged couple sprung to him, exclaiming, "This is Mr. Wilder!" and almost overwhelmed him with their tears and caresses. "Let us pray," said the father; and they unburdened their hearts at the throne of mercy.

Scarcely were they again seated, when the mother took from

the shelf a new quarto Bible, saying she hoped her friend would not blame her for paying ten dollars for it out of the fifty he had sent her a few months previous. "Our old eyes," she said, "could not well read the small print of the other Bible. I told Mr. King I did not believe we could make any better use of the money, or should ever be the poorer for buying a Bible that we could read; it is a great comfort to us." Their friend expressed his approbation of the purchase, admired the Bible, and before he returned it to the shelf slipped into it unperceived a ten-dollar bill, which she afterwards wrote him had been found on the floor when they were reading the Bible, and which she recognized as from the hand of God, having no knowledge by what means the exact amount expended had thus come again into their hands.

After a brief interchange of confidence and affection, she said to her esteemed guest, "I presume, sir, you have not dined, and must be in need of refreshment. I am very sorry we have not a cup of tea to offer you, but we have some nice ham and fresh eggs, which I will immediately prepare." Her friend remarked, "There is a bag in the wagon containing several articles from 'your son;' perhaps there may be tea among them."

The bag, with no little effort, was transferred from the wagon to the cottage-floor, and the mother addressed herself to the task of taking out its contents. Among packages of flour, rice, loaf-sugar, coffee, chocolate, raisins, and other articles, each of which she held up with new expressions of delight, as received from one she so much loved, she at length came to a package of four pounds of hyson tea, when she held it out to the father with streaming eyes, saying, "Look here, papa; Jonas is the same dear good boy that he always was. He knew we were out of tea sometimes; he do n't forget his poor father and mother." Then opening a package of Turkey figs, "And is this also," said she, "from Jerusalem? Papa, was there ever such a son as Jonas?" By this time all hearts were overflowing. "Let us pray," said the father; and the exploring of the treasures was suspended while they again united in thanksgiving to God.

It was not long before the little company were seated at a well-furnished table, refreshed by the gifts of the kind "son," mingling their sympathies and recounting all the way in which they had been led. While thus conversing the merchant affectionately asked,

" Do you never regret the sacrifice you have made in giving up your only son to be a missionary?" The aged father replied,

" 'God so loved the world, that he gave his only begotten Son, that whosoever believeth in him should not perish, but have everlasting life;' and shall I withhold my only son from obeying the command of our ascended Saviour, 'Go ye into all the world, and preach the gospel to every creature'?"

All present were deeply affected, a tear standing in the eye even of the young driver. They again bowed in prayer; both the father and the merchant led in turn, commending the little company, the absent son, and a sin-ruined world to the God of missions.

The interview was an hour bright with the beams of the Sun of righteousness amid the dark pilgrimage of life, an oasis in the desert, a season never to be forgotten by any one of the four persons who thus met for the first and the last time on earth.

That young driver, as he afterwards distinctly stated, here first had his mind impressed with the sacredness of the work of foreign missions. He gave his heart to Christ, pursued a thorough course of education, went forth to the heathen, and was no other than Henry Lyman, the noble martyr who fell by the side of Munson, in 1834, among the bloody Battas of Sumatra.

The aged father, in his will, bequeathed to the merchant, for the purchase of a book in token of his love, the sum of five dollars, which at his death was paid to the widow for the old small-print Bible, which is still preserved as a precious memento. The widow has entered into rest; and the stranger passing a rural graveyard in South Hawley, where the scenery opens in magnificence and beauty, reads on the tombstone of the father his reply just quoted to the question whether he ever regretted the gift to missions of his ONLY SON.

www.ingramcontent.com/pod-product-compliance
Lightning Source LLC
Chambersburg PA
CBHW021717110726
47902CB00005B/1236